The Villa Girls

The Villa Girls

Nicky Pellegrino

First published in Great Britain in 2011 by Orion Books,
an imprint of The Orion Publishing Group Ltd
Orion House, 5 Upper Saint Martin's Lane
London WC2H 9EA

An Hachette UK Company

1 3 5 7 9 10 8 6 4 2

A CIP catalogue record for this book is
available from the British Library.

ISBN (Hardback) 978 1 4091 0092 8
ISBN (Trade Paperback) 978 1 4091 0093 5

Typeset by Deltatype Ltd, Birkenhead, Merseyside

Printed in Great Britain by CPI Mackays Chatham ME5 8TD

The Orion Publishing Group's policy is to use papers
that are natural, renewable and recyclable products and
made from wood grown in sustainable forests. The logging
and manufacturing processes are expected to conform to
the environmental regulations of the country of origin.

www.orionbooks.co.uk

Love is not a thing to understand.
Love is not a thing to feel.
Love is not a thing to give and receive.
Love is a thing only to become
And eternally be.

Sri Chinmoy

Whatever 'in love' means.

Prince Charles

Love? I'm happy enough without it.

Rosie Goodheart

Prologue

I'm happy being single, really I am. There's no space in my life for a man. No room in my cupboards for his socks and jerseys, nowhere for his jars of hair wax or shaving sticks. I don't want his pictures hanging on my walls or his TV taking up my living room. I don't need any company. My life is absolutely fine the way it is. There's nothing that needs changing.

Most people find that difficult to believe. They insist on offering eligible friends and throwing awkward dinner parties. It's as though choosing a path so different to the one they've followed is almost an insult. And that's odd because I'm happy for them. Marriage and babies, they're perfectly good things. It's just that I don't want them. Not at all.

So what do I love so much about my life? Well, waking early every morning to the dirty London light and hearing the hum of the city beyond my sash windows. Drinking the first exquisite cup of dark-roasted coffee as I lean against the bench in my clean, white kitchen. Eating a slice or two of toasted sourdough from the bakery around the corner.

I really love my flat – the two lower floors of a tall house in Belgravia, bought with what was left of my parents' money. The walls are painted in pale shades and the floors are bleached wood. There's hardly any furniture and yet there's still a place for everything – shoes in a cupboard by the door, magazines in a neat pile with white spines aligned, surfaces empty and clean. I love the way it looks.

And I love my morning walk past the shops to catch

the tube eastwards to the studio I share with my business partner Johnny Wellbelove. Here light streams through long windows and there's another kitchen, all gleaming silver and industrial. One entire wall is lined with shelves to house the oddments of crockery I've collected over the years, drawers are filled with folded coloured linens and mismatched cutlery.

It's here that Johnny photographs the food I cook and style for him. We work for magazines and book publishers, mostly together but sometimes apart. Johnny is what my mother would have referred to as 'camp as a row of tents'. He's funny and flamboyant, and I like that about him. It means I don't have to be.

As Goodheart & Wellbelove the pair of us have been together for long enough to be an effortless team. And yes, we love what we do.

So I'm that unfashionable thing: content. To me there's no reason to be constantly striving for the next triumph or trying to reach a higher rung on the ladder. I'm happy with what I've got. Why would I need more?

And yet even I understand why we need to climb out of our lives now and then, no matter how well arranged they might be. I can see that it's good to visit new places, to dip in and out of other people's worlds before coming back to our own.

I love my life in London but there are times I need to get away from it, just like anybody else. And I guess that's one of the reasons why for all these years I've carried on being a Villa Girl.

Rosie

The Villa Girls happened by accident, and I was the least likely part of them. It all began during the final summer of our sixth form. I remember the day quite clearly. It was one of those mornings when we were supposed to be sitting in the library revising quietly for exams but instead I'd sloped off for some time on my own, just as I did whenever I got a chance those days. Often I caught the tube up to Hampstead and walked over the heath or wandered aimlessly around shops and markets. I spent hours in galleries and museums or sat in parks. Anything rather than go back to the place I was supposed to call home.

I was fairly new to skiving off but had discovered the secret was to do it in plain sight. So I never tried to run or sneak away. Instead, I walked confidently, head held high. And if the worst did happen and a teacher loomed then I made sure I had an excuse ready: 'Off to the doctor; women's troubles.' It worked every time.

On that particular day, I'd shaken off school and was walking through the Barbican Centre, skirting the hard edges of a building to shield myself from the wind, when I noticed Addolorata Martinelli sprawled on a bench near the lake, smoking a cigarette and wearing a bright blue hat pulled over her dark curly hair. She must have been bunking off too and clearly didn't care who saw her.

She glanced over as I walked by and I heard her calling out to me far too loudly. 'Hey, Rosie Goodheart. Aren't you supposed to be at school?' The heads of several curious passers-by swivelled and I kept walking as though I didn't have the faintest idea who she was.

If everything had been normal that summer then Addolorata would have left me alone. The pair of us had been in the same class for years but we'd never come close to being friends. Even now she's got one of those personalities that seems to seep over the edges, and in those days there was always some sort of drama going on: boyfriend trouble, break-ups, pregnancy scares. Addolorata was noisy about it, too, as though the rest of us were only there to be her audience. As a general rule I hardly ever spoke to her.

But this was the summer everyone in my class had been told they had to be nice to me. To keep an eye on me, even. And so instead of letting me walk on alone, Addolorata got up from her bench and followed.

'Hey, Rosie, are you all right?' she called, again too loudly. 'Where are you going?'

I stopped to let her catch up so she didn't have to shout. 'Nowhere in particular,' I told her.

'So why aren't you in school?'

'I'm sick of revising.'

'Oh yeah, me too.' Addolorata lit another cigarette and offered me a drag, which I refused with a shake of my head. 'I don't care about the exams anyway. When I've finished with school I'm going to work in my father's restaurant and it's not like I'll need A levels for that.'

'I guess not,' I said economically, hoping she'd give up trying to coax a conversation out of me.

She might have left me alone then if not for the ten-pound note that came blowing down the street straight towards us in a strong gust of wind. Addolorata bent to pick it up and we both looked round, trying to see who might have dropped it. There was no one in sight.

'What do you think we should do?' I asked.

'Spend it, obviously. That's the rule with found money: you have to get rid of it as quickly as it came to you.'

'I've never heard that one.' I was interested now.

'Well, possibly I'm making it up,' Addolorata admitted, laughing. 'But let's spend it anyway. We could go and get dim sum.'

I had no idea what she was talking about. 'Get what?'

'Dim sum. Chinese dumplings. Haven't you ever had them?'

I shook my head. 'Don't think so.'

'Really?' She sounded amazed. 'I'll take you to my favourite place. You'll love it.'

We caught a bus to Chinatown. I don't know how Addolorata knew about the restaurant she led me to. It was down a narrow side street and you had to ring on a buzzer beside a scruffy-looking door and climb two flights of bare wooden stairs that led to a long, undecorated room. The place was crowded with Chinese people and between the packed tables unsmiling women pushed huge stainless-steel trolleys piled high with steaming bamboo baskets.

Addolorata wasn't the least bit intimidated by any of it. She found us two seats at a shared table and chose the food she wanted. With a finger she waved away the shrivelled chicken feet, a nod brought crescent-shaped fried dumplings, sticky rice wrapped tight in dark green leaves, doughy pork buns.

'Taste this,' she told me, plucking a prawn dumpling from a basket with her chopsticks. 'Oh, and this is really good too.'

'Do you come here with your family?' I asked, watching Addolorata load up a dumpling with hot chilli sauce.

'What? God no, my father wouldn't eat stuff like this. I come by myself usually. I really enjoy it.' She poured some tea from a dripping pot. 'Sometimes I bring a book or magazine, but often I just sit and watch the expressions on people's faces as they eat.'

5

It seemed an odd idea to me. 'You like to watch people eat?'

She nodded as she grabbed at another dumpling with her chopsticks. 'Especially Chinese people because they sit for a long time over their food, talking and drinking tea, savouring little mouthfuls. They're interesting to watch. It's like witnessing a tiny slice of their lives.'

Curious now, I looked more carefully at the old man and the young girl across the table from us. They were making their way through a shared plate of crab, cracking the claws with a hammer and sucking out the sweet white meat inside. Beside us was a larger group feasting on steamed leafy greens covered in a silky sauce and platters piled high with fried squid. The whole restaurant was filled with the sound of friends and family gathering over food. It hummed with happiness.

'So what do you think of the dim sum?' Addolorata asked. 'Do you love it?'

'I like the way it looks,' I told her, 'the baskets and little dishes of dipping sauces. It's pretty.'

She gave me a sideways look. 'But do you like the flavours?'

I'd thought most of it tasted pretty good so I nodded and Addolorata used that as an excuse to take more from the trolleys: gelatinous rice-noodle rolls, little squares of shrimp toast, deep-fried silken tofu. Far too much for me to eat. I worried this was going to cost more than the ten-pound note we'd found and tried to make her stop.

'Don't worry,' she said. 'On weekends I do waitressing shifts for my dad. I've always got a bit of cash on me.'

It was only once we were out on the street again, full of dim sum and not sure what would happen next, that Addolorata asked me the question I was sick of hearing.

'So how are you doing anyway, Rosie?' she said awkwardly. 'Are you all right?'

I gave her the reply everyone seemed to want: yes, I was fine. And then I tried to get away from her.

'Thanks, that was great,' I said, moving off a few steps. 'Really delicious. I'll see you tomorrow, I expect.'

'Hang on, Rosie.' Addolorata looked worried. 'I didn't mean to upset you.'

'You're not ... I'm just ... going somewhere.'

'Not back to school?'

'Of course not.'

'Well, where then?'

'To Liberty.' It was my favourite place back then, still is really. 'I'm going to look at scarves and handbags.'

Addolorata laughed. 'Really? Why?'

'It's what I like to do.'

'So can I come with you?' she asked.

'I'm fine on my own, you know; I don't need company.'

'Maybe I'd like to come.'

I gave up trying to shrug her off and together we walked through the side roads of Soho and down Carnaby Street. She seemed to know this part of London as well as I did. But she didn't know Liberty, with its small rooms filled with luxury. She hadn't ever visited its collections of designer clothes or browsed its glass cases of costume jewellery, the squares of screen-printed silk scarves, the boxed stationery – all of it chosen by people with taste. We spent ages walking through each floor, touching things we couldn't afford and ended up in my favourite place of all, the beauty room, spraying our wrists with perfume and smearing our skin with samples.

'Mmm, this is lovely.' Addolorata misted the air with Chanel No 5. 'I wish I could afford a bottle.'

'Didn't you just say you always had loads of cash from waitressing?'

'Yeah, but I'm hopeless at saving up enough to buy anything proper.' Addolorata set down the bottle and smiled at the sales assistant. 'I spend it all on things to eat.'

By now it was growing late and outside London's treacly light was thickening into gloom. Liberty had switched on its lamps and seemed even more like a jewel-box, its counters heaped with things anyone would want to own, its air smelling of new fabric, polished wood and empty afternoons.

'I should go,' Addolorata sounded reluctant. 'My mother will be expecting me home.'

'Yeah, I guess I should head off too,' I agreed.

It wasn't until we were more than halfway back up Carnaby Street that I pulled the bottle from my pocket. 'Here you go.' I held it out to her. 'This is for you.'

'What?'

'The perfume you wanted. Chanel No 5.'

'You took it?' Addolorata looked astonished.

'It's only the sample. Half of it's been used up already, see?'

'But still, you stole it.'

'Hey, if you don't want it, no problem.' I shrugged.

'No, no, I'll have it.' She took the bottle and shoved it deep into her jacket pocket.

It wasn't that I was trying to shock Addolorata, or impress her even. The only reason I'd taken the perfume was that she seemed to love it so much. And stretching out my hand to scoop it up was the easiest thing in the world. But now I could tell she was looking at me in quite a different way.

'What if they'd spotted you?' she asked.

'Well, they didn't,' I pointed out.

'If I got caught doing something like that my parents would kill me.'

'But I don't have any parents.' I said it matter-of-factly. 'Not any more.'

'Oh no, damn it, I'm so sorry.' Addolorata looked appalled. 'I shouldn't have said that. I just kind of ... forgot for a moment.'

'Don't be sorry. It's not your fault.'

She fell silent for long enough for it to be uncomfortable and then, as we turned the corner into Broadwick Street, Addolorata asked me a question. Just one little question but it ended up changing everything.

'Hey, Rosie, what are you going to do once school is finished?'

'I don't know,' I admitted. 'What about you?'

'I'm going to Spain. Toni's aunt is letting us have her place in Majorca for a few weeks.'

'That sounds good. Lucky you.'

'So do you think you might like to come?' she ventured. 'It won't be very exciting or anything. We're just going to lie in the sun and live on San Miguel beer.'

'Me?' I said, surprised. 'Toni wouldn't want me, surely?' Toni was another girl I barely ever spoke to, part of that same crowd, with their noisy boyfriend troubles and the packs of condoms posing obviously in their handbags.

'Why not? A bunch of us are going. One more won't make any difference.'

'But Toni doesn't like me.'

'I don't think that's true. She doesn't even know you.' Addolorata fingered the outline of the fragrance bottle in her pocket.

It was true that I didn't have any idea what I was going to do once the exams were finished. School was the only constant left in my life. Yes, I hated the teachers and their dreary lessons, but at least they were something to run away from. Where would I be when I didn't even have that?

'You're living with your aunt, right?' Addolorata asked. 'Would she pay your airfare?'

'Things didn't work out with my aunt. I'm with an uncle now.'

'Well, perhaps he'd help out. It won't cost much, just the flights and food. My dad's paying for me ... It's meant to be an advance on my wages. Can you get the money somehow?'

I thought about being in another country, far away from here, with foreign voices I couldn't understand, different colours, foods and faces. 'Maybe … I don't know … I'll think about it,' I said.

'I'll tell the others then, shall I? It'll be fine, I'm sure it will.'

EXTRACT FROM ADDOLORATA'S JOURNAL

Oh bloody hell, I'm going to be in so much trouble when they find out who I've asked to come to Spain. My family's always telling me I'm too impulsive and now I see they may be right. But I can't go back on it now, not if she says she wants to come. Poor little thing. Her parents all smashed up in their car on the M6 and now she's living with some uncle and always seems so lonely, even though she must have some friends, I suppose. I'll have to make the others go along with it. I mean, it's only a few weeks and there'll be loads of us. Hopefully she won't start stealing stuff over there and get us all arrested …

God, she's a strange girl. I keep thinking how I'd be if my parents were wiped out like that. Not like Rosie Goodheart. I've never even seen her cry. No one has …

The Olive Estate

To Enzo the olive trees were like soldiers, climbing the hill behind the house in regimented columns, moving only to let the breeze shake itself through their silvery green leaves. There were so many of them now, thousands and thousands. They made the landscape what it was, stretching away in every direction. Only one small group broke the long, neat lines. On stony ground at the start of the rise, they fell about in an undisciplined straggle. Their trunks were twisted and split by time, their branches left unpruned. Hundreds of years ago some forgotten member of the Santi clan had planted them there. Enzo often wondered what he might think if he could see what his humble olive grove had become.

In this part of southern Italy almost everyone grew olive trees. If you owned a scrap of land you planted a few so you might pickle the fruit or press your own oil. Enzo's Nonna liked to dry the olives in her oven and store them in terracotta vases with salt and oregano as her own Nonna had taught her to years ago. She drank the olive oil like water. Each morning when she woke she took a long, grassy green sip of it. She swore that was why her skin was so soft and her face still unlined, and promised it would help her live for many more years.

Enzo knew that olive oil was the lifeblood of the Santi family. It had made them wealthy and respected. His great-grandfather was the one who had understood there was good money to be made from it. He had bought tne big stone press and begun to plant more trees, so many different varieties. From the beginning he favoured majatica, for it gave good crops and the oil was prized and plentiful. Those who tasted it for the first time found it difficult to describe: fruity, maybe slightly bitter, elegantly spicy, just a little peppery. His Nonna would roll her eyes. 'It tastes like majatica, nothing else. Why always try to complicate things?'

Enzo had grown up with the trees. His childhood harvest task had been to collect the fruit that fell from the panniers of the adults picking from their highest branches. Even then he'd known one day the whole grove would belong to him, the eldest son of the eldest son. These trees were his whole future.

Right now, though, he was only twenty-one, his grandfather was healthy, his father still young enough. One day Enzo would be the head of the Santi family but not for a long time. He wondered what he was supposed to do till then. Live with his five sisters in the house hemmed in by trees, waiting for each of them to marry and leave? Follow his father's orders as the years slipped by bringing the same tasks every season? Shake himself free now and then by driving too fast round the coast road, although his Nonna had begged him a thousand times not to?

The old lady fussed over him, she always had. Sometimes he found himself growing impatient with it. Now, for instance, as he sat in a kitchen chair while she took her time trimming his fingernails into neat squares and massaging olive oil into his cuticles with the pads of her fingers.

'I'm old enough to do this for myself,' he grumbled, marvelling at the firm grip of her worn hands. 'There's no need to keep treating me like a baby.'

'You wouldn't do it right,' his Nonna said briskly. 'I don't want people thinking my only grandson isn't well looked after. Let me put this towel around your shoulders and I'll trim your hair a little. Then you'll be my handsome Enzo again.'

He continued to mutter his complaints as she snipped at his hair. As a boy, he had liked all the attention. With his mother often busy cooking or cleaning and his father working on the land, only his Nonna always had plenty of time for him. Summer or winter they'd walk through the olive groves hand-in-hand and she'd tell him stories about the trees, how there were some in the world that had lived for thousands of years, perhaps even since Jesus and the saints had walked the earth.

'Imagine that, tasting the same fruit those holy people ate,' she liked to say. 'When we're gone and forgotten, these trees will be here still, Enzo. Never forget that. We are only guardians, here for a short while to care for them.'

At harvest-time she liked to take him to the pressing room and hold a small cup beneath the flow of fresh virgin oil. Together they'd take turns sipping from it, as though it were the finest wine. Always there was a lesson to be learnt. 'Wine ages well, oil doesn't,' his Nonna might remind him. 'All its goodness fades over time. That's why the Santi family is so healthy. We get the freshest and the best oil. The trees bless us with it.'

Enzo noticed how his sisters never walked in the olive groves with Nonna. Instead, they were put to work in the kitchen or given a bucket full of sudsy water and sent to mop the floors. He had heard the nickname they had for him – the little Prince of Olives – and knew how jealous they were. But he was the eldest son and they were girls; in their place he'd have felt bitter too. Still, what could he do?

His Nonna put down her scissors and held up a mirror so he could examine her work. 'Is that good or do you think I should take off a little more from the front?' she asked.

Enzo surveyed his reflection. His eyes were dark brown and his skin had turned the colour of liquid honey in the sun. Since his Nonna didn't like the fashion for hairstyles that touched the collar, she kept his short and sleek. His father's hair she cut in exactly the same way and his grandfather's too. 'It looks fine,' he told her. 'Don't take off any more.'

'*Va bene, va bene*. Go and wash your hands while I find a little something for you to eat. Some prosciutto and a few of my good olives, eh? That will keep you going until lunchtime.'

Enzo stood and hugged his Nonna, his arms wrapping easily round her tiny frame. He knew she was far from frail, despite her appearance. If she chose to she could still walk from one end of the olive grove to the other without getting breathless. And at harvest-time she'd be out with her basket from dawn to dusk gathering the fallen fruit. 'I am a Santi. We know how to work,' she often said. 'We take strength from it.'

Brushing a few stray clippings of hair from his shoulders onto the floor, Enzo went to wash his hands just as she'd told him to.

Rosie

London was wearing its weather like a grey shroud and every day seemed the same to me. Walking to school through the endless drizzle, lining up outside the exam hall, doomed to another day trapped at a desk, and then catching the tube back to my uncle's house where laundry hung from a rack that covered the kitchen ceiling and the rooms smelt of something they used to kill flies. As the exam weeks dragged by, it was only dreaming of the swell of the Mediterranean and the sound of Spanish voices that kept me going.

Addolorata must have regretted her invitation but once she'd offered me the words so impulsively there was no way she could take them back. I expect she was feeling sorry for me like everyone else and really hadn't meant me to accept it. I knew I wasn't welcome ... I wasn't particularly welcome anywhere. But the more I thought about it the more I longed to escape to an island, to sit in the sun, close my eyes and do nothing. To be anywhere but where I was.

The cash for my fare was easy enough to come by. My parents' house had been sold and there was a bank account full of money that had belonged to me since I'd turned eighteen a couple of months before. It might have funded the life they'd meant for me – the years at university, a place of my own, maybe even a little car. But there didn't seem much point in any of those things. My parents were gone, smashed up beyond recognition in the crash that had taken their lives. Bodies that once held me, warmed me, loved me had been turned into gruesome things, far too damaged for a girl my age to see. 'It'll only upset you, make it worse,' people kept saying in the run-up to the funeral, and I thought they were stupid because how could anything be worse than this?

I'd never had a chance to say goodbye. That final evening I ignored the sound of my mother's voice calling out to me, didn't glance out of my bedroom window to see them walking down the front path or wave as my father drove away – furiously and much too fast – in their little blue Citroën. Everything stopped with the last time I saw them, with my raised voice and a slamming door, with words I knew I hadn't meant at all.

It was the only thing I could think of. During sleepless nights and lonely days it weighed heavy on my mind. There was no way of changing it, nothing I could do to make it better. But if I could escape, run away from everything familiar for a while, then maybe I could forget that the last thing I'd ever said to my mother was that I hated her.

'I hear you're coming with us to Majorca,' Toni had muttered to me as we stood in the queue for an English exam. Her tone was offhand, her expression bland.

'I am ... if that's OK.'

'There'll be a crowd of us, I expect,' she replied with a slow shrug of her shoulders. 'So one more won't make that much difference.'

Toni didn't bother mentioning the trip to me again. It was Addolorata who gave me the dates and details of the flights they were on. She showed me the new bikini she'd bought and said she hoped it wouldn't look too awful on her. When I asked who else was going, her reply was vague. 'Me, Toni, Lou, possibly a friend of hers, maybe my sister Pieta. Just, you know, whoever wants to. We're really relaxed about it.'

It was turning into the wettest of summers. As London's streets filled with puddles I got through my exams by writing the first thing that came into my head. Like Addolorata, I didn't care about the results, couldn't see how they might possibly affect me. The old me might have spent every night revising then turned over the exam papers with a nervous intake of breath and written until my fingers hurt. I expect when it was over I'd have rushed to join the girls who used to be my friends to hash over the questions and our answers to them.

But that wasn't me, not any more. Now my life stretched ahead, decades and decades of it, and I wasn't interested in it at all. Couldn't see the point in literature, French and history. So instead of cramming in last-minute revision, I tried to fill my thoughts with Majorca. And I booked some flights and bought my own bikini.

My Uncle Phillip tried not to show his relief at getting rid of me for a few weeks. His wife, frowsy and fed up, was much less successful. She was shoving sausages, bread and ketchup into her two little boys when I waved my plane tickets under their noses.

'Majorca? Wish it was me. I could do with some sun. We all could,' she muttered. 'So, how many weeks will you be gone?'

'Three,' I told her. 'That's how long we can have the house for.'

'Three whole weeks, lucky you. And then what? When you get back what will you do?'

'Find a job and a room to rent,' I said with more confidence than I felt. 'I'll start looking as soon as I get back.'

'No hurry,' Uncle Phillip insisted. 'You've always got a home here, you know that. For as long as you like.'

I couldn't miss the sharp look his wife shot him then, just as I hadn't failed to hear her frantic whispering through their closed bedroom door night after night. I knew she felt as though her house didn't belong to her any more and couldn't wait to see me disappear out the front door with all my suitcases and boxes. Not that I blamed her, really. Most likely I'd have felt the same.

At first they'd tried really hard with me, moving their boys into bunk-beds in the box room so I could have the larger space, getting in my favourite foods, taking me on outings, and buying endless movie tickets and pizzas. They didn't understand why none of it worked, couldn't see that I felt as dead as my parents, as though nothing anyone did could bring me back either.

Eventually they gave up trying. To them I was just an awkward silence in a room. Someone who made laughter seem wrong and conversations stilted. How much nicer it would be if I was some place else. When she offered me the chance of three weeks in Majorca, Addolorata had no idea how big a favour she was doing us all.

The Majorca I'd imagined was all about sunburnt tourists and brash resorts but that first ever villa was backed by mountains and full of other people's books. A shabby old farmhouse, it had thick stone walls, a mossy terracotta-tiled roof and a long terrace with a view right down to the sea. There was quite a walk to go for a swim, down a path that was only sometimes shaded with trees and trekking back up it, salty-skinned and desperate for the first cold San Miguel of the day, seemed to take for ever.

These are the things I learnt about the others almost straight away. Addolorata worried she was fat. She'd eat a lunch of serrano ham, manchego cheese, salad and crusty bread, then squeeze her stomach into a roll of flab, groan and say, 'look at me; I'm huge.' Next she'd have an ice cream.

Toni had one weakness, a phobia about buttons. All her clothes fastened with zips, hooks-and-eyes or press-studs. She refused even to sit in a chair if someone else's button-covered cardigan was draped over the back of it.

Lou was a lot of fun. But she drank a glass of red wine five times faster than anyone else and sometimes in the morning, when she tried to cut up fruit for breakfast, the knife would shake in her hand.

There were only the four of us. The others had dropped out one by one, taken summer jobs or family holidays, been short on cash or enthusiasm. So it was just Toni, Lou, Addolorata and I with our bottles of suntan oil, our hats and sarongs taking a holiday in Majorca.

At night we drank wine and lay on our backs to look at the stars, wishing we knew what they were all called. Sometimes Addolorata played Michael Jackson and Prince, turning the sound up as loud as it would go, dancing like a mad thing with Lou on the terrace. During the day, if we weren't baking our bodies down on the rocks, we shopped for brightly coloured ceramic dishes and arranged fat green Spanish olives on them. They made so much noise the three of them, filled each day with their energy and laughter. It was a relief to let myself fade into the background of their lives for a while.

I'd brought my camera, a heavy old Russian Zenit my father had given me when I turned sixteen. While the others talked, drank and argued, I stayed behind its lens. I liked looking at life like that, restricted inside a frame.

When Toni bought little golden pyres of coconut cakes at the bakery one morning I photographed them arranged on a turquoise dish. Quietly I took shots of Addolorata as her skin turned to copper and glistened with sun oil. I looked through my camera at Lou, a glass in her hand, and at Toni while she spent an intrepid morning climbing the walls of rock that surrounded our little swimming bay.

'Do you have to photograph everything? Can't you put that camera away?' each of them complained at some point.

So then I started rearranging things in the villa, moving furniture around and gathering wildflowers to brighten up the brown-tiled kitchen. The décor in the whole place was a little tired, with faded fabrics and walls begging for a fresh coat of white-wash. But I put a bowl of waxy-skinned lemons on a table, collected shells, seeds and pebbles to layer into a clear glass vase, ordered stray books into piles and even organised the food we bought, bread on a board, tomatoes in a roughcast earthenware bowl, and it all looked so much prettier.

'Why don't you just sit down and relax?' they kept saying.

I couldn't explain why plumping up a cushion made me feel better. Or why I wanted to photograph a basket of bread before Addolorata's hand dipped into it greedily. Often I tried to be part of the group, lying out in the sun or sitting on the terrace talking about music, movies and boys. But far sooner than them I'd grow tired of it and wander off to find something beautiful to point my camera at.

After a few days I began getting up early, sometimes while it was still quite dark, and going to sit out on the terrace with a pot of strong coffee. Watching the light break through and hearing the birdsong that greeted it felt like time that was only mine.

That's where Addolorata found me one morning when it was barely light. She said she'd woken up hungry and decided to walk to the village for sticky almond cakes. When she saw me sitting on the terrace she looked startled.

'You're up already. Is everything all right?'

'Yes, I'm just waiting for the day to begin,' I told her. 'I really love it here.'

'That's good. I love it too.' She sat on the low rock wall that surrounded the terrace. 'I'm glad you came with us.'

'Are you really? I'm not driving everyone insane with my camera and my tidying up?'

She laughed. 'A little bit, maybe, but that's OK.'

I walked up to the village with her. The road was a gentle slope shaded by pine trees and Addolorata strode up it, panting a little as she neared the top. 'I've got to burn a few calories,' she said breathlessly. 'There are still two more weeks of eating to go. I'll be huge if I'm not careful.'

'You could just eat less,' I suggested.

She looked at me as though I were mad. 'But I'm in Spain with all this delicious food. I can't miss out. I want to taste everything: the tapas, the seafood, the cheeses. Don't you?'

'Well ...'

'Oh, please don't tell me you like the way it looks.'

I smiled. 'But I do.'

'You're strange. Food is for eating not photographing, you know.'

'But it makes a difference, doesn't it? Arranging it so it looks appetising? In your father's restaurant they must do that.'

'Yes, I suppose. But at Little Italy the flavours always come first. If things don't taste right it doesn't matter how good they look.'

'When we get back to London will you go to work there as a waitress?'

'No. I'm going to train as a chef. My father's big dream is that I should take over the place some day when he retires.'

'And do you want that?' I asked.

'Yeah, I suppose so. I want to cook. That's what I've always wanted.'

A part of me envied Addolorata her certainty. My parents would have pushed me through university and into some sort of career. Perhaps I'd have kicked against their plans, complained studying was dull or refused to take whatever course they wanted, but I'd have gone along with it in the end. I'd believed them when they said working hard was the only sensible option.

Now they were gone and it was entirely up to me to make all the decisions, to choose my own life. Even the idea of it was daunting. How was I supposed to start? To me it seemed a whole lot easier to fill my time rearranging cushions, putting flowers in glass jars and making life seem prettier when I looked at it through a camera lens.

WHAT ADDOLORATA SAID

'I know I shouldn't have asked her without checking with you first. I'm really sorry, OK? But they say that her dad had been speeding. That the car they were in was crushed and they were killed in an instant. I just felt so bad. Can you imagine how awful it must be? She must be trying desperately to hold herself together. How could anybody not feel sorry for her? Ah come on, Toni ... I know she's a funny little thing but she's turning out not to be that bad really.'

The Olive Estate

Around her neck Enzo's Nonna wore a small silver spoon on a long chain. When meals were being cooked she dipped it into the pans to test the sauces; nothing was ever put on the table until she was satisfied.

There was no part of the household she didn't have a hand in. Shopping lists were drawn up by her, the little vegetable garden outside the kitchen door was planted on her advice and she spent hours writing in her slow, large print in the ledgers where she kept the family accounts.

Her influence was felt beyond the house, well into the olive groves she walked through every morning. At harvest-time, other farmers saved time by using machines to shake the branches of their trees and laying nets to catch the falling fruit. But she believed shaking a tree hurt it right down to its roots so the Santi olives were handpicked by teams of workers with high ladders and then rushed to the pressing room and turned to oil within hours. Even the labels for the bottles weren't printed until his Nonna had checked that the words 'Single-estate grown, pressed and bottled' were large enough for her liking.

So many times now she had told Enzo how hard they'd worked in the early days, his grandfather busy planting and pruning while she raised their babies in two small rooms. Now the family owned a large house, painted pale orange and built right beside the highway where any passer-by could admire it. The basement was stacked with dusty jars of pickled artichokes and tomato sauce and hung with sides of prosciutto left to cure. Above it were three spacious floors that held modern bathrooms, well-equipped kitchens and comfortable living rooms but these apartments were used only for sleeping, for his Nonna still preferred the old house, with the lemon trees espaliered over the terrace, the television constantly blaring in one corner and the chickens underfoot. Ever since she was a newly-wed she had tended the shrine of Our Lady there; had swept the floors of its two rooms and gathered the family round its long marble-topped table to eat their meals. She liked the new apartments well enough – it was a pleasure to show guests through their cool, shuttered rooms and sense their admiration – but for the everyday business of living the old house was best.

As lunchtime approached, Enzo watched his Nonna setting the table that had been pulled outside into the shade of the terrace. She was calling instructions loudly through the kitchen door at whichever of his sisters was busy cooking. There had been some sort of squabble earlier, with tears at the end of it, although Enzo hadn't bothered listening so had no idea what it was about.

In the Santi family peace and quiet was hard to come by. Even when they gathered to share a meal, one sister would be kicking another beneath the table, there would be some reason for raised voices as the pasta was eaten, and before the meal was over someone would have stormed away from the table. Sometimes Enzo wondered if other families were like his. He remembered his parents' wedding anniversary when all of them had dined at the smart hotel restaurant in Triento. The entire meal had been eaten in silence, for unless they were fighting the Santi family had no idea what they should say to each other.

Often one look from his Nonna could silence any raised voices. Enzo didn't entirely understand why, as she was such a gentle-looking woman. One of his hands could crush her wrist easily, for her bones were like an insect's in comparison to his. And yet no one tried to argue with her or change the way she'd ordered things.

Even as she laid before him a dish of baked pasta or a platter of minnow-sized fish, rolled in flour, fried and doused in lemon, Enzo knew she did it because she wanted to. If she lit a cigarette and placed it into the mouth of his grandfather; or ate her own dinner in a rush over the sink while the rest of them dined at the table, it was because she chose to. This was her family and it brought her pleasure to look after them.

Taking his share of the fish, Enzo passed the platter down the table to his sisters. He nodded for his glass to be filled with the wine that his father had made and helped himself from the salad of rocket his mother had grown. Later he might take a nap then drive the few kilometres to Triento to meet his friends in their favourite bar by the marina and drink a coffee or a *limoncello*. Only during harvest-time or pruning was he needed much in the olive groves. His father could check the trees were growing free of disease; his grandfather would deal with customers. Summer had always been Enzo's time to please himself.

'Go and find a wife,' his Nonna always nagged when he left for the beach in the morning. 'Don't just sit there on your towel sunning yourself – think of your future.'

But when he was lying on the shingle listening to the waves crashing against the rocks and smelling the salt in the air, his future seemed such a long way away. Until then, what was there to do except enjoy himself?

By far the most important thing in Enzo's life was the red sports car he'd been given for his twenty-first birthday. It was kept in one of the barns and he was always careful to leave the roof closed up properly so he didn't find chickens roosting on its seats, their droppings spoiling the pristine cream leather. In summertime, especially, he loved driving fast round the bends of the coast road, although his Nonna had made him promise he'd be careful. The one time he'd persuaded her to come for a ride she'd complained endlessly about the dust and the sun in her eyes. Only when she was safely home again did she seem happy.

His Nonna didn't see much point in life beyond the estate. Other women her age might waste hours gossiping in the piazza or the bread shop, but she had no patience for it. Enzo knew far more than she did about the things that went on. He was aware, for instance, that his grandfather had a woman in the village, brassy-haired, many years younger and wearing a new gold necklace he was certain she hadn't paid for herself. He knew his father played cards for money and often lost the lot. He knew which of his sisters was likely to marry first and which one would get into trouble. His Nonna might have learnt all these things, too, if she'd spent more evenings strolling back and forth through Triento's narrow streets, stopping to chat or to take a coffee, just like he did.

There was a group of them that met most nights. They'd known each other for years, been in the same class at school, taken confirmation together. Now they dressed in pastel-coloured shirts, threw matching cotton sweaters around their shoulders, and moved in a flock from piazza to bar.

They might drink a couple of liqueurs, eat an ice cream or share a few slices of pizza, but none of that was the real point of the evening. For Enzo and his friends the hours squandered hanging round the streets or at the pavement cafés were for one thing only – looking at pretty girls.

And there were plenty of girls to admire in Triento. Often Enzo might let loose a whistle at a particular favourite – or even risk the pinch of a firm, young bottom – but that was as far as it went. Each girl had a mother who dreamt of seeing her in a pure white dress, standing at an altar, and Enzo was aware that the size of the Santi Estate was enough to waken any woman's ambitions so he'd learnt to be especially careful with the local girls.

Each evening, as he and his friends combed their hair and splashed on cologne, what they were really hoping for were tourists – foreign girls who'd stay only a few days and then move on to the next place. The trouble was there were so few of them. A little further up the coast were much richer pickings. Several times they'd driven all the way to Amalfi for the evening and been dazzled by what they'd seen: expensive girls, their wrists and throats glinting with silver, dressed skimpily in the latest resort wear and swaying on high heels. Enzo had tried to get himself noticed, talking in a louder voice and laughing more confidently at his own jokes, but somehow they seemed to know he didn't belong. None of his whistling and catcalling worked; the girls only laughed and shook their heads. He'd never had any luck in Amalfi, none of them had.

So mostly they stayed in their own village where the tourists were shod in ugly hiking sandals and interested only in staring at old churches or the famous statue of Christ on the mountain. Triento was an ancient place, caught between the mountains and the sea, a tangle of alleyways and steep streets shaded by the swell of the land behind it. Enzo always thought winter was a gloomy time there. But in summer, when the sun warmed the terracotta-tiled roofs and thick stone walls, he felt the place come alive. Then, on market days, people would travel from miles to buy waxy gourds of caciocavallo cheese, pink-speckled borlotti beans and peaches swollen with sweet juices. They stopped for espresso and rum-soaked cakes at the café, crowded the narrow streets and made the village more interesting.

Only in summer did the marina beneath Triento hold more than just the usual fishing boats. Enzo and his friends had wasted whole days sitting on the short stretch of sand waiting to see who would step off the smart yachts and shiny speedboats. Each year they teased themselves with the idea that some day their luck might change and the kinds of girls they were hoping for would finally appear in Triento.

Enzo finished his fish and nodded when his Nonna offered more. He wondered if this at last might be the summer it happened.

Rosie

I'd already taken loads of photographs of the café in the nearest village. Its wisteria-covered terrace, dotted with round metal tables, appealed to me and so did the people I found there.

Over the course of several days I'd managed to take surreptitious shots of the waiter, his tray balanced in one hand as he danced between his customers, and of the grizzled old men trying to make their cups of café Americano last for hours. I'd even photographed our milky morning coffees, which arrived with a little dish of sugary vanilla biscuits on the side.

Addolorata liked to settle at a table in the sunshine and pull down the straps of her dress so her shoulders would tan evenly. She lived in hope that a good-looking man might pass by and catch sight of her sitting there. 'I read that loads of movie stars have villas here – it's a playground for the rich arty types,' she told me, stirring spoonfuls of sugar into her coffee. 'So where exactly are they?'

'Sitting by their swimming pools, I suppose.'

'How are we meant to have any fun, then? There doesn't seem to be any nightlife, not even a disco.'

'There must be something, surely?'

'Yes, but it's all on the other side of the island where the hotels and resorts are. And we're here on this side … for weeks.'

'Maybe there's a bus that would take you over there.'

'But then we'd have to sleep on the beach and get bitten by mosquitoes and wake up with hangovers.' She made a face. 'I'd rather stay here and be bored, wouldn't you?'

'I'm not bored,' I told her.

'Really? Not at all? Just a nightclub and some male attention, that's all I ask. Then I wouldn't be bored either.'

I swung my camera lens over towards the bakery and focused on its doorway. 'Maybe there's a movie star in there, buying bread.'

'I doubt it. And don't bother pointing that thing at the wine shop either – it's only ever full of short, ancient men … I've checked.' Addolorata finished her coffee and forked up a mouthful of almond cake. 'I can't believe we've already done everything there is to do here. We should have rationed ourselves. We had way too much fun at the beginning.'

'There has to be something else.'

'Well, if there is then the locals are keeping it a secret.' Addolorata finished the last of her cake. 'I guess we could go and buy food now. Or is it too early? Maybe we should save the grocery shopping as a treat for later.'

I laughed at her. The emptiness of the days didn't bother me at all. I liked that there were so few expectations and hardly any choices. And I loved the hillside village, all its buildings made from the same pinky-grey stone and the landscape dotted with cypress and olive trees. I liked eating a lunchtime *bocadillo* at the café and buying fresh food in the tiny hole-in-the-wall store.

And I'd sent a postcard to my uncle's family purely to give myself an excuse to stand in the old post office where nothing seemed to have changed for a hundred years.

That morning we arrived at the food store at the same time as a delivery of fresh seafood: prawns in their shells, live mussels in a bucket, scary-looking octopus. At the sight of it Addolorata was more animated than I'd seen her in days. 'We could make a paella,' she suggested. 'I'm sure there's a proper pan in one of the cupboards and we could gather some wood and cook it over the barbecue on the terrace. What do you think?'

'Do you know how?'

She shrugged. 'I expect so. It can't be that difficult.'

I watched as she stripped the shop of everything she thought we might need: lots of seafood, Spanish rice, spicy chorizo, saffron, tomatoes and a bag of fresh green beans. 'Mmm, this is going to be fantastic,' she told me. 'We just need smoked paprika and then we're sorted.'

The walk down the hill with our heavy shopping bags was hot and exhausting. 'But it'll be worth it,' Addolorata promised. 'We'll go down for a swim first and then come back and have the paella as a late lunch with lots of lovely white wine.'

When we reached the house Lou and Toni were sitting on the terrace, still in their pyjamas and eating toast and jam. I'd noticed how they were beginning to form a pair, leaving Addolorata to keep me company. If she minded too much, she didn't show it.

'Have you guys only just woken up?' she called out to them. 'Jeez, Rosie and I have been out for breakfast, we've bought stuff for lunch and we've got the whole day planned.'

'We both have headaches,' Lou told her. 'Actually, we were just considering a couple of cold San Miguels for breakfast. Thought a beer might perk us up.'

'That's not a bad idea.' Addolorata dumped her shopping bags on the ground. 'Now you mention it, I might need some perking up too.'

The plan for a swim abandoned, the three of them sipped cold beers while I put the seafood in the fridge and restlessly scoured the garden for kindling, foraging in the long grass and weeds until I had enough fallen branches to get the barbecue fire started. Then I went back inside and searched the bookshelves for something that might have a paella recipe in it.

I re-emerged into the sunshine holding a tattered old volume called *The Beautiful Book of Spanish Cooking*. 'This has a paella recipe in it. But it says that it's traditional for men to cook it in an orchard over a fire of orange wood and pine cones,' I told Addolorata.

'Let's see.' She took the book from me and cast her eyes quickly over the recipe. 'Hmm, well, we don't have everything it says you need and we definitely don't have a man. But it also claims they used to put rat meat in paella so I don't think we should worry too much about sticking to the authentic recipe.'

All of us had imagined it would be easy to get a fire going beneath the barbecue, especially with the dry sticks I'd gathered. But in the end Toni and Lou had to walk back up to the shop for a box of firelighters. I stayed behind to help Addolorata, although she didn't need me really. She cooked in a relaxed way, almost as if it was incidental to everything else she was doing: talking, laughing, drinking chilled white wine. A meal was produced without her seeming to make any effort at all.

Once we'd managed to light the fire and it was burning well, I watched Addolorata pouring olive oil into the paella pan with a heavy hand. Crouching beside her, I started taking photographs as she threw in garlic, tomatoes and a chopped red pepper.

'Rosie, that does not seem like a flattering angle,' she said, shaking her black curls at me. 'All you'll be getting from there is loads of belly and chin. If you don't stop right now I'll feed your share of the paella to the stray cats.'

By now the scent of the wood smoke was mingling with the mouth-watering smells coming from the bubbling rice. Addolorata let the flames die down and left the dish to simmer gently.

'It'll be a half an hour before it's ready,' she told us.

'A bottle of wine, then?' suggested Lou.

This time I joined them, sitting in the shade of the terrace and sipping the wine far more slowly than they ever did. It amazed me just how many empty Rioja bottles and cigarette packets I found littering the villa every morning. Lou, in particular, seemed to be able to empty a glass without me even noticing her drinking.

By the time the paella was ready to come off the fire we'd finished the wine. Addolorata insisted on covering the pan and leaving it to stand for a while longer so Lou uncorked another bottle and I set the table, putting a vase filled with rosemary branches in the centre to make it look special.

At last Addolorata filled our plates with mounds of steaming paella.

'You've made so much we should have invited the whole village,' said Lou.

'Yes, we could have had all the local characters over,' agreed Toni. 'But sadly the grumpy old men and sour-looking women will have to eat their lunch somewhere else today.'

'Oh, they're not that bad,' I protested. 'A couple of them smiled and said "*hola*" today. By the end of another week they'll be treating us like locals.'

'I can't wait for that.' Addolorata laughed and picked up her fork. 'Anyway, have a taste and tell me what you think.'

The first flavour I found was the smokiness of the paprika, then the spicy heat of the chorizo and the lemony fishiness of octopus. All the broth had been absorbed by the rice but still the paella was slick with oil and tomatoes and difficult to eat without making a mess. As we peeled juicy prawns and licked golden rice from mussel shells, none of us spoke.

Addolorata and Lou piled their plates with second helpings but the paella pan was still half full when we'd finished eating.

'We can have it cold for supper with a green salad,' I suggested. 'Then there's no need to go shopping again.'

Addolorata licked the saffron from her fingers. 'I want to go up to the village later, though. I've just realised there's something we haven't eaten yet that we shouldn't miss out on for a moment longer: *churros* and chocolate.'

'Dessert? How could you even think of it?' I screwed up my face at the idea. 'Aren't you completely stuffed?'

'I am right now but in a few hours' time a fried doughnut dipped in chocolate sauce might be exactly what I need.'

'You'll regret it,' Toni told her.

'Probably,' Addolorata admitted, 'but I'm going to eat it anyway, I know I am. So what's the point of feeling guilty?'

After lunch we lay on sun-loungers that we'd pulled into the shade, idly reading books and magazines or doing puzzles. I kept thinking about the paella and wondering how Addolorata had been so certain it would be good when she'd barely bothered to taste it as it was bubbling away.

'Often I just know what flavours will go together,' she told me when I asked. 'It's an instinct, I suppose. And if I taste too much of a dish as I'm cooking then I'm bored by the time it's ready. So I prefer to rely on my instincts.'

'I've never really done any cooking,' I admitted. 'I wouldn't know where to start.'

'Not knowing how to cook is like not being able to swim. How do you expect to survive?'

'Would you show me, then?' I asked. 'Teach me how to make the spaghetti with bacon and olives you made the other night? And the risotto with asparagus?'

'Yeah, OK. Anyone can manage a bowl of pasta or a risotto. You'll love it once you get started.'

I couldn't imagine finding the joy in food that Addolorata seemed to have. Often she'd make plans for dinner before we'd finished breakfast. She hungered for new flavours, almost always ate too much, and it was astonishing the mess

34

she could make: the splatter patterns of tomato sauce up a wall, the stained clothes, the hot oil flicking from a flying pan.

But in those early mornings when I was the only one awake, drinking coffee out on the terrace as the sun came up, I'd started having ideas. I wasn't going back to my uncle's place, or to the aunt who I hadn't been able to stand. I couldn't bear living surrounded by other people's things or in the middle of their mess. I wanted to be on my own. For me to have a chance of managing it, Addolorata was right – I'd have to learn to start swimming.

EXTRACT FROM ADDOLORATA'S JOURNAL

I'm sure my clothes are getting tighter. That denim skirt never used to be so difficult to zip up and my jeans dig in to me when I sit down. That's it; I really do have to stop eating. From now on I'm only going to have fresh fruit for breakfast. And I'll get some exercise – go for a decent walk over the hills every morning. Rosie will come with me.

It's funny, I hadn't expected to end up hanging out with her. I can't see us being best friends when we get home or anything. There's something odd about her, she's not like the rest of us at all. Perhaps it's the way she looks, that light blonde hair and pale blue eyes, sort of glacial. She's so different to me – I always seem to be staining myself and spilling things, or I have dirt that needs scraping out of my fingernails and hair that needs washing. Rosie looks as though someone just pulled her out of a box. It's unnerving.

The Olive Estate

Some days Enzo hated the olive trees. Season by season they dictated how the Santi family lived. The olive trees were the reason Enzo's father spent so much of his time casting his eyes skywards and talking about the weather. They were why the whole family seemed edgy when a late spring brought hot, dry winds or heavy rains that might spoil the cream flowers, washing the pollen to the ground and wasting it. The trees were needy, they had to be fertilised, scrutinised constantly for disease and infestations. But mostly what they demanded was patience so they could grow their crop in peace until early winter when the harvesting began.

And then there was the pruning, with each tree shaped like a wineglass so the sun could touch the fruit to ripen it. Enzo had been taught how to prune properly as a young boy. 'Each tree should be trimmed until a bird can fly through it,' his Nonna had told him. 'We must let in light and keep the tree under control. But it's not so easy to decide which branches to take and which to leave. It takes years of experience to make a good pruner. Some day you will be one, though, I'm certain of that.'

Only on Sundays did the Santi family leave their estate untended. When the bells of all seven of Triento's churches rang out, the family changed into good clothes, the girls fussed with their hair and make-up, and they went to Mass together. Even his Nonna liked to wear a slash of orange lipstick, a red straw hat and a tailored skirt that never appeared any other day. She took her place proudly in the pew reserved for them in the church where they'd always worshipped. They had status within its walls, just as they did outside. As Enzo dabbed his forehead with holy water and made the sign of cross at the altar, he understood that even in church the olive trees were controlling him. He was a Santi son and certain things were expected of him, especially when he was under the watchful eye of his Nonna.

Sundays had been the same for as long as Enzo could remember. After Mass the family would return home to eat a leisurely lunch at the long marble-topped kitchen table. While the women cooked, the men grazed on antipasti and talked about the usual things: olive yields, the price of a new press, trouble with distributors. Then there would be pasta, often great trays of it baked in the oven, sweating with cheese and soaked in olive oil. Course after course would follow: a small dish of sweet-fleshed prawns, red peppers blistered over the wood-fired barbecue, eels baked in terracotta with wine and garlic, artichokes stuffed with parsley and steamed in lemon, sardines cooked with vinegar and onions. The dishes changed with the seasons, and sometimes a neighbour and friend would join them at the table, but everything else remained the same. They ate and talked together for half the afternoon.

Afterwards, while the women were in the kitchen cleaning the mess of dishes, there was time for a rest on starched, cool sheets until the family gathered again in the early evening and returned to Triento to make their *passeggiata*. Usually they broke into groups, Enzo met up with his friends, his father headed to his preferred table at the corner bar and his sisters linked arms with their mother. Up and down the narrow streets they would walk, back and forth, even on chill winter evenings. And the same thing was happening in every town around them. In the old days it had been how an Italian mamma showed off her daughters of marriageable age, and even now, when the girls were less carefully chaperoned, it remained a way to make a match.

Some Sundays his Nonna chose to join them and then Enzo's sisters walked slower and carried their heads more proudly. Ever since they were tiny they'd been taught to think of themselves as prizes. Each sister knew it was important to find a good husband, for beyond a dowry they could expect little from the family.

All were aware that the Santi Estate would never be broken up and parcelled off into smaller groves. Enzo was destined to inherit it whole and serve the trees for the rest of his life. The day would come when it would be up to him to oversee the harvest, take the first taste of each season's oil, balance the ledgers full of numbers his grandfather kept in his office and maintain the worn stone press that had crushed the olives that generations of the family had grown.

The Santi pressing room was at the heart of the estate. It was built into the side of a hill and behind it was another space, windowless, cool and dark, carved into the rock. It was here the family stored litres of precious olive oil in giant glass demi-johns. One of Enzo's jobs was to decant the cloudy green-gold liquid into smaller vessels for use in the kitchen. Salads would be tossed in it, onions fried; it was spooned into sauces and drizzled over nearly everything they ate.

Often his grandfather asked him to decant a little for the visitors who came to the estate. Some were expensively dressed with gold rings on their fingers, others looked more like ordinary farmers, but his grandfather treated all of them with the same careful respect. Enzo knew exactly who they were. Here on the edge of Calabria people whispered the names of their families. Each was important in his town or village, reaching into everything, influencing all. Every one of these men, who stood and chatted amicably to Enzo about football as he poured out their olive oil, came from a family that had the power to decide who lived and who died in the places they held sway over.

Usually they would take a drink with his grandfather, perhaps enjoy a snack of rough bread, prosciutto and olives, and then they'd walk between the trees where no one could hear them talking. Enzo had never asked what their business was. Like everyone, he knew enough to be wary.

He and his friends were scornful of the American Mafia films they'd seen on television, for here in the mountains of the Italian south that was not the way things were. These people were ruthless and mysterious; their families were loyal and feuds were settled quietly, not in a blaze of guns and pools of blood. Each clan had a different area they specialised in – protection rackets, drugs, kidnap, contraband, fraud – and they made a lot of money. If they'd wanted it these men could have bought every drop of the Santi oil as well as the land the trees stood on. But Enzo thought they liked the ritual of standing in the dim light of the cave as he poured out a bottle or two for them. They were men who understood tradition.

Before they left they would shake his grandfather by the hand, Enzo, too, if he was standing by. Each man's hand felt different: some smooth, others calloused; one strong-gripped, another not. There was no suggestion of a threat in the squeeze of their palms. These men might have been neighbours or old friends. They might have been distant family. Still, Enzo was glad to see the dust raised by their cars as they drove through the gates of the estate and away from his olive trees.

Rosie

My parents were very ordinary, not particularly clever or beautiful, just my parents, the people I loved and who cared for me. Both of them liked to do things properly so we had a comfortable house, a decent car and took package holidays every summer. My mother ate healthy food and exercised; my dad paid the bills on time and bought good insurance. They were nice people with nice lives.

But what was the point of them doing everything right if it was all going to end on a wet road in the crunch of metal on metal, their nice lives gone in an instant? If everything was utterly fragile and no one could tell what the next hour might bring, then why bother trying? Why plan anything at all?

Those were the thoughts that occupied me as I walked over the Majorcan hills with Addolorata in the cool of an early morning or sat on the terrace and stared out at the horizon bleeding into the sea.

The others had plans in place. Toni was going to university, Lou had signed on to a secretarial course, Addolorata would start work as a trainee chef in her father's restaurant. Often, as we lay baking in the sun after a morning swim, they would talk about how their lives were going to be.

'I want to have some money in the bank so I can afford to buy a house some day when I get married,' Lou said, sitting on the lip of a rock and churning her feet through the sea below. 'I'm not going to waste three years living on a student grant just to get a qualification that might not get me anywhere.'

'Yeah, but I will get somewhere,' Toni said, sounding sure of herself. 'I'll do my degree and then I'll train to be a teacher ... or a journalist ... I'm not certain yet.'

Addolorata was wallowing in the shallows like a seal. She reached out for her beer and balanced it against the rock. 'We're all going to lose touch with each other after this, aren't we?' she said regretfully. 'We'll go off in our separate directions and never have another holiday like this one.'

'Not necessarily,' said Toni. 'We can stay in touch, can't we?'

'Yeah, but we won't. You'll go to college and find new friends. Then you'll forget all about us.' Addolorata said it matter-of-factly. 'That's what happens.'

'It doesn't have to happen, though,' Toni insisted. 'We've been friends for years and years. Why would that stop because I'm going to college?'

'It just will. Everything changes. It has to.' Addolorata hauled herself out of the water and rolled onto the rock, her hair streaming like wet seaweed across her shoulders.

'OK, what say we make a deal, then?' suggested Lou.

'What sort of deal?' Addolorata asked.

'We could promise to have another holiday exactly like this one, couldn't we? No matter where we are or what we're doing, in three years' time – when Toni graduates from college – we'll meet at this villa.'

Toni looked doubtful. 'My aunt might not let us have it again,' she pointed out. 'And anyway, wouldn't we want to go somewhere more exciting?'

'We'd still need the sea, though,' Lou mused. 'And beaches, sunshine, delicious food and wine.'

'Italy,' Addolorata decided. 'In three years' time we should meet at a villa in Italy. No matter where we are or what we're doing, let's all agree to be there.'

'In three years' time? Anything could have happened by then,' I said in a quiet voice.

'But that's the whole idea, isn't it?' Toni sounded impatient. 'That's the point of promising.'

'OK, I'm in,' said Lou. 'Italy in three years' time. I'll be there.'

'Me too,' agreed Toni.

'I don't know where I'll be the week after we get home,' I protested. 'How can I think about three years from now?'

Still, I did like the idea. It seemed like a fixed point for me to aim for. My life was so uncertain; it was comforting to know there might be one thing tidily stored away for the future.

Addolorata stretched out her legs to dry in the sun. 'I can tell you exactly where I'll be for the next three years: pulling double shifts in a kitchen. Lou will be in an office, Toni will be writing essays late into the night. We'll be working, that's where we'll be. We won't have any choice.'

'You sound as though you're dreading it,' I said.

'Not really. It's just I've grown up in that restaurant. I know the menu back to front and all the waiters are old friends. I even know where the teaspoons are kept. Going to work there full time will be great but it's not exactly an adventure.'

'Is an adventure what you want?' I asked her.

'Isn't that what everybody wants? Not that there's much chance of it for me. My father seems to have my life all mapped out. He wants me to work hard at Little Italy and save up to buy a home of my own because owning property is the most important thing, apparently. Still, at least we've got another holiday planned. Surely we'll manage to find some sort of adventure in Italy?'

That afternoon Addolorata showed me how to prepare courgettes in a southern Italian way. We sliced them into long strips then placed them on a wooden board covered with a cloth to dry in the sun. Afterwards she fried them in olive oil and left them to steep in mint, garlic, vinegar, oil and salt. We ate them with a linguine she tossed with cherry tomatoes roasted softly in the oven, their flavour woken with lots of basil, garlic and chilli.

Addolorata laughed as I arranged the food on the plates, wiping a cloth round the rim, carefully clearing away oily splashes of tomato juice.

'You're funny, you know,' she told me. 'But actually I think you could be quite a good cook, even with all that fussing around you do. I can't believe you've never tried it before.'

'My mother did all the cooking at home,' I told her.

Mentioning my parents always drew the same response from people. Their eyes shifted, they sucked in their breath and settled their faces into an expression suitable for conversations about the dead. I suppose they were worried about upsetting me or didn't want to be reminded that life has to end at some point. That's why I rarely mentioned my mum and dad – everyone seemed to find it easier, even me.

Addolorata didn't flinch, though, when I brought them up now. 'Was your mother a good cook?' she asked lightly.

'Yes, I think so, but her food was all low fat and healthy,' I told her. 'She wouldn't have believed the amount of olive oil you put into everything and we only ever ate brown pasta.'

Addolorata pulled a face. 'Ugh life is too short for brown pasta.' Then she realised what she'd said. 'Oh God, I'm so, so sorry. I'm saying the wrong thing again, aren't I? I always seem to.'

'You're right, though,' I told her. 'Life is too short ... for lots of things.'

Lou tipped some red wine into a glass and quickly handed it to me. 'None of us can imagine what you've been through, Rosie,' she began. 'We all feel—'

'It's OK, you don't have to say all that sympathetic stuff,' I interrupted. 'It's not obligatory.'

For a moment the silence was so awkward I thought I'd have to leave the room.

'What is the right thing to say, then?' Toni asked, her voice almost icy. 'None of us knows.'

I drained my glass and handed it back for Lou to refill. 'I don't know. There isn't a right thing, probably … Look, I'm sorry, I know how difficult it's been having me around. But I'm really glad you let me come.' I said it as brightly as I could. 'It was so kind of you.'

The three of them were staring at me again. 'You'll come to Italy with us too,' said Lou, and it sounded like she meant it.

'Yes, you will,' agreed Addolorata. 'Definitely.'

'OK then, let's drink to Italy.' Lou raised her glass. 'We'll all be there in three years' time whatever happens.'

She uncorked another bottle of Rioja and, once we'd finished that, rummaged about in the cupboards pulling out half-drunk bottles of mysterious liqueurs. One tasted of blackcurrants, another had a picture of an artichoke on the label and even she couldn't swallow that one down. We emptied sticky bottle after bottle, drinking with determination. None of us thought about the morning, the headaches we might have or the hours in the night spent bent over the toilet bowl. The four of us drank as though it was the only thing that mattered.

WHAT ADDOLORATA SAID

'I know it's awkward and I keep putting my foot in it but we can't avoid ever mentioning her parents, can we? Or ignore what happened to them? Rosie's so prickly. As if having people feel sorry for her is the worst thing of all. That doesn't make it any easier.

'You know there are so many things I don't get about her. Like what's happened to all her friends …? She never mentions them. Surely they should be rallying

round? And do you think she really has no clue what she'll do when we get back home? She must have something, surely – people to catch up with, places to go. You can't ask her, though. She just gets that look on her face and freezes you out.

'I'm glad we've made a plan to go to Italy. It'd be cool to meet up there in three years' time and see how everyone's changed ... especially Rosie ... It seems as though nearly anything could happen to her.'

The Olive Estate

Surrounded by friends, with a glass of *limoncello* in his hand and the evening sun touching his face, Enzo was aware of the picture he made. He expected his share of admiring glances, had dressed for them, even, choosing his clothes carefully, smoothing gel through his hair and splashing his body with cologne, taking longer to get ready than his sisters did. They teased him for it, called him vain, but Enzo shook off the word easily enough. He knew how important it was to have style. All his friends felt the same. Even Gianpaolo Sesto, whose father was only a fisherman, had his mamma press his best shirt, combed his hair in place and carefully cleaned the fish scales from beneath his fingernails before walking to the bar near the marina, the one they tended to drift towards in the hotter months.

It was pleasant there, with a cool breeze lifting from the sea. There were plenty of outdoor tables shaded by striped umbrellas and often the patron would bring little plates of food for them to snack on – olives, of course, croquettes of potato, salty crackers and *suppli*, the little fried rice balls with mozzarella melting in the middle. The patron liked keeping them there, especially on a Sunday evening when everyone, young and old, made a *passeggiata* back and forth past his bar, the women showing off their best outfits, their finest jewels and their pretty daughters.

'Look out,' Gianpaolo warned, nudging Enzo with a sharp elbow. 'Here comes Maria Luisa Mancuso again. Her mamma gets a hungry look whenever she sees you. Had you noticed?'

'Yes, yes, I see her staring.' Enzo laughed, nudging his friend back just a little harder. 'Perhaps it's not me she wants for her daughter. It might be you instead.'

'I don't think so.' Gianpaolo shook his head ruefully. 'Maria Luisa is a pretty girl. Her mamma will want more for her than a boy like me. She is hungry for olives not sword-fish.'

Absent-mindedly, Enzo reached for a fat green olive, putting it in his mouth and rolling it round with his tongue, tasting the sourness of the brine as he watched the mother and daughter walk by. Gianpaolo was right when he said Maria Luisa had turned into a beauty. Her figure was shapely and the way she walked graceful. As a child, Enzo had played with her, chasing her through the olive trees on the estate for hours on end until his Nonna called them in for chocolate *gelato* and they giggled together as they made their faces messy with it. Eventually, Maria Luisa's body had changed, her breasts had rounded, her narrow waist flared into fuller hips. At the same time Enzo's voice had deepened and he'd begun to use a razor on his face. After that, they'd been awkward with each other and Signora Mancuso had begun to wear the hungry expression that Gianpaolo had noticed.

'I don't want a wife, not yet,' Enzo reminded his friend. 'I'd rather have some fun first.'

'Perhaps Maria Luisa's mamma thinks if she walks past often enough you'll fall in love and forget about fun.'

Enzo couldn't imagine being in love. Nor did he understand what made a man choose one woman over many. Yes Maria Luisa had a beautiful face and he'd always liked her, but to stand in front of a priest and vow to be with her always made no sense. Perhaps the next week he might meet another girl he liked more? Or change his mind entirely? Marriage seemed so final, so serious, and Enzo knew himself well enough to realise he wasn't ready for it.

47

'Come on, let's stretch our legs and see who else is about,' he said to Gianpaolo, draining his glass and pulling a comb from his pocket to fix his hair in place.

They strolled towards the seafood restaurant on the far point, nodding their greetings as they went. Enzo paused to talk to a couple of his cousins and perform the usual kissing of cheeks and shaking of hands. Then he spotted his sister Concetta, with Ricardo Russo and his mother walking on either side of her like guards.

Enzo was almost certain she would be the first of his sisters to marry – it was all she wanted. She and the others liked to imagine their wedding gowns and plan names for their babies. One time he had caught her signing the name Concetta Russo on the back of an old envelope and, embarrassed, she'd tried to hide what she was doing. Now here she was out with Ricardo and his family, wearing the white dress that only ever came off its hanger for special evenings and would be put away again as soon as she got home.

For a while they swapped pleasantries, then he and Gianpaolo moved on, walking slowly until they reached the end of the point. Circling back, they retraced their steps, Enzo finding more familiar faces amidst the crowds: old friends, uncles, people he'd known for years.

Feeling Gianpaolo's elbow nudge into his ribs again, he realised Signora Mancuso was steering her daughter back towards them.

'*Salve*, Enzo,' the signora called out when she was still a few feet away, her face creasing into a smile.

Enzo returned her greeting. 'How are you this evening?' he asked politely.

'Oh, well enough, but how very hot it is.' She rolled her eyes, fanning at her face with her hand. 'Tell me, how is your Nonna? I've been meaning to come over and bring her some bottles of my husband's wine. I know how much she always enjoys it.'

'That is very kind of you, Signora. I'm sure my Nonna would appreciate it.'

'We'll come over soon then, won't we, Maria Luisa?' The signora smiled at her daughter, encouraging her into the conversation. Enzo noticed how the girl's colour deepened and wondered if perhaps she was embarrassed.

'Yes, Mamma,' Maria Luisa murmured, her cheeks still flushed. 'And how are you, Gianpaolo? How is your family?'

'They are well.' Gianpaolo seemed to be looking down at the ground rather than at Maria Luisa. 'I'll tell them you were asking after them.'

'Yes ... yes ... it was good to see you,' Maria Luisa managed, as her mother began to tow her onwards, walking more briskly than before. 'I hope to meet you again soon.'

Watching the awkward exchange, something dawned on Enzo. He waited until the crowds had closed around Maria Luisa before playfully punching his friend on the shoulder. 'You're sweet on her,' he said, laughing.

Gianpaolo's eyes slid sideways. 'No, no ...' he began. 'Not really.'

'Don't lie to me. I can see right through you ... and Maria Luisa, too.'

His Nonna had always said Gianpaolo had the face of a cherub, with long lashes that swept to full cheeks and a head of tightly curled hair. He'd long been the best looking boy in Triento and since he'd started working on the fishing boats his face had tanned deeply and his body hardened.

'Like I told you, I think she's pretty,' his friend said defensively. 'If I was looking for a wife I'd want a girl like her. But I'm in no hurry. Some day, when I manage to buy my own boat, that will be the time to think about marrying.'

'Maria Luisa might not wait that long,' Enzo warned.

Gianpaolo shrugged. 'Money likes to marry money, doesn't it? Even if I had a boat I wouldn't be rich. I'll never stand a chance with her.'

'What are you talking about? You could have your pick of any woman in this town.'

'No, no, you're wrong.' Gianpaolo's tone was resigned. 'It's different for you, Enzo. You have land ... expectations ... Who wouldn't want to marry an olive farmer? But a fisherman's wife has a hard life. Every time Mamma sees my father head out to sea she worries a storm will blow up and the boat he's on might not survive it. Signora Mancuso won't want that for her daughter. She'll keep her away from me, you'll see.'

Later, as he was driving home, Enzo thought about his friend's words. He suspected that Gianpaolo was giving up too easily and was certain there was no way he would do the same. If he wanted a girl like Maria Luisa then he'd try whatever was necessary to get her. To Enzo it was as simple as that.

Rosie

In Majorca I'd been nudged along by the slow rhythms of island life. The pace of the days had lulled me – the heat, the music of the cicadas, the way my skin felt after I'd plunged into the sea then dried off in a warm breeze. I could breathe there; it was like I'd taken a holiday from grief as well as from everything else.

But then we returned to London and the city sliced right back into the old wounds. Majorca had changed nothing really. My life was still there waiting for me.

The first thing I did was change the thing I hated most. Desperate to escape my uncle's house, I went through the flat-share ads in the *Evening Standard* and spent my days, *A-Z* in hand, zigzagging the city looking for a place I thought would suit me. Eventually I found a basement flat in a stone-faced Georgian building on Fitzroy Square where I had to sleep on a mattress on the floor and could hear the tube trains rumbling beneath me. It wasn't ideal but I liked the fact that it wouldn't leach too much from my savings and that my two flatmates were politely disinterested so long as I did my share of the washing-up and didn't steal their cheese.

Both were older than me. One had an office job and left early each morning suited up smartly; the other was an out-of-work actress desperate to score a part in *Starlight Express*. She put in hours of practice, roller-skating in circles round the square or back and forth across the linoleum kitchen floor when it was raining.

I quickly found there was a comfort to living among

strangers. No one ever asked where I'd been or what plans I had. Even the actress, who spent a lot of time hanging round the flat drinking tea, didn't seem to care. And when I heard the front door shut behind her I knew I was completely free. I could cry as loudly as I wanted, hit my fists against the worn old carpet. The outer walls of the flat were thick; we were almost buried underground; no one could hear me.

Sometimes I'd go for a walk round the square and stare up at the blue plaque of the house where Virginia Woolf had once lived. I'd read her novel *To The Lighthouse* in the final year of school and even though I'd never loved the book I'd been fascinated by the story of its author, especially her ending. Virginia Woolf filled her pockets with stones and walked into a river. They called it suicide while the balance of her mind was disturbed. She'd left behind so many people to grieve her. It occurred to me that barely anyone would notice if I were to do the same.

Often I didn't get round to leaving the flat at all. I lived on baked beans and spent hours lying on my mattress reading trashy old paperbacks that my flatmates lent me. There were times when I craved real pain instead of the endless mugginess. Then I'd pinch the skin on the insides of my upper arms, twisting hard enough for it to hurt. I liked seeing the bruises there the next day. At least they were visible scars.

I didn't always feel so bad. Some mornings I made myself get out of bed at a decent time, showering and breakfasting like a normal person. I had promised to send my uncle a postcard once a week so he'd know I was OK and on those days I had to leave the flat. Once I'd written a few words and mailed the card off, I'd walk down to Berwick Street market to buy fruit. From there it was a short stretch to Liberty but I never went through its doors any more. I couldn't bear its glitter. I sat at a café opposite, drinking coffee and watching other people wandering inside.

It was while I was there, browsing idly through a copy

of *Time Out* that someone had left behind, that I saw the advert.

> *Have you suffered loss? Are you struggling with pain and sorrow? Renowned and gifted psychic medium Bella Luna can act as a bridge between this world and the next. She has the power to help you have that final conversation you always wanted with your loved ones. She will help you find closure.*

It wasn't that I even believed in mediums. And Bella Luna ... well, anyone could see what a fake sort of name that was. It was the idea of a final conversation, the one I'd always wanted – that's what got me. If there were a chance, just a tiny, slim one, that she wasn't a hoaxer, then wouldn't I want to take it?

I called the number from the nearest phone box and listened to her answerphone message. Bella Luna was in a reading right now but if I left my name and number she'd contact me as soon as she was free ... The flat in Fitzroy Square didn't have a phone so I had no number to leave. I wasn't going to be deterred. Already I felt a lifting of my spirits at the thought that my parents might not be completely out of reach.

I left Bella Luna the number of the phone box I was calling from and then stood outside waiting for it to ring. I was there a couple of hours and every time someone went in to make a call I'd glare at them. When at last I heard the phone ringing I rushed to grab the receiver.

'Hello, Rosie Goodheart speaking.'

'Hello, Rosie, my name is Bella. You need me.' Her voice was low and kind.

'Yes, yes, I do. When can you see me?'

'Well, I'm not sure. I have a long waiting list. A lot of people need my help.'

'Can't you fit me in somehow?'

'Let me see …' She was silent for a moment. 'I do seem to have a cancellation later this week – Friday morning at eleven. Would that suit you, Rosie?'

'Yes, I can be there.'

She gave me an address in Clapham North and told me it was only a short walk from the tube station. 'Don't be late, though,' she warned me. 'I only have an hour free and I cannot rush the spirits.'

Once I'd put down the phone I felt foolish. As if some woman in south London who'd given herself a fancy name could help me. Most likely she'd take my money and feed me a load of rubbish. Still, I'd made the appointment and I had no other plans for Friday morning so I might as well give it a go.

It turned out that Bella Luna lived in a tall Victorian terrace just off the main road. She answered the door herself, a tiny bleached-blonde woman in her fifties, and led me up several flights of stairs to an attic room with sloping ceilings that had been painted peppermint green. There was sunlight streaking the walls and potted palms in the corners. It didn't seem spooky at all.

In the middle of the room were two chairs and a small side table. We sat there, face to face, and Bella Luna, who must have sensed how nervous I was, gave me a reassuring smile.

'So, Rosie, there is someone you want to contact in the spirit world?'

'My parents. They died last winter.'

'Don't tell me any more. Let the spirits give me the rest. This is the way I work. I'd like to lay my hands on you, if I may. Very gently, like this, see. Touch is most important to me.'

Her hands seemed to burn where they rested on my arm.

'Rosie, are you OK?' she asked in a slow, calm voice.

'Yes, I think so.'

'I have guides who help me cross to the spirit world. I need to wait for one of them to reach me. It may take a few moments. Be as still and quiet as you can.'

I could hear a clock ticking somewhere and beyond that the high-pitched scream of a child and the roar of buses and lorries. But the only thing that seemed to matter was the weight of her hands on my arm.

'I see her, Rosie,' she said at last. 'I see your mother. She's an elegant woman, yes? She has fair hair like yours and the same beautiful, pale skin?'

I nodded. 'That's right.'

'Your father is with her. They are sitting together. I think they used to sit like that, side by side, when they were watching television at night, yes?'

'Yes, they did.' I was feeling a tiny bit less sceptical.

'I'm sensing they were good people. They had a happy marriage. They loved each other a lot.'

I nodded, not trusting myself to speak.

'But you didn't always get on with them, did you? Sometimes there were silly quarrels. And often they were your fault really, yes?'

I'd got really good at not crying in front of people but now hot tears began to slide down my cheeks.

'Your parents are worried about you, Rosie. They say the connection was broken too soon. It was very sudden the way they died, yes? There was no time to say goodbye.'

'No time at all.' I wiped my eyes with a tissue she offered then balled it up in my hand. 'I'd been so mean to them that day. All Mum wanted was for me to tidy my room but I wouldn't. I slammed my bedroom door in her face. We had a fight and I told her I hated her. Then I was sulking so much I didn't even say goodbye. My mum called out when they left but I ignored her. She left thinking that I didn't love her.'

It was the first time I'd told anyone about the quarrel, or even said the words out loud. I felt so ashamed that I couldn't look Bella Luna in the face.

The pressure of her hands on my arm grew firmer. 'They want you to stop worrying about that, Rosie. Your mother says it wasn't important, that the pair of you always made it up in the end. She knows you didn't ever hate her. Sometimes late at night she'd come and sit on your bed and talk to you, yes?'

'That's right.'

'She says you'd have been friends again by bedtime. It was just a little quarrel. It makes her very unhappy that you're worrying. She says you have to stop.'

I wanted to believe her. To hold on to this small comfort that she'd offered. 'Can you tell Mum that I'm sorry?'

'She knows that, Rosie, I don't have to tell her.'

I was crying so hard now the tears seem to come from the back of my throat. 'Can you please tell her I love her?'

'She knows that, too. But your father wants to speak now. He wants to make sure you've got all the life insurance, all the money. He says there should be plenty, that he was always careful to make sure you'd have no financial worries if anything happened to them. There's a box of papers, yes? He wants to know if you found it, Rosie.'

'Yes, it was in his office. My Uncle Phillip found it. He sorted everything out.'

'Your father doesn't want you to waste the money, Rosie. He wants you to be sensible and invest in something. He's worried about you frittering it away. He's saying you should put the money into something solid, a property. A decent place in a good area, security for your future. Your mother is agreeing with him. He's got an area in mind.'

'Where?' I asked.

'It's not so clear now. Something beginning with a B … Bel… is it Belgravia? Would that be a place he was fond of?'

I'd never heard my father mention Belgravia but didn't like to say so. I lied and said it was.

Bella Luna seemed tired. She lifted her hands from my arm. 'I'm sorry; I can't stay in the spirit world any longer. But I hope I've given you what you needed, Rosie. I hope I've helped you.'

'Yes.' The tears were drying on my face. 'Thank you, you really have.'

I paid the fifty pounds I owed, and as I followed Bella Luna back down stairs I asked when she could fit me in for another session.

'I'm not going to do that, Rosie. It wouldn't be a good idea.'

'Why not?'

'Look, I could keep taking money from you. There are lots of mediums that would. But that's not how I work. I don't think it's wise to keep bothering the spirits. They need their peace. And those of us they left behind ... well, we need to learn to live without them. Do you understand?'

I was close to tears again. 'Yes,' I said huskily.

Bella Luna opened the front door and showed me out. 'Good luck with the house-hunting then, Rosie. Belgravia's a lovely area.' She said it so chirpily it was as though for the past half-hour we'd been having a normal conversation rather than reaching into the spirit world.

I didn't go straight home. Instead, I took the tube to Victoria and walked down past the coach station and into the area my *A-Z* said was Belgravia. I could see straight away it was pretty exclusive. The white stucco houses were freshly painted and had big grand porticos. There were Sloaney women wearing strings of pearls and Barbours shopping at little delicatessens. Even the pubs looked posh, with outdoor tables surrounded by pots of blooming red geraniums that reminded me of Majorca.

It was a complete mystery to me why the clairvoyant had

thought my father might suggest I buy a place here. And yet I wanted so much to believe in her and everything she'd said.

EXTRACT FROM ADDOLORATA'S JOURNAL

I'm worried about Rosie. It's like she's disappeared off the face of the earth. When I started working at Little Italy I was so busy I sort of forgot about her and now I feel guilty. I even went into Liberty the other day thinking I might find her browsing round the counters but of course she wasn't there.

The trouble is I don't have an address for her or know the name of the uncle she lives with. She may not even be with him now. I know she said she hated it.

I'll try to ask around. There were girls she was friends with at school – most will have headed off to university but perhaps I can track them down and find out if she's kept in touch. Toni keeps saying I shouldn't worry, that Rosie's not my responsibility and she can look after herself. But I'm not sure. I talked to Papa about it and he agreed with me. I have to do something.

The Olive Estate

Stripped to the waist and sweating, Enzo worked the patch of ground he'd cleared of spent crops, driving in his hoe and turning the earth while his Nonna sat and watched him from beneath the shade of the terrace.

'Oh, what heat, what heat,' she complained, fanning at her face with a brown, speckled hand. 'I really think this summer might kill me.'

'It's not so bad,' Enzo replied, bent over his work. 'It's always the same this time of year, isn't it? And it will be winter soon enough. Then you'll be complaining about the storms.'

'Maybe, but when you're my age you'll feel it worse. You won't be capable of digging out in the midday sun any more. And the winter cold will force itself into your bones. I only hope by then you have plenty of sons to help you on the estate. Otherwise you'll have a big problem.'

Enzo nodded and kept hoeing.

'You are a man now,' his Nonna said with a sigh. 'Where have the years gone, eh? Tell me that.'

Enzo said nothing. He knew what was coming.

'Don't imagine I don't know what you get up to – wasting your time hanging around in Triento with your friends, eating too much pizza, staring at the boats in the marina. Your father was exactly the same. You're not doing anything different.'

'You're forgetting about the time I waste at the beach, Nonna.' His tone was resigned.

'Yes, yes, the beach.' She sighed again. 'You spend too much time there also. Although in this heat it must feel good to swim in the sea. I haven't done that for so many years.'

'Come with me then.' Enzo meant it. 'Why don't I take you this afternoon?'

'No, no, it's impossible. Even if I managed the steps down I'd never climb back up again.'

'But you're fit, Nonna. And I could help you. It would be fine.'

She shook her head. 'I'm an old woman and my place is here. You'll be old too soon enough and then you'll understand. The years go by fast, Enzo. The music seems to speed up. And then suddenly you notice people around you are starting to look worn and lined. And you glance in the mirror and find the same is happening to you.'

Enzo couldn't imagine being old, his face pleated with wrinkles, his eyes sagging out of shape, his whiskers grey.

'Yes, Nonna,' he said automatically.

'You shouldn't waste too much more time,' she warned, 'or you may run out of it altogether. A woman is made to bear children when she's young. And if you don't move fast enough the good ones will be taken. Had you thought of that?'

'Yes, Nonna, I know.' Enzo paused to wipe the sweat from his face with the shirt he'd cast off earlier.

'What are you waiting for?' Nonna asked. 'I don't understand it. Your father was the same. I remember having this exact conversation with him. You're so like he was at your age. Nothing is any different at all.'

'I know that, Nonna,' he repeated, although by then he was only half-listening to her.

Sometimes Enzo wondered which of the local girls he'd end up marrying. He suspected his family favoured Maria Luisa simply because her father owned a block of land bordering the Santi Estate. She was an only child and once he was gone

60

the vines could be cleared and the land used to plant more olive trees. But there were others, Ilaria Conti and Donata Esposito. Their names were mentioned from time to time, their families asked to share a meal on Sundays.

An invitation to eat at the Santi Estate was always welcomed, for Enzo's mother and sisters were good cooks and his grandfather famed for having a heavy hand with the wine. Meals with guests attending went on all afternoon and, while Enzo chafed at the hours sitting at a table as yet more food was brought, he knew better than to show it.

The dishes served depended on the season. In winter his mamma liked to warm her guests with soups of rice and finely sliced Savoy cabbage flavoured with salami or with creamy vegetable broths of green lentils and golden chicken stock. Afterwards there would be a tray of baked pasta snowed with cheese and to follow shanks of meat cooked on the bone in an oily stew of tomatoes.

During the hotter months the food she served was lighter but there was still plenty of it. Summer brought Enzo's favourite dishes: fresh sardines soured with vinegar and sweetened with sultanas; the nutty, earthy flavour of artichokes braised with garlic and anchovies; a salad of crisp fennel sliced thinly and paired with nuggets of blood orange. Even then, the eating and talking dragged on and he was always cheered to see dessert appear, sliced fruit soused in wine or a sweet tart of vanilla, ricotta and candied orange peel. Once it had all been savoured and the coffee drunk, their guests might stand and make a move to leave but still there was never any hurry. Most would linger, standing by their cars while they found new things to talk about or accepting an invitation for a final stroll beneath the olive trees to aid digestion.

His Nonna never seemed to tire. She sat, spine straight, alert to every nuance of the conversation, no matter how many hours the meal lasted. Afterwards she might comment on some little thing about the day's guests, note that Maria Luisa's mother had to prompt her to offer help in the kitchen, wonder why Ilaria Conti needed to spend so long in the bathroom. It seemed there was nothing she failed to notice about the girls who came to the estate with their hopeful mothers.

'Nonna, what if I never fall in love?' Enzo asked as he finished hoeing her vegetable garden and making it ready for re-planting.

'You will sooner or later; everyone does,' she reassured him.

'It doesn't seem that way now.'

'Well, you can't always rush things. Sometimes love grows slowly. I myself had known your grandfather for many years before he asked me to be his wife. It can take time to look at someone you knew as a child and see her as a woman.'

'I think Gianpaolo is in love with Maria Luisa,' he confided.

His Nonna tutted. 'He is a beautiful boy your friend – the face of a cherub, like I always say – but he would do well to look elsewhere. Rosaria Mancuso hasn't raised her daughter to marry a boy like him.'

'But if they are in love …' Enzo began.

'It will make no difference.' His Nonna shook her head. 'Not with Maria Luisa. He's a good boy but she is the only child they have and she'll inherit all that they've worked for. Things are expected of her.'

Enzo left his Nonna to her planting and cleaned the hoe carefully before putting it away as he knew how much she hated finding it with earth hardening on the metal. Then he went to make himself presentable so his grandfather wouldn't frown to see him sitting down to eat with dirt on his hands or sweat drying on his body. Enzo wondered why older people liked having so many pointless rules to live by. To him it seemed they only complicated things that ought to have been simple.

Rosie

My mother always had a proper place for everything. She hated to leave the house if surfaces weren't wiped down and cupboard doors closed on all the clutter, and I'd been trained to be the same. But in the short time I'd lived in the half-light of my basement room I'd made a nest of my belongings. When I got back from my session with Bella Luna that Friday afternoon the sight of it almost shocked me. I hadn't realised how far I'd let things slip. Straight away I set about restoring order, picking up clothes from the floor and hanging them on the rail, piling books against one wall and lining shoes beside the other. I found a vase for the bunch of sunflowers I'd bought on a whim from a stall beside the tube station and put them on the floor beside my mattress. Even then it was gloomy but at least it looked like the person who lived there cared for it ... and for herself.

I thought a lot about what the clairvoyant had said. During the long days I spent alone, hibernating behind my closed bedroom door as the sunflowers withered and turned their water milky green, my mind kept returning to her words. Sometimes the memory of them caused me to cry, but softly and quietly, in a way that made me feel better rather than worse. Curled up in bed, listening to my flatmates clanking pots and pans in the kitchen as they made themselves supper or slamming the front door as they headed out, I felt so far from the world. I wasn't sure how to rejoin it.

I suppose I'd been cutting myself off from people ever since my parents died. Nothing about life had been the same after that. My old friends with their study groups and their mania for getting good grades seemed pointless and pathetic. I was angry with them for thinking life was as simple as passing exams. I didn't want their pity or the offers of study notes they'd taken at classes I'd missed. I turned down invitations to visit their homes because I knew their parents would only look at me sorrowfully then talk about me in another room. I kept saying no to people and I found if you refuse enough invitations, if you're rude enough, they stop asking in the end. I hid in my room in the ugly basement flat and told myself I'd rather be alone anyway.

It was only the idea of buying an apartment that coaxed me out. It was the one solid piece of advice I'd been given that didn't make me roll my eyes and walk away. I liked the idea of having a place of my own, with more than one room and new things in it to arrange. The more I thought about it, the more I could imagine my father being concerned about me investing in something solid. The psychic had been spot on there – financial security was just the sort of thing he cared about. Still, I was confused about Belgravia. He had no connections in the area, as far as I knew. It had looked so expensive; I was certain it would use up a lot from the sale of the house and the life insurance policies.

Yet it was the only clue I'd been given about the next step I should take. It was a direction to head in, a reason to get out of bed, take a shower and find clothes to wear. The more I thought about it, the more I wanted to believe it was the answer to everything.

I found myself drawn back to Belgravia, wandering aimlessly, sitting in cafés and staring through the windows of shops that sold paintings, expensive furniture or over-priced baby clothes. It seemed such a safe, genteel sort of place: a perfect part of London for a young girl on her own.

What I needed was advice from someone who knew about buying property. The obvious choice was my uncle but I didn't want to involve him. He'd been so uptight when he'd seen how much money I'd been left, muttering about family trusts and offering to manage the funds until I was older, wanting to take it all over. When I'd refused there was nothing he could do. Legally it was mine.

The only other person was my aunt but we were barely speaking. Things went wrong between us after I moved in with her. She would have been a nightmare for anyone. My aunt's the type of person who has a special way of doing everything, from folding towels to packing groceries at the supermarket. She even managed to make my mum seem messy and disorganised. I tried my best to fit in but no matter how tidy I was there was always something I got wrong: clean dishes put away in a place they didn't belong, newspapers left spread out on a table. I swear she followed me round the house polishing off the marks my fingers left on her brass doorhandles. It all blew up into a series of fights and I didn't want any more slamming doors. There'd been enough of that.

While I was mulling over the problem of where to turn, I found myself edging a little further into the world of clairvoyants and healers. It was impossible to resist trying each new thing I read about. One day I had my aura swept, the next my tarot read; I had crystal therapy and colour healing and chakra balancing massage; I read my horoscopes obsessively and bought self-help books. Some of it was comforting but nothing helped really. It didn't give me any answers or change the way I felt. My life never felt mended in any way.

And so the idea of buying my own apartment crept over me and took hold. It filled my mind and seemed like an answer.

I remembered Addolorata telling me how keen her father was on buying property. She'd complained he was always lecturing them about the importance of investing in bricks and mortar. 'Papa thinks everyone ought to live the way he does,' she'd said, 'otherwise they're all idiots.'

Hoping he might give me advice on where to start, I looked up their restaurant, Little Italy, in the *Yellow Pages*. I hadn't seen Addolorata for weeks and felt guilty knowing I was only considering it now because I wanted help. Then I discovered the restaurant was a manageable walk away from Fitzroy Square and wondered what it was like. I imagined the bustle and the sound of Italian voices, the dishes on the menu and the way they'd taste and smell. It would be so easy to wander over there at lunchtime and maybe I'd find a quiet table where I could eat a bowl of pasta. For all this time I'd been living on a relentless diet of sweet, mushy baked beans or tinned soup, as opening a can seemed the most I could manage. I hadn't cooked any of the dishes Addolorata had taught me and was craving proper flavours: the sharp sweetness of cooked tomatoes, the oiliness of fried aubergines, the creaminess of seafood, lemon and Arborio rice.

So late the next morning I dressed in the cleanest clothes I could find and, feeling unexpectedly nervous at the prospect of being with people again after weeks spent mostly alone, I walked slowly towards Little Italy. I found it on a street where there was a bustling market, just around the corner from a delicatessen where they sold cheeses and salami so strong you could smell them from the pavement. Little Italy looked exactly how an Italian restaurant should, quite a big place really with a white canopy shading the pavement at the front, silver aluminium tables and chairs beneath it and planters filled with neatly trimmed green bushes separating it from the rest of the street.

Awkwardly, I paused before going in. It was still quite early and a couple of waiters were standing chatting near the entrance. One of them called over, smiling and friendly. '*Ciao, bella*, have you come for lunch?'

'Yes, but I'm on my own.' My barely used voice was croaky and hoarse.

'That's fine.' He smiled again. 'I have a very nice table for you. Come this way.'

Inside Little Italy the tables were topped with red and white chequered cloths and the roughcast stucco walls covered in old black-and-white photographs of people I assumed were the Martinelli family. In one, a dark-haired girl and boy were laughing together as they sat astride a Vespa. In another, a young couple in old-fashioned clothes stood beside a big baroque fountain smiling nervously at whoever was behind the camera.

The waiter showed me to a corner table where I had a sweeping view around the whole of the dining room and brought over a menu and a carafe of chilled water. 'I'll be back in a moment to tell you the specials,' he promised.

'Oh, wait,' I called as he turned away. 'If Addolorata is in the kitchen would you mind telling her I'm here? We know each other from school. I'm Rosie ... Rosie Goodheart.'

'Rosie? Yes, of course. But she is busy right now. She may not have time to come out.'

Within minutes Addolorata was there, wiping her hands on a tea towel, her cheeks pink.

'Oh my God, Rosie, I can't believe it.' She sat on the bench beside me and squeezed me into a fierce hug. 'I've been so worried about you.'

'You have?'

'Yes. I wondered what had happened. It was only after we'd said goodbye at the train station that I realised I had no idea how to find you. You should have given me an address or a phone number. I asked around but no one from school had any idea where you were.'

'You asked around about me?' I said stupidly. 'Why?'

She looked at me properly. 'Bloody hell, you're looking skinny, Rosie. How have you done that? Look, I can't really

68

talk now as lunch service will start any minute. But I do want to catch up. Are you hungry?'

I nodded that I was.

'Good. Well, don't worry about ordering. I'll make sure you get something you'll like. Just promise you won't disappear again, OK?'

There was a lot of food. A hearty risotto of roasted squash and creamy taleggio cheese, a peppery watercress salad, a dish of sticky slow-cooked pork and sweet peperonata and another of seared squid with rosemary and lemon. Some of it I barely managed to taste, and when the waiter returned to sweep up the plates they remained nearly full.

Gradually other people claimed the tables round me. Some seemed like regulars, greeting the waiters by name and hardly bothering to glance at the menu. They ordered bowls of soupy mussels and platters piled with ice and seafood. As I grazed on my meal, I listened to their conversations about office politics and unhappy relationships; saw how they fell silent when the food arrived and how they lost themselves in its flavours; watched them sign credit card slips and heard them promise to come back soon.

Only when every table was empty did Addolorata emerge from the kitchen.

'Did you enjoy your lunch?' she asked, taking the seat opposite mine. Her skin was dewy from the heat of the kitchen and her hair more frizz than curls. She seemed all keyed up. 'What did you think of the squid? Papa is worried there is too much rosemary and it's overwhelming the flavour but I think squid is a bit tasteless on its own, don't you?'

'It was all really lovely. It tasted great.'

'Papa believes we should make everything the same way he has for years. Honestly, he drives me insane.' Addolorata reached for my water glass, took a couple of sips and paused for a breath. 'But anyway, what about you? Tell me what you've been up to.'

'Oh, nothing much.'

'But where have you been all these weeks?'

'Just down the road, actually,' I said lightly. 'I moved out of my uncle's place and found a room in a flat share.'

'Is it OK? Lou's found a place near King's Cross but it's a hovel. Renting sounds like a nightmare. So expensive. I'd much rather stay with my parents than move somewhere awful. What are your flatmates like?'

'They're fine but actually I'm hoping not to be there for too long.' I braced myself before saying the words out loud. 'I've decided I want to get a flat with the money my mum and dad left me. The trouble is I'm not sure how to go about it. I've never had anything to do with buying property before.'

Addolorata nodded, not seeming to think it a crazy plan at all. 'A place of your own would be fantastic. Perhaps my father could give you some help. He knows all about that kind of thing.'

'I wondered if he might. But do you think he'd mind?'

'Are you kidding?' She laughed. 'Papa would be thrilled to tell you how best to do it. Giving advice is his favourite thing.'

Addolorata's father turned out to be even more dark and dramatic than his daughter. He bustled from his kitchen and, as I stood to shake his hand, swept me straight into a hug. '*Cara, cara*, I've heard all about you,' he said, his accent thickly and richly Italian. 'Such sadness. No wonder you have no appetite. But still you managed to eat a little? The risotto and the salad. You liked that?'

'It was all delicious, Mr Martinelli,' I said politely.

'Beppi ... you must call me Beppi.'

'It's just there was too much. I couldn't manage it all.'

'Don't worry. I've had it packaged up for you along with one or two other little things from the kitchen. You must eat, *cara*. When you have suffered sadness, good food is very important.'

I'd known he was Italian but still Beppi's foreignness took me by surprise. I hadn't expected his accent to be so strong or for him to speak with his whole body – waving his arms in the air to emphasise every word.

When I explained what I wanted he became even more animated. 'A property? Yes, of course I can help. I bought my own house and this building we are in now. I know how to deal with the estate agents. You have no family to guide you? I am very glad you came to me, then.'

'All I need is some advice on where to start, really.'

'Yes, yes, *cara*, you need lots of advice,' he agreed, nodding energetically. 'You will come to my house for lunch on Sunday and we will talk about it again then.'

'Lunch …' I said uncertainly.

'Yes, come at midday. You will meet the rest of my family, my wife Catherine, my other daughter Pieta. And I will make my lasagne – everyone loves it. Come hungry, though. My lasagne is rich and very heavy so don't fill up on bread first. You will need your appetite.'

I was taken aback. I'd only come for a few tips and hadn't wanted Beppi to go to any effort. But talking to him was like being caught up in a crowd and swept along. There was no way of resisting once he'd made up his mind.

'Lunch would be lovely, thank you,' I agreed, because it seemed the only thing to say.

It had been so kind of Beppi to invite me but for the rest of the week I dreaded going. It was the idea of being pulled into a family again, of being reminded of everything that I was missing. As I listened to the rumble of my flatmate's roller skates going back and forth across the grubby kitchen floor, I wondered if I could make some excuse to get out of it.

Before I'd left Little Italy, Addolorata had made me write down my address on a paper napkin she'd shoved into the front pocket of her apron. 'I'll see you at my place on

Sunday at midday, then,' she'd said. 'Try not to be late. Papa is unbearable if everyone isn't at the table the moment the food is ready.'

I considered phoning and feigning illness but suspected she might come and find me. After all, I'd asked for their help – it would be churlish and rude not to turn up. So, reluctantly, on Sunday morning I ironed a skirt and top, picked out a pair of flattish sandals and walked all the way to Clerkenwell.

The house they lived in was opposite a churchyard. It was one of those tall, narrow buildings with shuttered windows that never look like there is anybody home. But Beppi answered the door after just one knock, a smile beaming from his face. 'Rosie, you are here at last. Thank goodness.'

'I'm not late, am I?'

'No, no, but now there is time for you to meet the family and see my garden. Come in, come in.'

Inside it felt homely and welcoming. There was Italian opera playing loudly and the sound of voices straining to be heard over it. Beppi led me to the kitchen and introduced me to his daughter Pieta who looked entirely unlike Addolorata – very slender with dark hair in a sleek bob and her lips stained red. His wife Catherine was sitting at the table grating a big block of parmesan. Looking up, she gave me a tired smile. 'Rosie, I'm so glad you've come,' she said over the strains of Pavarotti soaring into an aria. 'Please make yourself at home. Why don't you help yourself to a drink? There is a jug of fresh lemonade in the fridge.'

'No, no, first I will show her my garden. You won't believe, Rosie, how many different vegetables it is possible to grow in London. I would like to have chickens, too, for the eggs. But my wife, she says no. She doesn't want to hear the "bawk, bawk, bawk" all day long. Such a pity.' Beppi shook his head sadly and held open the back door for me.

Every inch of the garden behind the house had been

cultivated. It was almost autumn now and yet still there were fruiting tomato plants climbing bamboo stakes, bushes of basil, runner beans and rosemary. 'This is amazing,' I said. 'My dad used to grow the odd lettuce in his flowerbeds but I've never seen anything like this before. I'd love to come back with my camera and photograph it.'

'Photograph my vegetables.' Beppi started to laugh. 'Why would you want to do that?'

'I like the way they look,' I explained; 'some all neat in rows, and others tangled and messy.'

'Well, today we will be eating the food not taking pictures of it. Come back inside now. As my wife says there is lemonade in the fridge. And Addolorata is around somewhere. I will call her down.'

The lasagne Beppi had made was divine, thin leaves of pasta, a slow-cooked beef sauce and creamy béchamel sauce. When he offered me seconds I almost said yes until I noticed Addolorata shaking her head at me and heard her hissing, 'It's only the first course.'

'Is there more to come?'

'Loads.'

By the time we'd made our way through the tender little meatballs simmered in Beppi's special sauce, the aubergines smothered in mozzarella and parmesan, the sliced courgettes dipped in flour and egg then fried, I could hardly move. Beppi, though, seemed energised by the eating. Every few moments he'd leap up and return to the stove.

'Sit down, for goodness' sake,' his wife told him. 'None of us can manage any more anyway. You're wasting your time.'

Once we'd eaten, Pieta made coffee in a Moka on the stovetop while Addolorata started on the dishes. The kitchen was a terrible mess, the sink piled with dirty pans; and somehow Beppi had splattered red sauce halfway up the wall behind the cooker. But he wouldn't hear of me helping clear up. Instead, he produced piles of estate agents' brochures and began a rapid monologue, talking about things like lease extensions and service charges, stuff I hadn't known I needed to worry about.

'And the prices these days, *cose da pazzi*.' He threw his hands in the air. 'If you go a bit further out of the city it gets better. So where? Which area would you like? Dalston? Stoke Newington? Or maybe south of the river?'

'What about Belgravia?' I asked hesitantly.

'Belgravia?' Beppi sounded shocked. 'It is very exclusive, too expensive. You can't buy a place in Belgravia. No, no. It is impossible.'

'But could we just look there?' It was ridiculous clinging to what the clairvoyant had said but I couldn't shake the idea there might be a place there meant for me. 'Perhaps we'll find something I can afford.'

Addolorata had been flicking through a few brochures piled on the table. 'It can't do any harm to go and see a few apartments, can it? I'll come with you if you like.'

'No, no. I will go,' Beppi insisted. 'I will take care of it. Maybe you will have to settle on a place that needs some work but I can help with that, too.'

I happened to glance at his wife then and caught an expression on her face: a brief pushing together of her lips and a lowering of her eyes, not a scowl exactly but she didn't seem pleased.

'Mr Martinelli, I don't mean for you to spend all your time flat-hunting for me,' I said quickly. 'I'm sure you're very busy with your restaurant.'

'Don't be ridiculous, I am happy to help. And call me Beppi, *cara*, please.'

When I glanced back at his wife, she smiled in a resigned sort of way. 'He likes to help people,' she said and it sounded like an accusation.

If Beppi noticed her tone, he didn't show it. He was

scribbling some notes on an old envelope and I saw that even his handwriting looked foreign and illegible.

'*Va bene*, I will talk to some agents, get some ideas and perhaps make some appointments for us to view four or five places to begin with. When are you available, Rosie?' he asked.

'Whenever it suits you.'

'But can you get the time off work? Is that going to be a problem?'

'I don't have a job.' I said it casually not expecting the words to have the effect they did.

'No job?' Beppi was astounded. 'No work at all? What do you do all day then?'

I had no real idea how I got from one end of the day to the other. 'Well, I read and take walks ... and things,' I offered.

'But, Rosie, that is no good.' Beppi still seemed shocked. 'You must work.'

I stared back at him. 'Why?'

'These years are very important.' He tapped his hand on the table as though trying to be sure he had my attention. 'This is when you build the foundation for your future. You must get experience, learn things. You can't sit around doing nothing and living off your inheritance.'

'I've been looking for a job.' It was a lie but I felt forced into it.

Everyone was looking at me now, waiting to hear my plans. Pieta was wiping a tea towel over a dripping dish, Addolorata sipping espresso from a tiny cup, Catherine fiddling with the edge of a brochure. But everyone's attention was focused on me.

'What sort of job?' Beppi asked.

'Um, office work ... you know. Answering phones ...' I hated this.

'But you've had no luck?'

'Not so far.'

75

Beppi shook his head in disappointment. 'I think you must try harder,' he said. 'This bequest from your parents, perhaps it will buy the flat you want but you can't live on it for ever.'

'Yes, I know that.' It was another lie. I'd been careful not to look that far into my future.

'When I was your age I was supporting my family – my mother and my sister – with the money I earned working in a big hotel in Rome. I didn't love it but I knew that one day it would lead to something better and see: here I am today with a restaurant of my own. You have to do the same, Rosie. You must work towards what you want or you won't get anywhere at all.'

Thankfully, Addolorata rescued me before her father could go on lecturing me for too long. Escaping the house, we went and sat in the grassy churchyard with her sister Pieta who painted our toenails purple as we lazed in the afternoon sun, the two of them sharing a couple of cigarettes they'd sneaked out of the house, casting guilty looks back at the windows and hoping they wouldn't be spotted. We might have been three sisters sitting there together except they were so dark and I so fair.

'There was way too much food as usual.' Addolorata pushed her thumb into the waistband of her skirt to feel how tight it had become.

'And so much washing-up afterwards,' I added. 'I couldn't believe it.'

Addolorata laughed. 'Don't worry, we're used to it, aren't we, Pieta? It's always the same in our house.'

I remembered the Sunday food of my childhood, always a roast with crunchy potatoes and the best gravy, eaten in the dining room – never the kitchen – and with my mum's good napkins to cover our laps. I missed her food. She'd never really loved cooking but she did it well. And afterwards we'd clear up the dirty pots together, talking about the coming week or perhaps a holiday we were planning, just little unimportant things usually, until one day we ran out of Sundays.

'There, what do you think of that?' Pieta had finished my toes. 'Pretty good, eh?'

'Really good,' I told her. 'I love the colour.'

'Now you have to sit still for at least ten minutes while they dry properly. Don't smudge them or I'll be furious. Won't I, Addolorata? She never has the patience to stay still long enough.'

'I know, I'm hopeless,' Addolorata agreed. 'I take after Papa. He can't sit still either.'

'He's very ... forceful.' I chose my words carefully.

Addolorata laughed again. 'Bossy, you mean? Yes, we're used to that, too. I hate to say it, Rosie, but he's probably right. It can't be good for you not working. Don't you get bored ... and lonely?'

'No,' I lied.

'But who have you been hanging out with? No one from school has seen you for weeks.'

I turned my head and looked towards the church. 'I've been fine,' I insisted.

'You don't work, you don't see anyone. Rosie, how can you be fine?'

'Because I am.'

Suddenly it felt like the Martinelli family was smothering me. It had been good of Beppi to open his arms and welcome me in, good of them all. But I didn't need this interference, this poking and prodding at my life. I didn't want their family at all, actually – I wanted my own.

Forgetting about the fresh polish on my toes, I got to my feet. 'I really am fine. I don't know why it's such a big deal. I'll find a job eventually.' Turning away, I tossed my final words over my shoulder. 'Just stop going on about it, OK?'

As I strode across the churchyard away from them, I heard Pieta calling after me.

'Oh no, Rosie, you've ruined it completely.'

WHAT ADDOLORATA SAID

'Already Papa is spending half his time shouting down the phone at estate agents. It's quite sweet really. He keeps saying he hopes someone would do the same for his daughters if something happened to him. But I'm not sure Rosie is ready for it. She is so difficult and touchy sometimes and you know how interfering he can be. Already he's taking over things completely. Last night he even suggested she do some waitressing shifts in the restaurant. He thinks she's depressed and having a job might help. Now I'm supposed to talk to her, convince her, but I'm betting she'll hate the idea. Waitressing doesn't seem her kind of thing at all. And anyway, I've got a better plan.'

The Olive Estate

Enzo had never known his mother scream like that before. The sound was so piercing he heard it from the bottling room where he was stacking crates. As he ran back towards the house he could hear his Nonna's cries too. There was something odd about them. She sounded like a small bird calling for food.

Heart thudding, he barrelled through the back door and found them in the kitchen, their arms around his eldest sister Concetta, all three with tears on their faces.

'What is it? What's happened?'

His Nonna wiped the wetness from her eyes. 'Such wonderful news. Your sister is to be married.'

'Married?' Enzo said stupidly. 'Why did Mamma scream, then? Why are you crying?'

'*Stupido*.' Only his Nonna would dare call him that. 'Concetta is to marry Ricardo Russo. He is a good boy from a good family. That is why I'm crying. I am happy.'

Enzo smiled and murmured his congratulations but still he didn't understand what the fuss was about. Everyone knew Concetta and Ricardo wouldn't wait much longer. Very few of the young people managed to, for when a boy was only ever allowed to kiss a girl and perhaps touch the skin beneath her clothes, marriage seemed the only option.

'*Auguri*, Concetta,' he said, even though a wedding had been as inevitable as this year's harvest.

'*Grazie*, Enzo.' She kissed him, her eyes still glittering with tears.

For the next weeks the Santi family lost interest in everything except talk of wedding gowns and guest lists, bonbonnière and bridesmaids. Every time Enzo went near anyone he heard snatches of their conversation.

'The tables for the wedding feast will run between the olive trees,' declared his Nonna. 'The Russo family is large. We will need twenty of them at least.'

'We will have fireworks that people can see from miles around,' promised his father.

'There must be champagne, lots of it. And a horse and carriage to bring Concetta and Ricardo from the church.'

'We will kill a pig for the feast.'

'All the girls should be bridesmaids. It will be charming, no?'

Each day they continued, until it seemed to Enzo the wedding had nothing to do with Concetta any more. Their plans were so big and she so tiny.

'Are you OK?' he asked one morning as he helped her feed the pigs with kitchen scraps. She had always been his favourite sister, the one closest to him in age who never seemed to resent him as much as the others did.

'Nonna thinks there may be three hundred guests,' she said in wonder. 'Do I know that many people?'

'You're the first of us to get married and they are excited,' he told her. 'That's why it's grown into such a big wedding.'

Concetta laughed. 'Oh, when you marry it will be much bigger, Enzo. If I get three hundred guests, then you will have six. The whole town will be invited. We will have to plant more olive trees to fit the tables under. And raise more pigs. Can you imagine?'

'Yes.' He looked at the fleshy snout of the animal destined for Concetta's wedding table. 'I can imagine it. Yes I can.'

Tipping out the rest of the scraps, Enzo carried the empty buckets back to the house. He wondered at Concetta – so willing to go into a lifetime with the only boy she'd ever known. As a little girl she'd run wild, always making some sort of trouble. There was the time she managed to start their father's old truck and drove it nearly to the highway. At school the teachers scolded her for cheekiness, she wrote on her hands, stole her mother's lipstick, didn't care about rules. Enzo had loved her for it.

Then when she was a teenager Ricardo Russo had been herded towards her by their mothers. There had been endless Sunday-evening strolls and family dinners until it was accepted they were intended for each other. His sister had become so docile then, so happy to walk with tradition. Still she seemed to care for Ricardo well enough, although they rarely had time alone together – there was always a nonna or mamma somewhere close by, often a younger sister, too.

Now she was caught up in this frenzy of talk about flowers for bouquets and sugared almonds for the wedding favours. She spent her time taking counsel from the family's priest or reading magazines meant only for brides. Enzo remembered his mother's scream, so high-pitched and excited, as though marriage was the best thing she could want for a daughter. Perhaps Concetta thought the same now.

Putting the lids on the buckets, Enzo lined them up beside the kitchen door. By tomorrow they would be full again with vegetable peelings and rotten fruit. Concetta would carry them back to the pens and tip in the whole stinking mess for the pigs to snuffle through. It had been her job since they were little children: that was one thing that hadn't changed.

Rosie

Addolorata reassured me. She said she was from an Italian family and they fought all the time. She wasn't offended that I'd stormed off from the churchyard and nor did her sister Pieta care if I'd smudged my polished toenails. None of that was important. They only wanted to make sure I was all right.

It was late one morning when she came to check on me. I was still curled up on my mattress and heard my flatmate roller-skating to the front door to answer the knocking. Her voice called out, 'Hey, Rosie, visitor for you,' as she skated back to her room.

Addolorata hesitated before she pushed open my bedroom door. 'It's only me. Can I come in?'

I was ashamed of the way I'd behaved and of how she'd found me, lying in pyjamas that might have been cleaner, hiding away in my shabby little room.

'I'll make you a cup of tea,' I offered. 'There's some milk in the fridge that should still be OK.'

Addolorata's arms were crossed and she was looking around her in dismay. 'I think my bum's too big for this room, Rosie. Why don't you put on some clothes and we'll go out for a coffee instead. I've come up with an idea I want to tell you about.'

She teased me by refusing to explain it until we were sitting in the nearest café sipping on coffee she dismissed as being 'nothing but crappy hot brown milk'.

'You know how we've got all those old photos on the

walls of Little Italy?' she began. 'Well, I think it's time to add something new. So what if you brought in your camera and took some really cool black-and-white shots, just of stuff like the chefs working in the kitchen and the waiters serving food, what do you think?'

'Why don't you get a proper photographer?'

'Because Papa wouldn't like it. He's only agreed to this because it's you. Honestly, Rosie, it's a huge deal. Papa hates me suggesting any sort of change to the place. He likes things to be the same. But miraculously he's said yes to a few new photos. So please, please, will you give it a go?'

'I don't know if I'm good enough ... I don't have the right equipment and ...'

'But the photos you had developed while we were in Majorca were amazing. We want the same kind of thing. Nothing posed and fake ... just sort of alive, like the others were. And Papa will pay you for them.'

Photography had only ever been something I did to please myself. I loved playing with the old Zenit my father gave me. At first I'd taken the usual shots of people smiling self-consciously into the lens – my parents, neighbours, friends. Then I'd moved on to other things: flowers in gardens, graffiti on walls, interesting faces of strangers. I liked reducing the wide expanse of the world into just a few details, forcing them into a frame, and my walls at home were always covered with prints of the latest shots I'd taken. Now I looked at all those pictures I'd fired off – my father clipping the hedge or my mother at the ironing board, just snatches of ordinary moments in their lives – and it seemed as though I'd found a way to steal time.

I'd never thought of photography as a proper job before and was intrigued by the idea of someone thinking it was worthwhile paying me to take pictures. Still, I might never have agreed to the plan if Addolorata hadn't told me her father's original suggestion.

'Waitressing shifts?' I couldn't imagine myself coping with that. 'But Little Italy is so busy and I've never done anything like it before.'

'That's what I told Papa,' she admitted. 'But with the photographs you'd get to hang out and work at your own pace. So will you do it?'

'I'll think about,' I agreed, still uncertain. 'I can't promise I'll take any shots worth hanging on the walls, though.'

At first the idea seemed ridiculous but then I went out to buy some film and a special cloth to clean my camera lens, and I began to get excited. What had struck me most about Little Italy was the constant movement: waiters rushing back and forth to the kitchen, people coming, going and eating. I wondered if it was possible to capture that in a picture, if I could somehow manage it.

Pulling out the envelopes of shots I'd taken in Majorca, I looked at them with a critical eye. Some scenes I'd framed badly, other images lacked interest. Still, as I set aside the ones I thought really worked, I began to feel faintly pleased. The pictures of us basking on the rocks and of the old men on the terrace of the café I liked especially. They brought back the feeling of being there. I'd meant to put these photos in an album but instead had shoved the envelopes in a box and forgotten about them. Now I was grateful to Addolorata for giving me a reason to look through them again.

Not that I liked the idea of turning up at Little Italy with my old Zenit in my hand. The thought of standing in the middle of a restaurant holding a camera made me cringe. I'd always hated being the centre of attention and dreaded people staring at me as I worked. Trying to distract myself from worrying about it, I loaded some film and went to take some practice shots around Fitzroy Square: details of buildings, people hurrying past, an old tramp rummaging in a dustbin. It felt really good to look at the world through a lens again. I'd missed the feeling of recording a moment, of having it to keep for ever.

I didn't want to waste a lot of film so decided to spend the first day at Little Italy wandering around and framing shots but not clicking the shutter. At first I felt shy and embarrassed but after a while it seemed most people were so intent on their work or the food on their plates they barely registered I was there.

Feeling more confident, I loaded some film and began to shoot for real. I captured Beppi shouting at a young chef for messing up an order, his arms windmilling. I photographed plates lined up on the pass just before they were whisked away, customers dabbing at themselves with napkins or forking spaghetti to their mouths, waiters wielding giant wooden pepper grinders. By the end of that first lunch service I was exhausted from holding the heavy Zenit to my eye and concentrating so hard on firing off shots at exactly the right moment. At the same time I was almost buoyant. Surely I must have some good stuff already.

I came back the next day and the next, running through far more film than I'd intended. By the end of the week Addolorata seemed the only one still conscious I was there. 'Don't take photos from that awful angle,' she kept reminding me.

The film was delivered to the lab in one big batch and I ordered contact sheets because someone there told me that's what the professional photographers did. Beppi had agreed I could choose the frames I liked but said the final selection would be his. Then we'd have the shots enlarged, framed and hung on the wall. It was scary but exciting imagining the customers pausing between courses to look at my work. I wondered what they'd think.

In the end I did help out a little in the restaurant, just setting tables and tidying up a few things that looked out of kilter to me, the arrangement of the plates on the big old wooden sideboard and a pinboard covered with postcards that customers had sent back from Italy to Beppi.

'You're quite sure you don't want to waitress for me?' he asked several times and each time he shook his head sadly when I refused. 'What will you do then, Rosie? You must work. Everyone has to work.'

Picking up the bagged contact sheets from the lab was like being given a gift to unwrap. I spent hours poring over them in the nearest café because the light in my room was too dim even in the middle of the day. My favourite shots were of Beppi. His face was so mobile and his moods so apparent. Whether he was laughing, shouting or in a brief moment of stillness he made the most interesting subject of all. Addolorata was more guarded and some of the waiters a little self-conscious, winking at me when they saw the lens swing in their direction. By the end of my editing session I'd covered thirty to forty shots with little yellow stickers and pencilled stars on a few I liked especially. There had to be some worth hanging on the wall.

Beppi had suggested I take the contact sheets over to his house on Sunday lunchtime. It was the one meal he insisted they all eat together as a family and he wanted everyone to see the shots before he made the final choice. 'Little Italy is a family business so all of us will have a say in the decision,' he told me.

I caught Addolorata's eye at that moment and saw her mouthing over his shoulder: *As if!*

So I walked to Clerkenwell again, cutting through back streets and across squares, crunching over fallen autumn leaves. On Sunday mornings London always felt like it was waiting for something. The traffic didn't hum so loudly, the sandwich bars were closed; the people were dressed differently and didn't move so fast. That Sunday it seemed as if I was the only one with a sense of purpose for a change.

I'd taken my camera with me so while the family spread

the contact sheets across the kitchen table I went out and photographed Beppi's garden. I did it partly so I wouldn't have to watch their faces as they scrutinised my work, but also because I liked the look of this place where only food was grown. There were things I'd never seen before: leafy green plants with ruby-red stems and spreading herbs. The tomato vines were dying back, the bean shoots had given up producing and some patches of the garden were bare but still it made for interesting images. I even liked photographing the tools Beppi used, the rusted old spade and fork, the ancient trowel dusted in soil.

For a while I stayed in the garden, playing with the light and different angles, until at last Addolorata poked her head out of the door. 'We're still arguing but I just wanted to let you know they're fantastic. Really they are. Well done.'

Only then did I realise how tense I'd been. I sank down into an old deckchair that had been placed to catch the midday sun and closed my eyes for a moment. I wondered if I felt a tiny bit happy.

When I plucked up the courage to go back inside and check which shots they'd preferred it surprised me how many of Beppi had made the cut. I thought he'd hate the ones of him shouting and losing his temper but he seemed flattered if anything. I'd given him a box of green stickers to highlight his favourites and he'd used them liberally.

'You'll have to peel some off,' Pieta was saying as I came through the kitchen door. 'You'd need to extend the restaurant again to fit this many shots on the wall.'

'God forbid. Don't even suggest that to him.' Catherine looked genuinely horrified.

They persuaded him to think about it some more once we'd eaten. But even as he served the ravioli that Addolorata had stuffed with beetroot, shards of walnut and melting goat's cheese, the chicken he'd braised with orange and prosciutto and the dishes of greens from his garden steamed and drenched in olive oil, even as we sat round the table to eat it together, he kept returning to the pictures.

'I think there are too many of Frederico,' he complained, staring at a shot of the head waiter. 'Perhaps we should get rid of this one, see.'

'But that big bowl of spaghetti he's holding looks so fantastic,' said Addolorata. 'And anyway, Frederico's been with you almost since the very beginning so surely he deserves a few photos on the walls? Why don't we ditch this one of me instead?'

'There are so many I like. How do I choose?' Beppi lamented.

'You're going to splash sauce on them if you carry on like that,' his wife warned. 'Put them away for a minute.'

They bickered throughout the meal, at times voices were raised and Beppi grew quite heated, but the argument was punctuated by laughter. It was so unlike the way fights had been in my family. I remembered the shock of sudden shouting from my father or my mother, then tears and the long days afterwards when no one seemed able to look at each other, never mind speak. They hadn't argued very often but when they did it was horrible.

Here among the Martinellis arguments were commonplace. Something was always rippling the surface; they never expected calm to last long. It surprised me. I hadn't realised other families were so different to my own.

It took more than a week for them to make the final selection. I left the contact sheets with them and Addolorata told me Beppi talked of almost nothing else. Stickers were peeled off and repositioned, then peeled off again. In the end they went back to some of my original choices, although I was disappointed one or two of my favourites had been left out.

'Don't say that to Papa,' Addolorata begged me. 'If you do then he's bound to start all over again. He can't change his mind any more. None of us can bear it.'

She'd taken to coming round for coffee in the mornings before her lunchtime shift began. I never knew if she would appear but it meant I had to get out of bed early and make sure I was dressed just in case. We'd walk down to an Italian place on Charlotte Street because they knew her there and often gave us little plates of fresh biscotti to taste.

'Better than your father makes, eh?' the owner would say cheekily. 'Be sure to tell him that.'

The Martinelli family started expecting me for lunch every Sunday. I was treated less like a guest and more like one of the family: Beppi even allowing me to help scrub the dried tomato sauce from the plates and wipe its splatter from the walls. At times, I wondered if his wife minded. I still remembered her odd expression on the first day, almost as though she resented him paying me so much attention. But I'd never seen it again. Now she seemed as welcoming as the rest of the family.

Every Sunday had the same pattern: there was always too much food, always some sort of fight, and always the same lecture about me looking for work. But I was growing used to it. To me it was starting to seem how Sundays ought to be.

WHAT ADDOLORATA SAID

'I hate to admit it but Papa is completely right when he says that Rosie needs something to occupy her. She seemed so much happier while she was busy taking pictures. He's so proud of himself now you'd think it was all his idea, not mine. He's even planning to throw a little party – an unveiling ceremony – and serve free Prosecco and antipasti to his friends and some of the regulars. He's totally over-excited.

I've noticed that Rosie seems a bit flat, though. It's as though the fun part is over for her now and she's back to having nothing to do with her time.'

The Olive Estate

The summer had burnt itself out and Enzo could sense a chill in the air and a strengthening of the sea breeze. His mother had put away her light cotton dresses and was wearing wool, his father's impatience was growing as he circled the groves, checking the trees and worrying about the weather.

Every member of the Santi family was building towards the harvest. Tools that had been stored since last year were pulled out again, cleaned and checked; bottles and labels were readied. No one could walk past a tree without examining a leaf for the telltale scars of fungus or the signs of an infestation.

There were so many things that could hurt an olive tree: moths, cicadas, beetles, flies or roundworms. Most destroyed them slowly, feeding on the flowers, leaves and fruit, attacking the roots. Defending the trees meant constant vigilance and care, nursing them towards the harvest that this year was expected to be bigger than ever.

Enzo didn't mind the extra work – it was too chilly for the beach now, anyhow. The Lido had been closed, the sands abandoned. He and his friends had moved on and now spent whatever free time they had up in Triento or down at the port, drinking beer at the bar with the best view of the few boats still nudging in and out of the harbour.

Among them most days was Ricardo Russo, his sister's fiancé, but the chatter never turned to weddings. There were better things to discuss: football, music, cars, the latest Sony Walkman. Often they talked about the same things day after day, had the same arguments. Like Enzo, many were eldest sons whose futures had been decided. Soon Ricardo would step into his family's linen business; others had herds of cows waiting or shop counters they would stand behind. Enzo could imagine them thirty years from now sitting round this table, their hair grey, their paunches swelling, still having the same conversations.

He drained his beer and refused another, cutting short the afternoon. He had promised his father he'd check the machine they used for labelling as last year it had been unreliable and slowed production. The last thing they needed was a repeat of the problem. Nothing should stand in the way of the bottles being filled and packed, ready to be transported to places Enzo was certain he would never visit. Santi Olive Oil sat on the shelves of smart shops all over the world. New Yorkers drizzled it on their salads and Londoners dipped their bread into it. All were happy to pay a high price for their taste of Italy.

There were plenty of other growers who would stretch a harvest – secretly blending what they'd pressed with inferior oils – but Enzo's Nonna would never countenance that. The Santi Oil had always been completely honest and the family prided themselves on it. Each drop came from olives grown right there on the estate.

Enzo knew what everyone liked to say about them in the village: 'The Santi family knocks down houses to plant olive groves.' His grandfather would even repeat those words himself whenever he bought more land with plans to raze the buildings and extend the reach of his estate. Each year he planted new trees, rows and rows of them; although it would be years before some began fruiting properly and he might not live to see it.

'The future,' Nonna would say. 'He is thinking of the future. Those trees are for you.'

Enzo's earliest memories were of planting days, toddling

after his mother as she helped mark out the rows and stake the spots in the flinty sun-baked earth where the trees would stand. Once they were planted no tree would be disturbed, so his grandfather always walked the rows before the healthy saplings were set in shallow holes and the earth piled round them. Enzo could measure out his childhood against those trees. They had grown as he had.

'In hundreds of years they will be still fruiting, even though their trunks will be wrinkled and gnarled,' his Nonna reminded him whenever they visited the newer groves. 'These trees are your grandfather's legacy.'

In her room she kept a book about olive trees and some nights she would read it slowly and memorise facts to share with him. She liked to talk of their history, how the Persians had grown them and the Greeks helped spread them right across the Mediterranean, how other trees might be more beautiful but none was so sacred and blessed. These were the things his Nonna considered just as important as anything he might learn from his teachers at school.

So much of Enzo's childhood was tangled up with the trees. He remembered the smell of wood smoke at pruning time, with fires dotted over the hills as every farmer in the area burnt his discarded branches; the hard bread softened in peppery oil his Nonna gave him to chew; the long days of harvest-time when bedtimes weren't so strictly enforced and meals were snatched. He remembered how the taste of olives infused whatever he ate, probably even the milk suckled from his mother's breast. And he still remembered the Bible class when the teacher told them how the sight of an olive branch had been what showed Noah the deluge was over. She looked straight at Enzo as she spoke the words, as though the branch had come from the Santi Estate. All the class knew his family had more trees than the rest and that still his grandfather went on knocking down buildings to plant more.

Enzo wondered when it would stop. Would future generations keep planting until the Santi groves touched the edge of Triento? What would people in the village say about them then?

Rosie

While we were waiting for the prints to come back from the lab, Beppi's plans grew grander. His little unveiling ceremony had turned into a proper party, with the guest list lengthening and Little Italy officially closed for the occasion. All the staff were caught up in the excitement, the chefs busy coming up with ideas for finger food, the waiters planning changes to the dining room to accommodate the numbers that were expected.

To me it seemed a lot of fuss and I was concerned that after such a big build-up people could only be disappointed. Purposely I stayed well away from Little Italy. I wasn't there when the prints came back from the lab or when Beppi got the finished frames and had them hung on the wall. He told me he'd taped a black cloth over the top to hide them from view so now I couldn't see how they looked until everyone else did.

The week before the party Addolorata wanted us to go shopping for new frocks to wear but somehow we ran out of time. So instead Pieta took us upstairs and said we could choose something of hers that we liked. She had an entire room hung with clothes, a giant walk-in wardrobe – I'd never seen anything like it. There were racks of vintage dresses and gypsy-style skirts, shelves of handbags and shoes. I stood in the doorway lusting after it all.

Pieta smiled. 'So do you like my collection?'

'Where did you get it all?' I was still gaping at the room.

'Oh, markets and second-hand shops. Some of the clothes

I made myself. Come in and we'll choose some pieces for you to try.'

I'd lost so much weight since I'd moved to Fitzroy Square that I had no trouble fitting in to even the tiniest of Pieta's outfits. It was intoxicating playing dress-up, transforming myself into someone else entirely with each change of style.

'This is better than trying on clothes at Liberty,' I said, staring at my reflection in the mirror propped against the wall. 'How on earth do you decide what to wear every morning?'

Addolorata wasn't having such a good time. Her curves were more generous than mine and, even when she squeezed into an outfit, its buttonholes pulled or the zip wouldn't fasten.

Sucking in her stomach, she modelled a lacy sixties mini-dress. 'If I don't eat between now and the party do you think I could get away with this?'

'It'll never happen, Addolorata.' Her sister was laughing. 'Try this one instead. I can let it out for you around the hips if you like.'

We both settled on black dresses. Mine had a halter neck and a skirt that swished when I walked. Against the dark fabric my skin and hair looked paler, and I might have stepped out of one of my own photographs.

All of us felt jittery on the night of the unveiling. Lou came over to the Martinelli house and Pieta helped us get ready, smudging shadow on our eyes and glossing up our lips, as we drank glasses of bubbling Prosecco and got in the party mood.

'What a shame Toni isn't here,' said Lou. 'Then all the Villa Girls would be together.'

Toni was at university in Leeds and, although she spoke to Addolorata on the phone now and then, seemed to have been falling away from her old friends just as we'd predicted. I couldn't pretend to be sorry. There had always been a spikiness about her, a harder edge. Toni was a person of strong likes and dislikes and I was pretty sure I knew how she felt about me.

Lou, though, was very different – softer and more fun. I couldn't imagine her disliking anyone so long as she had a full glass of wine in her hand.

'The Villa Girls? Is that what you're calling us?' Addolorata smiled. 'It's a good name. I like it.'

When we were ready, I set up my camera on the new tripod I'd bought and took some shots of us outside in the soft evening light. As I clicked off a few frames I imagined looking back at the images in ten years' time, seeing the smiles on our faces and the champagne flutes in our hands and feeling nostalgic. I even caught myself wondering who I might be by then, how I would have changed. It was the first time in ages I'd thought about my future and it took me by surprise.

We took a taxi to Little Italy, all of us giggling, intoxicated by bubbles and excitement. Beppi had organised a red carpet to be laid at the entrance to the restaurant and he was standing on the edge of it, greeting guests as they arrived.

'Where have you been all this time? I thought you weren't coming?' He hopped from foot to foot with impatience when he saw us.

Already waiters were circling with trays of drinks and platters of food. The tables had been moved aside and people were grouped, laughing and chatting, beside the long wall where the covered photographs were hung.

Addolorata saw me glancing up at the dark mass of them against the white stucco. 'Don't be nervous, it's all going to be fine,' she promised.

'That's easy for you to say.'

Lou lifted a glass from a passing waiter's tray. 'Here, have some more champagne,' she advised. 'I'd be nervous too, if I were you.'

Before he unveiled the photographs, Beppi made a speech. He talked for a long time in his rolling accent, telling his audience of friends and customers how he had married his wife in Rome and come to London with nothing. He told of the early days of Little Italy when they'd lived in a tiny apartment above the restaurant and worked long days and nights. Although at times his English wasn't perfect, Beppi held his audience.

At long last the head waiter helped him pull away the tape that held the cloth to the wall, and, with a final flourish, Beppi revealed my photographs. There were twenty in all, set in thin black frames against a white background. I could see straight away what a good idea they'd been. For the diners it brought to life the behind-the-scenes world of Little Italy: the frenzy and heat of the kitchen; the perpetual motion of the chefs and waiters. The finished prints took me by surprise, they looked so slick and professional it felt almost like I was staring at another person's work.

Addolorata pushed me forward to stand by her father and everyone clapped us loud and long. Beppi wanted me to speak but I thought if I tried I might cry so I shook my head and only stayed beside him for a few moments before bolting back to the safety of my friends.

The rest of the evening went by in a blur. I never got a chance to examine the pictures properly because every time I got close people would stop me to offer congratulations. Some told me I should be a professional photographer; others asked if I would take pictures of their children or pets. My face ached from smiling. When Lou suggested escaping to a vodka bar she knew of in Soho, I was quick to agree.

Thankfully, Beppi was in his element, the centre of attention, and didn't notice us slipping away. We hailed a cab and Lou abandoned the champagne flute she'd been carrying beside a tree as we clambered into the back.

'You did a great job, Rosie,' she said woozily, as London's lights blurred past.

'Yeah, you did,' agreed Addolorata. 'I'm so glad I bossed Papa into it.'

For the first time, in the back of that taxi speeding towards more alcohol, I got a taste of what success felt like.

Once the distraction of the unveiling was out of the way, Beppi focused his considerable energy on flat hunting. He began without telling me, exhausting several estate agents as he compiled lists of places he thought worth considering. Even when he did agree to let me see a few apartments, he seemed on edge.

'Don't sound too keen on anything or they will put the price up right away,' he kept warning. 'Better if I do all the talking.'

Flat hunting turned out to be an unsettling experience. The places we visited were clean and tidy, all ready for inspection, yet still there were traces of other people's lives in them. In one first-floor flat a withered old lady sat in an armchair chain-smoking as we moved through what had clearly been her home for many years. In another there was a child's drawing stuck to the fridge with the words 'We still love you Mummy' scrawled beneath a collection of stick figures, and I wondered how exactly this family's life had been pulled apart.

Each flat told a story; I began to see just how much pain and heartache there was out in the world. In a way it was comforting because I realised it wasn't just me, I wasn't alone. While Beppi looked for signs of rot and subsidence, I looked for the unhappy lives of strangers.

And then we saw it, the flat I fell in love with. It was on the very edge of Belgravia, closer to Victoria really, and looked like no one had cared about it for quite some time. Beppi pushed his thumb into its soft walls and peeled away paint, muttering about its many faults, but I could see beyond them. Perhaps it was because the place was completely empty, no one's furniture cluttering the rooms, no ghosts of the people who had been there before. The basement was dingy and the courtyard the estate agent had enthused about nothing but cracked concrete and weeds, but still, from the moment I walked through the front door, I could imagine living there.

'It needs a lot of renovation.' Beppi was resoundingly negative. 'It will be a big job. And it's not in such a good street, is it?'

'Yes, but the price reflects all that.' The estate agent was brisk. 'You won't get a better buy around here. This place won't be on the market long, I promise you.'

'Actually, I do quite like it—' I began but Beppi shook his head violently and hustled me out as quickly as he could.

We saw several more flats that afternoon but either the price was too steep or the lease too short, or the rot was too advanced.

'We'll never find anything,' I said, despairing by the end of the day. 'It's hopeless, isn't it?'

'But I thought you liked the basement with the ugly courtyard?' Beppi flicked back through the brochures in the file he'd made up for me.

'Yes, but you said that one needed too much work,' I reminded him.

'Ah, that was only for the agent's ears.' Beppi risked a grin. 'I know how these things work.'

'So should I buy it then?' I was eager.

'Not so fast, *cara*. There's a builder who worked on Little Italy for me. I will get him to take a look and find out what he thinks. But you know you would be better moving further out – you will get more for your money. Are you sure about Belgravia?'

'Yes, I think so,' I told him. It wasn't really about what the clairvoyant had said any more. My need to believe in her wasn't as strong, not since I'd started taking the photographs at Little Italy and life seemed to have a point to it again. Still, I liked what I'd seen of Belgravia, it felt welcoming and looked right. I could imagine what the empty apartment might become.

Back at Fitzroy Square that night it felt like the walls of my tiny room were closing in on me. Already I was envisaging myself with two entire floors of my own, shelves to put my books on, a proper wardrobe for my clothes, space to stretch and move. Beppi had warned me not to get too excited in case his builder didn't give the flat the thumbs-up, but I had so much time for dreaming I couldn't help it.

The next morning I woke before either of my flatmates. Hanging my heavy old camera over my shoulder by its thick strap, I caught a tube up to Highbury and walked the familiar streets to the only real home I'd ever known. It was where I'd grown up, where I'd peddled my tricycle down the front path, had a rabbit hutch in a corner of the garden and a swing on the lawn. Strangers were living there now; they'd turned on a light in the room where my parents had once slept and I guessed they must be getting up and ready for work. Perhaps they had the same routine we'd had: breakfast before they were really hungry, the quickest of showers and a struggle through the traffic to get to places on time. Did they grow pots of herbs in the backyard like my mother? Had they changed the colours of the walls and put their beds in different places? It seemed extraordinary that I couldn't slide my key in the lock and push the door open to see for myself.

There had been a For Sale sign in that front garden just a few weeks after my parents had died. I'd begged my Uncle Phillip not to do it but he didn't listen. As always, everyone thought they knew what was best for me.

The place had been snapped up so quickly. I'd been allowed to keep some things I really wanted: my mother's blue-and-white striped Cornishware, my father's desk. Those went into storage and the rest was sold or found its way into the homes of aunts, uncles and cousins. Then I'd been whisked away from this plain, terraced house on its very ordinary street without ever saying a proper goodbye.

Now I stood for a moment and stared over the neatly clipped hedge. My mother had touched those brick walls; she'd pulled weeds from that tiny patch of front garden and swept the steps clean of fallen autumn leaves. My father had painted the wooden window frames a dark blue he'd never much liked and stood on a ladder to wash down the windows once a month. My parents had been here and now they were not.

Holding my camera to my eye, I fired off a couple of shots of the front gate where my mother used to stand, waving me goodbye whenever I headed off on school trips or outings. Then I lowered my camera, took one final look at the place and turned away. As I walked down the street I imagined my mother still standing at the gate and waving long after I'd disappeared out of her sight.

When I got back I found Addolorata waiting for me outside the flat in Fitzroy Square. She took one look at my face and quickly asked, 'Is everything all right?'

'Yes,' I lied. 'I just went for a walk to take some early-morning pictures. Everything's fine.'

'Let's go and get a coffee then.' She gave me a triumphant little smile. 'I've got some news.'

We walked down to Charlotte Street, Addolorata doing that irritating thing of refusing to give me a hint of why she'd come until we were sitting down sipping our coffee.

'You've met a new guy,' I tried to guess. 'Your father's let you change the menu. Well, what then?'

'None of those things.'

She ordered a cappuccino with extra chocolate and, once

she'd licked off the froth, said, 'I've done something very clever.'

'Just tell me.' I was laughing now. 'Stop torturing me.'

'I've found you a job.'

'What sort of job?'

'Well, to be honest I'm not entirely sure. There's an old Italian bloke that comes into the restaurant now and then who always likes to have a chat with my father. So yesterday Papa was showing off your pictures and the old guy said his son is a photographer and right now he's looking for an assistant. Papa got completely over-excited and came running into the kitchen. Once I'd managed to calm him down, I got a number for the son.' Addolorata produced a slightly greasy serviette from her pocket. 'You should call him straight away.'

'A photographer's assistant? Could I do that?'

'It's worth phoning him, isn't it?'

'Yeah, I guess so.' Those shots on the wall of Little Italy had boosted my confidence. 'Even if he doesn't want to hire me he might give me some good advice, right?'

Addolorata might have come and stood over me to make sure I made the call only she was running late for work. So I headed back to my room, the serviette stuffed into my pocket, and dreamed a little more. In my head I was already a photographer's assistant living in my own smart flat in Belgravia. I put off calling the number for as long as I could and comforted myself with daydreams.

EXTRACT FROM ADDOLORATA'S LETTER TO TONI

So we're helping Rosie find a place to live and a job, sort of taking over her life really. Weird, isn't it? I keep thinking that if her parents hadn't died I'd have left school without bothering to talk to her again. I never really liked her crowd. Remember how we used to call them 'the Worthies'? They were always collecting funds for charity, scoring 90 per cent in tests and telling us not to smoke in the toilets. I think she must have changed or maybe she never really was that worthy after all.

The Olive Estate

Everything about his Nonna's kitchen was familiar to Enzo: the old wooden dresser so worn and carefully oiled, the Pyrex dishes covered with garish pictures of chilli peppers, the Moka pot on the stove, the paint peeling from the walls and ceiling, even the ugly plastic-backed curtains decorated with red and white flowers. Nothing there had changed for years.

Enzo knew without opening any drawer or cupboard door what lay behind it. He could find the pile of table linen crisply ironed by his mamma or put his hands on the tomatoes his sisters had bottled over the summer. He knew where the dried pasta was stored, the jars of beans and drums of Arborio rice. All of it was where it had always been.

Even the sounds and smells were as he expected. Coffee first thing every morning, earthy and strong, sipped to the sound of the cockerel crowing shrilly and his Nonna swearing that some day she would wring its neck. By mid-morning that had been replaced by the frying of onions and garlic, the bickering of his sisters and his mamma's voice, louder and more insistent. Searing meat and bubbling sauces meant lunchtime was approaching. And then the afternoons, with the sweetness of baking bread or the jolting of the table as a pasta dough was kneaded.

Usually Enzo didn't mind the certainty of home. He saw how it brought comfort, especially for his Nonna who was old and liked things to be how she had arranged them. But sometimes, early in the morning, woken by the familiar sound of his father snorting into his handkerchief or his mother's heavy footsteps, Enzo would pull the bed covers over his head at the thought of yet another day of it.

Even in Triento the signs of change were rare. Much the same people sat outside the cafés or gossiped in the piazza. In summer they complained of the heat, in winter of how cold and windy it had turned. Each year Enzo recognised some of the same tourists even, returning a second or third time to visit their favourite churches and monuments.

And since Gianpaolo had pointed it out, he noticed how often Signora Mancuso paraded her daughter by. He saw them all the time. At the market helping Concetta carry the shopping, they would drift into his line of vision. Drinking a coffee with his grandfather or a beer with his friends, they would be a few tables away or might call a greeting through the doorway. Late in the summer Maria Luisa had cut her hair so it curled around her face and now she looked more grown up. Other than that she hadn't changed much either.

He supposed he must seem equally familiar to her. Maria Luisa knew most things about him: the jokes that made him laugh, the foods he preferred to eat, the shows he watched on TV, the music he enjoyed listening to. There was no mystery, nothing undiscovered, about either of them it seemed.

They even knew the lines their conversations would follow. Each time they met they'd talk about the weather, the harvest, the health of their families, Concetta's wedding plans. Since the day her cheeks had pinked at the sight of Gianpaolo, Maria Luisa always made sure to ask for news of him, ignoring the frown the question brought to her mother's face. Enzo noted this quiet rebellion and wondered at it. Perhaps there was a part of Maria Luisa he hadn't seen, some mystery after all, although as hard as he looked he could never find more signs of it.

'She is so determined, that Signora Mancuso,' Gianpaolo remarked one evening as they shared their usual jug of beer.

'She never misses an opportunity to put Maria Luisa in front of you.'

'She's wasting her time,' Enzo told his friend. 'I'm not interested.'

'Perhaps not now but you might change your mind.'

'I don't think so. I can't imagine what would make me want to marry Maria Luisa. And anyway, like I keep telling you, it's you she prefers. She likes having a chance to say your name.'

Gianpaolo stared down into his glass. 'Rubbish,' he said gruffly but he sounded pleased.

Sinking back down in his seat, Enzo looked around the bar and thought how even here nothing ever seemed to change. The same dusty bottles of whisky were lined up on the shelves behind the patron, the same old men were playing cards in the corner and accusing each other of cheating.

'Do you think we should try a different bar instead of coming to this same one all the time?' he asked Gianpaolo

His friend looked surprised. 'In winter we come here, in summer we go down by the marina. They're different, aren't they?'

'Yes, but our habit is the same. What I mean is we should drive down the coast and find somewhere new.'

'But why? We wouldn't know anyone there. They'd all be strangers.'

'That's the whole point,' Enzo told him. 'They would be new people, different.'

'But they'd be the same really,' his friend pointed out. 'They'd only seem different until we got to know them.'

Enzo found the thought depressing. 'Perhaps we should go back up to Amalfi then ... or Napoli. In the spring when the tourists start coming back.'

Gianpaolo didn't seem keen. 'I suppose so ... if you like,' he agreed reluctantly. 'But it's a long way to go for a beer. What's wrong with this place anyway?'

'It's boring. We know exactly what we'll drink, who we'll see, even what we'll talk about. It never changes.'

Gianpaolo laughed. 'But that's what I like about it. After a day out fishing in the wind and rain it's good to be safe and dry here with a drink in my hand. It's what I look forward to.'

'Yes, but don't we need some fun ... a little more excitement? We're young – isn't this when we're meant to be having a good time? Otherwise I might as well give in to the signora,' Enzo shrugged a little bitterly, 'and be like my sister and Ricardo Russo and do all the boring things everyone expects of me.'

Rosie

Roberto Olivieri was the photographer's name, although he answered to Rob and spoke with a slightly forced Cockney accent. His studio was in Camden in an old warehouse on the edge of the canal. It looked very cool, the leather sofas, the white-painted floors and walls, the old Gaggia coffeemaker on the counter and the pinball machine in the corner. My portfolio had been hurriedly assembled and when I pulled it out I was certain he would laugh me out of the place.

'Who taught you?' Rob asked, frowning as he looked through some of my Majorca shots. Even the way he dressed was cool – a pork pie hat on his shaved head and his jeans held up with red braces.

'No one taught me,' I admitted. 'I just play around with an old Zenit I've got. I don't really know what I'm doing.'

'But you have fun with it, right?'

'Yes, I do,' I agreed. 'But you're probably wanting someone with more experience?' I could see by the way he set the portfolio aside without looking at anything for long that I didn't stand a chance of being his assistant.

'Look, the truth is I've got loads of other people after this job,' he admitted. 'They've graduated from photography courses, have the technical knowledge, the understanding of light. You've definitely got a good eye and I'm impressed with some of your candid shots, but I'm not going to hire you as an assistant, sorry.'

I got to my feet, not feeling particularly disappointed since this was exactly what I'd expected. 'Thanks for your time—' I began.

'Hang on, I haven't finished.' Rob handed me back my portfolio. 'There is something you might be interested in. My studio manager has just quit. It's only an admin job. You'd be making coffee, answering the phone, looking after studio and gear hire, that sort of stuff. I can't pay much but it'd be a good way to find out if photography is really what you're interested in.'

I didn't bother asking myself why Rob had lost his assistant and his studio manager in quick succession. Naively, I let him hire me for around half what he'd paid my predecessor, although I didn't find that out till later – around the same time as I discovered the power of his temper and his unpredictable mood swings.

My first week there I was absorbed in learning where things were kept and how stuff was done. Most of the time it felt like I was play-acting at working: chirping down the phone 'Canal Photographic Studios', frothing milk for coffee, filing rental agreements and keeping the studio spaces tidy. It was easy work and I enjoyed it. Rob had a tendency to bark instructions and never explained himself properly but we seemed to rub along OK.

Then he had his first big meltdown. It started with a lot of shouting followed by the sound of something plastic smashing as it was hurled against the wall. Two seconds later Rob emerged from his office. 'My phone is broken,' he barked. 'Get me a new one.'

After that there were frequent inexplicable rages. Chair were thrown, things were destroyed. In between times, Rob was charming but it was nerve-racking never quite knowing when he would snap.

I think I'd have quit the job if it hadn't been for Johnny Wellbelove. He was the photography student who had scored the job as Rob's assistant and the one who bore the brunt of his rages. If a film cartridge wasn't loaded quickly enough or he was a bit slow setting up the lighting then Johnny got it in the neck. He had a knack for acting like he didn't care and that enraged Rob all the more because, no matter what he said, he couldn't get a rise out of Johnny.

Behind Rob's back we'd laugh at him. Johnny did funny, rather camp impersonations of him losing his temper, called him Benito Mussolini and pranced around imitating his Cockney accent and making up ridiculous rhyming slang. Sometimes I'd find myself still laughing hours later.

I'd assumed Johnny was gay but then he introduced me to his girlfriend, a tiny doll-like thing who always wore black leather pants and a tight top. After work the three of us would often go for a couple of beers. Johnny was into live music and was always dragging us off to see noisy, pub bands. He looked a bit like a rock musician himself, with his hair patchily lightened in home-bleaching sessions, his jeans carefully ripped and his Doc Martens covered in graffiti.

'Guess what Benito did today,' he'd yell, as some amateurish musician thrashed his guitar loudly onstage. And then there'd be a half-heard tale of the latest tantrum and Johnny would vent his anger at last.

I'd have been more envious of him going out on shoots if I hadn't known how often he was humiliated. Still I missed my own photography and worried that there didn't seem any time for it now I was working. It had been ages since I'd bothered pulling out my old Zenit. Sometimes I helped to clean Rob's lenses and pack them away and I liked the feel of them in my hands but the more I learnt about the technical side of photography the more difficult it seemed to actually take a picture.

All of Johnny's work was really punky and alternative. His portfolio was full of pictures of heroin addicts shooting up and filthy street people down on the embankment with their sad little cardboard kingdoms and dogs tied up with bits of rope. So when he told me about the weddings I was astonished. It was a sideline he had going on the weekends that had started with him photographing the wedding of a friend as a favour and snowballed from there. It turned out he was a genius at capturing romantic images of girls in frothy tulle and he got away with charging what seemed like a ridiculous sum for them.

'Weddings are bloody hard work, you have no idea,' he told me. 'I wish I'd never started. Thank God it's winter and there aren't as many.'

'If you like I could give you a hand some time,' I offered. 'Just for the experience. Don't tell Rob, though. Yesterday he called me a tragic little wannabe photographer.'

'Jesus, Rob doesn't know about this.' Johnny looked horrified. 'He'd go nuclear if he had a clue I was moonlighting. He'd have the biggest Benito moment of all time.'

I giggled. 'It's almost tempting to tell him just to see that.'

'Don't even think about it, Rosie, he'd have a stroke.'

'He's such a pig. Remind me again why we don't just leave like all the others did.'

'Because we're learning,' Johnny said. 'And because we have a laugh together.'

The next weekend I helped him with a wedding and understood very quickly why he found them so tough. You had to be perky and polite – this was a couple's special day, after all – but you also had to deliver the goods. If you shot all day from the ceremony to the reception it was a long, long job and I had no idea how Johnny had been managing without an assistant. There was so much for me to do: loading film, fiddling with the light meter, numbering the finished rolls, carrying his gear and wrangling the guests. Every now and then I set up a shot – a detail of the dress or a bridesmaid's bouquet. It was exhausting but quite good fun.

'That was so much less stressful today, you wouldn't

believe it,' he told me later as we unwound over a couple of beers. 'Would you be up for assisting me every time, if I pay you a share of the loot? You could put together the couple's finished album, too, if you like. I hate that side of it.'

'All right then,' I agreed. 'I could do with the cash, actually.'

By then I'd made an offer on the flat in Belgravia. The reality of owning bricks and mortar was starting to sink in and even though my inheritance would cover the costs, I'd decided it was time to start earning decent money.

With the two of us working the weddings we had some good times. Johnny lent me one of his cameras and, when there was time, I took candid shots of the guests and the ceremony. People seemed to love them, said they brought the day back to life, so eventually Johnny included the candids as part of his package and put his price up even further.

I got used to yelling things like 'now can we have the family of the groom please', holding bouquets for nervous brides or fluffing around with their dresses getting them ready for shots. The funny thing about doing weddings is that never once did it make me dream of my own – quite the opposite, really. I couldn't imagine standing up in front of everyone I knew and repeating those vows. I certainly didn't lust after a big meringue of a dress. Sometimes I'd let Addolorata and Lou look at the wedding albums I'd made up and I never understood what made them coo over them.

'It's romantic,' Lou said, 'and so beautiful.'

'Yes, but it's just the one day,' I pointed out. 'And it's not real. Life has bad things in store for some of these people. Half of them will probably get divorced.'

'That's a miserable way to look at things,' argued Addolorata. 'My parents are still together, aren't they?'

'So you want the whole business: the white gown, the bouquet, the speeches, the big tower of a cake?' I asked.

'I don't know about that, but I want to be married some day,' she told me.

'Yeah, me too,' agreed Lou.

'Well, I don't,' I said and I meant it.

'You'll change your mind when you meet the right guy,' they both insisted.

And that's what everyone always said ... but somehow I couldn't imagine it.

EXTRACT FROM ADDOLORATA'S JOURNAL

It's ages since I've written anything in here. I like the idea of keeping a journal that I can reread when I'm old and grey but there never seems enough time to keep up with it. I've been working crazy hours at Little Italy, pulling double shifts, and all I want at the end of the day is to sit down with a beer and a cigarette. Oh and Papa has been driving me crazy. He's totally resistant to any sort of change, convinced his way is the only way. I've got so many ideas, so many things I'd like to do, but he barely even listens. I'm sick of it, really. I know it's a completely terrible thing to say but sometimes I look at Rosie with no family at all and envy her freedom. She can be whatever she wants ... do anything at all ...

The Olive Estate

Enzo found his Nonna in the pressing room, sweeping the stone floor as she did once a week to keep the place free of dust and cobwebs. When olives were being milled and all the machines working at full tilt the noise was deafening. But the rest of the year the sunless room was peaceful and cool and Enzo knew it was one of his Nonna's favourite places. She went there often if her mind was worrying at a problem.

She looked up as Enzo stooped beneath the doorway but kept sweeping and didn't offer him her usual smile. He thought she seemed exhausted, the dented skin beneath her eyes stained purple, the fine mesh of wrinkles more noticeable even in the half-light.

'Why don't you rest, Nonna? I will finish in here,' he offered.

She shook her head stubbornly. 'It's not the sweeping that is tiring me.'

'What then?' he asked. 'What's wrong?'

She clucked at him. 'Nothing is wrong. The trees are healthy, the fruit looks plump; the harvest should be a good one.'

Enzo was certain she was lying. For days now the atmosphere on the estate had been strained. First the wedding talk had stuttered into silence, as though no one cared any more what style of dress Concetta would wear or what the guests might eat. Conversations were hushed and hurried; even disagreements took place in voices that couldn't be overheard. His grandfather spent hours on the phone, the door of his office firmly closed, only emerging to sit at the head of the table at mealtimes. Even his sisters had picked up on the shift in mood, their usual squabbling subdued. Enzo didn't like this silence. He found it strange, worrying.

And then his father had disappeared early one morning and not returned that night. 'Away on business,' was his mother's explanation but Enzo had thought she seemed anxious, jumping when the phone rang and leaving a sauce unattended on the hob for so long that it caught.

It was as though the Santi family was preparing for the harvest as normal, but their minds were somewhere else entirely. Enzo couldn't work out what had changed. There had been no cancelled orders or unhappy customers as far as he could tell – nothing out of the ordinary. The weather hadn't been especially stormy; no trees were showing signs of disease. There was a wedding to look forward to.

His Nonna ought to have been smiling, not leaning her broom against the wall and agreeing with him tiredly. 'Perhaps you are right and I should rest,' she said. 'Don't worry about the sweeping, I will do it another day.'

Taking the brush from where she'd left it, Enzo finished the task for her, even though the floor looked clean enough already. As he worked he thought about the unease that had crept over his family, the sense that everyone was watching and waiting. He wished he understood what lay behind it.

On the surface everything seemed to go on as normal. The weeks went by, winter deepened and Enzo watched the firm green olives slowly change, swelling and blushing purple then darkening to black. It seemed to take forever before his grandfather declared them ripe for picking and then a tremor ran through the whole family. Each knew what the harvest expected of them. His mother and younger sisters were bound to the kitchen producing food to fuel the workers, the others stayed in the groves, where they climbed high ladders and gently eased the olives from the trees by hand.

On other estates they might use wooden rakes to pull off the fruit and nets to catch it as it rained down, some even beat at the branches with sticks. Here on the Santi Estate they didn't hold with anything that might bruise or damage what was picked. Even clutching an olive in a hot hand or squeezing it too hard was frowned upon. Up on the ladders with their heads in the branches, each worker heeded his grandfather's words: 'Take hold of each olive like you would the hand of a shy, beautiful woman,' he liked to call up to them through the silvery leaves.

In the pressing room his Nonna held sway, making sure the fruit was crushed and turned to oil a few short hours after it had been picked, for, as she constantly reminded Enzo, stale olives would make for a bitter oil that was no reward at all for the year-long cosseting of the trees and the back-breaking work of harvest.

There were so many things that might taint the oil and turn it musty or rancid: light, air, too much heat, even the tiniest bit of dirt. It took kilos of fruit to make just one precious litre and his Nonna was careful there was never any waste. She made soap from the third or fourth pressings and the paste that remained was burnt on the fire where the workers went to warm themselves and rest for long enough to drink a cup of rough red wine and swallow down a thick wedge of bread topped with mortadella sausage and goat's cheese that his mother had brushed with olive oil and aged for a year like the mountain people did.

Harvest-time brought its risks, hands grew sore and dirty, pickers had been known to fall from ladders and bones were sometimes broken. The work was hard from dawn to dusk, as the crates were filled with plump shiny olives. Only when the light had faded did they make their way back to the house where his mother had set up trestle tables in the biggest of the barns. Enzo's sisters brought out the food they'd spent the day preparing: warm pizza breads folded and stuffed with softly steamed broccoli and smoked Provolone, soups of pasta and beans, pork sausages hot with *peperoncino*, stews of lamb and wine slow-cooked in clay pots, and Enzo's favourite dish of all – *cotechinata*, the skin of the pig stuffed with salted pork, garlic and hot red peppers then simmered in tomato sauce.

On the final night of harvest his grandfather would always spit roast a pig that had been raised and killed on the estate. Everyone toasted the new season's oil and the noise around the trestle tables grew louder as the wine jugs were emptied. All of the olives were picked, the oil was pressed and now the trees would be left to rest until pruning time when the cycle of life on the estate began again.

Usually the Santi *festa* went on all night long, his grandfather remaining at the head of the table until the last worker had gone or fallen into a drunken sleep beneath the trees. This year it ought to have been no different: the harvest had been successful, the bottled oil was already turning greeny gold as the sediment settled, and when his grandfather raised the first glass of wine he said as always, '*Una buona annata*, a good year.'

But once the meal was finished Enzo saw him slip away silently from the table and with his place empty everything seemed off key. The harvest songs were sung less joyously, the braziers were allowed to burn down and, feeling the shift in mood, the workers were all gone well before dawn.

Rosie

As hard as I tried I couldn't ever be the perfect shiny thing I thought my parents wanted. I let them down over and over again, slamming doors or souring a weekend treat by swinging into a bad mood. Even I didn't understand why I behaved that way.

I suppose all teenagers are temperamental and think no one understands them so I wasn't worse than anyone else. The difference was my parents expected more of me. If I'd had a sister or brother it might have been different, but I was the only one there to soak up their attention and give them reasons to be happy.

They were lovely parents, so encouraging, so ready to cheer me on. They wanted to be proud of me and so often I wouldn't let them. Looking back now I'm ashamed to remember myself. Bad grace, bleak moods, sulks … my nasty little repertoire for pushing them away and somehow ruining a triumph.

Now at last I'd done something worthwhile. My name was on the deeds of a flat in Belgravia. I'd sat in the office of a solicitor, signed documents and made the place mine. In a few weeks the keys would be in my hands. It felt like I'd changed, become ridiculously grown up, and I wished my mum and dad were here to see me now.

'I can't believe you have your own place,' Addolorata kept saying. She was looking exhausted and it had been weeks since she'd had time to catch up for a coffee because Little Italy had been short-staffed and busy.

'I can't believe it either,' I admitted.

'You'll be able to do anything you like – even bring a guy home and spend the night with him.' She said it as though it was the best thing she could imagine.

'Yeah, I guess so.'

'You don't sound particularly excited.'

'There's still so much to do,' I explained. 'Building work, redecorating, finding furniture. I can't get excited about it being all finished and actually living there. It seems a long way ahead.'

'Are you going to stay in that dump in Fitzroy Square until it's ready?'

'I suppose I'll have to.'

Now that my time in the light-starved basement was coming to an end I realised how depressed I'd been there. The roller-skating flatmate, the unfriendly girl in the business suits, the kitchen in what was really a corridor, the mattress on the hard floor; all of it was horrible. I'd stuck it out for months when I should have been looked for something else.

'It'll be Christmas soon,' Addolorata pointed out. 'You can't spend it in that place.'

'I'll be OK,' I lied.

'But, Rosie, this is your first Christmas without your parents. I bet even those freaky flatmates of yours have places to go. You'll be completely on your own.'

It was something I'd been worrying about for weeks, ever since I'd found out Canal Studios would be shut over the holidays so there would be nowhere for me to go to every day. Johnny would be smoothing down his bleached quiff into respectability and spending time with his parents in the Home Counties, the awful Rob would be away somewhere terrorising other people, and I'd be stuck below ground with only the rumble of tube trains for company. It seemed a pretty bleak prospect.

'There's always my uncle ... or my aunt,' I said. 'I'm sure I could go to them if I felt like it.'

'Or you could come to our place,' Addolorata said it casually.

'For Christmas Day? That would be lovely. But are you sure I wouldn't be intruding?'

'No, what I meant was you could move in with us until your flat is finished.'

'But I couldn't ...' This wasn't what I'd expected at all. 'It would be too much ...'

'Oh look, I might as well come clean.' Addolorata screwed up her face. 'Papa has already decided you're coming. He's put a single bed into my mother's old sewing room. It'll be a bit of a squash in there but no worse than your room in Fitzroy Square.'

The arguments I put up were half-hearted. Becoming part of a family again, even one so different from mine and only for a few weeks, was such a seductive idea. I was ready for it now. There was something about the way the Martinellis behaved together I found reassuring. They argued constantly, shouting like they hated one another, and then it was over, like summer rain, and everything was calm again. The fights were usually about such unimportant things – Addolorata's smoking, Beppi trying to force more food on someone who wasn't hungry. I liked their predictability and I loved the sense of permanence about their tall house full of old things. To settle in it for a while would be a good thing; to have a big, noisy Italian Christmas with nothing to remind me of home.

Addolorata and Lou helped me move the next weekend. They'd brought a few empty cardboard boxes and we filled them with the belongings I'd accumulated since I moved in. There wasn't much stuff really – all my precious things were still in storage – but stripped of them the room seemed even more miserable. I wondered how I'd stood living in it for all that time.

The boxes were loaded into the back of a white van Beppi had borrowed from one of his suppliers and he drove us, slightly erratically, with one hand on the horn and talking the whole way. 'If I had seen where you lived before today I would have made you come sooner, Rosie,' he kept saying. 'Why did nobody tell me how horrible it was, eh? Cellars are for keeping wine in not people. *Cose da pazzi*, you girls shouldn't have let her stay there.'

'Papa, we're in a bus lane.' Addolorata was laughing. 'No, don't hoot at him, you're the one in the wrong. Look out for that car turning right. Brake, Papa, brake!'

Fortunately their house was only a short drive away. Catherine was waiting at the gate and looked genuinely relieved to see us pull up. 'Did he hit anything?' she asked Addolorata.

'No, not this time.'

Catherine turned to me. 'Rosie, I'm so sorry. I tried to persuade him to send one of the waiters to drive you but he insisted on doing it himself.'

'Tsk, I have never heard so much rubbish.' Beppi emerged from the back of the van, already clutching a box in his arms. 'I am a very good driver.'

Lou and I tried to hide our smiles. We'd never felt in any danger but Beppi had driven almost exactly how we knew he would. It was how he cooked too: excitable, almost out of control, chopping an onion so fast it was amazing he didn't take a finger with it, always half distracted by something.

Shrugging off our help he ran up and down the stairs with my boxes, piling them up in the sewing room. The place still had a musty spare-room smell but they'd done their best to make it look cheerful. Someone had put a jar of white flowers on a table, Pieta had wheeled in one of her clothes rails and Addolorata had covered a pinboard with shots of our trip to Majorca and hung it on the wall.

'I know it's not much,' she said. 'But at least when you look out of the window you see trees instead of a brick wall.'

'It's fantastic, really it is. I don't know how to thank you all.' I was embarrassed to feel the tears welling in my eyes. Addolorata pulled me into a hug and when she let me go she was a little bit teary too.

'Don't thank us until you've tried living here,' she warned, laughing and wiping her eyes. 'I only hope we don't drive you crazy.'

It was odd lying on the bed after she had gone to her own room, leaving me to settle in. I could hear the crashing of pans downstairs; footsteps on the floor above; the creaking and complaining of old wood in an unfamiliar house.

I wasn't sure what to do with myself. Should I go down and help Beppi in the kitchen? Sit in the living room with a magazine? By now I'd grown so used to sharing a flat with people who weren't remotely interested in me, it felt strange to think that here I would be noticed.

I must have fallen asleep for a good couple of hours because I woke to the tempting smells of simmering sauces and roasting meats and Addolorata calling out that the meal was ready.

As I took my usual Sunday lunchtime seat beside her at the kitchen table, Beppi opened a bottle of Prosecco. 'Today I think we must make a toast to Rosie, to her new flat and her new life,' he declared. 'But also to her parents who would be so proud to see how well their daughter is doing and how strong she is.'

'Thank you.' Clinking my glass against his, I felt more unwanted tears clogging my eyes.

Beppi told me there was no need to keep thanking them and that I was to treat their home as my own.

'If you're hungry then help yourself to anything you want.

You will have you own key and must come and go as you please. This is your home for as long as you need it.'

It was Catherine who passed me a box of tissues to mop up the tears I couldn't seem to hold back.

'We're all glad you're here with us,' she told me. 'And we're proud of you, Rosie, really we are.'

WHAT ADDOLORATA SAID

'There was this big emotional scene over lunch. Rosie was in tears then got all awkward and embarrassed. My mother started crying as well and my father was furious because no one would eat. Then there was an argument about … actually, I'm not sure what it was about … but the whole mood of welcoming Rosie was kind of ruined, although as Pieta pointed out later she's going to have to get used to it. Rosie says her family had a different way of arguing to ours. That they hardly ever yelled – just sulked mostly or slammed the odd door. It's very English, isn't it? Personally, I'd rather have a really good shout. But still, it would have been nicer if it hadn't happened on Rosie's very first day.'

The Olive Estate

Enzo woke in the night and thought he heard the squeal of a truck's brakes and the whispering of men's voices. He rolled out of bed and opened the shutters but rain clouds lay over the moon and the sound, if there'd been one at all, may have come from beyond the barns, well beyond his line of sight. Yawning, Enzo considered going to investigate. The barns were mostly empty but the storage areas behind the pressing room were stacked with cartons of freshly bottled olive oil. If someone were to steal them the losses would be great.

His muscles still sore from the hard work of harvest, Enzo bent to pick up his jeans from where he'd dropped them earlier. He pulled on a woollen jersey against the cold and picked up the heavy metal torch from beside his bed that would serve as a weapon if necessary.

The torchlight wasn't needed for him to find his way across the familiar yard in the darkness and skirt around the edges of the old buildings. He moved softly across the hard-pressed dirt, his feet in sneakers, making barely any noise at all. As he neared the stone barns he slowed and stepped more carefully. He heard the sound of an engine running and something heavy being moved from place to place. By now he was round the back of his Nonna's kitchen, as close as he dared to get. He could see that the truck was backed right up to the open doors of the biggest barn, its headlights dimmed. Enzo was confused. This was where the harvest supper had been held two nights earlier. He had helped his sisters clear away the trestle tables just that morning and now the barn lay bare. There was nothing in there to steal.

He risked moving closer, frustrated that the high barn doors were blocking his view. Now he could see the truck's ramp had been lowered and two men were moving up and down it. After a moment or two he realised what was happening. These men were not stealing from the Santi family. They were carrying boxes into the barn and leaving them there.

For a moment Enzo considered hurrying back to the house and waking his father. Then he remembered the closed expressions and whispered conversations of the past few weeks. Whatever was going on, it was likely his father knew about it. He watched the two men working as he tried to decide what to do. The easiest thing would be to turn away, return to bed and say nothing, to come back in the morning and investigate the boxes when no one was around. But it angered Enzo that his father had not confided in him. He was a grown man, so much was expected of him, and yet still they treated him like a child, leaving him out of discussions, deciding everything themselves.

'What the hell is going on?' Enzo spoke loudly and suddenly. Flicking the switch of his torch, he shone the light directly at the barn doors.

He heard the sound of a box being dropped. '*Merda!*' someone said, and Enzo thought he recognised the voice.

'Who is it? What's going on?' he hissed.

'*Cose da pazzi,*' the man swore again.

Enzo strode up to the barn doors and shone the torch inside. The light picked out a stocky man, a woollen hat pulled over his head and a scarf hiding all but his eyes. The other one was silent and out of sight, perhaps hanging back behind the stacks of boxes they'd been busy piling up.

'I'm Enzo Santi.' His voice sounded shaky. 'This is my barn. Tell me what you're doing in it.'

'Go back to bed, Enzo.' Now he was certain he knew this man. 'You didn't see anything here.'

'First tell me what's in the boxes?' he insisted.

'Forget it, boy. This is not your business. Go back to bed and stay away from the barn.'

'You have no right to be here.'

'You don't know what you're talking about. It would have been better if you hadn't seen anything but now that you have just shut up about it, OK? And get that light out of my face.'

Reluctantly, Enzo flicked off the torch. He wished he could place the voice but he couldn't be certain where he'd heard it before.

'It's only a few boxes,' the other man said, this voice deeper and unfamiliar. 'They'll be gone again soon enough. Go back to bed and let us finish. Go now … I'm warning you. We're running out of patience …'

Enzo took a few steps backwards, then turned and moved quickly through the darkness back to the house. He locked the door behind him and lay on his bed, too furious to sleep. It wasn't long before he heard the truck rumbling away into the distance but still he waited until dawn to get up and creep back to the barn. There was a strong padlock holding the doors closed that hadn't been there before. Enzo rattled it impatiently. He needed to know what was in those boxes, what kind of business his father had involved the family in.

The other barns remained open so he took a look inside but nothing there was unexpected. One stored ladders and nets, equipment for spraying trees, empty crates that had held olives. The other contained his prized red sports car. Beside them were the hen houses and the sty where his mother and Concetta raised the pigs. All was normal there, too. It was just the big barn that held a secret. Enzo stared at its padlock as he passed by and wondered how difficult it would be to break in.

He remembered the stranger's words: that this was not his business, and felt anger rising in him again. This estate would be his some day. Didn't he have every right to know what was happening on it?

Rosie

The keys to my flat were scarred bits of metal that had rolled around inside a stranger's pocket with loose change and used handkerchiefs. They seemed like dirty things to me and I didn't like the dried-blood smell of them. It was a bit of a let-down, really. I'd been so impatient for the day they'd be handed over and now I didn't even want to touch them.

It was Addolorata who got excited for me. She bought some champagne and she and her sister Pieta insisted on taking a taxi to Belgravia, picking up Lou along the way.

'The flat is yours at last; we have to celebrate,' she said.

'Yes, but it's a real mess in there,' I said. 'It'll be horrible, really.'

Beppi's builder had left his mark on the place when he'd come to examine it. Rot had been dug out of the floors and plaster pulled from the walls. It didn't matter – eventually everything would be stripped back and restored. But standing there, in the middle of what was to be my living room, I began to feel overwhelmed by the work that lay ahead.

'I just want it finished,' I said. 'I thought it was only going to be a few weeks but from what the builder says it sounds more like months.'

Addolorata had brought a picnic rug and was laying it on the dusty floor, determined to make the moment special. Lou was already opening the champagne.

'How cute is the builder?' she asked as she filled the glasses.

'He's about forty and he's got a beer gut,' I told her.

'Shame.' Lou grinned. 'Still, maybe he'll have an apprentice.'

Neither of them had boyfriends and had been acting like they were missing a limb. They talked about it constantly, sizing up likely candidates wherever they went. I'd noticed that when they did have guys in tow they were different, like they'd switched off a part of their personalities. To me it seemed they were better off staying single but I'd never had the nerve to suggest it. Perhaps I was the odd one, not seeing the need to partner up, happy enough with the company of my friends.

Once we'd drained the bottle of champagne Lou decided it was time to go and check out the local pubs. 'We need to work out which one's going to be your local,' she told me. 'I like the look of the place up the road so let's try that one first.'

It felt strange to think this was going to be my neighbourhood. As we walked towards the pub I tried to imagine my life here, shopping for cheeses at the little delicatessen, drinking coffee in the café on the corner.

'This is a lovely area,' Pieta said when we'd ordered our drinks at the bar and Lou had already declared the place too full of old people. 'Does it feel like you've made the right decision?'

'I don't know,' I admitted. 'Perhaps I'll feel different when it's all finished. It'd be good to have a proper home again.'

'Pretty amazing to have your own place,' said Lou. 'If I came into that kind of money I'd blow the lot travelling the world.'

Addolorata sipped her wine and looked thoughtful. 'I'd live in Italy for a year and learn to cook really brilliantly,' she declared.

'I know, but it's different for you,' I pointed out. 'You have places to come home to when you've finished travelling and having adventures.'

The Martinelli girls had shown no signs of moving out of their parents' Clerkenwell house and Lou, who'd rented her own bed-sit the moment she could afford to, still appeared on her mum's doorstep every Sunday lunchtime with a sack of dirty laundry and a hunger for pork crackling, crisp roast potatoes and gravy.

'I hadn't thought of it like that. I guess you only realise how important home is when you don't have one,' Pieta said gently.

The three of them were wearing that expression on their faces people got when they were feeling sorry for me. I hated it so much. 'I'll have a home soon enough,' I said briskly. 'Once it's been re-plastered, re-floored, repainted and who knows what else.'

'Until then you've got a home at our place,' Addolorata reminded me. 'You know you can stay for as long as you need to. My parents love having you there.'

'Are you sure?' I was onto my third wine and feeling bolder. 'Even your mother?'

She looked at me. 'Yeah, of course. What do you mean?'

'It's just the first time I was there … I got the feeling … oh, never mind, I was probably wrong.'

'But she's made you feel welcome, hasn't she?' Addolorata asked.

'Yes, but sometimes I worry about your father helping me too much. I've taken up so much of his time. I get a sense that she isn't entirely happy about it.'

Both sisters stared at me but it was Pieta who spoke. 'Mamma struggles sometimes.' She said it so softly I had to strain to hear her over the bar-room noise. 'It's tough for her. Papa is hardly ever at home. He's always busy with something. Always on the go.'

Addolorata flicked her an anxious look. 'They're not un-happy, though. They love each other,' she said, sounding uncertain.

'Yes, they do,' Pieta reassured her. 'It's just there are times when I notice that Mamma seems a bit low and perhaps that's what Rosie picked up on too. But she's been that way for as long as I can remember. There's always something distracting Papa from her. So it's nothing to do with you really, Rosie, and you mustn't worry about it.'

The sisters huddled together after that, talking intently about their parents, bickering a little. Lou was chatting to an oldish guy at the bar, leaving me alone to sip my wine and think about how sadness was everywhere – even in the Martinelli house. I'd never realised how much of it there was in the world. Glancing at the people drinking and laughing at the tables around me, I wondered if there was something that was breaking their hearts right at that moment. Perhaps the blonde woman with the irritating laugh had lived through tragedy; maybe her companion had all sorts of hidden secrets and sorrows. It changed things for me when I started to think of strangers like that.

Then Lou returned from the bar, giving me a triumphant smile. The guy she'd been talking to was carrying a champagne bucket and following her to our table. For the rest of the night he bought us drinks, leaning over to light cigarettes, talking loudly about the things he owned, the boat he sailed on the Solent at weekends, the car he drove fast to get there.

'I'll take you girls with me some time, if you like,' he offered and Lou was nodding and agreeing that she'd love to go, even though he was way too old and likely interested in just one thing.

He was slickly good-looking, though, hair gelled, shirt pressed, shoes polished. He wore the lightly tanned look only a rich person has in winter and I could see Lou was impressed with him; that her mind was already spinning with possibilities.

But I knew something she didn't. Most people were

liars. The way their lives looked from the outside could be misleading, they were putting on a show the same way I did everyday when I stepped out and faced the world.

You never knew the heaviness others carried with them, not anyone, not really.

EXTRACT FROM ADDOLORATA'S JOURNAL

I feel so terrible about what I wrote last time. How could I have wished my family away? It's the dumbest thing I've ever said. The truth is I can't imagine having no home; no place I can go back to no matter what happens. Listening to Rosie today made me realise how much I take it for granted – my father growing his vegetables and cooking us huge meals, my mother always around. I should make more of an effort to appreciate it because some day it won't be there any more and then I really will be like Rosie.

She's been so calm about buying this flat, barely even excited. I hope it's what she wants, that she'll be happy living there all by herself. I can't think of anything more lonely myself.

The Olive Estate

Every time Enzo walked past the barn he felt his mood grow bleaker. No one else seemed to have noticed its doors were padlocked, no one ever mentioned it. His father, grandfather, even his Nonna were hiding something from him, he was sure of that now.

In the evenings he sat with his friends at a table in the corner bar and only half-listened to the familiar banter about football and cars. He wondered if among them there was one who knew about the boxes in the barn, if they had a father or an uncle who had helped to put them there.

Wherever he went Enzo listened for the voice he'd heard that night. But the weather had turned colder and the streets of Triento were empty. Even the bar closed early, the drinkers hurrying home to the warmth of a log fire and a steaming bowl of *pasta e fagioli*.

Each new winter seemed harder than the last. As the wind blew up from the sea and snow dusted the mountains beyond the estate, life grew slow and ugly. The girls of Triento wrapped their bodies in thick, quilted jackets, their skin paled and sallowed and, instead of parading through the streets collecting whistles and admiring glances, they stayed at home and helped their mammas in the kitchen. Even the food dulled over winter. By spring Enzo knew he would be tired of his Nonna's spicy *minestre* of chickpeas and pasta, of his sisters' hearty soups and heavy savoury pies. Tired of rain and thunder, tired of watching the wind whip through the branches of the olive trees and, this winter at least, tired of sidling past the barn to see if its door still lay bolted and locked.

He tried to rouse his sister Concetta's interest in the mystery. 'Why do you think the big barn has a lock on it these days?' he asked as he helped her unload bags of shopping from their mother's rusty old Fiat.

She shrugged. 'I don't know.'

'But what's in there, do you think?'

'Who cares?' She looked at him as though he were crazy. 'The barn has nothing to do with me. Ask Papa if you really want to know.'

Enzo had considered it. But lately his father's moods had been as stormy as the weather. Most days the sound of his shouting echoed through the house, his flash floods of rage sending his sisters running to their rooms in tears and leaving his mother living life through gritted teeth.

'Papa will tell me to mind my own business,' he said to Concetta who was busy filling the cupboards with the dried beans and pasta she'd shopped for in Triento earlier that morning.

'Well, maybe he's right and that's exactly what you should do.'

'But something is going on, don't you think? Something is wrong.'

'What makes you say that?' Concetta seemed curious now.

Enzo struggled to explain it. 'Nothing is as usual, nothing at all. Surely you've noticed?'

She shook her head. 'Not really. Give me an example.'

'Well, Nonna keeps taking to her bed. That's not normal, is it?'

'It's winter and she's old. Every time she catches a cold it goes to her chest. And she worked long hours at harvest-time. Nonna is run down and she needs her rest. That's why she's been spending so much time in bed. It's no big mystery.'

'OK then, what about our grandfather? Have you seen

him lately? Why is he always locked away in his office? Last week Mamma even took some of his meals for him to eat in there. Don't you think that's strange?'

'Not really. He's busy working. Every year the estate gets bigger, we make more oil, get more customers. It must be a huge job to manage it all. Some day it will be you who is shut away in that office for hours on end and then you'll find out for yourself how difficult it is.'

Concetta filled a pan with white beans, put it on to boil and then began chopping onions and celery for that night's broth. 'So you see, nothing is wrong,' she told him. 'Everybody is busy, that's all. Perhaps if you did a little more to help around here it might make things easier for them, eh?'

Enzo had been on the verge of telling his sister about the truck he'd seen and the strangers unloading boxes but now he bit back the words, his voice sulky as he said instead, 'I do plenty. More than you.'

Concetta gave a dry little laugh. 'That's what you always say.'

'I worked hard over harvest-time, picked more olives than anyone,' he said defensively. 'I filled cartons with bottles of oil, loaded them into trucks, it was proper work. You were hiding in here the whole time gossiping with the other girls; you didn't see any of it.'

'Yes, yes, if you say so, Enzo.' Concetta poured a slick of olive oil into the bottom of her soup pan.

'You always stay here in the kitchen; you don't see what is going on. You know nothing.' He tossed the words at her.

Concetta tipped the finely diced vegetables into the pan and the hot oil sizzled. 'So the barn is locked. So what? I really don't care. I've got better things to think about and plenty of work to get on with,' she said.

Scowling at her one last time, Enzo left his sister to her soup. As he walked round the back of the kitchen and towards the big stone barn, it occurred to him he hadn't checked it since the day before. What he saw as he came closer was entirely unexpected. The padlock had gone, the door lay slightly ajar. He pushed it open with the flat of his hand, but inside there was nothing to see. The barn was empty and the boxes might have never been there at all.

'*Cose da pazzi*,' Enzo swore beneath his breath.

Rosie

Things were changing, moving at last. The first thing Beppi did was have new locks put on the windows and doors of my apartment. 'Anyone could have keys to the place. It isn't safe,' he pointed out. So now I had three shiny new keys in my pocket and each evening after I'd finished work I jumped on to a tube train and went to see how much the builders had got done.

Some days they hadn't been there at all and nothing was different. Other times I'd find them still busy, filling the air with a raw sawdust smell as they put in extra hours.

Addolorata met me at the site as often as she could and it didn't take me long to work out she wasn't interested in the renovations.

'Don't you think builders are sexy,' she kept saying. 'I love the way they can *do* things. And their tool belts are kind of hot too ...'

The builder she was most interested in was called Eden. He had skin the colour of milk chocolate and long black dreadlocks that swung around as he worked. I understood what she saw in him, actually. His smile was appealing and he was laid-back and softly spoken.

'Why don't you ask him out for a drink?' I asked her.

'Yeah, maybe. There's no rush though, is there? He's going to be here for ages. They all are.'

It was a depressing thought. As the builders dug away at the rotten flesh of the house they found more problems, more things that needed surgery. 'Do it properly now and you won't have to worry about it again,' Beppi kept telling me. But I was impatient to move out of his wife's sewing room and into my own little place, and every time the builders shook their heads and made that heart-sinking tutting sound I knew that day was moving further into the future.

'I'll tell you another thing, that Eden is the only man alive who looks good in denim dungarees.' Addolorata would have talked about him the entire time if I'd been prepared to listen. In actual fact, there was no point in either of us turning up at the flat so regularly. Progress on the building work was too painfully slow for me and Eden, despite all the extra effort Addolorata had been making, didn't seem to notice her at all.

'What I need is to find out more about him. How old is he do you think? Where does he live? Is he with anyone?'

'Why don't you ask him?' I was getting impatient.

'That's not how it works, Rosie. I can't ask him. Then he'd know I'm interested.'

'But you want him to know you're interested, don't you?'

'Oh dear,' she shook her head at me, 'you've got so much to learn.'

Addolorata might have been joking but at times it did feel that way to me. All I seemed to do was learn. There was so much to get to grips with: the language of building, the things these men were doing to the place I owned, the costs and budget blow-outs. It was difficult and exhausting.

As the weeks went by I found myself longing for small comforts: hot baths and cups of tea, the feeling of the duvet lying heavy on me when I lay down at night. And I began to understand how consoling food can be.

On a cold winter's night, I'd take refuge in the soft creaminess of a buttery risotto, in the flavours of fried cauliflower and taleggio cheese or the earthiness of field mushrooms. I grew hungrier and greedier. When Beppi wasn't at home I rummaged in his food stores searching for things to cook and eat. The kitchen was a treasure trove. I found bundles of home-made pasta, carefully dried and wrapped in linen tea towels; sauces and soups neatly labelled and packed away in the deep freezer. I started to play with the ingredients I unearthed, making a salty, pungent dressing from anchovies and garlic to drizzle over vegetables, simmering a meaty shin bone in a sauce of tomatoes and red wine to serve with rigatoni. One night I made what I considered my triumph, a huge fish soup with prawns and mussels that Addolorata had brought home from Little Italy, flavoured with lots of fresh flat-leaf parsley from the pot on the window sill and slugs of peppery olive oil.

Beppi was never particularly complimentary about the dishes I served up to him. 'That was not too bad,' he would declare once he'd wiped a crust of bread around his plate to soak up the last of a sauce. 'Quite nice, I suppose.'

'Take no notice,' Pieta told me later. 'He never has a good word to say about meals other people have cooked. The tastier they are the grumpier it seems to make him.'

Pieta was the only one who noticed how the food looked. Each time I served up a meal she commented on the plate I'd chosen or the way I'd arranged it. 'You've got a really good eye,' she told me once or twice.

To me it never felt as though what I was doing was clever. 'I'm only trying to make the food look as delicious as it tastes,' I told her.

Sometimes I got things wrong. I'd forget to stir a sauce and let it stick to the bottom of Beppi's cracked old Le Creuset casserole. Or I'd fry a delicate fillet of white fish until it was dry and rubbery. Beppi was kinder to me when I failed. He gave advice and even offered to teach me a few dishes.

'Watch him like a hawk,' Addolorata warned me. 'If you don't pay attention he'll sneak in a pinch or two of some secret ingredient so that you never can get your food to taste quite the way his does.'

But Beppi showed me flavours I'd never have thought of myself. Red mullet baked with raisins and pine nuts the way the Romans cooked it. Laid out in the dish ready to go in the oven it looked so pretty. When I told him I'd never made pastry he taught me how to make a tart of ricotta custard topped with cherries cooked in brandy. Desserts opened up a whole new world of eating for me and for the first time ever I felt my stomach strain against the waistband of my jeans whenever I sat down.

For a while I didn't care if my thighs spread and my stomach bulged because I'd discovered there were other delicious things you could do with ricotta like bake it with lemon zest and saffron or stuff it into soft pillows of ravioli.

Cooking was an easy way to lose myself and make a bad day seem a little better. When I was piling a rich purple beetroot risotto into a clean white bowl or resting a roasted leg of chicken on a mound of gently stewed caponata I forgot about things like builder's dust and dry rot. Instead of worrying about the apartment or the latest drama at work, I planned the next thing I would try to make and pestered Addolorata for the ingredients. I wanted squid ink for a risotto, smoked paprika for a stew, spicy sausage laced with fennel, interesting new bowls and platters to display them on.

I grew used to listening to the noises of the house, and when I could tell Beppi wasn't in his kitchen, I'd creep in and find something to quickly chop and bury in olive oil. I loved mixing flavours, colours and textures, often firing off a couple of photographs of the finished dish as I anticipated the moment of spooning it into my mouth.

Eating became my way of punctuating each day with pleasure. I couldn't understand how I had taken so long to discover it.

It's driving Papa crazy having Rosie taking over his kitchen. I almost feel sorry for him. He doesn't want to upset her so won't say anything but I see the way he sets his face when he finds her cooking there. It's quite good really. He's so worried about what she's up to he's loosening his grip at Little Italy. Yesterday I slipped some lime zest into a seafood risotto even though he's always insisted it overpowers the clean flavours of the fish. He didn't even notice! Now I'm wondering if I could do something rebellious with the meatballs. Drizzle in some Worcestershire sauce or even a little harissa. Spice them up a bit.

It's odd the way Rosie's got into food all of a sudden. She seems so all or nothing about life ... so driven and focused. Anyone else would have noticed by now that it's Papa who likes to be the best cook in the family.

The Olive Estate

Enzo kept finding new things to worry about. If the olive oil she swallowed first thing every morning was so good for her then why was his Nonna sickening? And when exactly had she turned her face from his grandfather? It seemed to have happened without anyone else noticing. On the days when she was well enough to cook she still placed the food before her husband and made sure his glass was full of wine. But no words had passed between them since well before the harvest.

Enzo watched them at mealtimes and saw how their eyes never met. There had been no argument as far as he could remember; no raised voices, no single sign that his Nonna might have discovered one of her husband's discreet flirtations with another woman. Just this long, unaccountable silence they'd all grown used to living with. He wished he understood it.

In winter the family spent more time in the kitchen. The old wood-fired stove was lit and they sat around the kitchen table in a fug of warmth and cigarette smoke, the old television in the corner blaring as they raised their voices to talk and argue. Usually his Nonna was there in the centre of things, spooning soup into a bowl for anyone still hungry, preparing the food they would eat the next day. But this year, once the evening meal was over, she wrapped a woollen shawl round her shoulders and hurried to the main house and her bed. There she would cover herself in quilts and thick blankets and stay sleeping until late the next day.

Enzo had been wondering whether his grandfather still slept beside her as he had for all the long decades of their marriage. One morning to satisfy his curiosity he woke especially early and sidled through the big house until he came across the old man snoring in a narrow bed in one of the spare rooms. There was something sad about finding him lying there alone, one of the old brightly coloured children's blankets pulled up over his shoulders. He had been such a powerful man but now he seemed diminished. Enzo stood in the doorway watching him sleep.

These days it felt to Enzo as though he was always waiting for something. Daily he walked across the estate, through the house and garden, constantly checking all was as it should be. He didn't bother trying to discuss things with Concetta again, nor did he raise his concerns with their parents. For now it seemed wiser to keep his eyes and ears open until he understood things a little better.

At night, when it was dark and silent, he slipped out of the house and walked a circuit that took in the old barns and the pigpens. He moved his bed closer to the window and left it ajar despite the winter cold so he would hear the rumble of any truck or the sound of a stranger's voice. Some nights it was stormy and wet and he had to force himself to leave the comfort of his bed, to put the bare soles of his feet on the icy floor tiles and brace himself for the rush of cold air.

But Enzo was determined to find out what was going on. This was his estate, he reminded himself as he struggled out of sleep. When the old men were gone he would be the one to make all the decisions. He felt fierce about the place now, possessive about each centimetre of the land and every tree that grew upon it.

During the day he walked over the estate with his father, turning the silvery leaves as he went, checking them for signs of disease. Together they made sure water wasn't pooling around a tree's roots after a heavy storm or that a high wind hadn't caused any damage. His father never asked where this sudden interest in the olives had come from. He didn't question him at all. It seemed to Enzo that he enjoyed having his son at his shoulder day after day. His mood always seemed a little lighter when they were out together.

Even on Christmas Day they spent an hour or two lapping the estate and, during the grey, wintry weeks that followed life seemed to settle into its more usual rhythms.

And then one wind-blown night Enzo closed his window tight to stop it rattling in a storm. He slept deeply despite the howling of the weather and didn't force himself out of bed but stayed glued to the warmth his body had cast on the sheets. And the next morning when he filled a cup with strong black coffee and walked out to the barns he found what he'd been watching and waiting for all this time. The doors were closed and locked again.

Who knew what lay inside this time?

Rosie

My body was starting to spread and let go, spilling in folds over the tops of waistbands that had once been loose. My breasts were growing bigger, too, swelling another cup-size. Even my face was changing, becoming plush and voluptuous. Food was doing this to me.

Some days I vowed to stop eating. *Tomorrow I'll count calories*, I would promise myself. Over a hundred of them in a banana, forty in an apple. But then I'd find a bowl of leftovers in the fridge – firm tubes of rigatoni blanketed in home-made pesto, preserved peppers saved from Beppi's summer harvest – and I'd spoon a little into my mouth just to test the flavours, shave some parmesan over the top and take a second bite, until half the bowl was gone and then I thought I might as well finish it.

Growing fatter was very nearly a sensuous thing. It was as though I was exploring the possibilities of my body, testing its limits. I avoided the scales because I knew already from the mound of my belly and the surplus of my thighs what they would tell me. And I kept on eating.

Beppi's kitchen was filled with Italian foods but I wanted to go further than that. So I sneaked across the border to France and after a love affair with wine-soaked casseroles and creamy sauces, moved on to more exotic destinations. I bought a book on curry and found an Indian spice shop in north London, coming home with bags of ground turmeric, cumin and coriander. I was so entranced by the colours, spooning them, red, yellow and gold, into a pan of sizzling onions. And I loved the flower-shaped seeds of star anise and knotty little cloves, and learning how to use them.

Beppi would raise his eyebrows when he found an aromatic stew of lamb and coconut milk flavoured with green cardamom pods simmering in his kitchen or saw his fridge stocked with fresh ginger roots and fragrant coriander. 'Very nice,' he'd grunt when I offered him a spoonful of something new to taste. 'Different.'

I filled his cupboards with strange ingredients: tamarind to sour a prawn curry, palm sugar and salty fish sauce to spike an Asian dressing. I bought a wok for stir-fries and pretty blue, crackle-glazed bowls to serve them in. I pounded my own curry pastes with a mortar and pestle and grew used to having fingers scented with onions and garlic. And I discovered textures and tastes that reminded me of that first meal of dim sum that Addolorata and I had eaten together: squares of silken tofu simmered in chicken stock and light soy sauce, the briny slipperiness of freshly shucked oysters, the sharp bite of Sichuan peppercorns.

One Saturday afternoon I followed a recipe for tea-smoked duck and had to fling open the back door despite the cold outside because Catherine was coughing so much from the fumes that filled the kitchen.

'At least you clean up your mess afterwards,' she said, eyeing the blackened fowl dubiously. 'Not like my Beppi. So many dirty dishes, so much tomato sauce everywhere.'

Catherine only enjoyed the plainer foods I gave her: the wonton soups with noodles, the chicken poached with spring onions and Chinese wine. 'I'd be perfectly happy with a poached egg on toast,' she would often say when she noticed me opening the food cupboard and wondering what to make for our dinner.

As for Pieta, she tasted everything but only ever managed tiny portions. She liked to keep herself slim so she could fit into all the clothes on the racks of her walk-in wardrobe and turn herself into a different picture every day.

If the others were busy working in Little Italy then I'd ask Lou over to help us finish whatever I'd made. She didn't enjoy cooking much but did like to eat and never objected to me spooning a second helping onto her plate or insisting she try just one more dish.

If there were still leftovers I'd package them up to take into work for Johnny. Or I'd drop them off for the builders if I got a chance. I even bought stainless-steel tiffin tins and Chinese noodle boxes to carry them in. What I'd begun to enjoy was watching people's face while they ate what I'd cooked. Johnny loved red meat. His eyes lit with expectation at the sight of it and, as he chewed a hunk of brisket I'd braised with cinnamon sticks and kaffir lime leaves, his expression spoke of pure enjoyment.

I liked the appreciative noises people made when they were eating and was pleased if someone wiped a finger round the rim of an empty plate and licked it clean, greedy for more of the flavours.

And so I continued to eat, growing larger week by week, my bottom hanging down like two dew drops, my face filling out, my wardrobe of jeans and T-shirts replaced with looser smocks, long cardigans and flowing dresses.

I'll stop eating, I promised myself. *Just one more feast.* Perhaps I'll bake a pie of flaky pastry with smoked fish and butter-softened leeks or stain my hands with beetroot juice and simmer a sweet, hearty borscht dolloped with sour cream.

I'll stop eating on Monday, I promised myself. *Or maybe the Monday after that.*

WHAT ADDOLORATA SAID

'Remember how Rosie never seemed to care about food?
Well, now she's obsessed with it. The fridge is always

full of stuff she's cooked and she eats even more than I do these days. I hear her late at night rummaging round in the kitchen looking for leftovers. No wonder she's putting on weight. She fits my fat jeans – you know, the ones I bought when we got back from Majorca? She's quite big, honestly. You won't believe it when you see her.'

The Olive Estate

Enzo thought his Nonna was reviving with the season. As the wildflowers tangled beneath the olive trees and his father sighed and talked of mowing them down, she emerged from hibernation and criticised all that had been done while she was sleeping.

'The trees haven't been pruned with enough love,' she complained more than once. 'I heard the chainsaws roaring away day after day. Too much has been taken off. The next harvest will be terrible, you'll see.'

She even found the strength to lecture Enzo, to remind him how the finest olive oil was made with nothing but fruit, passion and hard work. And she spent hours each day cleaning what had already been cleaned, scouring out the demi-johns that had held last season's oil, complaining as she did so that everything their neighbours made was no better than *lampante,* so acidic it was good only to make soap. 'Most of them don't care,' she lamented. 'They blend it with a better oil and cook their meals with it. Perhaps it is musty or rancid but they've been eating it that way for so long they think it is normal. They have no passion, none at all.'

She had said these things to him so many times before but Enzo didn't mind. He was glad to see his Nonna more like her usual self again.

'Surely a bit of dirt won't do any harm?' he said, coaxing her to keep on talking. 'A tiny scrap of leftover sediment in a container can't hurt the new oil that much.'

'Enzo, Enzo, have you not been listening to me properly all these years?' His Nonna paused in her scrubbing. 'The olive oil is fragile, a living thing. If you don't care about producing the finest then don't worry about little things like dirt and heat. People will still buy it, I expect. But that is not how we do things here. The Santi Oil has to be the very best. It has to be.'

'Why, though?' Enzo had never thought to ask that question before.

She stared at him as though she couldn't believe the words she'd heard. 'Why? What do you mean, why?'

'If we can still sell our olive oil even if isn't perfect then why worry so much about the quality?' Enzo pressed her. 'Maybe there are ways we could make more money if we lower our standards a little.'

'Lower our standards?' His Nonna practically hissed the words as she repeated them. 'How exactly?'

'Well, haven't we always refused to process any other farmer's olives in case they are bad and taint whatever comes after them on the press?'

'That's right. And you think we should change that?'

'Why not? We could keep the press running longer, increase our profits,' Enzo pointed out. 'Doesn't it make sense?'

'You have been talking to your father, then?' she said acidly.

'Is that what he thinks, too?' Enzo was surprised. 'I didn't realise he thought we should make changes.'

His Nonna shook her head. He could sense her disappointment. 'I will be dead and buried before anything is allowed to taint the Santi Oil,' she told him, her voice harsh. 'Especially money.'

And with that she bent low over the demi-john and resumed her fierce scrubbing, refusing to speak another word to him for the remainder of the afternoon.

Once all the cleaning had been completed to his Nonna's satisfaction and the soil beneath the trees was tilled and fertilised, there was little to do on the estate except wait for the blossoming to begin. Enzo always waited impatiently for the delicate cream flowers and liked seeing them hiding shyly behind the olive trees' silvery leaves, fragrant and pretty. For his father, though, this was an anxious time, when the weather could wreak havoc on the crop that was to come.

'This season has to be a good one,' he kept telling Enzo as they walked the rows and looked for flowers. 'There is Concetta's wedding to pay for, the dowry we must give her. A lot of expenses and debt.'

Lately Enzo had been feeling a new closeness with his father. He thought he'd begun to understand how he must feel, trapped between the old and the new, longing to make changes but never allowed to take charge.

'Papa, if we used machines to shake the trees then we'd harvest faster, wouldn't we?' he said as they strode between the rows. 'We wouldn't need to hire in so many workers, to feed them and give them a share of our olive oil. And we'd still get a good price for it.'

'Your Nonna won't hear of it,' his father said shortly.

'But if the family needs the money surely we should do whatever it takes to get it?'

His father stopped walking and gave him a long, hard stare. 'Stay out of it, Enzo,' he advised.

'Papa?'

'Don't think I haven't seen you sniffing around the barn all winter and heard you creeping about at night.'

'But ...' Enzo was shocked.

His father held up his hand. 'Out of respect for me don't say any more.'

'I'm only suggesting we should think about making the harvest easier.'

'I know exactly what you're saying. There is just one

thing you need to know: nothing here is going to change. Nothing.'

'And if the harvest is bad and we don't make enough money to pay our debts?'

'Then your grandfather and I will handle it, just as we have before.'

Enzo tried to contain his fury. 'And what about me? One day this estate will be mine to run. Don't you think I need to understand what is going on here? What is happening in the barn?'

'Not yet,' his father said shortly.

'Why not?' Enzo demanded to know.

'You are young, hot-headed. That is fine, so was I at your age. But a hot head is not what is needed right now. This is a time to be very careful. To watch what you say and what you do. Are you listening to me, Enzo? Trouble isn't very far away. And you are my only son so don't blame me for wanting to protect you from it.'

His father's tone was so serious that suddenly Enzo felt afraid. He looked down towards the cluster of buildings nestled in the crease of the hill, the olive trees marching out on either side. Such a short time ago all this had seemed so reliable, so permanent. He had thought his life here was all laid out for him. Now he understood it had never been the case at all. This land, the trees that grew on it, even the house the family lived in, none of it was certain. And in that moment it felt a lot more precious to Enzo than before.

Rosie

The final part was the best. Choosing the shades of paint for the walls, the fabric for sofa covers and curtains, the finish of the kitchen cupboards, the tap-ware for the bathroom. I haunted furniture stores, bought piles of magazines and stared at photographs of other people's interiors. As I busied myself doing the usual things that filled my days – working, cooking, eating – I let myself dream.

My flat in Belgravia was taking shape at last. Every time I visited it things were looking better rather than worse. Even Addolorata had sensed that soon the builders would be finished. She had swallowed her pride and asked Eden out for a drink. By now they were in an awkward dating phase. She wasn't ready to call him her boyfriend but still they saw each other most days. That meant I hardly ever caught up with her, even though we were living in the same house. Lou was the one who came along on my forays to shops and building suppliers, and the business of filling a space with beautiful things seemed to bemuse her completely.

'How can that toilet be so cheap and that one so expensive?' she asked on one trip. 'They're both used for exactly the same thing, aren't they? Why wouldn't everyone just buy the one that costs the least?'

'Because it has to look right, fit the style of the décor,' I explained.

'Why?' she demanded, but I couldn't really explain.

'It just has to, that's all.'

'I'd rather drink a good bottle of wine than sit on a fancy

toilet,' I heard her mutter as she moved away to examine the shower cubicles.

Whatever Lou said I was determined to buy the best I could afford, to surround myself with things that pleased the eye. My months in the basement in Fitzroy Square had helped me realise it was what I needed. I wanted my belongings to be arranged around me not piled into corners of a room. I wanted proper furniture, cupboards stacked with things that matched, crisp white bed linen and fluffy towels. Thankfully, Johnny and I were getting busy again. With spring had come the wedding season and already our weekends were filling up. Neither of us really loved photographing brides and grooms but we wanted the cash. Johnny longed for his own studio and I needed my little flat to look perfect.

'What about some posters to brighten up the walls?' Lou asked, bored with bathroom suites by then. 'I know a place in Soho where you can get really cool film ones.'

I wrinkled my nose. 'No, I don't think so. The walls won't need brightening up.'

'But everything you're choosing looks washed-out and pale. Isn't that going to be boring?'

'It won't be, you'll see.'

I felt very confident about it; as though there was an exact way the place was meant to be and all I had to do was work it out.

'Well, you'll need a sofa bed so your friends can stay over, won't you?' pointed out Lou. 'You're going to want to have company. Especially after living at Addolorata's place. It will be pretty quiet on your own.'

'I don't think so.' I ran my finger over the clean modern lines of the tap I liked best. 'I think I'm going to enjoy it.'

There was no doubt I'd miss the Martinelli family, with their sudden clamours and passions. I'd miss my quiet chats with Catherine over cups of tea and buttery shortbread biscuits. I'd miss seeing how Pieta had chosen to transform herself with clothes each day and of course I'd miss Beppi. But it wasn't as if I'd never see them again. I'd still be invited for Sunday lunches and I'd always go back to Little Italy.

It wasn't the food alone that drew me to their restaurant, although I'd been savouring the winter menu of robust pasta soups and roasted butternut risotto. What I liked most was to visit the photographs I'd taken, to make sure they were still hanging where I'd last seen them, their frames carefully dusted and their glass fronts polished. While I spooned through the rich coffee-cream layers of a tiramisu I remembered those hot, intense days when, camera in hand, I'd recorded life behind the scenes in Beppi's restaurant. I still took lots of pictures – shots of Johnny's brides or of the food I cooked – but it never gave me the same feeling I'd had back then. Looking at my photographs on the wall reminded me of that.

It was working at Rob's studio that had really thrown me off my stride. Up until then photography had seemed such an adventure. But then I'd realised all the things I didn't understand. There was so much gear, so many technical terms and ways to sculpt with light and shadow. I'd been so naive to think it was only about staring through a lens, framing a scene, capturing a moment.

Occasionally I would ask Rob to explain something to me but he was usually less than encouraging. 'I pay you to manage my studio, not to ask me questions,' he complained once. So I tried to learn from watching him, and I would pester Johnny with queries when Rob wasn't about. It was frustrating and slow. After a while, it seemed easier not to worry about it and instead to get on with my job and escape the place as fast as I could at the end of every day.

There was nothing terribly difficult about my work in the photo studio; it was just a matter of being organised. Often Rob managed to make things stressful by changing his mind at the last minute or coming up with reasons to keep us later than necessary. He seemed to take pleasure in flinging piles of paperwork on my desk just as it was turning six o'clock and demanding it be sorted by first thing next morning.

'Another one of Benito's little power trips,' was Johnny's usual response.

Sometimes, though, Rob could be encouraging. He helped Johnny get an exhibition at a little gallery in Camden and let me keep some old gear he didn't want any longer. Then, just as we were thinking he wasn't so bad after all, he'd throw us off balance with an acid aside or lose his temper over something trivial.

'If he was horrible all the time it'd be easier almost,' I said to Johnny one night as we recovered from one of Rob's especially septic moods. Lou had come to join us in the pub and we were well into our third round of drinks and feeling a little mellower.

'He *is* horrible all the time, Rosie,' Johnny insisted. 'You just don't see it.'

'Well, he sorted that exhibition for you. That was nice of him, wasn't it?'

'Not really. I'm indebted to him now and he knows it. So it's just another of his power games, isn't it?'

'I hadn't thought of it like that.'

'Yeah, it's like giving you a few bits of worn-out gear. You feel grateful. But try asking him for a pay rise. Then you'll get the whole "after all I've done for you" speech but you won't get any more money.'

Lou shook out another cigarette from the shared packet on the table. 'Show me a boss who isn't a complete psychopath,' she said out of the corner of her mouth as she lit it. 'At least you guys work somewhere interesting. You should try sitting in my office all day. It's hideous, like being in prison.'

'What exactly is it that you do all day?' Johnny asked her.

'Make coffee, answer the phone, file bits of paper, type things, hang out until it's time to go to the pub at lunchtime.'

'That's pretty much the same as me,' I admitted.

'Yes, but you work in a photographic studio. That has to be more glamorous than being an admin assistant in a building suppliers', surely?'

'Oh yes, it's endless glamour.' Johnny was laughing now. 'It's like a little piece of Hollywood in there, I tell you.'

'Well, what are we going to do?' Lou sucked hard on her cigarette and blew out a long stream of smoke. 'Is this it for the rest of our lives?'

Johnny shrugged. 'I hope not.'

'What is it you really *want*, though?' Lou pushed him. 'What are you going to be when you grow up?'

'I want to take photographs.' Johnny sounded certain. 'To work for myself not for some idiot like Rob Olivieri.'

Lou turned to me. 'And you, Rosie?'

'I'm not sure yet. I just want to move into my apartment, get settled. And then I'll work it out, I guess.'

Draining her glass and stubbing out what was left of her cigarette, Lou shook her head. 'Well, I'd like to be there already, with the husband and kids, the nice car and the big house. I need to know how long I have to wait for all that. It's what I want. So why can't I just have it now?'

We drank until it blurred life's edges and we'd spent more money than we ought to. By the end of the night, our table was a mess of crushed potato crisps, empty glasses and over-full ashtrays.

'One more round?' Lou slurred hopefully.

'Nah, I've had enough,' said Johnny. 'Got to be up early and ready for the next lot of glamour in the morning, hey, Rosie?'

'That's right,' I agreed.

Johnny walked us to the nearest bus stop and waited until we were safely onboard. As I took my favourite seat, at the very front of the top deck, I wished the bus were taking me to my apartment in Belgravia instead of my makeshift camp

157

in Catherine's sewing room. I wanted to climb between clean white sheets in a room that was perfectly ordered. I wanted my own little bit of the world, to be certain of my place in it at last. Just like Lou, I longed to be there already.

But even when it was finished and the builders had taken their ladders away and there was no one strewing the floor any more with greasy pie wrappers or empty Coke cans, it seemed unbelievable to me. When the furniture was arranged and the cushions plumped, when there was food in the fridge and hot water flowed from the taps, I didn't quite know what to do with myself in all this space that belonged to me. I sat on the sofa, then lay on the bed, opened the curtains then closed them again, turning and turning like a cat trying to settle.

Lou had wanted me to have a house-warming party but I wasn't ready for an invasion yet. Instead, I let people visit in smaller groups, poured them tea from a pretty china pot and served them little cakes of coconut and sour cream that I'd baked myself.

The Martinelli family came first, then I invited Lou and Johnny and finally I gave my uncle and his wife a reluctant welcome. Their two little boys sprayed cake crumbs all over the floor and dabbed at everything with sticky fingers, while the pair of them gaped around in astonishment.

'How much was that? What did that cost you?' Uncle Phillip kept asking. 'What did you pay for it?'

'When I was your age I lived in a squat in Stockwell,' his wife told me waspishly. 'What does a young girl like you need with a flashy place like this?'

I didn't bother trying to explain that I wanted a home, a place to come back to. It was so unlikely she'd understand me. That clairvoyant had seen it though – she may have been a sham but she'd sensed how I needed somewhere to anchor myself. By now I'd stopped trying to believe Bella

Luna had really seen my parents in the afterlife. It was a nice idea, something to cling to for a while when I most needed it, but I'd let it go. She'd been perceptive enough to recognise what might bring me comfort and it was worth the money I'd paid her just for that.

Having a home of my own didn't make me braver, though, as I'd imagined it might. If anything, the opposite was true. I settled in and nested, resenting anything that took me away from the place. Instead of going to the pub with Johnny after work, I hurried home, desperate to slide my key in the lock, open the door and smell the vanilla-scented candles I'd set out in the hallway.

Lou couldn't stand how tidy the place was. She'd knock over a pile of magazines or jumble up stuff on a shelf when I wasn't watching. 'It's not natural to be so neat,' she told me. 'It's a sign of mental illness.'

She was always trying to drag me out to the pub but I preferred to open one of the bottles of wine I kept chilling in the fridge and arrange some soft creamy cheeses and sharply peppered bread sticks on a platter. 'Isn't it more comfortable here?' I'd say as I lit lamps and pulled the curtains closed.

It was Lou who first mentioned Italy. 'I need a holiday,' she said one night as she tipped the rest of the wine from the bottle into her glass. 'We've got to plan one for this summer. If I don't have something to look forward to I'll curl up and die.'

'Um,' I said non-committally.

'I've got a brilliant idea. Why don't we bring forward our next Villa Girls trip? Do it this summer instead?' she suggested.

'I thought the rule was once every three years.'

'Yeah, but we made the rule, we can break it,' she pointed out. 'We can go to Italy sooner if we want to.'

After that, Lou must have spoken to Addolorata who talked to Toni and suddenly everyone was excitedly sending off for brochures filled with villas to rent and talking about Italy almost non-stop.

'What about Tuscany?' Lou suggested over coffee and croissants at Patisserie Valerie one Sunday morning. 'We'd be right in the middle of wine country then.'

'But surely we want to be near the sea?' countered Addolorata. 'I think we should go further south.'

'The Amalfi coast?'

'Too expensive and touristy. Further south than that.'

'Let's just make sure it's somewhere a bit more fun than that place in Majorca,' Lou said. 'No more artists' colonies, OK?'

'Yes, somewhere with a nightlife,' agreed Addolorata.

It was a while before I managed to interrupt them. 'I'm going to give this trip a miss,' I said once they gave me a chance to speak. 'I'll come with you next time.'

'Oh no you don't, Rosie,' Lou said.

'But I've only just moved into my flat and I'm still getting settled in. I don't want to make plans to leave it yet.'

'You've got to come. We're the Villa Girls. There are four of us. That's how it is,' Lou insisted.

'Well, there'll be three of you this time.'

'Oh please, don't be so boring.'

Addolorata was more brutal. 'You know, Rosie, that's a bit selfish. Without you we probably won't be able to afford to rent anywhere halfway decent. Toni's on a student grant, remember. If you don't come then you'll be leaving us in the lurch.'

So that's how I was railroaded into being a Villa Girl the second time. I really didn't have much choice. Addolorata and her family had done so much for me and asked for nothing in return. I could hardly refuse to take a holiday with her.

'When were you thinking of going?' I asked, reluctantly caving in.

'Well, definitely not till summer proper. We want the weather to be hot and sunny and we need to save some money. Oh yeah, and also if I'm going to appear in public wearing a swimming costume I need to lose at least half a stone.'

I stared back at her, suddenly conscious that Addolorata wasn't the only big one in the group any more. My body had a new shape, rolls and folds that hadn't been there last summer, a tumescent belly and thighs I'd hidden beneath loose skirts and long layers during my winter of eating.

'Yeah, me too, I guess,' I agreed, wondering if my summer clothes would even fit me any more.

'We could all go on a pre-holiday diet,' Lou suggested. 'Shall we have a group weigh-in first?'

'No!' Addolorata and I spoke simultaneously.

I'd never dieted before. In my teens I hadn't given much thought to what my body looked like. It didn't seem all that important. Other girls discussed calories and ate joyless lunches of cottage cheese. I played lots of sport and mostly thought of food as fuel.

Pushing away the plate covered in curls of croissant crumbs and greasy smears of butter and jam, I wished I hadn't eaten so much. Food had changed my body and I'd been willing to let it. But if I was going to Italy in the summer, I'd have to wear light dresses, short skirts and little tops, maybe even a bikini.

It was time to stop eating.

EXTRACT FROM ADDOLORATA'S JOURNAL
I know it must be amazing for Rosie to have a home of her own but I don't see why she has to hide herself away and be so anti-social. Lou says she rushes straight back after work and never wants to stop for a drink. She hasn't dropped into Little Italy for a while. And we practically had to force her to come to Patisserie Valerie

for a croissant. It reminds me of what she was like when she lived in that awful basement in Fitzroy Square and disappeared for all that time. The place may be different but she's behaving the exact same way.

The Olive Estate

Concetta's wedding had been set for late summer so the weather would be hot enough for her guests to sit beneath the trees, feasting all afternoon and well into the night. But no one was surprised when the plans were changed. They had seen how Concetta's waist had thickened, watched her running from the kitchen when fish was being gutted, heard her in the bathroom early in the morning.

'This is the perfect time for a wedding anyway,' Enzo heard his mother say more than once, a forced note to her voice. 'And if it isn't fine we'll put the tables out in the big barn like we do at harvest-time. It'll still be lovely, Concetta, you'll see.'

There was a rush to finish the dress and send out invitations. All his sisters were conscripted to help. But it seemed to Enzo that the fuss they made over every little task only slowed them down. He heard them squabbling over who had the neatest handwriting and was certain he might have addressed the envelopes in half the time it took them to decide. Their raised voices became the soundtrack of his life and he did all he could to avoid them.

Mostly he busied himself outside the house, shifting crates of wine and beer into the cellar, helping his father wipe cobwebs from the folding chairs and trestle tables stored in the small barn. Whenever there was time he worked by his Nonna's side in the garden for she was determined the estate should look perfect when Concetta's guests arrived.

'Weeds are a sign of laziness,' she told him, busily ripping them from the ground. 'You can tell all you need to know about a man by the state of his garden, his house and his shoes.'

'Is that how you decided my grandfather was the right man for you?' asked Enzo, half-joking. 'Were his shoes highly polished?'

'Yes, yes,' his Nonna said seriously. 'And the collar and cuffs of his shirt weren't grubby; his suit was pressed, his fingernails and hair tidy. He looked like a man who knew how to take care of himself so I thought he'd be able to care for me too. And I was right, he always has. So you see how important clean shoes can be.'

'But it's different now. Women today don't need a man to take care of them,' Enzo pointed out. 'They have jobs, money in their pockets. The world has changed since you were a girl, Nonna.'

She snorted. 'Do you think so? It may seem that way but the truth is things have changed far less than you imagine. A woman still wants to feel a man can provide for her, no matter what she says.'

'Some women might, yes,' Enzo agreed, thinking of his sister Concetta. 'But not all of them, I'm sure. In the cities there are career girls. They are more independent.'

His Nonna snorted again, louder than before. 'Independent? They have a job, a house to look after, children to raise – how much time is left over for independence? None at all. These career women will understand that eventually, you'll see.'

Enzo stared at his Nonna, wondering if for once her wisdom had failed her. 'The world is changing,' he insisted. 'Nothing can stop that.'

'What you don't realise is that marriage can be a fragile thing,' she insisted. 'A woman must truly need a man for it to survive. And I suppose he must need her too.'

Enzo remembered his grandfather lying alone night after

night in the small children's bed in the downstairs room. He wondered if that was what had gone wrong. Had her need for him gone and then something had broken because of it? He longed to ask his Nonna but her expression was fierce as she uprooted weeds and shook out the soil from their roots.

'Search for a woman who needs you, Enzo,' she advised, tossing the weeds onto a pile in the wheelbarrow by her side. 'And when you find her, marry her fast, that's my advice.'

Later, as he was burning the garden waste, Enzo tried to imagine being responsible for a woman all his life, keeping her housed, fed and clothed. Year after year there would be more people depending on him – first their babies, then aged parents, an unmarried sister or two. So many of them relying on him alone; the thought of it made him dizzy. No wonder his father's face showed strain with every change in the weather and his grandfather drank himself sleepy with rough red wine every night.

Enzo poked at the fire with a stick, listening to the weeds hiss as they curled up in the flames. Was that really how it would be for him? He stopped adding wood to the fire and stood watching for a long time while it flickered and slowly died down to glowing embers.

In the end everyone agreed Concetta's wedding went off better than they could have hoped. It was a fine day and his sister looked pretty in the dress that had been let out for her at the very last minute. While the photographs were being taken she held her bouquet stiffly over her swelling belly and later, during the wedding feast, Enzo noticed her new husband stroking it with one hand as he chatted to an uncle or cousin. This is mine, he seemed to be saying, and for the first time Enzo wondered if Ricardo Russo would be a good husband for his sister. He had known him all his life but wasn't sure that he'd ever really liked him. Ricardo was just another member of the group, someone to stand with on street corners and whistle at girls. Now he'd married into the Santi family things were different and Enzo wished he knew him better.

Once the photographer had finished, Concetta tossed her bouquet at her younger sisters and there was an outbreak of shrieking and giggling as they rushed to catch it. All of them dreamed of a day like this, yards of tulle and flowers in their hair. Enzo had never met a girl who didn't.

That night he stayed up late drinking with the other men, gathered at the longest table beneath the olive trees. As the day closed and the sun's warmth faded, his mother brought out thick rugs and glasses of warmed wine spiced with orange zest, cinnamon and cloves. She lit cigars and served little plates of food in case anyone still had an appetite.

There had been dish after dish to feast on that afternoon, all of it made by his sisters. They had eaten the traditional wedding soup of meatballs and rice, as well as lamb cooked in earthenware pots, hot peppers and scented cheeses, swordfish steamed with chicory, pork roasted on a spit. Later there were sweet foods, little knots of biscuits dusted with sugar and dense with butter and almonds, and the triumph of the wedding cake itself, covered in sparkling fireworks instead of candles. Enzo counted fourteen courses in all – a proper wedding, just as everyone would have expected.

As for Ricardo, he seemed changed already. Even the way he was talking was different, stronger and more confident, as though now he was married he was on an equal footing with anyone. As he topped up the glasses with brandy and wine he was quicker to share his opinions, to shout another man down, fast to use the words 'my wife' with pride sounding in his voice.

Enzo suspected this was how every new husband was supposed to be on his wedding night.

Rosie

Dieting turned out to be so much more difficult than I imagined. I'd start the day well enough with a healthy fresh fruit salad and a low-fat yogurt. By mid-morning my stomach would be growling and the supply of chocolate chip biscuits Johnny kept at the studio calling to me. The trouble was I couldn't eat just one biscuit. It was like a reflex to reach for another and so easy to polish off half a packet without properly noticing.

I bought some bathroom scales so I could weigh myself every morning and I filled my fridge with vegetables and anything that said 'lite' on the label. But after a week or so of steamed fish and undressed salads I found myself craving the kinds of foods I'd never particularly enjoyed before, sticky buns with unnaturally bright pink icing, supermarket flapjacks, blocks of fruity nutty chocolate. They were so quick to buy, unwrap and eat I could almost kid myself they didn't count at all.

When the scales showed no change, the needle sitting stubbornly in exactly the same place, I promised myself I'd try harder. I bought a pile of magazines that had the words 'Diet' or 'Lose Fat Fast' emblazoned on their covers and tried to follow the advice I read there.

One weekend I made a giant pot of cabbage soup, seduced by the promise of shedding ten pounds in seven days. But it tasted bland and pointless and after just a couple of days I had a headache and felt grumpy. There were other diets I tried. They promised a quick-fix and involved eating huge amounts of grapefruit or egg, drinking endless glasses of freshly squeezed lemon juice and warm water, counting every single calorie. All were so revolting I couldn't stick to them for long.

On days I thought of as 'good', I'd keep going on fruit and a handful of nuts then nibble on toast and Marmite at dinnertime. But if I ruined things by snacking on something 'bad' in the morning there didn't seem any point in depriving myself for the rest of the day. So then I filled up on bakery pies, sweet tarts of baked custard or hot salty fish and chips, and promised myself I'd be good again in the morning.

I felt guilty when I ate and ugly when I was full. It was easier to avoid food altogether. Very soon I began to dread going to places where I knew there'd be lots of it, turning down invitations to the Martinelli Sunday lunch and avoiding mealtimes at Little Italy. My whole life seemed in better order when I felt light and empty.

When the needle on the scales started to shift downwards, I was encouraged to try harder. I took to writing down everything I'd eaten in a little notebook that I carried with me. Johnny couldn't understand my new obsession. As he saw me open a lunchbox filled with carrot sticks and celery, his face would fall.

'I miss the curries and the noodle dishes you used to bring in,' he complained. 'Now you've finally got a kitchen of your own and you never cook anything in it.'

And he was right. The stainless-steel pans I'd hung from hooks above my stovetop were gathering dust, the placemats and little dishes I'd planned to bring out for special dinners were still in the cupboards. It had been so much fun to fill my kitchen with pretty things but I'd barely used any of them.

So that night I made a rich spicy dhal, ate a tiny bowl of it myself and packed up the rest in a tiffin tin to take for Johnny the next morning. The following Sunday I baked a tin-load of brownies that I left beside the coffee machine for Johnny and Rob to pick at as they pleased and, while the dense chocolatey squares preyed on my mind all day, I was proud of not touching even the tiniest corner of one.

It was good to shop for ingredients again and spend hours in the kitchen mixing and melding them into something delicious. But it felt almost as satisfying being the one not eating, shaking my head and pretending to be full, lying that I'd already had a big breakfast.

At last I was seeing some results, my clothes were feeling looser, my body looking more how I remembered it. To speed things up I bought a pair of running shoes and woke an hour early every morning to sweat my way around St James's Park. I told myself that as soon as the weight was gone I'd ease up on the exercise and go back to eating normally. But I wasn't sure I could remember exactly what normal was.

Every time I saw her Lou seemed completely over-excited. 'What's Italy like, do you think?' she kept asking. 'How different will it be to Spain? Will the sea be cold? What shall I pack?'

I was trying to share her enthusiasm but the nearer we got to the trip the less real it seemed. I'd read all the details about the place we'd rented – a small, green-shuttered apartment in a bustling port within walking distance of a busy market town – I couldn't imagine myself with any of it as my backdrop.

Going through the motions, I ironed my clothes, laying them in neat piles on the bed, packing them into my case methodically. Almost everything I owned fitted me again. I liked my body so much more now it was slimmer, and I could see that others did too. Men's heads turned as I passed them in the street. Even the plumber who'd come back to fix a leak beneath the sink whistled when he saw me: 'Well, look at you,' he said, as though I'd managed something clever.

I still missed food and there were days I ate too much of it, giving myself permission to spread butter thickly on a slice of sourdough or fill a bowl to the brim with creamy cauliflower and blue cheese soup and blanket it with parmesan. Usually the eating didn't satisfy me, though, it only made me feel guilty, and the next day I'd nibble on a carrot or a handful of almonds to make up for it.

Italy would be an endless feast of food – I knew that because Addolorata couldn't stop talking about it. The tomatoes were different, she promised, and the basil too. Even the simplest meal had more flavour and the poorest peasant ate well. No one there survives on baked beans, white bread and fish fingers, she said disdainfully, not like here. Italians care about food. They keep chickens for fresh eggs, cultivate vegetables on any spare scrap of earth, raise caged rabbits to slay for a casserole. Every meal is important to them and taste is everything. If an Italian serves you a plate with only a sliced pear and a wedge of cheese on it then you can be sure the pear will be perfectly ripe and the cheese the best they can afford.

'And Italian food is still so regional,' Addolorata said joyfully. 'There'll be no pesto sauce where we're going, no cream or butter in the dishes. The meals there are based on spicy local sausage flavoured with fennel and lots of chilli, fish soups and stews of peppers and pork. Oh, and divine little cakes and pastries, too, of course. I've been reading all about it. There'll be so much to try.'

'But we won't only be eating, will we?' I said, concerned. 'There'll be other things to do.'

'Yes, yes, drinking, swimming, sunbathing,' she promised. 'And the brochure says "bustling port", remember, so that has to mean there's something going on after dark. A few bars and a disco, at least.'

'I bloody well hope so,' Lou said it fervently. 'I'm badly overdue for some fun. Every morning on my way to work

I tell myself this won't go on for ever, that some day things have to change – but they never do.'

'You can't hate your job that much, surely?' asked Addolorata.

'Oh yes I do. Once we've had our Villa Girls trip I'm going to start looking for something new. The day I hand in my resignation will be the best ever. But I need a holiday first.'

The three of us were going on the same flight and Lou had sworn she'd be drinking glasses of bubbly the whole way there. Toni had independent plans. She'd bought a Eurorail pass and was taking a longer trip, stopping off in France and northern Italy, and arriving at the apartment we'd rented two days before us. I hadn't seen her since she'd left for university and now I was dreading the prospect. It wasn't that she'd ever been completely awful to me but her words tended to have a sour bite and often I felt as though she were silently judging everything I did.

From time to time Addolorata passed on little snippets of news about her. Toni had a boyfriend. Then she didn't. She was studying for exams, going to summer balls, making new friends. Her life seemed foreign to me. I wondered if we'd have anything left in common.

The last thing I packed for Italy was my old Zenit camera. It was stowed in my hand baggage, even though it weighed a ton, because it was far too precious to risk with the baggage handlers. I could have afforded a newer, better camera but this was the one I loved. In fact, for me the only exciting thing about the whole holiday was the prospect of finding things to point that camera at: shrunken old ladies dressed from head to toe in black, colourful painted tiles, strings of chilli peppers hanging from a market stall, pallets of dusty ciabatta. If nothing else, I'd be coming back with a new collection of images printed on paper and seared on my brain.

When it came time to leave I shut the door of my flat

behind me, testing it was properly closed with a push of my hand and double-locking it carefully. I didn't know my neighbours yet so there was no one I could ask to keep an eye on the place. I'd have to trust it would be OK on its own.

The wheels of my suitcase rumbled over the pavement as I dragged it behind me and the bag with my camera in it knocked against my side with every step. I was going to Italy and knew I was lucky, that I ought to be pleased, but the truth was I couldn't wait to get home again.

WHAT ADDOLORATA SAID

'Rosie's being boring about the holiday. She couldn't make it much plainer she'd rather not come. She's been refusing to get excited about anything. I hope she's not going to ruin the whole thing. She was a lot more fun when she was into food, that's for sure. You know, I'm beginning to wonder why I was so insistent she came. We'd have a better time without her if she's going to carry on like this.'

The Olive Estate

Enzo couldn't believe his eyes, none of them could. This was what they'd been hoping for every summer, the reason they'd wasted so many hours milling about near the marina or in the main piazza. There were four of them, all pretty in different ways, and they were sitting at a café table, in the shade of a striped sun umbrella, drinking beer and sharing a dish of plump green Sicilian olives.

Moments earlier they'd strolled straight past him and his friends. Enzo suspected they'd come from an apartment on the steep slope above the port, one of them wearing high heels she could barely walk in, one with very Italian hair and olive skin, one with her face pinched tight by a sour mood, and the final one, the girl his eyes were drawn to, fair-haired and with a heavy-looking old camera slung over her shoulder.

Enzo hadn't managed the smallest whistle, not even an appreciative hiss. He could only gape as the four girls strolled by and then swivel his head so his eyes could follow them. Now he was standing there like a fool, still staring and unsure what to do.

'You go and talk to them, Santi.' The whispering among his friends began. 'Ask their names. See how long they're here for.'

'Why should it be me?' Enzo demanded. 'Gianpaolo can do it. He's the best looking of us, isn't he?'

Flushing, Gianpaolo fell back a few steps and barricaded himself behind the rest of the group. 'You're the one with the sports car, Santi,' he pointed out. 'You could offer to take them for a ride.'

'Yes, it should be you who goes first,' the others agreed. 'Come on, what are you waiting for? Not scared, are you?'

There was some laughter and a little jostling. Breaking away from the group, Enzo took a few steps towards the girls, conscious of so many eyes on him.

'*Vai, vai*, Santi,' he heard Gianpaolo call out and then there was another rattle of laughter.

Drawing closer he heard the girls' talking and straight away knew their words were English. At school they'd studied the language and he'd made an extra effort to learn so he could understand the words in the music he liked listening to and sing along to Michael Jackson and Madonna. But these girls were speaking too rapidly for him to follow the conversation properly. There appeared to be some sort of argument going on, the dark one and the sour-faced one clearly weren't too happy with each other. Enzo hesitated, unwilling to interrupt a quarrel and not sure what he should say if he did.

Then the fair girl looked up and met his gaze. He watched her pull the lens cap off her camera, saw her point it straight at him and heard a click as she took a picture. As he stood, silent and indecisive, she wound on the film by hand and, lifting the old camera to her eye again, fiddled with the lens and fired off another one.

'Are you taking my photograph?' Enzo spoke slowly, his tone polite. 'Why?'

The girl seemed surprised and her fair skin flushed pink. 'You and your friends were staring at us, weren't you?' she said, clearly enough for him to understand.

'Yes,' he agreed, 'I suppose we were.'

'So you like to stare … and I like to take pictures.' She turned her attention back to her camera.

Enzo moved a step closer. 'What's your name?' he dared ask.

But it was the girl in high heels who answered his question. 'Hi, I'm Lou,' she told him, speaking more clearly too now. 'The girl who took your picture is Rosie. And the two that are having a big stupid fight are Toni and Addolorata.'

'Addolorata, that is an Italian name,' Enzo said.

It was Lou who spoke again. 'Yes, that's because her father is Italian.'

'Is he from this region?'

'No, he lives in London. That's where we're all from. We've booked that apartment up there – the one with the green shutters – for three whole weeks. But Toni's been here for just two days and reckons she's already bored with the place. She says it's all pebble beaches, ancient buildings and old people. Is that true?'

Enzo laughed. 'Slow down, slow down. I can't follow you if you speak so fast.'

She repeated her words more slowly and, encouraged by her friendliness, Enzo drew closer. 'But I'm not old, am I?' he said. 'And neither are my friends.'

'That's true.' The girl smiled at him. 'So, can you tell us if there's anything much to do round here?'

'Lots of things.' Enzo waved his hand in the air expansively. 'Further south there are some beautiful sandy beaches. They are a drive away but that is fine – I have a car so I can take you if you like. And if you sit here for a while longer you will see the *passeggiata*. There'll be lots of people in the port and up the hill in the village, walking, talking, taking a drink and doing a little shopping. It happens every single evening, although always it is busiest on Sundays.'

'But are there any clubs? Or discos?' the girl wanted to know.

'This is Italy. You can dance anywhere you want.' Enzo was pleased with the smoothness of his reply and with how well his English was holding up. He felt more confident. Pulling a chair from a nearby table, he edged it inside their circle. Behind him he heard a few approving whistles from his friends.

'Do you mind if I join you?' he asked cheekily once he was safely seated.

His friends were now drawing closer too; Gianpaolo even daring to take a seat beside him. Enzo introduced them one by one and asked the waiter for more glasses and another jug of beer. 'We must have a drink to celebrate your arrival in our town,' he told the girls. 'We'll make sure you have a good time here, won't we, *ragazzi*? You won't be bored, I promise. We've lived here all our lives and know all the best places.'

Enzo had been hoping to talk to the fair-haired girl but she'd picked up her camera and was walking around the outside wall of the marina taking photographs of the fishing boats.

'Those boats are old and dirty. I don't think they will make a very pretty picture,' he remarked. 'Better if she took a photograph of a yacht or a speedboat, instead. That would look much better.'

'It's Rosie's hobby,' Lou explained. 'She takes pictures of everything. Trust me, if you hang out with us for the next three weeks you're going to get pretty tired of her pointing that camera at you.'

'We will have to risk it.' Enzo grinned at her and she smiled back encouragingly.

'Well then,' was all she said.

Rosie

Things started pretty badly. The plane was delayed, the train journey much longer than we'd expected and when we finally arrived at our rented apartment Toni was there, filling the place with her mess and her bad mood. She had left things everywhere: piles of clothing on chairs, damp towels flung over the balcony, magazines, books and lipsticks strewn about. She only had a small rucksack but an enormous amount of rubbish seemed to have come out of it.

In the two days she'd spent alone in Triento, Toni had decided she hated the place. 'Why don't we get hold of the rental agency, see if we can cancel this apartment and find somewhere better?' she nagged as Lou poured glasses of red wine and I made toasted bread and cheese.

'Look, we're all knackered. Can't we just relax and then have a walk around the town tomorrow?' Addolorata said reasonably.

'Yeah, but we want to get onto the rental agency as fast as we can, don't we?' Toni was insistent.

'Let's think about it in the morning, OK? Right now all I want is a couple of drinks and my bed.'

Standing on the balcony and staring out over the port I decided Toni was an idiot. This place seemed charming. Beneath us was a seafood restaurant and the air was thick with the scent of frying onions and filled with the sound of people's chatter. It was a tiny settlement, just a cluster of terracotta-roofed houses built into the rocky side of a mountain and curving around the small marina. There were a few cafés, a shop that sold *gelato* and a collection of boats, most of them ramshackle. As the sun began to set, the sky bled pink and made the view look like a scene from an old hand-tinted postcard. I grabbed my camera and tried to capture it before the light changed again.

From the moment we woke the next morning it was obvious there was going to be a big row at some point. Toni was taciturn and the mood tense as we walked up the steep mountain path towards the village. Even strong coffee and sweet pastries at a little café in the piazza didn't ease the atmosphere.

'Let's take a look around,' Addolorata suggested once we'd finished our breakfast.

'I think you've pretty much seen everything already,' Toni replied acidly.

But she was wrong. Beyond the piazza was a weave of narrow lanes that held surprises. We found an expensive-looking boutique in one, a shop that sold handmade silk scarves and woven baskets in another and a cute-looking pizza place up a tiny back alley.

'Perhaps we should come here tonight,' Addolorata suggested. 'I can't be bothered cooking. We could have a few drinks afterwards in that bar we saw on the corner.'

'Better not do all the fun things at once,' Toni warned. 'Remember last time.'

I could see Addolorata was losing patience, although she was managing to hold herself in check. It was later, down by the marina as we were having an afternoon drink, that she took the brakes off her mood and the quarrel began in earnest. Lou and I let them fight it out, their voices raised. Most likely it would have ended with someone storming off if the young Italian guys hadn't interrupted.

I'd noticed them staring our way; young, handsome, well dressed, they were difficult to miss. I was watching as they tried to decide who would approach us and wasn't surprised when they chose the tall one. There was something about him; he'd have stood out in any crowd. Not that he was more attractive, just more noticeable for some reason I couldn't put my finger on.

As he edged towards us, I couldn't resist taking a couple of shots. That seemed to encourage him, although that hadn't been my plan at all. Once he'd joined us they all swooped in. Still, Lou was pleased. I wandered off to take a few photos of some amazing-looking old fishing trawlers, and when I got back she was in her element, surrounded by men and topping up everyone's glasses.

All afternoon things stayed raw between Addolorata and Toni. It didn't matter too much because the Italian boys filled any awkward silences. One had an oddly high-pitched giggle, another soft brown cheeks that kept flushing red whenever Lou paid him any attention. But it was the tall one, Enzo, who seemed the leader of the group. When I caught him staring at me he held my gaze, smiling rather than being shamed into looking away. And after the third round of drinks he moved his chair closer to mine and trained his attention on me.

'So, Rosie, that is your name, no?' he said in his halting, heavily accented English. 'You take so many photographs. I would like to see them when you have them developed.'

'I don't think so,' I said. 'I hardly ever show them to people.'

'What if I drive you up to take some pictures of our statue?' His tone was teasing. 'Would you let me then?'

'The statue?' The moment we'd arrived I'd noticed it high on the mountain, a tall white figure of Christ dominating the skyline. At nightfall the moon had risen behind it and, brightly illuminated, it had seemed to hover above us in the velvety blackness. Now in the bright daylight, it gleamed white against the pure blue of the sky.

I hesitated. 'Would you take us all?'

'Of course. I have a car and my friends have Vespas. We will all of us go in a group tomorrow.'

'But aren't you busy? Don't you have to work? Or are you on holiday too?' I asked and he shrugged as though it didn't matter.

Perhaps there was something about Triento that had seduced me by then. As the afternoon wore into evening people were appearing, well-dressed women walking arm in arm with their daughters, old men with their wives. The port had a buzz to it, felt pleasingly foreign. I looked at Toni's face, still unrelenting and sulky. And then I made up my mind.

'We'd love to go to the beach and up the mountain tomorrow, wouldn't we?' I said brightly. 'I can't think of anything better.'

EXTRACT FROM ADDOLORATA'S JOURNAL

This place is perfect. I can't understand why Toni is so down on it. There are beaches and bars ... what else does she want? I'm sick of all this squabbling. All I want is to relax and have some fun. Isn't that the point of holidays? And there was me thinking it was Rosie who was going to be the problem. Aside from half-living behind that camera of hers she's being fine.

The Olive Estate

Enzo was convinced that the fair-haired girl liked him. Yes she was shy but she had taken his photograph and when he'd put his chair beside hers she hadn't seemed to mind. Of all four girls he thought she'd been the most enthusiastic about the prospect of a drive up the mountain to see the statue.

As soon as he got home he kicked the chickens out of the small barn and polished the dirt from his car. He spent a long time burnishing its bodywork with smooth strokes, buffing the leather seats and shining the windows. Tomorrow he would fold down the roof so she could feel the wind in her long fine hair as they drove fast round the coast road. 'Rosie.' He tested the unfamiliar name as he worked, rolling his tongue around it. 'Rosie.'

Only once the car was gleaming and he'd thrown a tarpaulin over it to stop the chickens fouling it before morning did he turn his attention to himself. He would pick out the perfect clothes, choose the right cologne and maybe even ask his Nonna to trim his hair a little. After giving it some thought, Enzo decided it might be wise to wear a little jewellery too but not too much in case it looked flashy – he didn't want the girl to think he was trying too hard. And then, to his surprise, he realised he was nervous.

That evening, as he took his usual place at the dinner table, listening to his sisters bicker and waiting for the meal to be served, Enzo replayed the scene of their meeting in his mind, wondering if he'd said the right things and made a good impression. He imagined the conversations they might have the next day, and couldn't help wondering how long it would be before he could take her hand, or even kiss her.

'Enzo, you've lost your appetite,' his Nonna said when he barely picked over his plate of pasta. 'Are you not hungry? Do the *vongole* not taste right?'

'No, no, they are good.'

'Then eat, eat. Have a little more of the sauce.' She stood to reach for the pan. 'Maybe your pasta is too dry.'

'I'm fine, Nonna, really,' he insisted.

'If you don't want it then give it to Ricardo rather than waste it,' she scolded him. 'He always has a good appetite.'

Even though Concetta and her new husband had their own apartment in the main house, still they came most nights to eat with the family, and by now his sister wasn't the only one whose belly looked swollen. 'Take it, Ricardo.' Enzo pushed the bowl towards him.

His mother looked concerned. 'Eat a little meat and some vegetables at least,' she begged him. 'Concetta, get your brother some food.'

'Mamma, look at me,' Concetta complained. 'The baby is kicking, my legs are swollen, I'm tired. Can't you ask one of the others to do it?'

'I told you, I'm fine,' Enzo insisted, raising his voice to be heard. 'I'm not hungry tonight.'

'*Va bene*, don't make such a fuss,' his mother said. 'I'll put aside a little something for you anyway in case you have your appetite later.'

Enzo refilled his glass and watched the others eat. He saw how Concetta pushed her pasta aside, soaking up a little sauce with dry bread and nibbling on it half-heartedly. Ricardo helped himself to her leftovers, oily tomato sauce flicking from the ends of the spaghetti and splattering down his shirt. His Nonna served herself a tiny portion but finished every last bite. His mother frowned after taking a mouthful as though dissatisfied with a flavour she'd found there. His grandfather ate quickly, head held low, not speaking until the bowl was completely clean. And his father ate as though it was just one more thing in life he had to do.

What would the English girl make of a family like this? If he brought her here to the Santi Estate would she share a meal with them at this long table? Would she be impressed by the rows of olive trees growing their fruit sedately in the stillness of summer? Might he show her the cave where the oil was kept cool and fresh, or take her to the cellar to see the giant fists of prosciutto his Nonna had hung there? Surely in England there was no place like this one.

Enzo hoped the English girl had liked him.

Rosie

I've always loved the smell of a room where food has just been cooked and that's what Italy smelt like to me. Every open window I passed seemed to leak the pungency of garlic fried moments ago or the sweetness of just-baked biscotti. It was as though you didn't even have to eat to taste the flavours because the air was so rich with them.

Addolorata had cooked for us in the end that first day because Toni screwed up her nose at the idea of pizza. She made a ragu from a local sausage so overstuffed with peppers and spices it turned the sauce orange.

'Fennel,' she said, as she tasted it. 'Lots of chilli, some sweetness too. It's good but very strong.'

Afterwards we went back to the bar near the marina and had another couple of drinks, arguing the whole time over whether we should stay in Triento or move somewhere more exciting.

None of us had really expected the Italian boys to come and meet us at the café in the piazza the next morning as they'd promised to. We went only because it seemed the best place to find coffee and pastries at that hour and Addolorata was in the grip of her usual craving for sugar.

'They'll be off chasing other tourists by now, I expect,' she said, swirling some fattening treat, rich with almonds and butter, through her milky coffee.

'They were cute though, weren't they?' Lou said wistfully.

We were about to head back to the apartment when we heard the sound of a car's horn hooting and the buzzing of

Vespas. A red sports car rounded the corner of the narrow street far too quickly and screeched to a halt right in front of us, in the middle of the piazza. Almost immediately an official-looking woman wearing a white peaked cap and a jacket with gold braid on the epaulettes shot out of the café and began blowing furiously on a whistle.

'*Porca la miseria*, Enzo Santi.' She blasted the whistle again, louder than before and gestured for him to drive on.

Enzo tried to charm her with a smile and said a few words in Italian. When he'd finished the woman took one sidelong look at us, shook her head and held a finger in the air. '*Un minuto*,' she barked, and stalked back into the café where her espresso was cooling.

'Are you not supposed to park there?' Addolorata asked as he and his friends came sauntering over in their bright shirts, pastel cotton sweaters thrown over their shoulders, designer sunglasses pushed up on their heads.

There was something rather arrogant about Enzo's shrug. 'Relax, order more coffee if you like. It will be fine. Then we will take you up the mountain to see our statue of *Cristo* and afterwards we will go to a beach.'

'And lunch, somewhere good for lunch,' Addolorata reminded him.

'Yes, of course,' he agreed. 'We will eat well.'

In the scramble to get into the vehicles I ended up beside Enzo in the passenger seat of the sports car. Lou was on the back of a Vespa, her arms already wrapped around the waist of the good-looking driver, and Addolorata and Toni had climbed in behind me.

'Do you like to drive fast?' Enzo asked, showing an even row of strong white teeth as he smiled.

'Not really,' I replied.

He laughed. 'Don't worry; you will like it in this car.'

The road to the statue wound steeply up the mountain and Enzo's tyres screeched as he attacked it in his car, the

Vespas trailing behind us. From behind I heard Toni yelling at him to slow down but the sound only seemed to encourage Enzo to press harder on the accelerator. Hanging on to a strap above my head, I thought how easy it would be for him to misjudge a turn of his steering wheel and for the car to leave the road, crash through the barrier and plummet down the side of the mountain. It was only a matter of a few centimetres, a split second of inattention, between living or dying in the same way my parents had. I wasn't afraid exactly, just newly aware that life was such a flimsy thing. Suspended in the moment, powerless to change anything, I didn't even scream at him like the others were.

By the time we reached the car park at the top, Addolorata was furious.

'That was bloody stupid,' she yelled. 'You might have killed us all showing off like that.'

'It was fast,' Enzo agreed, undaunted. 'But I've driven it faster.'

I was angry too but I didn't say anything. From what I'd seen so far, all Italians drove like lunatics. And to be fair, Enzo didn't know the reason fast cars didn't seem much fun to me.

There was a church up on the mountain as well as the remains of some ruined old buildings and a row of souvenir shops with a small bar tucked between them. Enzo offered to buy us a drink to settle our nerves but the syrupy black liqueur he ordered tasted of bitter herbs.

'It's Amaro, very good for the digestion,' he told us.

Only Lou looked to be enjoying herself. She was still exhilarated from the ride up the mountain and kept saying, 'Let's do it again. How fast do you think we can go on the way down?'

By the time we got close to the statue the sun was high and the heat shimmering. I paused to take some photographs, letting the others walk on ahead. Only Enzo stayed behind with me.

We climbed the steps to the statue, staring up at it together. To me it looked serene, yet somehow showy and domineering too. I wasn't certain if, close up, I liked it all that much.

'Why does it have its back to the sea?' I was curious. 'It seems strange. Shouldn't it face the other way?'

Enzo stared at the statue as though he'd never looked at it properly before. 'I don't know,' he admitted.

'What made them build it up here in the first place? Triento is such a small village and this is such a ridiculously big statue.'

'Second only in size to the one in Rio de Janeiro.' Enzo said it as though he was reciting something he'd been taught at school.

'Yes, but why?'

'I could ask my Nonna, if you like. She has lived here all her life so surely she must know.'

As we walked round the base of the statue, staring at the view, Enzo pointed out the landmarks he thought I might be interested in.

'Down there in the port, that is the roof of the apartment you are staying in. And right over there – almost on the horizon – do you see the rows of olive trees climbing up the hillside? Yes? That is part of my family's estate.'

'Do you live there?' I asked.

'Yes, with my sisters, my parents, my grandparents, all of us together. Perhaps I will take you there to meet them some day.' He smiled at me. 'The estate is very beautiful and our olive oil the best in Italy – at least, that's what my Nonna says.'

Away from his friends Enzo seemed different, softer and less certain, easier to talk to. All the swaggering arrogance had gone. He spoke with a quiet pride about his family, told me about life on the estate, the work he did there and how some day he would be responsible for it all. We took a seat at the base of the statue and sat there for a long time, his town spread out beneath us, talking about his life.

'And what about you, Rosie? Where is your home?' Enzo asked, climbing to his feet and carefully brushing clean the seat of his bone-coloured trousers with his hands.

When I told him I lived in a flat on my own his surprise was evident. 'Just you? Alone in an apartment?' he kept saying.

'Yes, just me,' I said.

'Here in Italy that is unusual. Most girls stay at home until they marry,' he told me.

'But I like living by myself. It's peaceful.'

'Peace?' Enzo laughed wryly. 'On our estate there is usually someone around, a sister, a neighbour, a worker. People are always coming and going. There are peaceful places, I suppose, out amongst the trees or in the pressing room when it is empty. Mostly though there is noise. I'm used to it.'

'I used to be ... but not any more.'

'You have no family with you? Not even nearby?'

'No one. I'm completely on my own.'

We were almost back at the car park and I could see the others. Lou was laughing at something one of the boys was saying, Toni was standing slightly to one side swigging from a bottle of mineral water, Addolorata leaning against the sports car.

'Enzo?' For a second I hesitated. I hated talking about this, but it felt important he should know. 'Both my parents are dead. They were killed in a car crash. That's why I live alone. And why I don't like driving fast – not even in a nice car like yours.'

WHAT ADDOLORATA SAID

'I wasn't going to get back in that car and go to the beach with them. It was only that you wanted to go so

much. And then, the weirdest thing, Enzo drove like an old man. All the way round the coast he crept along, that's why you overtook us so easily on the Vespa. I thought there was something wrong with the car at first. But then he drove like that the whole way back as well. Perhaps Rosie said something. They were together for ages up there by the statue. He doesn't seem like her type at all – just a flashy Italian boy who's been too spoilt by his mamma. Can you imagine what the car must have cost? And that watch? And his clothes?'

The Olive Estate

Even once he'd dropped off the English girls at their apartment Enzo drove like he never had before, braking gently, changing gears smoothly and letting the car drift into the bends and ease softly out of them. Gianpaolo overtook him on his Vespa, yelling something insulting that was carried away on the breeze, but still Enzo didn't pick up speed. From the engine there was a throaty rumble instead of the usual roar and, by the time he reached Triento, there was a queue of cars behind him, their drivers leaning on their horns.

Enzo knew plenty of people who had lost someone on the roads – he'd worn a black armband himself for one of his uncles. And yet he'd never believed it might happen to him or a person he really cared about.

He'd thought about it as they were eating pizza together at the little outdoor snack bar shaded by pines on the cliff above the beach. And as they were swimming, laughing and shouting, the boys doing handstands beneath the waves, the girls squeaking at how cold the water was. Lying stretched out on towels letting their bodies dry in the sun, he'd thought some more. But Enzo hadn't said anything. When words were difficult to choose he preferred to stay silent.

His thoughts remained confused. All Enzo knew was he liked the English girl better than any from Triento, although she wasn't as pretty as some. Her eyes were too large for her face; her nose had the hint of a hook in it. She seemed to hold herself slightly apart from everyone else. Enzo had never met anyone quite like her and he was intrigued. He longed to take her away from her friends, to drive her for hours and hours in his car and get to know her properly. After today he wondered if he had any chance with her at all.

When he got home he found his Nonna alone in the kitchen. She was baking bread, and the sweet, dusty smell of it instantly gave him a sense of comfort and belonging.

'Where is everybody?' he asked.

'Your sister Concetta is lying down, the others went into Triento with your mamma. Your father is somewhere on the estate. Your grandfather,' she shrugged, 'I don't know.'

'When will the bread be ready, I'm starving.'

She patted his arm with floury fingers. 'Sit down. I will find you something to eat.'

As soon as the golden crust had hardened she pulled the loaf from the oven and spread warm slices of it thickly with *Nduja*, the spicy, creamy sausage dosed with chilli that tasted so good topped with smoky sheep's cheese. While Enzo ate, she sat beside him, nibbling on dried olives she'd fried quickly in olive oil with oregano and shredded hot peppers.

'Nonna?' he began. 'Can I ask you something?'

She pushed the dish of olives towards him. 'Taste a few, they are good.'

He took one but only to please her. 'You told me a woman must need a man for them to be happy together.'

She nodded. 'That is true.'

'So how does the man know if the girl needs him?' He hesitated. 'Or likes him even? What are the first steps he must take? How is the right way to do it?'

'So many questions.' His Nonna poured a little fresh oil into a dish and tore another hunk from the still-warm loaf. As she dipped the bread and chewed she seemed to be thinking hard. 'There are things you can do to ensure you make the finest olive oil,' she said carefully. 'There is the best way to store it so it stays fresh and holds its goodness. There are wise ways to prune a tree and bad ways. All your life I've taught you everything I know about all those things. But women? There are a thousand different ways to win or lose them. We're not as simple as olive trees, Enzo, and I cannot help you understand us.'

'But—'

'Why must you know these things now?' she demanded. 'You've never asked me anything like it before.'

Enzo shrugged and took another olive, biting into its wrinkled, slightly bitter flesh, tasting the *peperoncino* that flavoured so much of what they ate.

His Nonna looked amused. 'Can it be you've found a girl in Triento that isn't charmed by you? Who is she? You should bring her here. I would like to meet her.'

'Maybe,' he muttered.

She took his chin between her fingers, turning his face towards her and he saw that she looked happy. 'Are you falling in love at last, Enzo?' she asked.

Embarrassed, he shook his head free. 'Nonna, don't ...'

'Perhaps I can tell you one or two things that will help, then.' She sat back and considered it for a moment. 'Be gentle, for a woman's feelings bruise as easily as a ripe olive's flesh. Be careful, because just like the *mosca* can attack a tree without you noticing—'

'Nonna, must everything always be about olives?' he interrupted, half-exasperated.

'Yes, Enzo.' She touched his face again. 'Yes, I think it must.'

Rosie

'You have to get us an invitation to that olive estate,' Lou kept saying. 'He did promise to take you there, didn't he?'

Every morning Enzo had come to meet us while we were having coffee at the café in the piazza. By now the woman in the peaked cap had given up whistling and yelling when he parked his car there. Instead, she nodded and said, *buon giorno*, when she saw us waiting. So did the man who sold linen and the butcher leaning in the doorway of his shop waiting for customers. We'd been staying in Triento for just over two weeks and already it felt as though people expected to see us, like we were becoming a part of the fabric of the place.

Usually when Enzo arrived we'd order more coffee and a plate of the dense high-calorie cakes stuffed with ricotta that were his favourite. He'd always have a couple of friends with him, Gianpaolo often among them because he and Lou had a holiday romance raging by then. One day they took us high into the mountains and we ate lunch in a dim little restaurant with walls that looked like they'd been carved from the side of the mountain. They fed us salt cod, fried aubergine, sweet red peppers, and I could feel my waistband tightening as we ate.

On fine days we went to a beach, driving a little further south every time so Enzo could show us a new one. It was always him who paid for the sun umbrella and the deck-chairs or fetched ice-cold Coke from the bar when we were thirsty.

I'd started photographing him almost compulsively. To begin with it was the planes of his face I was fascinated with. I liked to capture him when he was slightly turned away so I could see the line of his cheekbone and the way his lashes dipped and curved towards it. Or when his black hair was sleek from a dip in the sea and his tanned skin dusted with sand. He didn't seem to mind me pointing the camera at him, only laughing and sometimes saying, 'One day you'll have to show me all these pictures, eh, Rosie?'

Always when he took us somewhere I sat in the passenger seat beside him. He never mentioned my parents or what I'd told him that first day but he drove as though he was thinking of them, slowly and much more carefully.

If I went for a swim, Enzo came too; when I wanted to walk along the tide-line he would join me. To my surprise, the attention made me happy. It felt good knowing he was watching me, I liked the sound of him saying my name, I liked noticing how we smiled at the same things. Even a silence between us felt comfortable. When I wasn't with Enzo, I was thinking about him ... and missing him.

Photographing him turned into an obsession. I took pictures from behind with the sea before him, strong shoulders, long back, legs that were muscled and firm. Through my lens I watched him lying on a towel with his head buried sleepily in the crook of his arm, or play-fighting with Gianpaolo or in the middle of some sort of beach game with a bat and ball that all the Italians seemed obsessed with.

'Perhaps we should have a shot of us together,' he suggested finally and so I got Addolorata to take one and Enzo pulled my arm through his as we smiled into the camera.

He was always bringing me food from home, a jar of his Nonna's olives, a smartly labelled bottle of their oil, some bread she'd baked, little gifts that were for all of us to eat but given just to me.

'I think it's so sweet how he's wooing you,' said Addolorata. 'Very old-fashioned. Has he even kissed you yet?'

'No, but then we're never alone,' I pointed out.

'Well, maybe it's time you were.'

Even Toni seemed curious to see the olive groves. She'd relaxed a little and was letting one of Enzo's friends pay attention to her, although I don't think she was terribly serious about him. She still had her weird button phobia and a tendency to look for the things that were wrong in any situation. But barefoot on a beach, waiting for Enzo to bring us slices of pizza or chop up a watermelon, even she couldn't be entirely unhappy.

'Yeah, go on, Rosie,' she urged me now. 'Get Enzo to invite us for lunch with his family. Everyone says their place is amazing and we really have to see it.'

'I can't make him ask us there, though, can I?' I pointed out. 'It's up to him.'

'Well, you could throw out a few hints, at least,' Lou suggested. 'Or, you know, let him kiss you – that should soften him up.'

Enzo did kiss me that evening, as it turned out. There had been a plan for him to drive us up the mountain to see the view from the statue by night but the others came up with all sorts of lame excuses why they shouldn't join us: Addolorata was tired, Lou wanted to stay by the marina and have a few drinks, Toni preferred to stay there too.

Enzo didn't try to persuade them to change their minds. He seemed pleased if anything. Refusing the beer I offered, he suggested we should leave right away. 'We could watch the sunset from up there. I've never done that before and I'm sure it will be beautiful,' he said.

It was a windless, warm evening and there was no one else up on the mountain. Enzo and I chose a spot beneath the base of the statue and settled down to watch the sky change. By the time he kissed me its colours had dulled and the sun was disappearing. The next thing I knew it was dark and there were pinpricks of light beneath and above us.

'Are you cold?' Enzo asked at last.

'A little.' It felt awkward to be speaking to him again after so much kissing.

He rubbed my body briskly with his hands so the friction would warm me. 'Would you like to go back?'

'Not yet, I like it here.'

We talked for a while after that and I told him how the others were nagging me about visiting his estate.

'They want you to invite them for lunch. They keep going on about it.'

'Sunday is always the day we have guests,' he said hesitantly. 'So I suppose you could come then.'

'You don't have to have us if you don't want to.'

'I'd like for you to come, Rosie.' He rubbed his face into the side of my neck and his voice grew muffled. 'But if you do then you'll meet my Nonna. And when she sees you she will know for sure you are the girl I like.'

I had been imagining Enzo's family as very much like the Martinellis only bigger, noisier and more Italian. He talked about them often, always with affection, and, knowing they were there at the very centre of his life was satisfying to me. I'd been longing to meet them and see their estate just as much as the others, although I'd been trying not to make it too obvious.

'Have you told your Nonna about me, then?'

'Not really. But she knows that there's someone and she will realise it is you.'

'And are you worried about us meeting?'

Enzo looked thoughtful. 'My Nonna is the most amazing woman I know. All my life she's been the person I have most admired. I really want her to like you.'

'But you're afraid she may not?' I asked.

He nodded. 'You're not what she expects.'

'Well, I might not like her either,' I retorted, stung.

Enzo laughed and kissed me again for a long time as the moon glowed behind us and Triento's bright lights startled the night. I liked the way the kissing made me feel, lips, tongues, bodies colliding and everything beginning to burn.

Much later as we broke apart and, both slightly dazed, began the drive back down the mountain I realised that in a week's time I'd be back in London and my normal life would be closing around me again. The holiday was nearly over. Time was running out.

'There's only one Sunday left,' I told Enzo. 'And then we leave.'

'But there's still much more of summer to enjoy.'

I shrugged. 'Yes, but still we only have one more Sunday of it here.'

Before I climbed out of his car, Enzo kissed his fingers and pressed them against my cheek. It was an odd gesture, caring and familiar.

'I don't know if my Nonna will like you,' he said again and then he smiled at me. 'But I'm certain that I do.'

EXTRACT FROM ADDOLORATA'S JOURNAL

Three weeks isn't long enough. I wish we could rent this place the whole summer and spend every day at the beach and nights at our favourite bar. Lou's the one who's going to hate leaving most. She's fallen for Gianpaolo and is already planning to come back for a visit. Toni won't care so much. She's always talking about her new college friends so I expect she'll be glad to get back to them. And Rosie? I've seen a different side to her this holiday. She seems to have relaxed for the first time. She's so much easier to be around.

I don't know if the change is all because of Enzo. She likes him a lot, although she doesn't talk about him much. I'll admit he's a better person than I took him for at first. It'll be interesting to see this big estate they all keep going on about and to meet his family as well. I wonder what they'll think of us ... and what we'll think of them.

The Olive Estate

When Enzo heard the truck in the night he fought the urge to go out and take a look. He would only see the same sight as before: men carrying boxes into or out of the barn. It had been going on for so long now that, while he never could predict when they might arrive, he knew for sure they would come.

He slept very little that night and then fell into an unsatisfying doze. When he woke, later than usual, there was barely anyone around, only his father whose face was blank and his Nonna whose pallor seemed grey and tired. They sat around the table as the smell of fresh coffee flooded the kitchen and no one bothered to speak. Enzo wondered if either of them knew for sure what the boxes contained or if, like him, they assumed it was some sort of contraband – cigarettes, electronic equipment, fake designer handbags.

His Nonna laid out slices of her home-baked bread, a jar of bitter orange marmalade and a wide-lipped saucer filled with olive oil. She poured strong black coffee into his cup and spooned in sugar. 'Eat,' she told him in a morning-weary voice.

So many secrets lay between them now; Enzo kept turning them over in his mind until he grew dizzy with them. Each morning it was a relief to roar away from the estate and leave its problems behind. By the time he drove into Triento and saw the girls waiting for him in the piazza, his head was beginning to clear. It always amused him how foreign they looked sitting there. So many little things: the shape of their clothes, the way they styled their hair, what they wore on their feet, the fact that Rosie always carried her camera. All these things gave away that they didn't belong.

There was something particularly foreign about Rosie. Something different. It was as if there was more to her than other people; parts she kept hidden or disguised. Enzo had lived surrounded by women all his life and imagined he knew how they thought and what they wanted. But with Rosie he understood nothing.

He found it impossible to predict her moods. One day she might be reserved, the next quick to laugh. There were times she ate like an Italian – sucking the spaghetti greedily into her mouth, mopping up the sauce and demanding more – and others when she had no appetite at all, tasting only a few salad leaves moistened with a squeeze of lemon juice. And most mysteriously of all, some nights it was the easiest thing in the world for him to reach across and touch her, others she held her heavy old camera between them and he barely dared to take her hand.

It was tantalising to think of bringing Rosie to the estate and showing her all that he was and had, but Enzo wasn't certain he should try to mix the two parts of his world. He watched his Nonna absent-mindedly flicking chickens out from beneath the table with her dishcloth. '*Cose da pazzi* ... they get everywhere,' she was muttering. As much as he admired her, still he saw the old woman clearly. She could be difficult, overpowering, uncompromising. He feared that like oil and water she and Rosie might not mix at all.

'*Mannaggia chi te muort.*' His father was staring out the window, scowling at the sky that had held its blue for weeks now. 'This has turned into a dry summer and there's no sign of rain yet. Enzo, you must help me lay the pipes in case we need to irrigate the young trees this year.'

'Yes, but not today,' Enzo said quickly. 'Today I'm busy.'

His Nonna glanced at him. 'What is it you must do that

you'd put before making sure the trees don't go thirsty?' she asked.

'There is … I have … just plans,' he stammered in reply.

'Plans?' Disappointed, she shook her head at him. 'Don't you see how much harder Ricardo works since he married your sister? Instead of wasting precious time with you he's in his family's shop or helping here on the estate. You're not a boy any longer, Enzo. It's time for you to do the same. Life is a serious thing and you must be serious too.'

Enzo knew this hectoring tone. Usually when his Nonna used it he thought it wiser not to argue. But today he had promised to meet Rosie and drive her all the way up the coast to Amalfi to show her the picture-postcard scenes, the seaside churches with tiled domes, the narrow streets of boutiques and smart hotels. They were planning a whole day together and he wasn't going to forfeit it for hours laying water pipes in the olive groves, no matter what his Nonna said.

'I'm meeting someone,' he said. 'I don't want to let her down.'

His father shrugged. 'Tomorrow … next week … it isn't urgent yet. So long as we get the pipes laid before too long.'

'Thanks, Papa.' He grinned at his father gratefully. 'Next week I'll help for sure – every day, if you need me to.'

Draining his coffee cup, he stood to go but his Nonna held up a hand to stop him. 'Wait,' she ordered.

'Papa said I could go—'

'I heard what he said. But we know nothing of this girl you've been seeing, even though it seems she's more important to you than our trees. Whose family does she belong to? Who is she? Why do you have to keep her a secret?'

'She's just a girl,' Enzo said bullishly, not wanting to talk about Rosie when his Nonna was in such an abrasive mood.

'Just a girl you meet up with every day and most nights, too,' she continued, her anger making her into something more magnificent. 'You've barely been a part of this family these past few weeks. All of us have noticed that. And yet you won't bring her here to meet us. Who are you ashamed of, us or her? Tell me that, Enzo.'

He stared at her, unsure what to say.

'*Va bene*, go then.' His Nonna flicked him with her dish-cloth just as she had the chickens. 'Get out of this house.'

Enzo paused in the doorway. 'I'd like to bring her here but ...'

'But what?'

'She's not what you're expecting, that's all.'

'And what is it you think I expect?' his Nonna demanded. 'All I've ever wanted is that you should find a woman who will support you in everything you do; like your mother does your father; like I have your grandfather for so many years. You will need that if you are to some day take over the running of this estate. Life is serious, as I keep saying, Enzo. Perhaps it's time you realised just how serious it is ...'

His father touched her arm. 'Mamma,' he said gently, 'calm yourself. It's not so important. Let the boy go. Let him have his secrets if he wants them.'

She sank back onto her chair and her face seemed to crumple, all the magnificence gone from her suddenly. 'There's no respect any more,' she lamented.

Enzo stared at his Nonna. He felt sorry to be the one to have left her looking so defeated. 'This girl, my friend ... she has no family,' he began. 'She isn't even Italian and next week she will leave Triento and maybe never come back. I need to find a way to make her need me, just like you said. But perhaps it isn't even possible.'

And then a smile spread slowly over his Nonna's face. 'So it is still this same girl – I knew it, I did,' she said with some satisfaction. 'Don't give up too easily, my Enzo. Anything is possible.'

Rosie

There were times I forced myself to think about how stupid this thing with Enzo was. We were heading back to England soon and then everything would be over between us, so what was the point of spending all this time with him? And yet I couldn't resist. He made me feel adored and I weakened to that like I might a dish of tiramisu: bittersweet with chocolate and coffee, rich with mascarpone cheese and Marsala wine. Once I'd tasted it I wanted much, much more. It frightened me a little, made me feel vulnerable, and I wished I could find some sort of balance: a place between fat and thin, between eating too much and too little, between being alone and being infatuated. It seemed in all of life I struggled to hold myself steady.

We had one single night together, stolen time. Enzo drove me to the Amalfi coast where we walked steep streets until our legs grew tired and then he took me to a small hotel that seemed barely to cling to the cliffside. There we sat out on a wide terrace covered in potted hydrangeas while waiters in starched linen brought us seafood and chilled white wine that tasted of honey and apples.

'This is like a dream,' I said, raising the glass to my lips. 'Wouldn't it be wonderful to stay here, in a room with a view of all this?'

'Is that what you'd like?' Enzo asked.

'Yes, some day, if I ever come back.'

'What about tonight?' He said the words lightly.

'We can't.'

'Why not?'

'The others are expecting us, we have no things with us … lots of reasons.'

'Well, I can call the bar in the marina and get them to pass on a message to your friends,' he suggested. 'And we'd only be here for one night so we can manage without our things. As for the other reasons … well, they're up to you. But if you want to then we could have a night here, the two of us, in a room with a view of the sea.'

'We could?'

He nodded. 'Why not?'

I hung back, feeling awkward as we checked into the hotel. Enzo was very smooth. He told them our stay was an impromptu one and our suitcase still in the car parked just down the road. 'I'll fetch it later, no problem at all. It's so beautiful here we couldn't resist staying a night,' he said to the desk clerk.

There was another awkward moment when we reached our room, a tiny space filled almost entirely by a double bed. But Enzo seemed confident enough for both of us. Flinging open the doors that led out onto a cramped balcony, he said, 'Here is your view. *Bella*, eh? Tonight it is all for you.'

I'd never seen how sleeping with a man could be as amazing as people claimed. I'd thought they were exaggerating. But with Enzo the feeling of his skin on mine made me shiver. And he took things slowly, for at long last he seemed just as uncertain and nervous about what was happening between us.

'We have all night,' he reminded us both. 'All night for our first time.'

I wish I could remember it better. In my mind it's all heat and bodies colliding. It's a cool breeze coming through the open doors and the sound of the waiters on the terrace below setting up for dinner. It's watching Enzo change and lose control; then letting myself go as well. It's a night that seemed to go on for ever and at the same time end far too quickly.

In the morning he ordered breakfast to be brought up to our room and we lay curled up together until it was time to check out. I thought I saw the desk clerk's lips twitch as he looked up to find us standing there, still in the same clothes and with no suitcase, but I didn't much care.

'Signore and Signora Santi, have a good day,' he farewelled us and Enzo squeezed my hand and smiled.

On the way home we were mostly silent, both taken up with how wonderful it had been and how hopeless things were for us now. I knew I could write Enzo letters from England, make the odd phone call, promise to visit at Christmas or next summer. But was there any point in prolonging something that was going to end eventually? Wouldn't it only make the ending worse?

'Tomorrow is Sunday,' Enzo remarked as we neared Triento.

'Yes.'

'So you must come to meet my family as we said.'

'Really?' I was surprised.

'Yes, bring the others if you'd like to. Everyone will be made welcome.'

'Weren't you worried they might not like me? I'm not what your Nonna is expecting – that's what you said.'

He slowed the car and glanced over to me. 'I want you to come.'

'And will it be all right?'

'I don't know, Rosie,' he admitted. 'But I want you to come anyway.'

WHAT ADDOLORATA SAID

'Out of all of us isn't Rosie the least likely to go off and spend the night with a man? I still can't believe it. And look at her now, all lit up as if it was exactly what she

needed. I wish I'd been whisked off to a hotel on the Amalfi coast. It's not likely to happen to me, though, because Eden isn't that kind of guy at all. I'm not certain if he even likes me most of the time. But Enzo doesn't try to hide how crazy he is about Rosie. I'm envious, to be honest. I'd like to know how it feels to be adored like that. I mean, Enzo's not my type at all – don't get me wrong – but still I'd like someone to make me feel the way Rosie's obviously feeling right now.'

The Olive Estate

Enzo was nervous, lifting the lids off pans to check what was cooking in them, pulling the heavy old table out beneath the espaliered lemon trees, shooing away the chickens and shutting them up in one of the barns.

Concetta kept laughing at him. 'I've never seen you like this about anyone. This girl must be special.'

'She's just a girl,' Enzo said self-consciously. 'I don't want everyone making a big fuss.'

Concetta laughed again. 'You're the one who's making the fuss.'

He had skipped church that morning so he could make sure everything was perfect. He'd spent an hour or so pulling stray weeds from the garden, taking his father's ugly old truck and parking it out of sight, even mopping the kitchen floor, although it was usually someone else's job.

'You're in my way,' Concetta had complained. 'Go down to the cellar and choose some wine for your friends to drink. And bring back plenty of olive oil, too. I'll need it if I'm going to cook all the dishes you've requested.'

Enzo had thought about the food very carefully. He had wanted octopus cooked in its own juices with tomatoes from his Nonna's garden but she'd been certain the English girls wouldn't care for suckered tentacles, no matter how delicious they might seem to him. Instead she had suggested they start with a simple pasta filled with ricotta and soft-leafed herbs. Then a braised swordfish, stuffed with salted capers and olives, and bathed in a piquant tomato sauce.

Perhaps some veal shin cooked slowly with red wine and bay leaves. A dish of sweet onions baked in olive oil and vinegar; another of grilled radicchio. And a large tray of glossy aubergines cut in meaty slices and baked with layers of parmesan and tomato sauce until they were golden and bubbling. Already the smells of the ingredients cooking and combining were filling the kitchen and drifting deliciously out over the yard.

When the rest of the family came back from church no one changed out of their best clothes as they usually would. His grandfather poured wine into carafes instead of putting out bottles. His sisters polished the cutlery as they laid it on the table. But most surprising was his Nonna who brought bunches of wild flowers she'd picked from the olive groves, arranging them carefully in mismatched vases and setting them down the centre of the table.

At midday Enzo drove to fetch the girls. They were waiting in the piazza as always, Rosie wearing a pale blue dress he'd never seen before, Lou in heels that were too high, Addolorata waving and even Toni deigning to smile.

There was lots of high-key chatter and laughter as they drove but when they pulled up at the high metal gates of the estate and saw the sweeping tree-lined driveway beyond them, the girls fell silent.

'Remind me again of your sisters' names,' Rosie said, sounding jittery. 'There are so many of them I'm sure I'll never remember.'

His Nonna was standing at the kitchen door, waiting to greet them. She kissed all the girls on both cheeks, leaving Rosie till last and taking an especially long, careful look at her.

'Ask your guests to sit down,' she urged Enzo. 'Once you've eaten you can walk around the estate, show them the trees and our mill, explain how we make our oil. But first they must taste the food we've cooked for them.'

When they'd taken their seats at the long table, his mother brought out dishes of antipasti for them to nibble on as they sipped their glasses of chilled Prosecco: courgette flowers fried and sprinkled with salt, bruschetta with tomato and basil, some of his Nonna's preserved olives, a little sliced salami.

Addolorata seemed utterly at ease, fitting in instantly. Lou and Toni were looking about them curiously. Only Rosie was uncomfortable, thought Enzo, glancing over at her, as though this hadn't been what she was expecting at all.

'Are you OK?' he asked. 'Don't eat the things you don't like just to be polite. My brother-in-law Ricardo will make sure there are no leftovers.'

She touched the camera she'd set beside her on the table. 'Do you think your family would mind if I took some photos of the food … and of them eating it?'

'No, go ahead. It will be fine.'

'Are you sure?' She sounded relieved. 'It looks so beautiful the way they've set it out.'

Enzo saw how his Nonna's eyes followed Rosie as she circled the table with her camera to her eye and wondered if she realised how closely she was being observed. There was an expression on the old woman's face he found difficult to read. She didn't seem disapproving but neither did Enzo think she was ready to like the English girls yet.

Just as she had predicted, they all enjoyed the pasta parcels with their delicate flavours of basil and parsley, drizzled in a light butter sauce fresh with torn mint. By the time the swordfish and the veal was served everyone had drunk enough wine to wash away much of the awkwardness. Enzo heard Addolorata laughing, noticed Lou with a carafe in her hand and saw how even Rosie had succumbed to the food, clearing her plate of the warm, vinegary radicchio and nodding when she was offered another small spoonful.

Even his Nonna seemed less watchful now. For the first

time, Enzo felt it was safe for him to relax. He ate a dessert of moist almond tart sweetened with honey that Concetta had baked. Then there was coffee, some little sugar biscuits, a slab of pecorino cheese and a bowl of fruit. Only by late afternoon, after hours of eating, was the meal considered finished.

As the food was settling in their stomachs, Enzo suggested a walk. 'We will go between the olive trees, up the far hill where there is a beautiful view,' he told the girls. 'It will be good for our digestion.'

He shepherded them across the estate, showing them the press and the cave where the tall demi-johns of greeny gold oil were stored. As they walked, he glanced over at Rosie every now and then. She was following a step behind the others, not even bothering to take photographs, her expression closed, her voice silenced. Enzo wondered what was wrong.

On the way back he took them past the barns because Lou was keen to see the pigs. It was almost second nature for him to glance over as they neared the largest barn to check whether it was padlocked shut. He did so now without really thinking.

'Strange,' he muttered, seeing the door slightly ajar. He was certain it hadn't been left that way the day before and yet he couldn't remember hearing the rumble of a truck in the night. 'You go on ahead,' he called out to the others. 'The pigpen is just around the corner. I need to check on something first.'

As Enzo stepped inside the barn he saw that several wooden cartons had been piled close to its entrance in careless stacks, as though whoever left them there was hurrying. He paused, wondering what he should do. It might be wiser to shut the barn door and forget what he had seen, but Enzo couldn't resist taking just one look. Once he knew what lay inside the boxes everything would be clearer and this might be his only chance.

Carefully he levered the lid from the carton nearest to him and brushed aside a layer of shredded paper. He expected to find packets of foreign cigarettes or electronic equipment; things he knew could be sold easily on the black market. But this was something different. Reaching in, he pulled out a zip-lock bag filled with a lot of smaller wax-paper packets. He opened one and looked inside. The white powder might have been slightly dirty flour or icing sugar.

'What is this …?' he said out loud.

'Oh my God—'

Enzo wheeled round when he heard the voice. He saw that Toni had slipped into the barn behind him without being noticed and was standing there, staring at the packet in his hand, her eyes wide. 'Is that drugs?'

'Drugs?' he repeated stupidly.

'Yes.' Toni came closer so she could get a better look. 'I don't know … heroin, maybe. What the hell is it doing here? Are all these boxes full of it?'

Enzo felt a rush of fear. 'I'm not sure.'

'It's on your property. You must know what it is.' Her voice was accusing. 'What's going on, Enzo?'

'I don't know yet. But no one must find out you've seen this,' he told her. 'That is important. Do you understand?'

Toni shook her head. 'I don't know—'

'This is serious … dangerous,' Enzo said in a low voice. 'Trust me, you don't want to get involved in it. Leave it to me to sort out.'

Toni's expression had hardened. 'Does Rosie know your family is involved with drugs? I bet she doesn't.'

'You don't understand. None of this belongs to us. It's been stored for a while for someone, and in a week or so it will be gone. My family has nothing to do with it. Nothing. I'm sure of that. None of them can possibly know what's inside these boxes. I didn't know it myself till now.'

'But it's on your property,' Toni repeated, beginning to

back away from him. 'You must have something to do with it.'

He shook his head. 'I can't explain because I don't understand myself what it's doing here. But please don't tell Rosie. Or anyone. Promise me that.'

'OK then ...' Toni said, edging out of the barn as though she were afraid of him now. 'OK, Enzo, OK.'

His hands were shaking. Pushing the plastic bag back into the box, he covered it again with shredded paper, replacing the lid as best he could and hoping no one would notice it had been touched. For a moment he stood alone in the barn wishing he felt braver. And then he followed Toni out into the bright sunlight, pulling the door shut firmly behind him.

He found her beside the pens, looking flustered and anxious to leave, hurrying the others on, claiming the pigs made her feel sick and she couldn't stand to be near them. Enzo insisted they stay a little longer. He took his time showing them through the main house, hoping for another moment when he might talk to Toni, but she stuck close to the others, avoiding him. When he offered them more coffee, Toni shook her head. 'We've been here long enough. It's time to go,' she said.

'But surely you want to rest for a moment before you leave?' He was desperate for a chance to be sure he'd won her silence.

'No, what I want is to leave,' Toni insisted.

All the way back in the car, she was quiet. She didn't exclaim about the food they'd eaten or question him about his family. She left that to the others. Enzo was panicking. When he pulled up outside the apartment he was so frightened and furious, he barely bothered trying to kiss Rosie goodbye.

And then, instead of heading home, he pointed the car south and took the coast road, driving faster than he had in weeks, throwing the car angrily into the bends so hard the tyres squealed. He heard the horns of other cars as he swung wide around a corner and saw their lights flashing at him but he didn't care. Concentrating on the road ahead, he emptied his mind of everything else.

As he passed through towns he met with traffic and was forced to slow down. It was strange watching the usual Sunday-evening scenes through his windscreen, people making a *passeggiata* along the main streets, families with lots of children, couples hand in hand, the tables full at nearly every café. Everyone else's lives were still normal, only his had changed.

Enzo drove further south than ever before, following roads on a whim, taking pleasure in the roar of the engine as he dropped down a gear and pressed his foot on the accelerator. He might have driven on and on if the light hadn't been fading and the hairpin bends of the bumpy mountain road grown so treacherous. Skidding through a patch of gravel Enzo scared himself, the fear a dose of reality. When a glance in the rear-view mirror showed him the moon was rising, he knew it was time to turn back.

Heading home he slowed his pace, driving more carefully, as though Rosie were there beside him. Once he reached roads he recognised there was no need to concentrate on handling the car and Enzo's mind was free for worries to crowd into it.

He had promised Toni that his family wasn't involved but he didn't know for sure if that was true. Perhaps his father was responsible or his grandfather. Enzo had always assumed his family's wealth was founded on the olive trees but it might so easily have been something else that had paid for all the land they'd bought, the house they'd built, even this car.

He was no innocent. He had smoked a little pot like all his friends and it had left him feeling slow and stupid. He had heard of pills that made you dance all night long and thought it might be interesting to try them. But heroin?

Never – it was a drug that destroyed people, everyone knew that.

It was time to face his father down, to demand the truth from his grandfather. Enzo regretted not doing it sooner. He was angry at them, disappointed in himself, and dreading the confrontation to come. Of all the quarrels the Santi family had ever had, this was bound to be the worst. He couldn't begin to imagine how it might go.

Enzo slowed his car even further. He was in no hurry to get home.

Rosie

From the moment I saw the elaborate metal gates of the estate and realised how much land Enzo's family owned, he started to change in my eyes. Yes, I'd seen how easily he dipped his hand in his pocket, how there always seemed to be enough to pay for whatever we wanted. I knew the car he drove must have been expensive. But I didn't realise what it all meant: that Enzo was rich, properly rich.

There was too much of everything that afternoon: too much food, far too many people, and from the moment we arrived I felt overwhelmed. Only Enzo seemed to notice; and perhaps his Nonna, too. Certainly her eyes were on me the whole time. She watched what I ate and what I left on my plate, stared at me as I took my photos. She was a tiny old lady with slightly hunched shoulders and an odd little silver spoon worn on a chain around her neck and yet still she had so much presence. I saw how Enzo's sisters waited for her to signal it was time to clear the plates and bring on the next course; saw how even his mother glanced at her for approval. And then I understood why he had been so uncertain about bringing me here. The Enzo that I knew was only a small part of him. This was who he really was, this estate, this family.

With every new thing he showed us the distance between our lives seemed to grow wider. It was all so impressive. The acres of fruiting olive trees, the room with the old press in it and the big, modern house with its large formal spaces filled up with uncomfortable furniture, hospital-ward clean.

I was glad when Toni insisted we leave, even though she was pretty rude about it. Both she and Enzo seemed off-key as we drove back but the others made up for it, buoyant with the pleasures of the afternoon, full of wine and food and noise.

The moment we got into the apartment I shut myself in my room and crept between the covers of my bed, closing my eyes and dozing in and out of sleep. I heard Toni calling out that she was going for a walk and the front door slamming behind her. Every now and then little bursts of conversation from the other two would pull me back into consciousness, but I lay determinedly still and kept my eyes closed until sleep blotted them out again.

It was Lou who woke me. 'Rosie, you'd better come and hear this,' she said tersely.

'Hear what?' My mind was still heavy with sleep.

'Come on, wake up. You have to listen to what Toni's just told us.'

On the kitchen table there was a half-empty bottle of red wine but it didn't seem as though they'd been having a good time drinking it. Lou's expression was grim, Addolorata looked as solemn, Toni seemed anxious.

They made me sit down and thrust a glass into my hand before they told me. Toni said the words twice before they sank in properly and even then I refused to believe her.

'But Enzo's not into drugs. He barely drinks alcohol,' I argued.

'I know, but that doesn't mean his family isn't involved with trafficking them,' Toni pointed out.

'Are you sure that's what you saw, though … heroin?' I tested the word, it sounded horrific. 'How do you even know what it looks like? Have you ever seen it before?'

'No,' Toni admitted. 'I suppose it could have been something else. But the way Enzo acted … and the odd way it was packaged up in those little wax envelopes that stamp collectors use ... I'm really sorry, Rosie, but it had to have been drugs. Heroin, cocaine – I don't know exactly but something bad. I wish I hadn't seen it. I don't know what made me follow him into the barn in the first place – nosiness, I suppose. But I did see it and I'm nearly certain what it was.'

I glanced over at Addolorata, perhaps hoping she'd have some other explanation but she shook her head. 'You have to remember things are different here,' she said gently. 'Corruption and crime are a way of life in places like this. It's the system ... how everything works.'

I felt very cold then, even though the breeze that was coming through the open window was a warm one. 'What are we going to do?' I asked. 'Should we call the police?'

Addolorata didn't seem sure. 'People like this are dangerous and the corruption taints everyone ... maybe even the police, for all we know,' she said. 'I think it would be safer not to get involved. We're leaving this week, after all.'

Lou looked devastated. 'But what about Enzo ... and Gianpaolo? Are we just not supposed to see them again?'

Toni gave a dry little laugh. 'You're incredible, aren't you? They've got a barn full of drugs and all you can think of is your love life.'

It was Addolorata who made an effort to calm things down. 'We're all shocked and upset,' she said reasonably, 'but there's no point in fighting and falling out. Let's take a moment to think about what we should do.'

Toni laughed again, a harsher sound. 'You can take as long as you like, it's not going to change anything. I've done it already.'

'What do you mean?' I asked.

'The police know. That's where I went while you were resting. I made a call from the pay phone down near the marina. I didn't give them my name but I told them everything else.'

'What did they say?' Addolorata asked. 'Did they believe you?'

'Yes, I think so. They wanted to send someone over to question us and that's when I hung up. Like you said, we don't know who to trust here. But when I gave them Enzo's name they knew exactly who I meant.'

For a moment no one spoke. It seemed impossible to find any words worth saying.

'I want to go home,' I managed at last.

'We will, in a few days' time,' Addolorata reassured me.

'Yes, but I want to go right now.'

'It's late, the trains won't be running. And don't you want to see Enzo? To at least say goodbye to him? He told Toni the drugs have nothing to do with his family. That might be true.'

'No.' I was adamant. 'I don't want to see him. I want to pack up my things and get the first train in the morning. You can come with me if you like ... or stay ... I don't care.'

Folding up my clothes and piling them into my suitcase, I heard the others arguing. Addolorata was furious with Toni for not speaking to us before she called the police. Lou was angry too. It sounded like they were both ganging up on her.

As for me, I didn't feel angry, only cheated and sad. I'd let myself believe in Enzo, trusted the face he showed me. But it turned out that just like everyone else he wasn't what he seemed. All his tenderness and charm had been nothing but surface gloss. Beneath it his life was a messy, damaged thing exactly like my own.

All I wanted was to run away from him and from my friends whose raised voices still echoed from the next room. Falling back into bed, I put my hands over my ears, muffling the sound of them. I tried to imagine myself at home; my head on my own pillow and the hum of London's traffic the only sound I could hear. I thought about burrowing as deep into my apartment as I could, drawing the blinds over the windows, ignoring anyone who knocked on the front door. Home felt like the only place I could be sure of anything.

EXTRACT FROM ADDOLORATA'S JOURNAL

I can't bear to write about any of this. It's all too horrible. I keep thinking about that family and what will happen if the police arrive. I know what they've done is wrong but today they welcomed us and I liked them all, I really did. I'm still struggling to believe they're not the people they seemed to be.

And I'm furious with Toni for not talking to us before she called the police. She might have given Rosie some warning. Couldn't she see how this would affect her? Poor Rosie, her heart must be breaking.

The Olive Estate

It was night by the time Enzo arrived home and at first the only noise seemed to be the singing of cicadas. But as he drew closer to the kitchen he heard women's voices and the sound of wailing.

He found his Nonna doubled-over in her seat, an apron thrown over her head to muffle the sound of her crying. Beside her, his mother wasn't trying to hide her grief, her sobs were lusty and wet, her face streaked with tears. Gathered round them were his sisters, tissues pressed to their faces, a chorus of crying.

The noise grew louder when they saw him. Enzo couldn't bear it. He begged them to say what had happened but his mother's sobs grew convulsive when she began to talk and his sisters were distraught at seeing her that way.

It was his Nonna who managed to speak. She pulled the apron from her face and tried to straighten in her seat. 'It's all my fault,' she told him, 'all of it.' And then she began to cry again.

For a while all Enzo could do was try to comfort them and only gradually did he manage to coax the story out. Concetta began it. She told him how the police cars had poured through the gates with lights flashing and sirens blaring. How their grandfather's head had fallen into his hands and how he had sat at the table beneath the roof of lemons and waited for them to come and find him.

When Concetta broke down and could talk no more his Nonna took up the story. Her voice sounded frail as she described the moment the handcuffs were snapped round the wrists of his grandfather and the rough way he was pushed into the police car. 'They took your father, too. Not to the local station either, somewhere else. That's all we know.'

Then his mother cried out, 'But who told them? Who can have known? We have been betrayed by someone.' And Enzo felt worse than he had ever believed it possible to feel.

Desperate to take some sort of action he found some milk and warmed it in a pan, persuading each of them to drink a little. 'There is nothing we can do tonight,' he reasoned. 'You must get some sleep. In the morning I will find a lawyer, contact the police, find out where they've been taken. But for now, all we can do is go to bed and wait.'

His Nonna couldn't be moved from her kitchen. She pushed away the glass of milk he offered and covered her face with her apron again. 'It's all my fault,' she repeated.

'How can it be?' Enzo asked. 'I don't understand.'

'If I'd allowed them to do what they wanted then none of this would have happened.' Her voice wavered, then cracked, and she began to cry again.

Enzo gave her a glass of brandy and she drank it like she was taking a breath.

'Nonna, I know about the boxes in the barn,' he said hesitantly, pouring out a little more brandy. 'I saw what was in them. But that's all I understand. You'll have to explain the rest to me.'

Somehow she managed to unravel the story. It took a while because it was a complex one and she was so ashamed of her own part in it. But he let her sip her brandy and held her other hand in his to stop it shaking.

'I did it for the olive oil,' she explained. 'I thought it was worth almost anything to keep it pure. But not this; never this.'

And then she told him about the visitor who had come one day to drink a glass of wine with his grandfather. He was one of the Calabrian men whose name people whispered with the most respect and fear. He headed a family that no one would cross if they could help it. And he had a proposal for them. He wanted to buy not just their olive oil but the Santi name.

'His plan was to dilute the oil with cheaper oils from other places – Spain, Turkey, Morocco – then sell it in our bottles beneath our labels so people would believe it was the very best quality.' Even now Enzo heard the fury ringing in his Nonna's voice. 'Your grandfather thought he might even be planning to mix in hazelnut oil so he could produce many, many more bottles and make a lot of money.'

'But why us? There are plenty of other farmers who grow olives. Why not take their oil?'

'Because our olive oil has a good reputation, fetches the best price. And selling it is a legal way to make money – a good way to hide cash you might be making from other things that are against the law.'

'So he had it all planned out,' Enzo said bitterly.

'Yes, yes, and your grandfather thought we would have to agree with it. It was me who refused. The pair of us had many arguments but I wouldn't back down. I was so sure there must be another way to keep this man happy without spoiling the oil.'

'And then what happened?' Enzo asked.

'He was very angry, of course. He threatened to burn our trees, to adulterate our oil, to destroy us. We took him very seriously because we knew he could do all these things if he chose to. And then one day your father went to see him and his attitude had changed. He didn't want our olive oil any more. He needed somewhere safe to store things – merchandise was the word he used. A safe place to hide this merchandise until the heat died down.'

'And you offered him the barn?'

'We had no choice. He threatened the most precious thing of all.'

'What do you mean?'

'He threatened you, Enzo. He stood and chatted while you poured off a bottle of olive oil for him one afternoon. And then he went back to your grandfather and talked about what a good boy you were and what a waste it would be if you drove too fast one day and misjudged a turn in the road, if your brakes were to fail and your car drive off a cliff and smash onto the rocks below. He told your grandfather to take great care, to look after you well. And he said that we'd best leave the barn doors open and see and hear nothing. So that's what we did.'

'Did any of you know what was in the boxes they stored there?'

His Nonna grimaced. 'We suspected. That's why your grandfather and I have barely been able to look at each other. The shame was so great. We tried to tell each other it was something harmless; fake designer bags and sunglasses, cigarettes even. But we knew what kind of business this man was involved in. All of us knew that.'

'And now?' Enzo asked. 'What can we do?'

She rubbed at her face with the coarse fabric of her apron. 'Now there is no hope at all. Someone has betrayed us like your mother said and we will pay the price.'

'Surely if we tell the police what happened …?'

'And name this man and his family? Tell them what we know? Testify against them? Better to take the blame and be in prison, I think.'

Enzo knew she was right. 'But they will die in there,' he said, despairing.

'Yes, and it is my fault. I should have let them take the olive oil.' His Nonna was beyond tears. 'I was so proud and now I have destroyed us all.'

Rosie

I threw away all the photographs I'd taken of Enzo, and the negatives too. The only one I'd allowed myself to keep was the shot Addolorata took of us together on the beach. I buried it in the very back of a drawer but I never forgot it was there.

It seemed the Villa Girls were well and truly finished. Everyone was still so angry with Toni, which seemed unfair really as none of it was her fault. She'd seen what she'd seen and what else could she have done? In her position the rest of us might have done the same.

We heard what happened afterwards thanks to Gianpaolo who wrote to Lou. He told her the police had raided the estate pretty much straight away and found the cartons exactly where Toni said they'd be. They were full of heroin, tons of it, worth a huge amount of money. And now Enzo's father and his grandfather were in prison waiting for their case to come to trial. Everyone thought it was bound to go badly. Drug trafficking was a serious crime and they'd been caught red-handed.

Mostly I tried not to think about Enzo, although sometimes, in the middle of the night, if I woke and couldn't get back to sleep, he'd sneak into my thoughts and I'd find myself wondering if he wished he'd never met me.

Every time I met up with Addolorata she insisted on defending him. She kept arguing that he might not have known the drugs were there, that perhaps he wasn't to blame. 'Remember how Toni said he looked really shocked when she found him there in the barn,' she reminded me one Sunday. 'He must have been just as horrified by what he'd found as she was.'

'Yeah, maybe.' I didn't want to hear it.

'Couldn't you at least send him a letter?'

My answer was the same as always: 'There's no point.'

I still felt so stupid, so angry with myself for trusting him and letting him close. I couldn't forgive him for not being worth it. There was no way I was going to change my mind.

That particular Sunday afternoon we were sitting in a coffee bar waiting for Lou to arrive. It was the first time the three of us had got together since Italy and I'd been dreading it because I knew exactly how the conversation would go.

'Why do you think there's no point in writing to him?' Addolorata pushed me.

'Because Enzo's not the person I thought he was.'

'None of us are.' She sounded exasperated. 'Surely you realise that?'

That's when Addolorata brought up the whole business of me stealing that sample bottle of Chanel No 5 from Liberty. She told me how shocked she'd been to discover I was a thief.

'But that was ages ago. I'd just lost my parents; was half-crazy,' I defended myself. 'I'm not a thief. That perfume is the only thing I've ever stolen in my life and I did it on the spur of the moment. It's hardly the same thing as a barn full of drugs.'

'Yes, but back then I thought it was how you acted all the time,' she told me. 'And it turns out that's not true at all – you're not the person I thought you were.'

'Fair enough. I agree you can't rely on first impressions. But still I don't understand what it's got to do with Enzo.' I was sick of raking the thing over. It only made it worse.

'I feel sorry for him,' Addolorata insisted. 'I'm sure he wasn't involved with whatever was going on. And now he's lost everything – even you.'

'He's hardly going to want to hear from me,' I reasoned. 'He must know one of us called the police. He'd hate us for that surely? And anyway, it was a holiday romance. It would have ended one way or another. It's shitty that it had to be like this but there's nothing to be done about it now.'

When Lou turned up she was carrying a large envelope stuffed full with photocopied newspaper clippings that Toni had sent her. She tipped them out and spread them over the table. 'I read some of these while I was at work today. They're all about drug trafficking in Italy. It's a huge problem, apparently. There are whole families of gangsters involved, like *The Godfather* or something ... only real life.'

'*Real life* ... you mean Enzo's life,' I said quietly.

'Yes, I guess so. Even Gianpaolo seems amazed. He told me he'd never have imagined they were involved in something like that.'

Addolorata was looking through the clippings, speed-reading bits and pieces from them as she went. 'Toni must have spent ages researching all this,' she remarked, 'and spent a fortune on photocopying as well.'

Reaching over, I took one of the shorter articles. 'I suppose she wants to prove she did the right thing, that the Santi family are criminals and they deserve what they got. This must be Toni's way of defending herself.'

The clippings made depressing reading. It turned out the gangsters, who called themselves the 'Ndrangheta, were involved with all sorts of horrible things. I didn't want to believe Enzo's family were a part of it. But then I remembered the flashy car he drove so casually, the reach of the estate, the big house with every floor furnished expensively. How could something as simple as olive oil have paid for all that?

Randomly I pulled out another article and read about how tight the families were. How the younger boys were trained up by their fathers to become 'men of honour'. And I thought about Enzo ... and it made me feel sick.

'Toni did the right thing,' I said. 'She couldn't have done anything else.'

'Yes, you're right,' Lou agreed. 'These people are evil, no matter how welcoming they may have seemed. At least now they're under lock and key.'

'Can we stop thinking about it now … and talking about it?' I pleaded, tossing the clippings at her. 'I can't stand it any more.'

That night when I got home I pulled out the picture of Enzo and me that I'd hidden in my bedside drawer. There was no need to take another look because I remembered every detail – his smile, the way my arm was tucked through his as though we belonged, his friends in the background pulling stupid faces, the colour of the sand, the light on the sea.

I wished my memories had ended there, with this one perfect moment.

WHAT ADDOLORATA SAID

'I told my father about it. He reckons Enzo was involved, for sure. It's still difficult to believe because he seemed such a nice guy but I guess you can't ever know what people are like. So I'm sorry, Toni. You did the right thing. I shouldn't have given you such a hard time but I was upset for Rosie and I was still having trouble believing what you'd seen. I should have remembered that you never lie. Even Rosie said that. She was the one who defended you. Anyway, we've all agreed to stop talking about it. But I owed you an apology. That's why I called. So I'm sorry, OK?'

The Olive Estate

In the mornings Enzo liked to walk through the olive groves and pretend nothing had changed. Often he put on yesterday's clothes and slipped his bare feet into his boots in the hurry to get out, always heading first to the old grove where the trees continued to fruit, even though their boughs were hollowed and twisted and their branches rarely pruned. These trees were untouched by all that went on around them. Lives began and ended, wars were fought, money was made and squandered, people fell in and out of love, and throughout it all the trees endured. Surrounded by them, Enzo tried to find the strength to face the hours ahead.

Life on the estate now seemed an endless struggle. Each day grief squeezed more tears from his mother, and Enzo was forced to harden himself to the sound of her keening. His sisters, too, could waste hours with their heads in their hands despairing of what might become of them. Only Concetta, her belly a heavy burden now and the baby just weeks away, seemed to understand the need to carry on. Often he heard her raised voice as she urged someone to mop a floor or scour a dirty pan.

It was his Nonna who worried him the most, for her determination to show strength seemed to be breaking her. In the mornings he would find her in the kitchen, the coffee already made, bread baking in the oven. 'What must we do today, Enzo?' she would ask him. 'Tell me how I can help.'

He saw how much she trusted in him to be the head of the family and Enzo couldn't let her down. If the estate was lost he thought the blow might fell her. So when he wasn't sitting in the offices of lawyers and listening to their grim predictions, he spent his days at his grandfather's sturdy old desk sifting through paperwork and trying to understand how the Santi business was run.

Money was his greatest concern. The first thing Enzo did was sell his car and now when he left the estate it was behind the wheel of his father's battered old pick-up truck. Despite that, there were still piles of unpaid bills for him to worry about. He told no one how bad things were, not even Concetta.

Nor could he bring himself to admit his share of the guilt or to think too much about how he might have looked the other way, minded his own business. If he hadn't interfered those boxes would have disappeared from the barn just as all the others had. He had been warned and he'd chosen to ignore it. Now all he could do was fight to save what his family had left.

Some of the things he found shocked him: how they had been living beyond their means for years, raising mortgages to cover his father's gambling debts, shirking taxes so his grandfather could offer whichever of the village women he was flirting with some expensive little treat. Most men Enzo knew played cards for money or cheated on their wives, and yet to know they'd done it, and put so much at risk, filled him with bitterness and fury. They were locked away now, powerless ... useless. Only he was left to find a way to sort it out.

There were days when Enzo was convinced it couldn't be done but then he'd uncover something – a payment due to them, a bank account he hadn't known existed – and he'd allow himself to hope.

Already his memories of summer were bleaching away. Days at the beach, evenings beneath the statue, the night in Amalfi – it all felt like it had happened years ago to some other person. There was no time to waste dreaming about Rosie or missing her. A couple of days after the arrests, Enzo had managed to drive down to the apartment she'd been staying in but there had been no sign of anyone and he suspected they'd gone away early. Later Gianpaolo offered an address so he could write to her but he shook his head. He had nothing he could say in a letter.

It was friends like Gianpaolo who surprised him most as he struggled with the shame of what had happened to his family. He'd imagined they would shun him, turn their backs, but the opposite was true. Some were admiring, others excited, as though he had turned into a sort of celebrity. Catching sight of him on his way to see a banker or an accountant in Triento, people would call out for the latest news: 'Enzo, Enzo, is there a court date yet? What's happening with the police? Are they likely to confiscate your land?' Quickly he learnt it was better to stay silent. Even those he was close to could not be trusted entirely.

Each evening at six o'clock he poured himself a large glass of brandy and drank it down like medicine. It was cheap and rough, burning the back of his throat as he swallowed it, but it warmed him instantly, taking the edge off the day. A second glass made him feel he might more easily find the relief of sleep that night. A third and he became so drowsy he couldn't resist resting his head on the desk and closing his eyes.

That was how Concetta often found him when she came to fetch him for dinner. She'd touch his face gently with fingers that smelt of rubbed oregano and raw onions and whisper him back to consciousness. 'Come to eat and then go to bed and rest. Don't fall asleep here. Enzo, *caro*, you are drinking too much.'

'I'm fine. It's just a glass or two to relax me,' he'd mutter. 'Don't tell Nonna, though. Don't mention it to our mother. It will only give them one more thing to worry about.'

Tonight Concetta too seemed as though she needed a sip of something to restore her. She looked exhausted, her hair un-brushed, an unhealthy sheen of sweat on her upper lip, the skin around her eyes swollen and shadowed.

'It would be bad for the baby,' she told him when he offered her a glass of brandy, sinking heavily into the armchair his grandfather had used for afternoon naps, 'otherwise I would happily drain that bottle dry.'

'Has Mamma had a bad day?' he asked, trying to keep the drink out of his voice.

'We all have.' Concetta stared at him with sorry eyes.

'What is it? What's happened?'

She let out a hiss of breath. 'The last thing we need right now ... Emanuela has fallen pregnant.'

Enzo looked at the brandy bottle, longing to take another glass. His sister Emanuela had only just turned sixteen. She was too young for this and he was much too tired to deal with it.

'Who is the father? Will he marry her?' he asked as Concetta must have known he would.

'A local boy ... one of Ricardo's young cousins. But who among us will organise a wedding? Mamma isn't well enough and I have all this to deal with.' Concetta sighed again and gestured towards the belly she was carrying high and proud. 'Look at me, I can't cook a wedding feast in this state.'

'There's no money for a feast anyway,' Enzo told her. 'They must marry quietly. That's all we can afford.'

'What about the money promised to each of us? The dowry? Emanuela will at least get that?' Concetta asked the question sharply.

Slowly Enzo uncorked the bottle, unable to resist the urge to pour another finger of brandy. 'There's no money for a dowry either,' he admitted, knowing his sister would be angry. 'What little cash I can find must go to pay the lawyers.'

'But that money is her right,' Concetta insisted fiercely. 'Emanuela is expecting it. And without it the Russo family may refuse to let the boy marry her. Had you thought of that?'

'In that case, Emanuela will stay unmarried. It will be one more shame for the family but that can't be helped.'

'No! You have to find the money somewhere.'

Enzo drained his glass quickly. 'I'm sorry, but things have changed, Concetta. The old promises don't count any more.'

'So you are to take everything – the whole estate – and the rest of us get nothing? Is that how it is to be?'

Enzo decided it was time to show Concetta the columns of figures he'd spent days wrestling with, to explain how even if the next harvest went well there would still be many challenges to face.

'Business was not looking so good even before the arrests,' he told her. 'We were spending more than we made. And now all of us must make sacrifices if we're to save the estate.'

'Then perhaps we shouldn't try to save it,' his sister argued. 'There is an alternative, after all. We could sell.'

'No, never.'

'Just think about it, Enzo,' Concetta urged. 'If we sold the estate, the *oleificio*, the label and everything, then there would be money for lawyers' bills and hopefully enough left over for everyone to take a share. All of us could make a new start.'

'It would break Nonna's heart,' Enzo argued.

'Her heart is already broken … all our hearts are.'

'This land will never be sold,' he said stubbornly. 'It was passed on to us and it has to stay in the family.'

'I know that's what Nonna has always taught you.' Concetta's tone was gentler now. 'It's a noble idea, but as you said things have changed. It's time to think about selling.'

'No,' Enzo insisted.

'I'm going to talk to the others. Maybe we will take a vote.'

Enzo coughed out a dry laugh. 'A vote? You have no rights to vote, Concetta.'

'Oh, don't I? Well, maybe I'll find myself a lawyer too. Find out if I have any rights at all.'

'You got your dowry, didn't you? When you married Ricardo?' Enzo said it wearily. 'Why are you making such a fuss?'

'Because it's not fair. Surely you can see that?'

Concetta heaved herself out of the chair. He noticed her ankles were swollen and that she gripped her lower back as though it were aching.

'Maybe it isn't fair,' he called after her as she lumbered from the room, 'but the estate won't be sold. I'll do anything to stop that happening. Anything I have to do.'

Rosie

Three things happened during the weeks after we got back from Italy. The first was that I wrote to Toni. I'd never had a thing to do with her outside of our Villa Girls' trips and never warmed to her much, but now I wanted her to know that I didn't blame her for how it all ended in Italy. In reply I got a sad little note apologising for all sorts of slights and snubs, half of which had gone unnoticed, and ending with the hope that we could be friends.

The second thing was that I weighed myself for the first time in weeks. All those heaped bowls of pasta dusted down with parmesan, the ricotta-stuffed pastries and the extra tastes of this and that had taken their toll. I didn't feel much bigger but the needle on the scales had moved upwards and that was enough for me. All the joy went from eating again and I fell into the bad old patterns. There were careful days, when I felt in charge of everything I put in my mouth, and there were others when I'd lose control and binge on fast, wasteful calories, little treats I couldn't deny myself like sugary doughnuts from the bakery I passed on the way to work, chocolate bars stuffed with nougat and nuts, late-night rounds of toast dripping with butter. I seemed to feel either guilty or hungry pretty much most of the time.

The third thing that happened was all because of Beppi and as usual it started with an idea that we dismissed as crazy to begin with.

'I have decided it is time to make a Little Italy cookbook,' he announced one Sunday afternoon after he'd served us all a long lunch. It was the first time I'd been to the Martinelli house in ages and it felt comforting to be sitting at their dining table laid with its mismatched old crockery. There were chipped-looking dishes that had belonged to Beppi's mother, cutlery she had been given by her parents as a wedding present; even the frayed linen napkins had some sort of family connection. Everything was well used and just the way I expected it to be.

'A cookbook?' Catherine rolled her eyes. 'Can you never be happy with life the way it is? Must you always be coming up with these new ideas?'

'It's a very good idea,' Beppi defended himself.

Only Addolorata seemed intrigued. 'It could be really cool,' she agreed. 'The only thing is it might backfire on us. If we tell people how to make the dishes themselves, would they still feel the need to keep coming to the restaurant?'

'Most people don't actually cook from recipe books,' Beppi said knowledgeably. 'They like to read them, look at the pictures and dream about cooking. And even if they do try to make something, it won't be as good as mine. They will still want to eat at Little Italy.'

'But how would you even go about it?' asked Catherine. 'Will you contact a book publisher? Is there anyone who comes to the restaurant who might help or know someone?'

'A publisher?' Beppi raised his eyebrows. 'Of course not. I will do it myself, my own way, just as I have done everything else.'

'But that would be so hard,' she argued. 'Things like photography and printing are expensive. And then you'd have to come up with a way to sell it.'

Beppi sighed. 'Always you must look for the difficulties, cara.'

'Yes, well, I'm only saying.' Catherine looked hurt.

'Nobody would do anything at all if they worried about how hard it was going to be,' Beppi lectured her. 'And we do have some connections. There is Rosie … she could take the photographs.'

'No I couldn't.' I was horrified. 'Food photography is a specialist job. I don't have the equipment, the technical skills, or anything.'

'What about your friend Johnny?' Addolorata wondered. 'He's only an assistant, I know, but doesn't he shoot a lot of other stuff in his own time?'

'Yes, but he photographs things like street druggies shooting up and rock stars backstage—'

'And weddings, right?'

'That doesn't mean he can take decent photographs of food, though.'

'We could do some test shots, couldn't we?' Addolorata suggested. 'Why not try a few next Sunday when the restaurant is closed? Will you ask Johnny? Tell him he can eat everything once he's finished shooting it. That might help.'

I looked over at Beppi and saw that he was beaming. Rummaging in a drawer, he found some scraps of paper and started making lists of the best dishes to include. 'I will write up the story of how I met my wife, how I came here with nothing and made a big success,' he said rapturously. 'I will put in some of my mamma's recipes, *cucina povera* is what they call it now … pah. And I will include the first dishes we served in Little Italy, the customer favourites we never take from the menu, food I love to cook at home. Oh, and some of the photographs Rosie took in the restaurant … they must go in as well. It will be quite a big book, I think, but very good. People will love it.'

All of us knew how pointless it was to try to argue with Beppi when he was in this mood and so, as he busied himself wrapping up the leftovers he insisted I take home, I promised to talk to Johnny first thing in the morning.

What surprised me was that Johnny was enthusiastic from the get-go. I think perhaps he'd been feeling like he needed a new project. Over the following week we gathered all the cookbooks we could lay our hands on and spent our evenings sitting in my apartment going through them carefully. We marked the shots we liked and the ones we didn't, examining and analysing endlessly, criticising the tiniest flaws and trying to work out how things had been done.

'It's all about light and detail,' Johnny decided. 'And see how some things are obviously tricky. Red meat can look pretty awful. So can slow-cooked dishes. Roast chicken can look ... disturbing. But if you get the light right and good props – that's half the battle.'

'Do you think you could do it, though?'

He shrugged. 'It's worth a try, isn't it? We could have a go at some test shots, like your friend suggested.'

'*We?*' I asked dubiously.

'Well, yeah, she could cook, I'd take the photographs and you'd style it, obviously.'

The idea of being involved gave me a lift. I thought it might be fun. So I gave him Addolorata's number and at work the next day when Rob was out I overheard Johnny on the phone with her discussing what she might cook. After several more calls and hours of deliberating they settled on a pasta dish, a risotto, a soup and a salad, all of which seemed relatively easy.

Johnny took charge in a nervous, intense sort of way, issuing endless instructions. 'We'll shoot at your place because the light in your upstairs room is good,' he told me. 'We need to have a really big think about colours and textures and then we should go out on Saturday and look for props. I'd like to start early on the shoot day and try a few Polaroids without the food so I can really get a sense of the light and framing. Although the morning light will be a lot bluer than it is in the afternoon, which might be a problem ...'

'They're just test shots, you know,' I reminded him. 'They don't have to be perfect.'

'Yeah, but we want them to look good, right? There's no point otherwise.'

He took a risk and borrowed some extra equipment from the studio without asking Rob – a steadier tripod than the old one he used and a couple of newer lenses. We had to smuggle them out of the place, as we knew Rob would be furious if he found out.

Johnny's excitement was infectious and I found myself spending every spare moment tearing clippings from magazines for reference, even cooking a couple of similar dishes myself and practising different ways to arrange them on a plate. Afterwards I tipped everything into the bin so I wouldn't be tempted to binge on it. That was the main thing worrying me: that the food I styled might end up in my mouth and the needle on the scales would keep creeping upwards.

Addolorata had dissuaded Beppi from coming along to the shoot so it was just the three of us, downing strong coffee to jerk ourselves awake early on Sunday morning. Everything had been prepped as much as possible in the Little Italy kitchens but still Addolorata made a mess in mine, spraying chicken stock across my stove-top and somehow smearing roasted butternut squash over one wall. There was no time to stop and clean. We didn't want the food to be sitting around, the rice congealing, the pasta growing limp, and all before it was photographed.

Straight away I could see this was going to be even more complicated than we'd imagined. A plate of food that looked fine to the naked eye seemed all wrong when viewed through the camera. The tiniest gap between salad leaves could cause a shadow that loomed like a black hole. Or we'd shoot a Polaroid and then I'd notice a bug had torn a tiny hole in one piece of lettuce that was blighting the whole image. Almost always something had wilted or looked messy by the time we were ready. Meanwhile, Johnny was wondering whether the background was too dull or fretting about the light.

'I hadn't realised so much went into one simple photograph,' admitted Addolorata, watching him fussing with his light meter.

Still, there was something unexpectedly pleasurable about having to be so rigorous. Concentrating on one thing completely blocked everything else from my mind. I even stopped thinking about what I arranged on the plates as food. It became something else entirely – different elements, things to be made beautiful. It almost felt like I was painting with it.

By the end of the day we were all exhausted. 'Do you think Papa is trying to kill me,' Addolorata complained as she helped me clean up. 'Imagine doing a whole book if that's how long it took us to deal with four simple dishes.'

'Yes, but it would get easier, surely?' I said. 'And it's not like we'd have a deadline – we could just work away on it whenever we had time.'

'Yeah, I agree.' Johnny was busy cramming cold risotto and limp salad leaves into his mouth. 'Let's see how things look when I get this film developed and then maybe we'll talk about doing another session.'

I opened a bottle of red wine and the three of us sat and plotted how we thought the perfect cookbook would look. There were loads of things I'd never considered, like typography and page layout, and we knew we'd need professional help at some stage. But still it seemed like a thing we might be able to do.

'Let's be honest, we have to,' Addolorata sighed, dipping her fork into a container of leftover pappardelle sticky with osso bucco. 'Just imagine trying to tell my father we think it's going to be too hard ...'

WHAT ADDOLORATA SAID
'I feel terrible. Rosie and Johnny have been sacked for

borrowing gear without permission. I knew that guy they worked for was a complete prick, but really! It was only a tripod, apparently, and a couple of lenses. You'd think he could have turned a blind eye. So now they're both out of work and it's our fault. At least they have the book to start on. Papa says he'll pay them and hire whatever equipment they need. He's so over-excited about the whole thing he actually thinks things have worked out well because this way it will be finished sooner.'

The Olive Estate

This was the most difficult harvest Enzo had ever known. The family was divided, his sisters against him and his mother far too beaten by grief to help. Lately she had been acting as though the arrests had never happened, turning away and refusing to listen if anyone tried to talk to her about them. Once or twice, Enzo had caught her putting plates of leftover food in the oven to stay warm. 'Ready for your father when he gets home,' she had explained brightly. He hadn't the heart to remind her that her husband was eating prison food. Instead, he waited till she'd left the room before removing the meal from the oven. She would assume it had been eaten, that his father and his grandfather had come home hungry and enjoyed every mouthful, but to Enzo it seemed kinder to let her carry on believing it.

He did not remember ever feeling as alone as he did now. There was no help to be had from Concetta who had retreated to her apartment in the main house, spending her days nursing her baby boy and shutting her ears to Enzo's problems. 'I've told you what I think. We need to sell the place,' was all she ever said.

As for Emanuela, her mood had grown fouler as her pregnant belly swelled. Unmarried and disgraced, she would cook for the olive pickers this harvest only because she knew she must. Enzo didn't want to think about how the food might taste.

Only his Nonna seemed to be on his side. 'The trees are thriving,' she would encourage him whenever she managed to get out into the groves. 'There has been no fruit drop, no *mosca*. It rained a little when the pits were hardening and again in late summer but not so much that the oil will be tasteless. It will be a good harvest. I can feel it.'

Enzo hoped so, for this was exhausting work. He needed to be everywhere: in the groves making sure the fruit was picked properly, in the *oleificio* to see it pressed, in the office to deal with orders. His grandfather had seemed to spend every harvest doing very little but stroll round the estate spreading goodwill, but Enzo felt as though he hadn't smiled for days, maybe even weeks. All he could manage was to deal with the next problem and then the next, hoping somehow he'd get through it and that litres of the very best oil would be his reward.

This year, once they'd finished with their own crop, they would be pressing oil for their neighbours. His Nonna had compromised on that at least, although she was already fussing about how best to clean the press so that no hint of taint from a half-rotted olive would be left behind.

'Perhaps we should do it the old way and put lemons and oranges through the crusher once we've finished,' she suggested.

'Yes, Nonna,' Enzo agreed automatically. He was glad to see her more energised but there wasn't space in his head for one more problem.

There was no feeling of celebration this harvest, not even when all the fruit was picked and the pressing nearly completed. No pig had been killed to be roasted on the spit and the bottles of wine Enzo opened had been found dirty with cellar dust and long forgotten. It tasted sour and effervescent on the tongue but still it was alcohol and the best he could manage.

While the olive pickers were forcing down a few glasses, he took refuge in his office with his bottle of brandy. Skin burnt by the weather, his chin scarred by hasty shaving, his clothes unwashed, Enzo felt defeated. Up on the wall there was a photograph of him that his grandfather had always loved. It had been taken the day he'd turned twenty-one and was presented with the keys to his car. In the shot he was laughing as though there was no reason to ever do anything else and, looking at it now, Enzo remembered how happy he had been.

Unhooking the frame from the wall, he opened a drawer and pushed it inside, out of sight.

Rosie

It was Johnny who panicked the most about being fired. I'd never seen him so upset. He told me he was certain Rob was bad-mouthing him around the industry and no one else would hire him now. Since I was the one who'd encouraged him to borrow the gear in the first place, I felt pretty guilty.

Getting sacked wasn't so serious for me – it wasn't as though I'd been on any sort of career path. And I was pretty sure I'd find casual work in a shop or wine bar, just like Lou had when she'd chucked in her office job. She was always telling me how she made the same money with a lot less stress and hassle.

Johnny's mood changed when he picked up the contact sheets of our shoot from the lab. 'I think they're OK,' he said almost incredulously, staring at the images through a photographer's loop. 'Perhaps not professional enough to go in a cookbook, but we've got something to work with here. Bloody hell, we're brilliant!'

Feeling more buoyant now, he and I spent an entire morning going through the proofs, painstakingly picking out what was wrong and what had worked in every image until we'd edited down our final selection.

'If Beppi's prepared to pay for it then I reckon we should tackle the book,' Johnny suggested. 'It's ambitious and we might stuff it up, but I think I want to try it.'

We started making plans and putting things in place. Johnny was determined to shoot in natural light so we discussed turning my upstairs room into a makeshift studio.

Addolorata offered to take time off work to help with the food preparation and I began trawling the shops and making notes about props.

All of us were captivated with the idea of seeing our names on a book, although it was daunting to think about how much we had to achieve to get there.

'Let's take it step by step,' said Johnny. 'The important thing at this point is for Beppi to decide on the recipes so we can write up a proper shoot schedule.'

Inevitably Beppi was finding it impossible to narrow down his choices. He was in love with every dish he'd ever created and there were heated discussions in the kitchens of Little Italy that leaked over into our Sunday lunches.

'I have decided that no one needs a recipe for *Melanzane alla Parmigiana*,' Beppi would announce suddenly, looking agitated as he stirred the Napolitano sauce that was bubbling on the stove while flipping meatballs in a frying pan with the spatula in his other hand. '*Melanzane* is too easy. A child could make it.'

'But I keep telling you that's how we're going to organise the book.' Addolorata sounded exasperated. 'There'll be recipes from our home kitchen and food from Little Italy. And some of it has to be really simple. It just has to, OK.'

'If I put in the *Melanzane* will I be able to fit the *Vignarola*?' Beppi asked. 'It is the Roman dish, you know, with the fresh spring peas and violet artichokes. And what about my mamma's beautiful *Zuppa di Soffritto*? Everyone keeps saying there must be fewer recipes but then they won't let me take anything out. This is impossible.'

'The trouble is we're wasting time,' I pointed out, in what I hoped was a reasonable way. 'If we can't get on with this soon then Johnny and I will have to look for jobs instead.'

'I am not going to rush things.' Forgetting for a moment that I wasn't his own daughter, Beppi raised his voice.

'Don't shout at her, Papa, she's only saying we need some

decisions.' Addolorata pleaded. 'We're going round in circles right now.'

I glanced over at Pieta, whose head was bent over a Sunday newspaper as she tried to hide her smile. 'There's going to be a lot more shouting before this cookbook is finished,' she whispered to me when Beppi shot out the back door to fetch some rosemary from his garden.

Still, the delay turned out to be quite helpful. It gave Johnny a chance to pick up some tips from a couple of professional food photographers he'd contacted, and then Beppi discovered one of his regulars at Little Italy was a graphic designer and we got lots more good advice from him, too.

By the time we were ready to shoot, Beppi had relented and agreed to let us make the final selection of recipes because it was clear, even to him, that it would never happen otherwise. Without the same emotional connection to every single dish, it was fairly easy for us to be ruthless, and within an afternoon we'd put a final list together.

Bursting with plans and ideas, Johnny couldn't wait to start shooting. While I didn't love the idea of my apartment being taken over with gear and bags of food, I kept telling myself it would be worth it.

To begin with we worked slowly, making our share of mistakes, learning as we went along. Gradually I picked up little tricks – perking up a salad by misting it with water and oil, blasting a chicken breast with a heat gun to make it a perfect golden brown. I built up a collection of tools and grew used to spending my days tweaking at things with tweezers, wiping tiny spills with cotton buds or dabbing at the food with artist's paintbrushes.

If I fiddled for too long with a dish the others grew impatient but I was determined to make everything as close to perfect as possible. Quite early in the piece Johnny and I had a couple of spats when he started playing with the food, twitching salad leaves around and putting sprigs of parsley on top of everything, which I thought looked terrible. It surprised me how passionately I felt about it.

Those photo shoots were long and intense, and, by the end of each one, none of us could face eating the food we'd been staring at for hours. Knowing I would only throw it out, Addolorata took to packing up anything that was still edible and taking it down to a homeless shelter so it wouldn't be wasted.

The more we learnt the less satisfied we were and the harder it seemed to get a perfect shot. There were times I was in tears as I re-plated a dish over and over, convinced it would never be good enough. Although Addolorata never raised her voice, often I could tell how irritated she was by the stiff set of her shoulders.

Somehow we got through it. The recipes were typed out accurately, the images edited and the whole lot sent off to the graphic designer who was looking after the page layout. For a while after that I think we all felt quite bereft. The book had been the only thing we'd thought and talked about for so long we'd lost track of life outside of it.

'Now we'll have to get proper jobs.' Johnny sounded depressed about it.

'Why don't you see if you could find some more work doing food photography?' Addolorata said. 'You make a good team the pair of you.'

She was the one who suggested we call ourselves Goodheart & Wellbelove. She said with a name like that she was certain people wouldn't be able to resist giving us work.

Ironically it was our old boss Rob who helped us onto the first rung of the ladder. He'd called Johnny in a panic one morning because his new assistant had quit and he was desperate for last-minute help on a big job. Reluctantly, Johnny agreed and afterwards risked showing Rob a couple of the Polaroids from the Little Italy shoot. Grudgingly impressed, Rob did a deal with him – he'd put us in touch with a few publishing contacts if Johnny would help him out until he found a new assistant.

Work built slowly at first – the odd job for a kitchen store catalogue here, a calendar there. As our reputation spread, the phone rang more often. People loved being around Johnny, he made them laugh and always remembered the names of their children or cats so he could ask after them. Clients seemed happy with the pictures we shot, booked us again, recommended us to other people.

When the Little Italy book was printed all of us were so excited. Naturally I found a few errors and imperfections, and that frustrated me, but the feedback from Beppi's regulars was fantastic. I suspect he gave away as many copies as he sold but the important thing for me was people liked it.

'I am so proud of you, Rosie,' he told me with tears in his eyes. 'Of all of you.'

And as with every time I had a success or triumph, I missed my parents and regretted that they weren't there to be proud of me too.

The Little Italy book led to other bits and pieces and eventually we scored a regular job with a magazine whose food writer didn't do her own styling. Each month she faxed through her recipes and we made them look pretty for her.

Eventually we were hired for commercial work and I found that much more challenging. There were soul-destroying days spent gluing sesame seeds on burger buns or sorting through endless packets of breakfast cereal to create a bowl of perfectly shaped cornflakes. The upside was the commercial rates were higher and, when Johnny heard about a great studio in East London, it meant we could afford to rent it. By then I was sick of having my kitchen cupboards overloaded with oddments of crockery and my fridge stacked with food. It was a relief to get rid of it all and have the place to myself again.

I settled into our new studio as I had my apartment, finding perfect places for everything. It felt good being there. There were ups and downs – assignments I found tricky, days that seemed as though they would never end – it's the same in every job, I suppose. But as I was icing cupcakes to arrange on a vintage cake stand or drizzling runny honey over a stack of pancakes, it felt like I was in the right place.

Occasionally as the years went by there'd be nights when I came home to a dark, empty flat and wished there was someone to drink a glass of wine with me and talk about the day. I imagined telling Mum some little thing or sharing a tricky problem with my dad. I tried never to wish for Enzo, though. I put him away, slammed a door on him in my mind.

My life was so good now, why waste too much time thinking about the things that had gone wrong in it?

EXTRACT FROM ADDOLORATA'S JOURNAL

We all seem so sorted and busy these days. Lou's been made manager of a wine bar, Rosie's got her own business, Toni's training to be a journalist, and Eden and I seem pretty happy together at last. I wonder if we'll ever manage another Villa Girls' trip? It would be a shame to finish things the way we did. The four of us had some good times, after all. And there are so many places to go, so many villas. I'm thinking Ibiza next time; or maybe Tenerife, or somewhere in Greece … Yeah, I reckon one more Villa Girls' trip at least. We owe it to ourselves.

The Olive Estate

This was a good day. Orders had come in, clients who owed money had paid up and Enzo was away from his desk, deep in the olive grove, trimming branches left bare by an attack of peacock spot. As he worked, he tried not to think about what lay ahead, the wedding or the way his life might change afterwards.

There had been ups and downs over the years, many times when Enzo thought for sure he would lose everything and others when he wondered if anything was worth the toll this work was taking on him. Finally he decided there was a better way and he should take it. Late in the summer Maria Luisa Mancuso would become his wife. The pair of them would move into his parent's old room and her warm body would rest beside his every night for the rest of his life.

Enzo expected her to be a good wife. Already she'd shown she could cook a meal for twenty people. She was tender with his sisters' babies, patient with his mother, happy to listen to his Nonna for hours on end. And he was glad for all of it.

It didn't pay to think too much, to worry why, when he walked into a room, he never sought her out with his eyes; why he didn't watch her face for signs of how she might be feeling or welcome her interruptions. Enzo needed a wife and Maria Luisa a husband. It would be a perfect arrangement.

Into their marriage she would bring a good sum of money and a parcel of land that backed on to the Santi Estate. There was the promise of more when her parents had gone.

Just the thought of it took much of the weight from Enzo's shoulders. And yet ... the months of courting had been like lifting a lid on his memories of Rosie. Wherever they went he was reminded of some little thing; and kissing Maria Luisa, he'd felt second-hand. He was looking forward to their first night together about as much as he did pruning the olive trees or laying water pipes in the groves, as just another thing that had to be done.

His Nonna had been wary about the match. He had expected a squeal of delight when he broke the news, maybe even tears, but she'd held her face very still for a moment and then had asked, 'Are you sure, Enzo?'

'I thought you would be pleased.'

'I would be ... only I cannot see the love this time.'

'Love isn't a thing you can see,' Enzo argued.

'But I did see it. With you I did.'

'How did it look, then?' he'd said with a sigh, tired of humouring her.

His Nonna seemed thoughtful. 'When love was a new thing? As if you'd had too much brandy and you were trying not to show it. You were extra careful in every movement, in all that you said. But there were things that gave you away, your eyes, your face, a feverishness, an excitement. That summer with the English girl I could see your love ... but not this time.'

'It's different now. I am older, life is more serious and love has to be more for me than a fever, Nonna. Surely you must understand that?'

'I do understand. But if a sauce burns the tongue you don't add more *peperoncino*. Nor do you keep pouring salt into the pasta pot. There is already too much unhappiness in this family, Enzo. There is no need for you to look for more.'

'Maria Luisa will make me happy,' he'd insisted.

'Happy yes; but only because her money will prop up the business and you can add her land to ours.'

'And I'll sleep all night long instead of my worries waking me,' he'd thrown back angrily. 'I'll support you, Mamma, Emanuela and her daughter, my other sisters. I will have cash to pay the bribes that make sure my father gets wine and cigarettes in prison, my grandfather a more comfortable mattress to sleep on. All these things are much more important to me than love, Nonna.'

'And what about Maria Luisa? Does she know this is why she is to become a Santi?'

'She says she wants to marry me. Surely that's good enough?'

'Enzo, please promise me that you are not walking towards unhappiness,' his Nonna had begged him.

He had looked into her eyes and sworn a promise. It had been easy enough to do. Enzo had grown used to telling lies, to letting his father believe there was hope and they would appeal his sentence, to saying 'business is good, never better' to his grandfather, to denying he'd received an accountant's letter or exclaiming that surely he'd paid a lawyer's bill. It seemed to Enzo that he lied all the time. Last year, when the harvest had been disappointing, he had increased production by buying in another grower's olives to bulk out his own. 'Single-estate grown, pressed and bottled' the Santi label promised, and now even that was a lie.

Once he'd finished trimming the olive tree, he moved on to the next one. He would teach Maria Luisa to do this. She would learn to pick and press and prune. At harvest-time she would cook for the workers. They would have babies and she would raise them, she would tend to his mother, clean his house. She would be a good wife.

He tried not to think of what his Nonna had said as he worked on alone in the grove until the light had faded. This was a good day and there was the hope of more good days to come. He didn't need a woman's love to make them better.

Rosie

The Villa Girls' trips were what punctuated my life. They were bright spots in a galaxy of everydayness. Without them the years would have merged with each other, big unchanging chunks of time. How would I have measured it passing? By the way Johnny's quiff was smoothed away and his girlfriend pulled out her piercings and put away her leather pants? By the birthday parties or the bigger apartments and better jobs people got? None of those things made all that much difference to me. The Villa Girls' trips – and the photographs I took on them – were the way I made sure I had memories.

Not that I was unhappy, quite the opposite. I was consumed by my life, especially when Johnny and I had a run of big projects. What filled my mind were the images we were shooting, a snow of icing sugar sifted over a chocolate cake or a plum soufflé welling over the sides of its ramekin. I was amazingly unobservant about everything else; didn't notice the trees in St James's Park losing their leaves or budding and unfurling new ones; didn't see that Lou's drinking had become a problem or know that Addolorata and Eden had split until it was all sorted and they were back together again. I was obsessed with my work and I liked it that way.

The Villa Girls didn't see much of each other when we were in London by that stage. We were all caught up with other things. Toni had worked her way up to a job on a tabloid newspaper, Addolorata had made her father cut down his hours and was taking more responsibility in the restaurant, Lou was unreliable when she was drinking and solitary if she wasn't. It was only those trips we took that glued us together as a group.

After the disaster in Italy our next trip was to Ibiza and it was a riot. Finally we had all the bars and nightclubs we could handle. The following year we went to the South of France and then, a year later, back to Toni's aunt's place in Majorca. Some things were always the same – days at the beach, nights staring at the stars. But friendships changed and alliances shifted. The things we fought about were different. We were grown up now, getting older and changing our opinions. Addolorata had begun talking about marriage, Toni about promotion and Lou about AA meetings. Gathered round a table with them, in whatever place we were visiting, it amazed me we'd stayed friends at all.

'I told you we would,' Addolorata often repeated. 'I don't think we'll ever lose touch now – marriage, babies, whatever. We'll always be the Villa Girls.'

The one thing we hardly ever talked about was that time in Italy. Lou had lost touch with Gianpaolo so there were no updates from him. We didn't know what had happened to the Santi family; if there had been a trial or prison sentences handed down; if they were even living on the estate because Toni had heard talk of Mafia land confiscations. It was extraordinary to think we'd touched these people's lives and changed them – a reminder, if I'd needed it, of how much of everything hinged on chance.

It was chance that took us back to Italy in the end. I'd certainly never planned to return. First there was the realisation Lou was depressed and badly needed to escape London; then the offer of a place to rent that seemed too good to be true.

'Still, Italy? Are you sure?' asked Addolorata. 'Aren't there too many memories there?'

I shrugged my shoulders. 'I can't avoid an entire country because I had a bad love affair there.'

'Yes, but this place – the Villa Rosa – is only a little way down the coast from Triento. Not so far at all from where we were.'

It was Beppi who had heard about the house. It belonged to an artist who'd been eating at his restaurant for years and lived in southern Italy for part of each year. She told Beppi it was on the edge of the coast, painted pale pink and surrounded by pomegranate trees. She said it had the most amazing sky.

'It sounds wonderful,' said Lou wistfully. 'It's been years since we were there. I wouldn't mind seeing Gianpaolo again, finding out what has become of him. Most likely he has a wife and children by now, but you never know.'

'Let's go then,' I said and they all stared at me, wearing the concerned expressions I hated so much.

'But what about Enzo?'

'We probably won't even see him. And if we do then I don't care. I'm over him, have been for a long time. I wasn't properly in love with him anyway, just infatuated and stupid. If this Villa Rosa place sounds perfect and Lou wants to go then I'm fine with it.'

We were at Little Italy having a late-afternoon coffee together as the waiters were setting up around us. It was only the three of us – Toni hadn't been able to leave her desk – and we'd come out of concern for Lou who was refusing to take the anti-depressants her doctor had prescribed.

'They don't work. They just make life feel all muggy,' she kept insisting.

'Lots of other people take them, so they must do something,' Addolorata pointed out. 'Won't you give them a try at least?'

'I'm managing this my own way,' Lou said stubbornly, sipping alternately from a glass of Diet Coke and a strong black coffee. 'They hand out these pills like sweeties and I think it's ridiculous. We'll all end up medicated at this rate.'

'No one's saying you have to stay on them for ever,' I weighed into the argument. 'But perhaps you do need help. What if you can't do it by yourself?'

I'd been concerned when Lou had chucked in the receptionist's job she'd had for the past few months. She was living alone now in an awful bed-sit, surviving on her savings. It was an echo of myself years ago and it frightened me.

'I have got help,' she told us. 'There's AA meetings, my counsellor, you guys. It's a bad patch, that's all. Maybe I'll catch the train down to Cornwall, stay in a B&B for a few days, get some fresh air walking on the beach.'

'On your own?' Addolorata asked.

'Yes, why not?'

'I might have a better idea.' That's when Addolorata told us about the offer of Villa Rosa, how she'd discounted it at first because of how close it was to Triento and the fact it had been barely a year since our last trip. 'Still, if you want to get away at short notice it's the best thing I can think of,' she said. 'Better than a lonely B&B, that's for sure. Papa's friend barely wants any rent for it, which would be good because Eden and I are trying to save for a place of our own. And all of us should go, that's the whole point of being a Villa Girl, isn't it?'

It took some juggling of work commitments and strong-arming of Toni who was deep in the ongoing tell-all of a politician's mistress. She was dubious about Italy, too – producing the same old concerned expression, asking if I thought it was such a good idea.

'What if we come face to face with Enzo?' she wondered when we sprung the idea on her that weekend over dinner. 'How would that be?'

'It doesn't worry me,' I promised.

'We're the ones who exposed his family,' she mused. 'Chances are he'll still be furious.'

I respected Toni's opinion now. She'd become a person who knew things.

'Do you think it would be dangerous to go there after what happened?' I asked her.

'No, not dangerous. I'm sure nobody would do anything to us after all these years, even if they remembered us – we're not in a bad Hollywood movie. And there might be a story in the whole Mafia thing. To be honest, I'm a bit over the politician's mistress. I keep having to buy her shoes to make her divulge more secrets. And in the office they've taken to calling me Tell-All Toni. Time to move on to something weightier, I think.'

So I pulled out the suitcase I only ever used for trips like these and chose the clothes to put in it. As I packed my swimming costume, sarong and sunglasses, I found myself opening the drawer where I kept that old photo of Enzo and me. It was so long since I'd looked in there that it smelt musty and damp. Staring at the picture, I tried to conjure up some emotions.

There had been a few other men since Enzo – dates in restaurants and movie theatres, one or two I'd even brought home. They'd been nice enough but once they'd left I was always pleased to put fresh sheets on my bed and spread myself across them. Would it have been so much different with Enzo? I tried to remember why I'd believed myself in love with him but the feeling had disappeared completely.

EXTRACT FROM ADDOLORATA'S JOURNAL
If anyone had told me we'd be going back to Triento I'd have said they were completely crazy. I hope this house is worth it. And I hope it does help Lou a bit. I can't believe the state she's in. Although now I think of

it she's always been a bit of a mess. It's just everyone was always so concerned about Rosie we never paid Lou much attention.

The Olive Estate

Sundays were Enzo's escape. Without them he'd have rarely left the estate, not with so many chores that needed doing, with endless problems piling up. But once a week his Nonna demanded he put on his good suit, forget about work, and accompany the family to Mass.

'We must hold up our heads,' she insisted. 'Let people in this town know that we are not ashamed. After all, we are not the only ones who have family in prison.'

Once Mass was finished she always lingered outside the church, exchanging pleasantries, determined to put on a good show. All of Triento knew her husband and son were serving years in prison – for a long time it had been the thing that fuelled their gossip. Yet bright in her favourite red hat, her face beneath it as wrinkled as an old apple, she'd appeared at church every single Sunday until they found some another person's scandal more interesting than her own. Enzo admired her now more than ever.

When they returned from Mass there was a long family lunch just like the old days. Neighbours and friends were invited and good food served all afternoon: silky handkerchiefs of pasta covered in basil and pecorino, red peppers roasted with almonds, fat meatballs bristling with pine nuts, rabbit stewed with white wine and celery. Even his mother ate heartily, although she was still so easily upset everyone was careful what was said around her.

Always Enzo sat at the head of the table, easier now in his grandfather's old position, with Maria Luisa beside him rehearsing her role as his wife. When the meal was finished and she'd returned to her own family, he would drive back to Triento, to the bar on the corner of the piazza where his friends were happy to drink a few beers and entertain him with meaningless chatter. Ricardo, Gianpaolo and the others, all were married now, and eager to escape their homes for an hour or two. It was reassuring to listen to the hum of their conversation, the usual arguments about football and cars, the complaints about prices, the weather and their wives.

Always at some point they would ask Enzo the same questions: 'Have you been to the prison? How are they doing?'

And he would lie and say, 'They are fine, they are good', and change the subject.

In truth, every time he visited, his father looked years older and his grandfather more defeated. Enzo was paying out a small fortune in bribes to be sure they had some comforts and yet still prison life was destroying them both. His father longed for the olive groves, fretting about his trees despite Enzo's assurances they were flourishing, he worried about his wife and daughters, he blamed himself for his misfortune. And his grandfather talked despairingly of things like honour and pride, doubting he'd live to see his estate again.

It was a relief for Enzo to leave the place, the sadness and the smell of it. Being here in the bar, softened by a few beers, surrounded by men he had known since they were boys, was a consolation. All of them had changed in some way: Gianpaolo's hair was thinning, Ricardo had grown even stouter, their faces were beginning to line. And yet each Sunday as dusk fell, nibbling at a dish of olives, arguing about things that didn't matter, Enzo's life felt nearer to how it used to be.

Rosie

What I loved about Villa Rosa was that it wasn't perfect but it didn't much matter. The place had a blowsy sort of beauty. There were stains on the ceiling from a leak over winter, varnish peeling on the shutters where it had blistered in the sea breeze and the gardens, supposedly looked after by an old woman who lived next door, were untamed and self-seeding. But Villa Rosa suited its flaws. It wore them well. There was a charm to the wild tangle of bougainvillea and the faded ceramic tiles on the terrace when you saw them with other things: the mossy pots of geraniums beside the kitchen door, the overgrown groves of blossoming lemon and pomegranate trees, the cowbells clanking on the hill that rose behind us, the smoke from peasants' fires flavouring the air.

'I'm so glad we came,' Lou said. 'This place is fantastic.'

She had been fascinated by the paintings that were hung throughout the place. Most were of the sky, shifting in its mood from midday blue to evening pink, and we assumed they'd been painted by the woman who owned the villa and whose books, art and music were scattered about it.

From the moment we arrived we treated Lou as though she might break: Addolorata cooking her favourite foods, Toni taking her on long walks and me spending hours sitting with her on the rocks below the terraced gardens watching the waves crash hard again them.

'I hope the weather warms up and the sea calms down so we can swim,' I said on our second morning. By then I'd found the iron ladder that was meant to be fixed to the rocks so we could reach a natural pool surrounded by towering walls of rock, but even there the waves looked too wild to risk it.

'I prefer the sea like this,' Lou replied, staring down at the boiling mass of it. 'So powerful and destructive, exhilarating to watch.'

'Perhaps if it stays sunny we should bring our lunch down here later,' I said brightly. 'Turn it into a picnic. Would that be fun?'

Lou was silent for a moment, then she turned to look at me and her face was as bleak as the rocks we were sitting on and her eyes as hard. 'The trouble is nothing is fun any more.' She sounded matter-of-fact. 'Not without a drink in my hand.'

It was the first time she'd opened up to me and I searched for the right words to say. 'That will change though, won't it?' I managed. 'You'll get used to not drinking?'

'Maybe,' she said. 'But life seems so one-note now. Drinking was always how I celebrated and commiserated; it was my treat at the end of a really shitty day, it softened everything and relaxed me. I'm not sure I know how to do anything without it.'

'I guess you have to find a way.'

'I know that.' Lou smiled ruefully. 'I've got to be successful at something, right? Even if it's only being sober.'

'You're so hard on yourself.'

'But it's true – I've failed at everything.' Lou sounded angry now. 'I haven't got a man or a career, not even a decent place to live. I haven't managed any of the things I always said I wanted.'

'It's not too late though, is it? We all have setbacks and disappointments; none of us gets through life without something bad happening along the way – you've just got to keep going.'

Lou was staring out at the horizon now. 'I don't know about that, Rosie,' she said. 'You lost your parents when you were still a kid, then you fell for a guy who turned out to be some sort of gangster. You've had hard knocks but you've coped. In comparison, I've had a dream run and still I don't seem equipped to deal with it.'

'Perhaps I haven't coped as well as you think,' I admitted. 'We all have our crutches, things we lean on.'

Lou swung round to look at me again. 'Oh yeah, so what are yours?' She sounded disbelieving.

'Food,' I answered honestly, surprising myself. 'I either eat too much of it or eat too little. It's all tied in with how I feel and what's happening. Sometimes I think I've got it under control but then I'll find myself at the fridge just before bedtime stuffing down a bowl of leftover pasta I was saving for the next day's lunch.'

'I didn't realise ... I've never noticed.'

'That's because I'm careful when other people are around,' I admitted.

'You're not anorexic, though? Or one of those people who make themselves sick?'

'It's not that extreme ... but still, it's not right. And I don't think I'm so unusual, actually. Addolorata is a bit the same.'

'But you're a food stylist.' Lou seemed confused. 'Why choose work like that if you can't control your eating?'

'When I'm working with food, I never want to eat. It becomes another thing entirely, something to mould, make perfect,' I explained. 'There've been times when I've spent a whole day cooking delicious things, then given it all to Johnny to take home and had a packet of crisps and a Mars Bar for dinner.'

It shocked me, how much I'd revealed to her. For years I'd been so good at being secretive, only ever showing pieces of myself, keeping the worst parts hidden. No one knew how I felt about food or that sometimes on empty weekends I still hid in my house too depressed to move. I didn't bore them with my bad days. But I'd wanted Lou to understand we weren't so different, she and I. Looking at her sitting there, knees pulled to her chest, chin buried in her scarf, I wasn't sure I'd been convincing.

We stayed a while longer, although the rocks made for a rough resting place and the wind had picked up and was blowing our hair round our faces, driving the waves more fiercely towards us and feathering the clouds across the sky.

'I've always admired you, you know,' Lou said at last. 'I thought you were so independent and brave. So sorted.'

'And the truth is I'm no more sorted than anyone else.'

'You've got a career, your own apartment.'

I gave a wry laugh. 'I'll tell you something about that apartment. I only have it thanks to a psychic. I went to see one because I was in such a state after my parents died and she told me to buy it.'

'A psychic, you?' Lou sounded amazed.

'For a while I even let myself believe she'd contacted my parents in the spirit world. It made me feel a bit better.'

'What else did she tell you?'

'Oh, that my parents loved me, predictable things. Still, it helped me at the time, crazy though it was.'

'You seem the least likely person to listen to a psychic.'

'Yes, but I'm not what I seem, not at all,' I told her. 'Addolorata once said that to me and she was right. It turns out none of us are.'

Perhaps it was only the wind making Lou's eyes water. She rubbed at her face with the end of her scarf as we stood and picked our way across the rock pools and back up the steps that led to Villa Rosa's terraced gardens. I could hear the old Italian woman from next door singing as she swept a pathway somewhere up ahead and above us in the trees pine martens were springing from branch to branch. I remembered

264

how hard it was to be unhappy when everything around you was beautiful and bathed in sunshine. How it was almost an affront, an extra unfairness in a way, that the outside world didn't look as ugly as the way you felt inside. I hoped being here didn't end up making thing worse for Lou. Or for any of us.

ADDOLORATA'S POSTCARD HOME

This is the best villa ever. So far no sightings of Enzo and his friends, although we've been keeping clear of places they might be. I keep expecting to see them round every corner. Slightly scary really. Still, it's beautiful here. Worth the risk! Love to all – Ax

The Olive Estate

Enzo wondered if the drink had made him stupid. He'd downed several beers and a brandy in the bar. Now he and Ricardo were in the pizzeria that lay down one of Triento's narrowest lanes, sharing a carafe of wine as they waited for their food. The familiar warm, relaxed feeling had come over him and his hand began to wobble, spilling a little of the Chianti.

'Careful, don't waste that,' Ricardo told him. 'I'll drink it if you don't want to.'

And then Enzo looked over towards the doorway and the glass fell clean out of his hand, shattering on the floor in a puddle of wine. He didn't see the patron of the pizzeria scowling nor was he aware of the waitress down on her hands and knees beside him, clearing up the mess. All his attention was on the woman who had just walked in, blonder and slighter than her friends, older than when he had last seen her, but still so much the way he remembered her.

Rosie hadn't noticed him yet. The light on her face was yellow and warm; she was smiling and looking pleased to be out of the chill breeze of Triento's early spring, breathing the smell of melting buffalo mozzarella and baking basil. Enzo wondered why she had come back.

And then he saw the others: Lou who had cut her hair short and was wearing flat-heeled shoes and sober clothes, Toni who seemed thinner and sharper, Addolorata a little rounder than before. The waitress came to his table with their plates of pizza, blocking them from view, and when he looked again they were sitting near the door, Rosie in profile to him, opening up her menu and filling her water glass. He tried not to stare, to make it too obvious, but the sight of the four of them was a shock.

Fearing Ricardo might notice something was off key, he struggled to act as normal, bending his head over his plate and forcing in small mouthfuls of his pizza, barely tasting the saltiness of the anchovies or the vinegary bite of capers. When he thought it was safe he risked another look at the four English women, certain they remained unaware of him. Rosie was looking over towards Lucio Ricci as he stood behind the counter making pizza, stretching the dough showily between his fingers. She still seemed like the outsider of the group, holding herself slightly apart just as she had before. Her fair hair hung down her back in the style she'd always worn it. Her smile was hesitant but when it came it changed everything. Enzo wondered if she would still smell the same way, as fresh and grassy as olive oil.

He'd never expected to see her again, never practised the words he would say or imagined how it might be. Enzo was bewildered. Trapped here in the far corner of the pizzeria, he couldn't leave without being seen. Ricardo had almost finished his food and soon they would be calling for the bill. He tried to think how best to behave but his mind wouldn't work properly.

'More wine?' he asked Ricardo, hoping for extra time. 'Shall I get another carafe?'

His brother-in-law shook his head regretfully. 'Concetta will kill me if I come home drunk. With this pregnancy she is even more bad-tempered than with the last two. They change when you marry them, eh? You'll find that out soon enough, I expect.'

For a moment Enzo's mind was blank and he wondered what Ricardo meant. Then he remembered the plans he'd made to join his life to Maria Luisa's. How cruel that Rosie should reappear now, of all times, a reminder of all the things that hadn't happened for him.

There was a tremor in Enzo's hands as he pulled out his wallet and tossed some money on the table. Standing to go, he forced himself not to glance towards the table by the door. He was certain they had seen him, though, could feel their eyes on him. One moment they had been laughing, the next they'd fallen silent and he knew they were staring in his direction.

Glancing up, he met Rosie's eyes. For a moment both were still and wordless, searching each other's faces, and then she turned, putting her hand over her mouth, and Enzo thought she seemed upset.

Edging round the tables, moving towards the door, he tried to catch her eye but she refused to look back. It was Toni who was staring now, coldly and boldly, sizing him up. She said something to the others and then put down her wineglass and, springing from her chair, followed him and Ricardo out of the pizzeria.

Enzo picked up his pace, but he heard her footsteps echoing behind them as she broke into a run. His face darkening into a frown, he turned to meet her.

Rosie

At first I'd avoided the bars down by the marina and only braved Triento on market days when we had to shop for food. There seemed no need to venture far; the Villa Rosa was so pretty, the weather warming up a little and all of us perfectly happy to pass a few lazy days there.

'Perhaps it's better for me not to see Gianpaolo,' Lou had decided. 'He'll only have changed, be old and fat probably. I'd rather remember him how he was ... and for him to think of me like I was back then too.'

Eventually we grew restless and more confident. There'd been no sign of Enzo or any of his friends when we'd visited the town. The only people we'd recognised were the butcher, still leaning idly in his doorway as he always had, the woman in the café still serving the same pastries and the traffic officer blowing on the whistle she wore round her neck with the same furious energy.

On the Sunday night when none of us could be bothered to cook food or deal with dirty dishes, Addolorata suggested we see whether there was still a pizzeria tucked away in one of the back alleys. We were tempted by the thought of a perfect wheel of it, blackened in places from the wood-fired oven, bubbling with buffalo mozzarella, crisped with prosciutto and singing with the flavour of Italian tomatoes. The smell when we walked in was encouraging. We were certain we were going to be served the most divine pizza we'd ever tasted.

Afterwards Toni told me she spotted Enzo right away

but managed not to show it while she tried to decide how best to act and what to say. I wish she'd thought to warn me because, when I looked up and saw him, I panicked so much I felt the pizza I'd just swallowed rise in my throat and feared I was going to be sick. I hadn't expected to react like that, had been so certain I'd stay calm and detached if I did bump into him. So many years had passed and I'd convinced myself that there had been so little between us in the first place.

When Enzo and his friend got up from their table, and made to leave, Toni stood to follow them. 'Stay there; I'll just be a minute,' she hissed and before I knew it she was heading out the door and down the lane towards the piazza.

'Shit,' was all Addolorata managed to say.

'We shouldn't have come. How stupid.' Lou rested a hand over mine. 'Rosie, are you OK?'

I shook my head, still too astonished at myself to speak.

Within a few minutes Toni was back at the table, her face flushed and her breath quickened.

'What did you say to him?' Addolorata asked.

'I asked if he was really Mafia. If he'd give me an interview, tell me his story.'

'You didn't.' Addolorata sounded shocked.

'I'm a newspaper journalist,' she said brazenly, 'that's what I do.'

'And what did he say?'

Toni flushed again. 'That I shouldn't go round asking people questions like that. He said it was dangerous. Told me to be careful.'

'And then?'

'Him and that fat guy he was with started walking off.'

I realised I'd been holding my breath. 'And was that it?' I asked. 'Was that the end of it?'

Toni looked at me. 'No, I went after them. I wanted to tell Enzo it was me who'd reported his family to the police, that you weren't to blame at all. But he wasn't prepared to listen.'

'Did he say anything else?'

'He was angry that I'd followed, gave me a look that made me think it would have been better not to. He said we should leave him alone to get on with his life and he sounded like he meant it.'

None of us could eat after that. The guy who ran the place made a big fuss, insisting on making up little packets of pizza for us to take away, wrapping them in greaseproof paper and tying them with string. Good-looking and flirtatious, he must have wondered why we were so immune to his charms.

We were subdued as Addolorata drove us back along the coast road, the sweet smell of baked pizza filling the rental car. 'Do you want to leave?' she asked as we neared the Villa Rosa. 'I could find out about trains and stuff in the morning.'

'No, we should stay here,' I told her. 'We've seen him now. It's over and we can stop worrying about it. Let's just carry on having a nice holiday like we were before.'

Toni agreed. 'He was in such a hurry to get away I don't think he'll be bothering us. But still, we'd all understand if you changed your mind, you know, Rosie. Don't feel bad if you do.'

At the house someone had switched on the outside lamps and as we drove through the gates it looked so welcoming. On the doorstep was a gift – a basket filled with vegetables: artichokes, asparagus, fat pods of fava beans. Villa Rosa felt like it had been waiting for us.

I thought about Enzo as I lay down to sleep that night. I wanted to imagine what he might be thinking and feeling but he'd seemed so strange, so different to the boy I'd known, that my mind refused to stretch that far however hard I tried to make it.

I can't quite believe how cool Rosie is being about all this. She seems fine about staying here, hasn't even seemed worried about going back up to Triento or down to the marina. It's almost like she wants to see Enzo again and have a chance to speak to him. Maybe that's it, perhaps she really does. But we haven't spotted him since that night in the pizzeria. We all got such a shock then. There was one moment when I thought he was going to stop and speak to us but I think he must have changed his mind. And Toni didn't exactly help the situation ... but then she never does.

I feel really odd about it; like it can't end like this, like something's going to happen. It's got to.

The Olive Estate

Enzo tried to imagine what she'd been about to say, the little sharp-faced one – Toni. He hadn't allowed her to speak, for Ricardo was already so curious and there were questions it was better not to answer.

He'd made some excuse to his brother-in-law, muttering darkly about journalists being a nuisance and later, back at the estate, had shut himself in his office and opened a bottle of brandy. He'd spent the night at his desk, sleepless and drinking, replaying the scene in his mind and imagining other ways he might have handled it. By dawn he had talked some sense into himself.

What he'd thought about were all the times it had seemed easier to give up; how it was only looking towards his Nonna, seeing how bravely she faced each day, that made him resolve to carry on. He reminded himself how the life he'd made had been hard won, how he'd built it from scratch, carefully and patiently, how by the end of the summer Maria Luisa Mancuso would be sharing it with him and then at last his future might be secure.

He was certain they understood each other, she and him. They came from the same world and all their lives had carried the same expectations. Between them there were only good things: fondness, respect. He hoped this was an arrangement that suited them both.

Enzo knew more troubles lay ahead for him. When his father and his grandfather were released from prison, they would come home changed men. He would have to care for them as he did for the rest – he would cope the way he always had, planning the next week and the next month, never looking too far ahead. Most likely he'd make more compromises, tell more lies, do whatever was necessary. He had saved the Santi Estate so many times over the years and it belonged to him now. He wasn't going to put it at risk.

The encounter with his past right there in the middle of the pizzeria had been disturbing. It had made Enzo think about the easy old days when the scrawled contents of his grandfather's ledgers were a mystery to him and a heavy fall of rain as the olive flowers were setting was his father's problem. The person he'd been then; so sure of himself and so stupid. What had Rosie seen in him? Perhaps she'd only wanted the promise of good times, of drives to beaches and bars in his beautiful car. He no longer had those things to offer.

Enzo knew what he must do. He would cancel Rosie from his mind, let go of the last shreds of memories he'd held onto for too long. The night in Amalfi, the endless, breathless kissing up by the statue – he'd talked about it to no one and was determined now to stop thinking of it.

He thought again of what he'd achieved and how he'd been forced to harden to manage it. Now he must harden once more, there was too much at stake to do anything else.

When the sky was marbled with light Enzo sluiced cold water on his face and backed his old truck out of the barn. It was a slow trip down to the port and the thing rolled like a pig in the corners, but it got him there in the end.

He found Gianpaolo's fishing boat moored at the far end of the marina and his friend onboard, toolbox open, hard at work already with his sander. When Enzo whistled loudly, the sanding stopped.

'*Salve, amico*!' His old friend smiled when he saw him. 'What do you think? She needs a bit of work but she's not too bad, eh?'

Enzo tapped at the side of the boat with his toe as though he was testing the strength of it. 'Why do you think boats are always female?' he asked curiously.

Gianpaolo laughed. 'They say it's because they're just as precious to us as our wives ... and just as high maintenance, too. Have you come to help me?'

Climbing over the rail, Enzo took the sander from him. 'For a couple of hours but then I have to get back.'

They worked side by side, the growl of the sander too insistent to bother trying to talk above it. Enzo knew Gianpaolo had saved for years to buy this boat and, once it was seaworthy, there would be more work and saving in store. He had married the daughter of another fisherman and together they lived in one of the tall, shuttered houses above the marina, a stone's throw from the place where he'd grown up. He seemed content with the way his life had turned out. When Enzo told him of his plans to marry Maria Luisa he only laughed and said, 'So it all paid off for Signora Mancuso in the end, then? I always wondered if it would.'

Before Enzo drove home they stopped for an espresso in the same bar where they always used to meet, standing at the counter and drinking it down fast.

'I saw some old friends up in the village last night,' Enzo remarked lightly. 'It was quite a surprise.'

'Oh yes, what old friends?'

'The English girls. Remember? The ones we met here years ago. They're back for some reason, having another holiday.'

'What all of them?'

'Yes, all four.'

Gianpaolo laughed. 'I wrote to her for a couple of years, you know, that girl Lou. I liked her. But then I stopped ... there didn't seem much point in carrying on. And eventually she stopped too.'

'She looked different, older,' Enzo said.

'I suppose we all do.' Gianpaolo pushed away his empty coffee cup. 'Still, I had a good time with her that summer. I had my fun.'

Rosie

Everywhere we went I looked for Enzo, expecting to see him standing out from the crowd as he always had. But we didn't find him in any of the old places, the cafés or the beaches, nor up at the statue or down at the marina. The others seemed relieved, even Toni gave up on the idea of her Mafia exclusive. As for me, the shock of our sudden meeting had eased and I was left with the memory of his face, the way he'd looked at me. I asked myself what I felt and the truth was only sadness. Whoever he was, whatever he'd done, I'd cared for Enzo once. Now I knew what I wanted most, a chance to speak to him, to see if I could put things right between us, to tidy up my past and make a proper ending.

Since I'd never managed to learn to drive, I had to get Lou to take me there. We woke early, took the rental car without telling the others and, map in hand, I directed her down roads neither of us remembered and made her drop me outside the tall iron gates of the Santi Estate.

'Are you sure about this?' Lou asked. 'How will you get back to the villa?'

'I'll find a way. Don't worry about it,' I said.

'I don't mind waiting here for you.'

I shook my head. 'I don't know how long this is going to take and the others might be worried. Better you go back. I'm sure they'll let me use the phone to call a taxi.'

Lou looked so anxious driving away that I waited there, standing and waving until she was well out of sight. Then I took a couple of deep breaths and turned towards the estate. It was as grand as ever, its gates free of rust, hinges so well oiled they swung open without creaking. Curving beyond them was the gravel driveway, the lawns on each side recently mown, and the olive trees marching away in long rows, as impressive as ever. The whole estate reeked of money just as it had the first time I saw it. Steeling myself, I started walking.

The first person I met was Enzo's old Nonna. She was hoeing the ground in her vegetable garden, dressed from head to toe in black, that strange silver spoon still hanging from a chain around her neck. I hesitated for a moment, concerned about her recognising me, worrying she might shout or even spit. Instead she looked up and, after what seemed like a moment of disbelief, I saw a smile begin to spread very slowly across her face.

Putting down her hoe, she called out a mild '*Ciao, signorina*', and spoke a few Italian words I didn't understand. In my memory she'd been stooped, grey-haired and wrinkled so I couldn't tell how much she'd aged but I did know for sure that she realised who I was. The intelligence in those keen old eyes was far too bright to miss.

She raised her voice, calling out for her grandson. '*Enzo, Enzo, vieni qua.*' and I was almost sick with nerves again. I think she might have suspected how I felt. Taking my hand, she squeezed it surprisingly hard in hers, as if to reassure me. Then she pointed towards the olive groves that stretched away behind the barns.

Enzo was up there amongst the trees, frowning at something he could see. He looked over as we approached, squinting at us from beneath the old straw hat he wore. I thought I saw the beginnings of a smile on his face but by the time I grew closer his expression was serious again.

'Peacock spot,' he said in a weary-sounding voice, showing me the blotchy yellowed leaves. 'It has been a wet spring.'

Standing this close to him, my hand still locked inside

the old woman's, felt surreal. 'Peacock spot?' I repeated stupidly. 'Is that bad? Will it kill the tree?'

Enzo shook his head. 'We will treat it with some spray and hope the fungus doesn't spread too far. But still some of the leaves will fall and the tree will not crop so well this year.'

'You have so many trees,' I said, staying on the safe ground he'd provided for me. 'Thousands?'

'Tens of thousands. And many different varieties – coratina, frantoio, leccino, pendolino and my Nonna's favourite majatica.'

'They all look the same to me.'

He nodded as though that's what he'd expected. 'Why have you come here, Rosie?' he asked.

'Because I didn't want to leave Triento again without saying goodbye properly, without explaining things a little.' I hoped he'd understand.

'But it's been so many years; does it still matter?' His voice sounded harsh and I was certain he was going to ask me to leave.

Then his Nonna spoke again; barking a few short words that were enough to make Enzo sigh and reply, '*Va bene, va bene.*'

'What did your grandmother say?' I asked.

'She told me to take you for a walk through the groves, to talk to you.'

'And will you?' I asked, surprised.

'If it's what you want.'

I nodded. 'I've come because I want to understand what went wrong, why it all turned into such a mess. I know it happened years ago, that after today we'll never see each other again, but I realised when I saw you in that pizzeria that it does still matter … it does to me, anyway.'

Enzo walked us to the top of the hill, to a place where we

could turn and look back at the sweep and fall of the land and the scope of the trees that covered it.

'I was so overwhelmed the first time I came here,' I admitted. 'I couldn't believe how much your family owned. It terrified me.'

'Yes, we have a lot; but still we nearly lost it all.'

'Because of us?'

He shook his head. 'I blamed myself, never you or your friends. I was the one who went into the barn and opened the boxes, even though I'd been told to stay away from them. I was too curious. What happened later was my fault.'

'Will you tell me about it?'

He sighed heavily. 'There's so little to tell and yet so much.'

We talked for more than hour and gradually Enzo showed me beneath the surface of his life. It all seemed so plausible, the threats made and the compromises, the boxes stored for someone else and so many lives spoiled because of it.

'If only Toni hadn't seen them; if only she hadn't gone to the police.'

'I've said that to myself thousands of times.' Enzo stared down at the groves. 'Tens of thousands – more times than I have got trees. But that's what happened. Life changed the way it did and there was no going back.'

'It must have been so hard for you.'

'Life as an olive farmer is hard,' he responded, 'and uncertain, too. There are many things to worry about – fungus, bacteria, olive fly, things that make a tree rot from root to tip. If you worried about it all you'd never plant a single thing. But in the end the trees survive and so do we.'

This Enzo seemed so different from the boy he'd been, the gaiety had been pressed out of him and the arrogance too. I wanted to reach over and touch his arm, feel his skin beneath my fingers one last time. Instead, I kept on talking.

'I thought your family would hate me but, if anything,

your Nonna seemed pleased to see me. Does she not know what happened? Surely she suspected who reported you?'

'I never told them,' he admitted. 'At first there were too many other things to worry about and, anyway, I was angry with them all. Later it seemed it would only make things worse if they knew. My sisters and I were fighting, my mother wasn't doing well, my Nonna was killing herself to keep up with the work we needed to do. I didn't tell them because it wouldn't have helped or changed anything. All I could think about was saving the estate. It's been my whole life since then.'

'You must love it so much.'

'More than anything,' he agreed.

I remembered how Enzo had made me feel all those years ago: defenceless and yet cared for at the same time. He'd reminded me what it meant to be loved and I'd sensed the family in him. But I hadn't ever known him, not really, not properly. Now he'd shown me the unhappiness he wore, revealed the scarred parts of himself, and I liked him all the more for it.

'I'm glad we had this chance to talk,' I said. 'It makes for a better ending, doesn't it?'

Enzo looked at me as though he couldn't decide what to say. 'I'm to be married soon,' he managed at last. 'A local girl. Her name is Maria Luisa. I've known her all my life.'

'Congratulations.' My voice sounded over-bright.

'And you? You aren't married yet?' he asked.

I shook my head. 'No, still alone. I'm used to it. I'm happy.'

Enzo walked me down the hill more slowly than he needed to and drove me to Villa Rosa in an old flatbed truck with a rattly engine. We were silent on the way – there seemed nothing left to say.

'Have a good holiday,' he told me as he pulled up outside

the gates. 'And have a good life too, Rosie. Stay happy. I like to think of you that way.'

Unexpectedly, he leant over and brushed his lips across my cheek. Springing out of the old truck as though I'd been scalded, not daring to try my voice, I only managed to raise my hand to wave a goodbye.

WHAT ADDOLORATA SAID

'So you just drove off and left her there by the gates? But why did she even go in the first place? I don't understand? Why didn't she tell me? Do you think she really wanted to finish things properly? Or was she perhaps hoping for something more? God, Lou, what were you thinking?'

The Olive Estate

Enzo knew his Nonna was furious with him. He took to avoiding her as much as possible, for whenever they met, she felt the need to share what she was thinking, and he was worn down with her lectures. Not a word she said made a difference anyway. Enzo had opened his fingers and let the happiness slip through them. What else could he do?

Now he was turning to face his future. He'd visited a tailor and been measured for his wedding suit, he'd asked Gianpaolo to stand up as his best man, he'd traded olive oil for good red wine, he'd bought a case of champagne and stored it in the cellar. Tomorrow he would take Maria Luisa to a jewellery shop so they could choose gold bands to fit their fingers and he would try to stay patient as she wavered over invitations and bonbonnière or talked of nothing but flowers and place settings. Sometimes he wondered if she'd looked ahead beyond the wedding to the marriage that would follow – he trusted that she must have.

'You are making a mistake.' His Nonna had caught him unawares as he wandered through the olive groves. 'Why are you so stubborn? Why won't you listen?'

'I listened for years and years,' he told her, turning over the leaves of each tree he passed to check for more signs of peacock spot. 'I don't need to listen any more.'

His Nonna looked shocked and then angry. 'So you've given up on love,' she said, falling in beside him even though he had quickened his pace to escape her.

'No, I haven't given up,' he said impatiently. 'Love is my

whole family, our estate, these trees, my friends. Love is the one thing I have plenty of.'

'And what about the English girl who came? I saw her. I know what she wanted,' the old woman said shrewdly. 'Tell me you don't want the same.'

Enzo tried not to sigh. Looping round to face the house again, he walked back along another row, his Nonna at his heels. 'I think men must be very different to women,' he told her. 'We don't waste our time wishing for the one thing we can't have. We don't let our emotions rule us.'

She folded her arms across her chest. 'And you think that makes men better?'

'Not better, just different.'

'I think it makes men stupid,' she said fiercely. 'You think you understand love but you don't know what it is.'

'Perhaps you're right,' he conceded, slowing a little, for he'd realised she was getting breathless. 'I have no idea what it is that makes one man and one woman choose to love each other. Does anyone? Surely it's one of life's great mysteries. That's why so many songs and stories are written about it, because no one truly understands.'

His Nonna's face had softened as he spoke. 'I like it when you talk to me like this, as though you were a boy again,' she told him. 'Remember how we used to walk through the olive groves and tell each other all our hopes and dreams?'

'I remember, of course I do.'

'Those were happy days. I miss them.'

'I miss them too,' he admitted, stopping for a moment to let her catch her breath. 'But when I was a boy I had no idea life would be like this. I didn't know it was so busy and so hard. And now even if I had time for dreaming I wouldn't have the energy. Every part of me is taken up with doing all the things that must be done each day.'

'This is not what I wanted for you.' She said it sadly.

'I remember exactly what you said you wanted: for me to

grow up, find a wife, inherit the estate, look after it well and have a son to pass it to. You told me we were the guardians of the trees. See, I haven't forgotten our conversations, Nonna. They are all still there in my head.'

She bit her lip. 'But I wanted other things, too – most of all your happiness.'

'I am not unhappy,' he promised, easing back into a walk as there were more trees he wanted to check before nightfall. 'Although if I find many more signs of peacock spot appearing then I may begin to feel that way.'

His Nonna halted and took his arm to stop him moving on. 'Forget the trees for a moment. If I made you believe they were the most important thing of all then I am sorry. I was wrong. Nothing is more important than love.'

Gently he pulled his arm free of her. 'Come back to the house with me,' he urged, 'you look tired. I can finish checking the trees tomorrow.'

'No, I have things to say so please listen like you used to,' she begged. 'I thought I knew so much back then, that I was so wise. But I've learnt some lessons and I need you to hear them.'

Then his Nonna told him what she believed love was; talking quickly, fearing he might move away if she paused to take a breath. He listened and understood how hard being without his grandfather for all these years must have been for her. And he reminded himself not a word of it could make a shred of difference.

'I am marrying Maria Luisa,' was all he said when she had finished talking.

Rosie

I don't understand why people can't be happy with the things they have, why everyone wants more all the time. If they're healthy and have enough to get by then what's the point of all this endless striving? People must think success will keep them safe, make them better, nicer or happier. Maybe they expect to be satisfied at some point but then it never comes.

The week after we got back from Villa Rosa I went to Liberty and spent half a Saturday exploring it floor by floor, soothing myself with the sight of beautiful things. I touched the Hermès scarves and tried on the Vivienne Westwood, daubed my wrists with perfume samples and stood before a mirror holding a necklace round my throat. I didn't buy a single thing. It was good to know it was all there, all that beauty and gloss, to spend a morning in its company but I didn't have to own it. I tried to tell myself I felt the same way about Enzo.

I'd got what I wanted – a chance to smooth things over, make them neat again. That had to be enough. So whenever I found myself wishing and wondering, or thinking about that last half kiss or remembering how Enzo had changed and all the ways he'd seemed the same, I told myself I had enough things to be happy with.

I was happy with my home. If I wanted change I could paint a wall a different colour or move a cushion.

I was happy with my friends. Addolorata's personality could be as jingly-jangly as the jazz music she'd taken to listening to, Toni was spiky and often selfish, Lou might

286

always need someone to lean on. But they were my friends and they were enough.

I was happy with my job. The hours spent sorting through bags of frozen vegetables to find the perfect peas weren't exactly joyful but there were moments when I cut into an onion tart and it oozed out, all brown caramel sweetness, or I found the perfect bowl for a rustic soup of autumn minestrone and I knew I was good at what I did, and that was enough. There was Johnny who made me laugh. There was the studio I looked forward to going to everyday. There was a vase of tulips singing on a polished glass desk, a neat stack of magazines, a pinboard filled with images I loved, shelves of crockery ordered by shape and colour.

I was happy with the family I'd found. With the Sunday lunchtimes watching Beppi attack the contents of a pan with his wooden spoon, with Catherine's gentle conversation and sharing smiles with Pieta. They weren't mine really but somehow they'd always made me feel like I belonged.

And I was happy being single, really I was.

EXTRACT FROM ADDOLORATA'S LETTER TO ROSIE
I know you'll read this and be angry with me. That's why I'm writing rather than saying it to your face. But you're making a mistake and if I don't tell you now then I'm certain I'll regret it later.

I remember years ago, after you lost your parents, you told me there was no point in trying too hard because life could be snatched away in an instant. I still don't think you were right but you weren't entirely wrong either. You can't latch on to a life and refuse to let it go. It won't allow you to anyway so what's the point in trying.

Things are changing for all of us. Eden and I are getting married and I hope some day we'll have kids. Lou's training to be a counsellor because she thinks she'll be able to help others even if she can't always help herself. Toni will be editor of that newspaper some day, mark my words, and she'll be even more terrifying when she is.

What about you? You're so quick to hide behind your own front door the minute it all seems too hard and messy. You won't ever talk to us about it, tell us what's wrong. Over the years there must have been times all of us have wanted to shake you but we made allowances because you'd lost your family.

Now it's time to be honest. You didn't go out to that estate just to tidy things up between you and Enzo, did you? You wanted more than that. You still care about him – I know you well enough to see that.

So why don't you take a risk? It won't be easy, but what's the worst that can happen? Tell him how you feel, Rosie. It's not too late, not yet. You keep insisting you're happy with your life the way it is and that's fine ... but perhaps there's more than happiness to be had. What about love? Don't you want that too?

The Olive Estate

Enzo had begun to write a letter. It wasn't easy because he wanted to find the right words and nothing he wrote seemed good enough. Locking the door of his office so none of his sisters could disturb him, he made false starts and wasted paper.

Some nights he kept going until the letter filled several sheets of paper and he'd written about things best left unsaid; how saving the estate had been a chore at first, how he was driven by guilt and duty, how slowly that had changed and now he understood at last what his Nonna had always tried to tell him about what the place meant to her.

Enzo could describe how he felt about so many things: the trees, the land, his family, his future, but not the thing that mattered. Every letter ended the same way, with blotches and words crossed out. Then he would sigh, lock away the sheets of paper in a desk drawer and vow to use his time better the next day.

Always as evening arrived he was drawn back to the letter, hoping this time he could start afresh, concentrate his mind and make it work. The words were close but flighty, even a glass or two of brandy didn't help him catch them. Yet still he wasn't ready to give up.

'Are you not sleeping, Enzo? Are you sick?' Concetta asked one morning when she found him, grey as the dawn, draining the last dregs of coffee from his cup.

'Why would you think I'm sick?' he said, his voice edged with irritation.

'You don't seem yourself, haven't for days now. Nonna is worried about you. So am I.'

Lately there had been a softening between them but they still weren't close as they'd been as children. 'Don't waste your time worrying about me,' Enzo said shortly.

Concetta busied herself grinding more beans and making fresh coffee. It was a moment or two before she spoke again.

'Are you sure, Enzo?' she asked suddenly.

'Sure that I'm not sick? Yes, of course.'

'No, I meant sure about this marriage to Maria Luisa Mancuso. She's never loved you. It broke her heart when she realised she couldn't have your friend Gianpaolo. I heard there were tears on his wedding day. And now here she is still unmarried and willing to settle for second best.'

'I'm not second best.' There was a flare of the old arrogance.

His sister gave him a cool look. 'For her, perhaps you are.'

'She may have loved Gianpaolo once but now Maria Luisa is happy to be my wife,' he argued.

Concetta leant back against the kitchen sink, her hips spreading a little. She sighed and Enzo thought she sounded like their mother. 'I would have thought you had some pride and that marriage would be more important for both of you,' she said.

'You married a boy from a good family, behaved the way everyone expected,' Enzo pointed out. 'You did your duty. Now I'm doing mine.'

'My duty? Is that what you think it was? I loved Ricardo, wanted to be with him. I'd never have married for any other reason. Only a fool would ... and you're not a fool, Enzo.'

He watched while Concetta poured another cup of black coffee, strong and sweet just as he liked it.

'I don't think you understand how hard a marriage can be, even when you love each other,' she told him as he sipped it. 'You never escape it. At night you're trapped with the smells and sounds of each other's bodies. Day after day you listen to them repeat the same things, put up with habits they probably don't realise they have. There are times I want to scream.'

'What times?' he asked, surprised to hear her admit it.

'Oh, when Ricardo's had a glass or two of wine and starts ranting on with criticisms of how things are done in his family's business. I have to nod and listen, no matter how often I've listened before, because I'm his wife and if I won't hear what he says, console him, make him feel as though he matters, then who will?'

'So you have regrets about your marriage.' Enzo shrugged. 'That doesn't mean I'll feel the same way.'

'You're not listening,' Concetta said impatiently. 'I don't regret marrying Ricardo. I still love him. But even with all that love it's difficult; so imagine the hell of a marriage without it.'

'You're hoping Maria Luisa and I won't marry and eventually I'll be forced into selling the estate. That's what this is about, isn't it?' Enzo accused her.

Concetta hissed out a breath through her teeth. 'Sometimes having a brother is just as impossible as having a husband.'

'Well, admit it, that's exactly what you want.'

'Yes, yes, I thought we should sell at first,' his sister agreed, 'but then I saw how your face was set against it and I did my best to support you. Surely you've noticed that? How I've stayed here, cooked and cleaned, run the house, fed the workers? Ricardo would have preferred us to get a place of our own long ago but I refused to move. I couldn't leave you, or Mamma and Nonna. You all needed me.'

Enzo stared at her.

'Why else did you think we were staying here?' She took his empty cup and swilled it clean beneath the running tap. 'I don't love this estate the way you do. I only love the people who live on it.' Concetta touched his shoulder. 'If you've finished your breakfast you can come and help me feed the pigs. The scrap buckets are overflowing and I could do with a hand.'

Helping her tip the swill of rotting fruit and vegetable peel into the pens, Enzo realised he'd never stopped to consider what Concetta might be thinking or feeling. Mired in the swamp of his own problems it had been easy to forget other people had them too.

She pulled the scrap bucket out of the pen as the piglets squealed and rushed towards the food. 'Surely my son must be old enough to carry these buckets by now. I'm passing this job on to him,' she swore.

'So you aren't planning to leave anytime soon?' he asked her. 'You'll stay and support me.'

'As long as you need me I'll stay,' she promised. 'You don't have to rush into a marriage with Maria Luisa. Find a wife who loves you, Enzo, that's my advice.'

He left Concetta to carry the empty buckets back to the kitchen, staying by the pens for a while longer, listening to the pigs snort with pleasure as they burrowed into their food.

Only when the day's work was done did he allow himself to be drawn back to the letter. This time Enzo didn't waste paper or words. He kept what he wrote brief and simple then sealed it into an envelope despite the lack of an address to mail it to. Perhaps it would be sent some day, perhaps it would stay on his desk and gather dust. Whatever happened, at least it was written and Enzo could stop thinking about it.

Rosie

There were two letters and one took its time to reach me. If it had been delivered any sooner things might have turned out differently.

For a while I'd been so angry I couldn't speak to any of the Villa Girls. Lou kept calling, trying to smooth things over, and even Toni rang once.

The part of Addolorata's letter that really offended me was where she had written about wanting to shake me at times. The idea that they'd been talking about me, making allowances for my behaviour because I'd lost my mum and dad. Every time I thought about it I felt more resentful, more furious.

Once she'd realised how upset I was Addolorata backed off completely. It was the others who told me she was worried, how she'd meant well and only wanted the best for me.

'Yeah, whatever,' I told Toni when she called.

'Oh, that's very grown up, isn't it?' Her tone was scathing. 'I suppose you're going to hang up on me now.'

I shifted the phone beneath my chin. 'No, of course not, but I do need to go. I've got things to do.'

'Can't you at least call Addolorata? She's really upset, you know.'

'Well, she shouldn't have written all that stuff.'

'She was only telling you what she thought, being honest.'

'Mmm, I know.'

Toni sighed. 'Oh come on, Rosie. This isn't like you.'

'I want to be left alone for a bit, OK? You lot can go out together and talk about me if you like.'

'We don't talk about you,' Toni insisted. 'Well, not in a bitchy way. We're concerned, that's all.'

'I don't want your concern. Surely you have problems of your own to worry about? Why does everyone feel they have to interfere with mine?'

'Fine ... call us when you've got over yourself.' And it was Toni who hung up on me.

It's only possible to be furious for so long. After a couple of weeks of finding ways to keep busy I ran out of cupboards to reorganise and surfaces to wipe down. Addolorata's letter had been screwed up in a ball but for some reason I hadn't thrown it away. Now I fished it from a drawer of paperwork, smoothed it out and read it through again.

She was right about some things. I could see how life was changing for everyone but me. Even Johnny had been talking about taking a break from work so he could shoot images for an exhibition that was coming up. He wanted to get back to his old, edgier style – instead of fluffing around with food, he wanted to shoot addicts in doorways and bikers with tattoos, that sort of thing.

There were other parts of Addolorata's letter that weren't entirely wrong. Yes, I had a tendency to retreat behind my own front door – I'd always been that way. Even as a child I'd loved my own room best: the faded flowery curtains, misshapen pottery bowls I'd made in art class, the posters of whatever pop star I had a crush on at the time. With my door closed and all those things around me, I'd felt happiest. So perhaps I hadn't changed so much after all.

But Addolorata wasn't right about Enzo. There was no point in digging over that old ground. He had his life worked out and so did I. Why disturb it just because there was a flutter of the old feelings?

I'd learnt the hard way that some things were better left to rest. Wiser to remember the happy times than the arguments, dwell on the successes not the failures. It was all a matter of discipline, of keeping the mind as tidy as one of my kitchen drawers and shutting out anything that might mess it up. Life had treated Addolorata very differently so how could she understand?

In the end it was her sister who made things right between us. Pieta Martinelli turned up on my doorstep early one Sunday morning with a bag of flaky, buttery pastries in her hand and I couldn't bring myself to be rude enough not to let her in.

She waited until the coffee had been made and the croissants arranged on a plate before she began to talk me round so gently I barely realised what was happening at first.

'Did you mind not having a sister or brother when you were growing up?' Pieta asked conversationally, settling in a pool of sunlight on the sofa nearest the window.

I cast my mind back to my childhood. 'Not really,' I replied. 'I was always happy with my own company. It wasn't until I met you and Addolorata that I realised what I'd been missing. It must have been good having a sister.'

'Mmm.' She tore off a corner of croissant, careful not to spill any crumbs. 'Sisters can be tricky, though. A lot of the time when we were kids I found Addolorata infuriating. Still do, to be truthful. She's untidy, stubborn, moody, self-centred ...'

I smiled despite myself. 'You've come to ask me to make things up with her, haven't you?'

Pieta didn't reply. Rather, she said: 'Addolorata is a bit like my father. When she's upset she won't admit it, instead she gets angry, works longer hours, smokes more.'

'That's what she's doing now?'

'Pretty much.'

'Look, it's just this letter she sent—' I began to explain.

'I don't really care why you've fought,' Pieta interrupted.

'I came to make sure you're OK and say we all miss you – not just Addolorata but me, Mamma and Papa. We all feel like you're part of the family.'

'I feel that way too,' I managed to say.

'Our family fights all the time. I'm not sure if we'd know how to talk without fighting. But it never means anything. It's just the way we are.'

'I know,' I muttered.

'And arguments are fine so long as they don't go on for ever.'

I relented. 'OK, it's really not that big a deal. I'll call her if you want me to.'

'That's not what I said. Anyway, there's no need. Papa is expecting you for lunch. He sent me over to make sure you came. He was stuffing sardines and artichokes when I left and there were two different sauces cooking on the stove.'

It had been a while since I'd sat at Beppi's table listening to him tell us how we should live our lives. I wondered what he was stuffing the sardines with. Parmesan, parsley, fresh white bread crumbs? He'd fry them in too much oil until they were golden brown and serve them with peppery salad leaves. There'd be something else, too, a pasta course or perhaps a risotto. The kitchen would sound with the impatient clattering of pans and the smell of whatever he was making would drift through open doorways and windows. I missed the Martinelli family and was tired of being angry with everyone.

'I haven't showered yet,' I told Pieta. 'I'm not properly dressed.'

'That's fine. I can wait.'

WHAT ADDOLORATA SAID

'I'm not going to apologise. Why should I? It's not my fault that Rosie's hypersensitive. Perhaps we should all

have been more honest with her in the first place instead of always making allowances.

'She's the one who dropped Enzo like he was something dirty the minute something went wrong. She's the one who refused to listen to any talk of second chances. I saw her face when she spotted him in that pizza place. I watched her afterwards. She's the one who's denying how she really feels. So why should it be me who apologises?'

The Olive Estate

Enzo told himself the letter didn't matter. But still he went to some trouble, driving down to the pink-washed villa on the coast and charming the old lady next door into passing on the details of whoever had rented the place to Rosie and her friends.

There was more charm needed when he rang the owner. She was reluctant to hand out information to a stranger, didn't have an address for Rosie anyway, but had finally given him the name Beppi Martinelli and the details of a London restaurant where he could be found.

Enzo copied the address onto the envelope but still didn't put it in the mail. For a week it sat on his desk, propped up against an olive oil bottle sample someone had sent him. He threw it a sidelong glance whenever he sat down but otherwise ignored it.

The letter might have been thrown away eventually had Concetta not been in one of her efficient moods. 'I tidied your office today, posted a couple of things, got rid of some rubbish,' she told him briskly one evening as she put his dinner in front of him.

'You posted the letters?' he repeated. 'The ones on my desk?'

'Yes, that was OK, wasn't it? One of them had been there for over a week. You've been so busy I thought perhaps you were falling behind with your paperwork. Is there anything else I can help you with?' Lately it seemed as though his sister couldn't try hard enough to please him.

'No, no, you've done enough,' he told her.

He finished his dinner before going to see for himself. Sure enough the desk was tidied, papers he'd left scattered had been marshalled into neat piles, and the envelope addressed to *Rosie c/o Beppi Martinelli at Little Italy* was missing. By now it might be in a mail-sack on its way to London.

Enzo tried not to think about it. Nevertheless, he took to telling his sisters he had errands to run and driving to Triento each morning to check what had arrived in his post office box. Finding it empty or with only a few bills waiting, he always felt a lurch of disappointment.

The person Enzo came close to confiding in was Gianpaolo. Late one sunny afternoon the pair of them were snatching a few lazy moments, drinking beer on the deck of the fishing boat, when Enzo felt tempted to share what was weighing on his mind.

'Everyone is telling me I shouldn't marry Maria Luisa,' he remarked.

'Oh yes?' Gianpaolo replied. 'And who is everyone?'

'My Nonna, my sister Concetta ... They think we don't love each other enough.'

Gianpaolo laughed drily. 'Women are obsessed with love, aren't they? I blame those magazines they read all the time. The other day Caterina wanted us to talk about our relationship. Crazy, eh?'

'What's wrong with your relationship?' Enzo asked him.

'Nothing, as far as I know. But women like to keep turning things over and over, examining them from every angle. If there isn't a problem they'll invent one. That's what your Nonna and sister are doing, most likely.'

Enzo hadn't thought of it like that but Gianpaolo had a wife and must know what he was talking about.

'Did you ever have second thoughts before you married Caterina?' he asked.

'Not really. I was ready to settle down and have a family.

Caterina and I had been together for a while.' Gianpaolo handed him another cold beer. 'Why? Are you having second thoughts about Maria Luisa?'

'Yes ... maybe.'

'Ah well, you've been a bachelor for a long time – it's probably normal to have a few jitters.'

Enzo hesitated. 'What if Maria Luisa's not the right one, though?'

'The right one! That's woman's talk,' Gianpaolo teased, swigging from his bottle of Peroni and letting loose a belch. 'They all expect some grand passion, for us to sweep them off their feet just like in the movies.'

'But real-life love isn't like that,' Enzo agreed. 'It's a practical thing, another building block of life, not the only part of it that matters.'

'That's right.' Gianpaolo finished his beer. 'And you're not such a young man, you know. If you don't get on with it there'll be no son to inherit the estate you've worked so hard for. Don't worry; I'll be there on the day to make sure you make it up the aisle. Once you've got that part over with you'll be fine.'

'Do you think so?' Enzo wanted to believe him.

'I'm certain.'

After Enzo left his friend, he drove up to Triento to buy a couple of things for his Nonna. The traffic there was worse than ever, choking the narrow laneways, and finding a place to park was almost impossible. Impatient to do his shopping, Enzo swung his old truck into the centre of the piazza, braking in the same place he'd always left his sports car in the old days.

Immediately he heard the traffic warden's whistle, loud and close. 'You can't park there. Move on, move on,' she called.

'Just one minute while I go to the pharmacy then I'll be gone,' Enzo told her through the open window.

She blew on the whistle again. 'No parking. Can't you read the signs?'

'You always used to let me stop here.'

She scowled at him. 'Yes, perhaps I did, years ago. But now there are other young men with shiny cars who think the rules don't apply to them and I've stopped making exceptions. So move your truck, Santi. Don't force me to give you a ticket.'

Enzo drove halfway down the hill before he found a parking spot, then had to head back on foot to pick up what his Nonna needed. As he walked he wondered when he'd stopped being counted as a young man. It wasn't that he felt old, not really. He was fit and strong, his brisk pace up the incline didn't leave him breathless. But he tried to see himself as others did and realised both Gianpaolo and the traffic warden were right. Life had changed. He wasn't so young any more, even if he felt it.

That letter to Rosie had been a mistake, an attempt to go back to a time when life had been more carefree. It was rash of him to write it and stupid to leave it out on the desk where Concetta might find it. Now all Enzo could hope was that no one would ever read it.

Rosie

The second letter was stalled for a while, lying beneath a pile of odds and ends pulled from Beppi's pockets – bills and loose change and old receipts – until he remembered it was there and thrust it at me in a panic that Sunday lunchtime between the pasta course and the sardines. I'd never seen Enzo's handwriting before but the Italian stamp on the envelope was enough to tell me who had sent it.

The atmosphere in the Martinelli house had been awkward up until then. Addolorata was quiet; Beppi even noisier than usual to make up for it and Catherine trying rather obviously to act as though nothing was different.

I'd done the usual things – taken a turn around the garden to admire Beppi's herbs and vegetables, helped him by grating the parmesan and mixing up a salad dressing, made Catherine a cup of tea – but there was still a sense that all of us were on our best behaviour.

The letter changed all that. Beppi pulled it from the basket where they tossed their keys and bits of junk mail. 'I couldn't imagine who in Italy would be writing to you anyway,' he said, flustered and apologetic. 'After all, you don't keep in touch with anyone there, do you? So hopefully it wasn't urgent.'

The envelope felt soft and creased from its time in Beppi's pocket, the corners were worn smooth. It was so light in my hand it didn't seem as if it could contain very much of anything.

'It's from him, isn't it?' Addolorata asked. She had been

distant with me so far but now excitement brought her closer.

'Yes, I think so. But why would he send me a letter?'

'Open it and find out,' she urged.

I paused, holding the envelope as though it were hot. 'I'm not sure,' I admitted, shocked to have even received it, wondering if I might be better not knowing whatever it said.

'Go on, open it,' Addolorata repeated, impatience ringing in her voice.

'I can't,' I said helplessly. 'I just can't.'

'Oh hell, give it here then.' Addolorata swiped the envelope out of my hand, ripping into it almost indecently.

The note inside was short, just a sheet of lined paper and not even closely written.

Addolorata's eyes flicked over it quickly. 'It's fine, really it is,' she promised when she'd finished. 'Do you want me to read it to you?'

I nodded, almost holding my breath as she began.

'Dear Rosie – I'm not the sort of man who thinks about his feelings much. It's been years since I've allowed myself to hope or dream but since you were here it's been impossible to do anything else. Will you let me come to you? Will you see me if I do? There are so many things I want to say ... things I should have said before. I hope you'll still want to hear them – Enzo.'

For a moment there was silence and then Beppi made a loud snorting sound. 'What sort of letter is that? He claims there are many things he want to say but then tells you nothing.'

'Maybe he wants to tell her in person,' Addolorata said softly. 'Perhaps it's not the sort of thing he can say properly in writing.'

I took the letter from her and looked through it again, trying to read more meaning into every line

'It's difficult to believe,' I said softly. 'I never expected this.'

'So will you see him, this boy?' Beppi sounded protective and I loved him for it.

'I don't know.'

'He is the one whose father and grandfather were arrested and put in prison? The same boy?'

'Yes, the same.'

'Meh,' Beppi said disgustedly. He might have added more but Addolorata gave him a firm look and he contented himself with a shrug of his shoulders and with throwing his hands in the air.

I didn't mind that the letter wasn't flowery and romantic. It didn't seem important. All I could think of was Enzo standing beneath his olive trees, thinking of me.

'What if he's given up waiting for a reply,' Catherine said worriedly.

'You'd think he'd have given a phone number.' That was Beppi. 'Or details of a fax, at least. It seems ridiculous to be communicating by letter in this day and age.'

'What will you do, Rosie?' Addolorata asked softly. 'Do you have any idea yet?'

I'd been worrying they'd gang up on me, try to force me into making what they thought was the best decision. But everyone seemed to understand it wasn't that simple. Even the Villa Girls left me alone for the next few days to work out what I wanted.

I read Enzo's note several times and composed so many replies in my head. Each one was different, depending on which way my mood was swinging.

It wasn't until I admitted to myself that every word in Addolorata's letter had been right that I realised I had to take a risk. I couldn't hang on to my life and hope it never changed. That wasn't happiness ... it was something else entirely.

But I didn't want Enzo coming to London and I wasn't ready to let him into my home; I didn't want that disturbed, not yet. If I were going to see him it would have to be in Italy.

Lou offered to keep me company but I thanked her and said no. It might have involved talking for hours, analysing the whole business over the course of a journey. Much better to be free – to go to Triento alone and see how things turned out.

I found other stylists to take over the jobs I'd lined up and told Johnny not to accept more bookings for me. I managed to rent that same pink house near the sea that we'd all loved so much just a few weeks ago. And I closed the door on my apartment not knowing when I'd be back to it.

It was the most fearless thing I've ever done. I suppose it must have been love that gave me the courage and that was strange because for a long time I'd imagined it was the thing that frightened me most.

EXTRACT FROM ADDOLORATA'S JOURNAL

I'm the one who's pushed Rosie into doing this and now I'm worrying. What if it goes badly and Enzo breaks her heart all over again? His letter left so much unsaid. Anything could happen really.

I went over to her place with a bottle of wine last night and we chatted while she packed her suitcase. All her clothes were ironed so carefully before she folded them away and the shoes were stowed in special bags. It made me laugh ... so organised, even when she's being impulsive.

Rosie says if nothing else she'll get a couple of extra weeks of summer holiday. That she's taking lots of books to read and her camera, too. She's not expecting anything from him, she kept repeating that. Still, I wish she hadn't gone alone. She ought to have taken Lou, it was crazy not to. I didn't tell her that, though ... I think it might be time for me to stop interfering in Rosie's life.

The Olive Estate

Enzo was in a panic but trying not to show it. Ever since he'd found her reply to his letter lying beneath a couple of bank statements in his post office box, his thoughts had been in chaos. He wanted to feel free enough to be excited but all he could think about was how impossible life had become.

The letter was safely locked in a desk drawer now but he knew it by heart:

I've rented the Villa Rosa for at least a couple of weeks, although the owner says I can have it for as long as I like as she has no plans to use it this summer. There is a Vespa I can borrow to drive to the port or up to Triento. But I'm not confident about taking it on longer trips so you must come to me to say all these things you want to tell me. I'm not sure whether it's too late for us or not, to be honest. Maybe we've missed our moment. Let's meet and talk, then we'll see. Love Rosie

Enzo was glad she'd chosen to stay in the little pink house. It was a few kilometres down the coast, far enough from the estate to be no risk in him visiting. He'd find a way to make her leave sooner than she'd planned, let her down gently and send her home. Gianpaolo was right: love was a woman's concern and it would be better not to waste more time thinking about it.

Why then did he take so long fussing about what he would wear? Why did he drive to Triento for a proper haircut and a decent shave, splash out on a bottle of cologne and even wipe the chicken dirt from his old truck with a soft cloth? He told himself it was pointless, there was no reason to make a good impression. Yet when he drove to Villa Rosa early that morning, well before any of his sisters were awake, his good shirt was carefully ironed, his comb tucked in the back pocket of his jeans and his skin smelt of citrus and sandalwood.

All the way there, as the truck jarred over the potholes and he felt a sweat breaking out on his brow, Enzo practised what he would say. There would be a quiet chat, he'd explain what a mistake that letter had been, and they'd part still friends. He was thankful Rosie had never seemed the type for outbursts or emotional scenes.

The moment he pulled through the open gates of Villa Rosa, he let himself be distracted. He'd been there briefly twice before but hadn't noticed either time how beautiful the place was. The tiled terrace covered in flowering bougainvillea, the lemon-laden trees against the pale pink house and the stretch of gardens reaching down towards the sea. Enzo thought it was charming.

Then he saw Rosie, coming out of a grove of fruit trees. She smiled at him and waved. She was wearing a loose sarong printed with red hibiscus flowers and he felt overdressed in comparison.

'*Ciao*, Enzo,' she greeted him.

'*Ciao*.' He leant down and kissed her on both cheeks. Her skin smelt of vanilla and he had to force himself to pull away.

'Would you like something cool to drink? The old lady next door has given me an enormous jug of home-made lemonade.'

They sat beneath a pomegranate tree, far enough apart that there was no danger of skin brushing skin. For an hour or so they talked and he failed to say any of the things he'd planned. Instead they discussed the summer weather and the chances of Enzo being able to attach the iron ladder to the rocks so that Rosie could take a swim in the sea when the waves calmed down. They talked of the estate and the olive trees, their families and their friends.

As the day warmed they took a walk, following a path shaded by pines that wound round the rocky bays beneath the house and Enzo pointed out views he thought she ought to come back and photograph. He showed her how easy it was to fix the ladder to the rocks and how safe it would be to climb down it. He was happy in her company. There seemed no urgency to reach the unspoken things. They would get there in time, Enzo told himself.

She insisted on cooking for him before he left. The food she made for lunch was simple enough: fennel baked with olive oil and parmesan, pasta shells creamy with fresh ricotta and scattered with parsley she'd picked from the garden, a little steamed broccoli drizzled with a paste of anchovies, garlic and lemon. He'd never watched her move about a kitchen before and thought she did so with a sort of grace he'd never seen in anyone else.

She photographed the food before they started eating then laughed apologetically. 'It's what I do for a living,' she explained.

As Enzo ate she told him about her life, so different to his and difficult to imagine. Listening to her talk of London reminded him of how small his own world was. He rarely moved beyond Triento, might never see the places she described. It wasn't that Enzo minded any more. But surely stealing a little of his life back, keeping some of it for himself, wasn't so wrong? All he wanted was a few weeks of summer, a small taste of happiness.

Enzo left the Villa Rosa that afternoon with an arrangement to go back to eat lunch there again the next day.

Rosie

Enzo and I were awkward at first. We edged around each other and sat with things between us – tables, dishes of food and glasses of wine, my camera. It seemed too difficult for either of us to say the things we needed to.

I served our lunches at the little shaded table out on the terrace. What I made was limited by how much I could carry in the panniers of the Vespa or pick from the garden but there was always something good: a spicy sausage of pork and fennel, a tangle of wild asparagus, a bunch of fresh chicory.

Life fell into a holiday pattern. Instead of being rattled out of bed by my alarm clock, I drifted awake each morning, then lingered over coffee and a crust of bread smeared with peach jam while I thought about what I might like to cook.

One day the fishmonger stopped by in his van and I scandalised the old lady next door by buying up seafood in abundance: fillets of swordfish to char-grill, calamari to stuff and prawns to fry quickly in olive oil with lots of garlic. There was so much pleasure in watching Enzo enjoy it all.

Always after lunch he kissed me awkwardly on both cheeks and drove home, tooting a last goodbye as he reached the first bend on the steep road.

I liked the romance of getting to know Enzo again. It was such an unexpected luxury. I loved closing the gates behind his truck and forgetting about the world outside. Often he'd had trouble finding excuses to get away from the estate and I knew he hadn't told anyone there about me yet. But when we were together – eating, swimming, soaking in the morning sun – it didn't seem to matter. Only later, in the afternoons, when he left me alone at Villa Rosa, did I wonder what either of us thought we were doing.

I'd started photographing him again and already there were canisters of film lined up waiting to be developed. He complained at first, pointing at the grey in the stubble on his face, the lines around his eyes. 'I'm not such a pretty, young boy any more,' he told me, laughing. 'Things have changed.'

Yes Enzo had changed but in ways you'd never tell from the images I'd captured. He was softer and somehow harder too. He seemed tired. For both of us this was an escape from our lives, an unreal time. I enjoyed the freedom of it, wearing loose sarongs, eating food from the pan, going barefoot and not brushing my hair. It felt like I was pretending – being someone who was far less like me and much more like Addolorata.

We never left the Villa Rosa, except to walk along the path around the bays. Then, after a week or so, Enzo borrowed a decent car from someone and drove me back to Amalfi. We went to the same hotel as before, with the wide terrace and the well-starched waiters, and ate a perfect lunch – delicate morsels of seafood we prised out of shells, fronds of salad dressed with oil and lemon. Afterwards he took me to the room he'd booked. Softened with wine and drowsy with food, we slept until the sun shone through the windows and lit our faces evening pink. I moved closer to him, smelt his hair, rested my cheek against his smooth shoulder. I heard him say my name, and said his name in return. That was our moment – we hadn't missed it at all. That was our coming together.

Only later, stretching out together in the dusky half-light, were we able to speak the truth to one another.

'Think of the life we might have had,' Enzo said, tracing the line of my arm with his fingers. 'If things had been different, if my family hadn't agreed to let the barn be used to store those boxes, what do you think might have happened?'

Lying there, taking warmth from his bare skin and smelling the muskiness of him, I tried to imagine a different ending. 'Perhaps things would have finished between us anyway,' I suggested. 'I'd have gone back to London, we'd have written to each other for a while like Lou and Gianpaolo did, and then gradually lost touch.'

'You think it was only a holiday romance? It was never more to you than that?' Enzo sounded almost disappointed.

'I'm not sure any more. It seems too long ago and what happened at the end flavoured everything else.'

'But tell me, why did you come back to Triento with your friends? Surely you knew we might meet? Was that what you wanted?'

'I thought I didn't care, that I wouldn't feel anything even if we happened to bump into each other. When I saw you in that pizzeria it felt as though someone had slapped me. It took me by surprise.'

'Me too,' he admitted. 'I never expected to see you again. Often I couldn't help thinking about you, though. Remember that night when we kissed for hours up by the statue? I used to let myself daydream about that. It was a nice memory to take out now and then.'

'The bit I liked remembering most was lying here in this hotel, feeling so nervous and shy of you, being with you for the first time. Whoever would have thought we'd come here together again?'

Enzo shifted in the bed, resting one of his bare legs over mine. 'I'm so happy we've had this time together.'

'It will be something else to remember, won't it?' My voice broke a little on the words.

'Rosie, I ...' he began and I heard the regret in his voice.

'It's all right, you don't have to say anything. I already know.'

'What do you know?'

'I understand the reality and how difficult it is. I have a life in London while everything you care about is here. How could we ever make a life together? There seems no way to make it work.'

'It's difficult, you're right.' Enzo hugged me tighter to him. 'But my Nonna thinks love is the most important thing. My sister Concetta does too. For them everything else takes second place.'

'Addolorata agrees with them. But I think things are more complicated than that.'

We were silent for a while and then Enzo squeezed my shoulders again. 'Let's not worry about it yet. We are in Amalfi, we are together and there are still a few good weeks of summer left. Why don't we let ourselves enjoy this time ... not look too far ahead?'

'All right then,' I agreed. 'Let's make more memories.'

WHAT ADDOLORATA SAID

'No I haven't heard a word from her. I called the number I have for Villa Rosa but there's never any reply. That has to be good news, doesn't it? Surely she'd be back by now if things hadn't worked out between them? I wish she'd at least send me a postcard. I'm desperate to know what's going on.'

The Olive Estate

The trestle tables had been pulled out of the barn and laid out beneath the trees. Everyone agreed they had never looked so pretty. Someone had trimmed the napkins with olive leaves and filled chipped, old enamel jugs with bunches of their branches, the fruit still clinging to them. They had gone to all the trouble of dyeing the sheets that served as tablecloths the softest of greens and of filling clear glass vases with heaps of polished waxy-skinned lemons. That same person had hung lanterns in the trees that were to be lit when the sun went down. There was champagne chilling in an old cattle trough and Enzo's Nonna had sacrificed a piglet to the spit. Music played and Concetta was singing along to it as her children played outside the kitchen door. His other sisters were busy slicing salami and cheese, watching over the trays of pasta baking in the oven and squabbling in high voices but only half-heartedly, for there was a celebration coming.

It had been a long time since the Santi family had anything to celebrate and Enzo had felt nervous from the moment he opened his eyes that morning. He'd spent the day fussing a great deal and achieving very little until in the end his Nonna sent him away to polish his shoes and tidy his hair.

'You can tell a lot about a man by the state of his shoes,' she reminded him. 'I may have changed my mind about so many things but that one at least still holds true.'

It was a golden morning with the lightest of breezes. No one could have asked for better weather. All week Concetta had been fearful of rain, insisting she could feel it coming in her bones. Enzo had never been happier to find her proved wrong.

There were still things to be finished, chairs to be shifted from the house to the olive grove, glasses to be polished clean of fingerprints, hard-crusted loaves to be sliced by someone with a strong-arm. 'Hurry, hurry, we will be late,' his Nonna was chivvying someone and Enzo smiled, for it was good to see her taking charge again.

There were so many more reasons to smile now but Enzo felt unpractised at it. He had grown used to being stern just as he'd become accustomed to waking at dawn and working hard until nightfall.

After today things would change here on the estate. Enzo wasn't sure how it would be but he knew it might not always be easy. Still, this was a celebration and he was determined to wear a smile for it.

Rosie

Enzo thinks the olive trees are like soldiers, lined up in columns, marching up the hill. To me they're far too feathery and feminine for that. Their leaves are pointed like fingernails, their branches move like hair in the wind. And the older ones, with their knots and wrinkles, all planted out of line and going their own way, rather remind me of his Nonna, although I'd never dare to tell her so even if my Italian was good enough.

Enzo's old Nonna seems so pleased with herself now. She stares at me sometimes the way I often stare at a plate of food I'm styling, at a tumble of salad leaves or a layered cake, as if she's scrutinising me for tiny flaws she might have missed before. And then, when she's finished, she beams and pats my cheek as though satisfied everything is in the right place at long last thanks to her.

His sisters stare at me too. So do strangers in the street. I know I look foreign, paler-skinned, fairer-haired, but it's not just that. People whisper about us. I am the girl who stole Enzo Santi from his fiancée. The gossip ripples from one side of the piazza to the other as we make a *passeggiata* on a Sunday evening. Enzo tells me to ignore it, says they'll find someone else to scandalise them in a month or two. His Nonna links her arm with mine and parades me almost proudly. She wears a red hat on her head so no one could miss her even if they wanted to and stops to speak to every single person she passes. The gossip doesn't seem to touch her.

For so long I'd imagined Enzo and I would only ever have our summer of stolen time together and so I'd squeezed enjoyment from every moment. There had been late, lazy mornings in the big double bed, the doors flung open onto the upstairs terrace, the sunlight pooling through; long walks along the coastal paths; meals beneath the bougainvillea. Everything appeared so idyllic and yet all of it was back-dropped with sadness.

There were so many things we tried not to speak about: how long I was planning to stay or what would happen after I left. We never mentioned the girl he was meant to marry. Instead, we acted like the future might never happen.

And then one day he didn't appear at Villa Rosa for lunch as I'd expected. Instead he arrived in the evening just as I was wondering if I could be bothered heating up leftover pasta for my evening meal. He was wearing his work clothes, the skin on his face sun-blushed.

'Jump in,' he told me, leaning over to open the passenger door of his truck.

'Where are we going?'

'You'll see,' was all he said.

As we drove up the hill he told me that instead of eating the lunch I'd made for him, the pumpkin gnocchi with rosemary and nutmeg, the salad of finely sliced fennel and blood oranges, he'd been with Maria Luisa having the con-versation he'd been dreading.

'I should have talked to her earlier,' he admitted. 'It was always wrong between us. To marry would have been a disaster, just as my Nonna and Concetta always told me. I see that now.'

Maria Luisa wasn't as disappointed as he'd worried she might be. Marrying him had only ever been her mother's dream. Now with their engagement broken she was free to do other things: travel, train for a career, make her own life.

I'd never met her but found myself hoping she'd find the courage to take the risks she needed to.

Enzo drove me to the estate that evening. No one there was surprised to see me. He'd told them already how things had changed and they were ready with bottles of sparkling wine and platters of food to graze on: home-cured prosciutto, long mild red chilli peppers stuffed with anchovies and capers, olives marinated with spices and garlic, a salad of cherry tomatoes bathed in oil. His sisters spoke to me in halting English and I understood enough to see they were happy for us.

I stayed until after the sun had set and Enzo and I walked through the olive groves in the dark while he whispered words to me that I'd never thought I hear.

'My Nonna insists you stay with us,' he said as he drove me home late that night. 'I was certain she'd disapprove but she thinks we've wasted enough time already and that I mustn't let you get away again.'

And I laughed because I could imagine the old lady saying exactly that.

'You're not planning to go away though, are you?' he said softly as we drew through the gates of Villa Rosa. 'You'll stay here with me ... for a while at least?'

How could I say no? How could I pack my clothes back into my suitcase and walk away from him a second time? My flat, my everyday life – I'd survived a summer separated from them. Surely I could manage to stay away longer ... a while at least?

It's a different way of life here – I'm discovering that. Enzo works long hours and I fit myself in wherever I can, helping in the kitchen or the olive groves. I take photographs of things that please me, jot down recipes I want to remember and listen to his Nonna tell me about the trees in a language I barely understand. I try to feel like I belong but I never quite manage it. Not so far anyway.

This morning we all woke with such a sense of anticipation. By the time I opened my eyes Enzo was up and gone already, his head full of lists of things he had to do. Everyone was busy, intent on their tasks, and I worked alongside them, doing what I could – carrying tables and chairs, making things look pretty.

Now every time they hear the sound of a car engine his sisters funnel out of the kitchen door in excitement. Any moment they will arrive, Enzo's father and his grandfather out of prison at last and coming home to the estate. There is a big feast prepared and lots of wine to be drunk. We are all waiting for it to begin.

Enzo thinks it will take a while for them to get used to life here again. He wants to wait and help with the harvest and the pressing of the new season's olive oil. Maybe he will stay until the trees are pruned. But then he will come with me to London and I'll open up my life to him. I'll clear a space in my drawers and cupboards, and on my bathroom shelf. It will feel strange, perhaps, but the thought of it makes me happier than I ever could have imagined.

'You'll hate the weather and how grey London can be,' I keep warning him. 'And I know you'll miss the estate, the trees, your family … are you sure you want to come?'

'Yes, I'm sure,' he promised. 'We'll come back here soon. I have to teach our children about the trees some day, the way my Nonna taught me. This is my home, the place I love. But I also love you, Rosie, and I want to know where you come from.'

Their car has arrived at last. Enzo's old Nonna has heard it. I see her pause, then drop the tea towel she is holding, unlace her apron and run her fingers quickly through her hair like a younger woman might. His sisters have set up their screeching again, pushing each other out of the way in the rush to get through the kitchen door. I stay behind, stirring the sauces, making sure some frying onions do not catch, rinsing salad leaves. This is not my family, at least not yet, and I feel awkward in it still. And so I don't watch Enzo's Nonna fall into the arms of her husband. I'm not there to witness his mother breaking down or to see Enzo solemnly shaking the two men by the hand.

Prison has changed them greatly – I realise that later when we're all sitting together at the long marble-topped trestle table. Just like me they are ill at ease here, more guests than people who belong, and dazed by the noise, the fuss and the food. His grandfather barely moves from his seat, his father excuses himself from the table once the first course has been eaten and walks alone between the oldest trees.

As for me, I understand so much more now. I see that life cannot be tidied up the way a room can. That it's a messy thing – uncertain, imperfect and full of compromises. That it can hurt sometimes but there's no way to avoid that.

I thought I was content with the way things were, happy being single, and perhaps I was. But now I see what I didn't before ... there is more than one way to be happy.

ACKNOWLEDGEMENTS

When I started writing *The Villa Girls* I didn't know much at all about styling food or growing olives. So thank you to food writer, stylist and photographer Julie Le Clerc, to Branka Simunovich of the Simunovich Olive Estate and to Margaret Edwards of Matiatia Grove – three impressive and talented women who generously shared their time and knowledge.

I'd also like to thank my friend Vicki Hoggard, the real-life Villa Girl who inspired the initial idea, and all the fantastic women who have helped keep me going through five novels so far: Justine and Mandana for looking after me in London, the Supper Club girls for always being available for emergency margaritas, all my horsey mates, Sarah-Kate for sharing the pain, Lisa for the chocolate macaroons, Sarah, Sido, Kerri, etc, for employing me ... loads more. Thank you all.

Thanks to everyone at Orion, most especially Genevieve Pegg, Yvette Goulden and Susan Lamb, and to Kevin Chapman, Jane McLean, Gemma Finlay and the team at Hachette NZ for masses of support and dessert wine.

Thanks to all the readers around the world who've found me on Facebook and sent lovely messages saying they like my books ... it's all for you, after all.

And thanks to Carne, as always. We made it through another one and I know I said I wouldn't do it again but the thing is I've got this really good idea...